"A great read with broad appeal, to even experienced cops and firefighters. Lynette Eason's blend of realistic, fast-paced action, suspense, twists and turns, and dynamic characters make this a real page-turner."

—**Wayne Smith**, FBI (retired)

"Lynette Eason once again pens a gripping thriller with her latest book, *Oath of Honor*. I can't wait for her next installment of the Blue Justice series!"

—**Carrie Stuart Parks**, award-winning author
of *A Cry from the Dust*

"Lynette Eason's *Oath of Honor* promises to be the beginning of another roller-coaster ride series. Readers are going to love Isabelle and Ryan's story while getting to know the entire St. John family. This engrossing novel will have them hooked from page one."

—**Lisa Harris**, bestselling and Christy Award–winning author
of The Nikki Boyd Files

Books by Lynette Eason

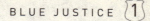

OATH OF HONOR

LYNETTE EASON

Revell

a division of Baker Publishing Group
Grand Rapids, Michigan

© 2018 by Lynette Eason

Published by Revell
a division of Baker Publishing Group
PO Box 6287, Grand Rapids, MI 49516-6287
www.revellbooks.com

Printed in the United States of America

Library of Congress Cataloging-in-Publication Data
Names: Eason, Lynette, author.
Title: Oath of honor / Lynette Eason.
Description: Grand Rapids, MI : Revell, a division of Baker Publishing Group, [2018] | Series: Blue justice ; #1
Identifiers: LCCN 2017036640 | ISBN 9780800727215 (softcover)
Subjects: LCSH: Policewomen—Fiction. | Murder—Investigation—Fiction. | GSAFD: Christian fiction. | Mystery fiction.
Classification: LCC PS3605.A79 O28 2018 | DDC 813/.6—dc23
LC record available at https://lccn.loc.gov/2017036640

Scripture quotations are from the King James Version of the Bible.

Published in association with Tamela Hancock Murray, The Steve Laube Agency, 5025 N. Central Ave., #635, Phoenix, AZ 85012.

18 19 20 21 22 23 24   7 6 5 4 3 2 1

Dedicated to the men and women in blue.
To all of the law enforcement workers
who risk everything to keep us safe.

LAW ENFORCEMENT
Oath of Honor

★ ★

On my honor,
I will never betray my badge, my integrity,
my character, or the public trust.
I will always have the courage
to hold myself and others
accountable for our actions.
I will always uphold the constitution,
my community, and the agency I serve.

★ ★

THURSDAY

Officer Izzy St. John plopped down at the table of one of Columbia, South Carolina's, finest Chinese restaurants and opened the fast-food carton of General Tso's chicken and white rice. The bell above the door rang and she glanced over her shoulder to see Chloe and her K-9, Hank, enter. "Hey. Here's yours." Izzy pushed the unopened food to her sister.

"Great. I'm starving." Chloe took the seat opposite her and opened her carton. Hank settled on the floor at her feet, while Chloe took a bite and sighed her enjoyment.

"Pork roast and mushrooms," Izzy said with a grimace. "Nasty. How are we even related?" Chloe, one of Izzy's five siblings, was two years older.

"You don't know what's good," Chloe said once she swallowed.

"I know what fungus is and there's no way we're meant to eat it."

"I beg to argue with that," a voice said. Izzy turned once more to see Ruthie, another sister, standing there, still decked out in her scrubs. At least they didn't have blood on them this time. Ruthie sat in the third seat and opened the food Izzy slid in front of her. "Mushrooms have many redeeming qualities," Ruthie said. "They have selenium. It's good for your bladder."

Izzy rolled her eyes. "I don't care. I'm not eating them."

"How about they're rich in vitamin D and boost your immune system?" Ruthie took a bite.

"There are other ways to do both without having to eat fungus," Izzy said and opened her can of Coke.

This time Chloe wrinkled her nose. "You won't eat something healthy, but you'll pour that into your system. You make no sense at all."

It was an old argument. A comfortable one.

The door swung open once more and Brady, Izzy's brother who was a former underwater criminal investigator turned homicide detective, joined them at the table. "What's up, brats?"

Ruthie raised a brow. "I finally break away from the hospital where I'm saving lives and this is the respect I get?"

"From the head brat, no less," Izzy murmured. Brady was the eldest of the St. John siblings.

He shot her a wink and dug into his sweet and sour chicken. "So, Rude Ruthie, you cut anyone up today?"

"Yes, two down, two to go."

Izzy caught the startled gaze of the customer just leaving the booth next to their table. "She's a surgeon," she hurried to reassure her. The woman's obvious relief made Izzy giggle. Once she was out the door, Izzy threw her napkin at Brady. "Seriously, you're rotten. You've got to realize not everyone gets our morbid St. John family humor."

"Sorry." He didn't look very sorry. He took another bite. "Who decided it was Chinese day anyway? I was kind of in the mood for Mexican."

"Derek decided," Chloe said. "Remember? Every second Thursday of the month is Chinese. He insisted."

"And yet," Brady said, "he's not here."

Izzy frowned. "Anybody seen him lately? I'm kind of worried about him. He wasn't at Mom's this past Sunday."

Her siblings stopped eating and looked at one another.

Chloe shook her head. "I haven't seen him, now that you mention it."

"Me either," Ruthie said.

Brady leaned back. "That's kind of weird."

Worry niggled at Izzy. "You think he's all right?"

Ruthie's chuckle sounded forced. "Y'all need to stop. Derek's probably on one of his undercover gigs again."

"Or got called out with the SWAT team," Chloe murmured.

Izzy sighed. Such was the life of a family in law enforcement. "You're probably right. Hey, is Linc coming? I got him sweet and sour chicken."

Brady glanced at the clock on the wall. "He texted and said he was finishing up some paperwork and would be about ten minutes late."

Linc, second oldest in the St. John clan, had finally been assigned to the FBI field office in his home city. It had been one of his greatest joys to move back to be near his family once again and he never missed a Thursday lunch unless he just couldn't help it.

"So, who's eating at Mom's this Sunday?" Chloe asked.

"I'll be there," Izzy said.

The others chimed in their plans to attend the weekly lunch. Sometimes only a couple of them could make it. Sometimes they all could. No matter the number, the food was always there and waiting, thanks to their father, who had most weekends off from his law practice—and loved to cook.

Izzy drew in a deep breath and glanced around the table. How she loved them. And admired them. Her phone buzzed and she unclipped it from its home on her belt.

A text from Kevin, her partner.

Can you go on a stakeout with me tonight?

Yes, I guess. What's going on?

I'll explain when you pick me up at 6:30.

2

The stakeout was a complete bust. Izzy's stomach growled and she pressed a hand to it while she contemplated leaving.

"I heard that," her partner, Kevin Marshall, said from the passenger seat of the Ford Explorer.

Izzy sighed. "People in China probably heard it. I'm starving."

"Sorry. Guess you blame me for that, huh?"

"Completely."

Kevin had complained so loud and pitifully about his lack of dinner before rushing to the stakeout that she'd rolled her eyes and passed him her brown paper bag. "You're the one that talked *me* into this. How is it I had time to fix some food and you didn't?"

"I'm a guy."

"So?"

"So, I don't think of things like that."

"That's a bunch of nonsense and you know it."

"No, it's not. It's why every good man needs a good woman—or a good partner who knows how to cook."

"Right. We'll leave that statement right there."

He'd grinned, pulled out her roast beef sandwich, and wolfed it down, followed by her chips and chocolate brownie. And now her stomach was mad at him—and her—for giving the food away.

12

"How much longer do you want to sit here?" he asked.

"This is your deal, Kev. Remember?"

"Right. Let's give it a few more minutes. Blackjack got out of prison last week but said the info was reliable."

"When did you start talking to Blackjack? You know he's my CI. Why would he trust you?"

"Because he trusts *you*. And you're my partner. And he couldn't find you. When he asked where you were, I told him you were indisposed."

"Indisposed?" She laughed, then frowned. "That wouldn't be enough."

"Well, I might have shown him the picture of us going bungee jumping together and I might have told him the story of how I talked you into it."

"You did what? For real?"

"Yeah. He laughed and said if you'd trust me enough to risk that, he'd trust me enough to talk to me."

"How much?"

"What do you mean?"

The innocent look didn't fool her. "How much did it wind up costing you?"

"A hundred bucks."

She gaped. "What? I've never paid him a dime for information."

"I pointed that out. Apparently you have to save his life to get the free stuff."

That sounded like Blackjack. She sighed. "You shouldn't be spending your own money on this."

He shrugged. "I don't mind when I think it's worth it," he said. "He was adamant this was going down tonight. I just need to get the evidence to pass on to the detectives."

"Blackjack. He's a card shark. What's he doing hanging out with gun runners?" Izzy murmured.

"I don't know that they *are* gun runners. He said they were, but it could be anything. He wasn't sure exactly what was going to happen, just that something was."

"Well, he's never led me astray before." She leaned her head against the window and thought about closing her eyes for a minute.

"We should make the bust ourselves and get credit for the collar," Kevin said. He practically vibrated with excitement.

"Calm down, partner. Make what bust? Nothing's happening. Anyway, we're off duty with no backup. We're not making any busts. This is an information-gathering stakeout, remember?"

To herself she added, *Maybe*. It all depended on the situation.

He grunted his disagreement. "What are we doing for your birthday?"

"That's two weeks away. And nothing."

He laughed. "Of course we are. What do you want to do?"

"To have enough evidence to shut these guys down if what you say is true."

"Izzy, Izzy," he said with a groan. "Please do not become such an old fuddy-duddy this early in your life. We're going to Xtreme Flips, so put it on your calendar."

"That place with the trampolines? Are you *trying* to kill me?"

"I took Lilianna there a couple of weeks ago. She loved it."

"Of course she loved it. She's seventeen!"

"So what? You act like you're a hundred years old." He paused. "Actually, I know a guy who's a hundred. He went skydiving for his birthday last month."

"Kev—"

"You went bungee jumping with me, but you won't go jump on an itty-bitty trampoline?"

"Death by bungee is instantaneous and most likely painless. I could be paralyzed for life if I land wrong on a trampoline. Have you looked at the statistics for injuries in those places? There's a reason you have to sign a waiver releasing them of any responsibility."

He shook his head, as though completely disgusted with her cowardice. "I'm taking you. End of discussion. And don't forget. Only twenty-three years to go."

She rolled her eyes. "You remember?"

"Of course. And I'm holding you to it."

"Right." As a teenager, she'd promised to marry him when she turned fifty if they were both still single.

He cleared his throat. "Now. Did I tell you that I told Lincoln about this?" He waved a hand at the warehouse.

"What? No. You neglected to mention that."

"I did."

"What'd he say?"

He shrugged. "That he'd look into it."

"And you don't want to wait on him?"

"Nope."

Kevin's eyes narrowed and Izzy could picture the conversation between the two men. One that would send Kevin out on his own, determined to prove he was right.

"He told you there wasn't anything he could do until you had something concrete, didn't he?"

"Yep."

Of course he had. She would have told him the same thing.

Which was why she now found herself on a stakeout on her day off, allowing her partner and childhood friend to talk her into this.

"What is it with older brothers anyway?" Kevin said.

"What do you mean?"

He lifted the binoculars to his eyes, then set them back on the dash. "They're so bossy—and arrogant."

"Nah. They've just lived more years so they have more experience."

"Linc, maybe. But not Derek. He has no excuse. He's, what . . . three minutes older than you?"

"Two and a half."

"But still older. And he rubs it in your face every chance he gets."

She grimaced. Derek really did. "I'll agree that he likes to share more than I like to listen."

Kevin cracked up. "You can be so diplomatic. You should go into politics."

Izzy couldn't help the smile that lifted her lips. "I'll leave that to Gabby." Gabrielle Sinclair was her best friend and campaign manager to Melissa Endicott, the woman currently running for mayor. Which still stuck in Izzy's craw. But that was for another time. "Derek just likes to push my buttons. It's what brothers do. Especially to sisters. You know you drive Cathy nuts."

"That's different. She's older. Little brothers are supposed to drive their big sisters crazy. But older brothers? Being older also seems to turn them into know-it-alls."

She huffed a low laugh and refused to take up the complaint until Kevin changed course.

"Speaking of Gabby, what's up with her taking that job as campaign manager for Endicott?"

"She and Endicott went to school together, then served in the Army together. It's a good chance for Gabby to make a name for herself."

But Kevin wasn't listening anymore, he was studying the area, his tension palpable. "Blackjack better know what he's talking about," he muttered.

"He does if his track record is anything to go by, so chill."

Izzy had met her confidential informant, Louis Harper, the night she pulled him from his burning home. She'd been patrolling his neighborhood after increased crime reports and had heard his cries for help. Since then, he'd been paying off his "debt" by feeding her information on various criminal activities for the past two years—in between the occasional visit to prison for minor infractions—and he'd yet to lead her astray.

Izzy didn't bother to tell him he didn't owe her anything, that she'd simply been doing her job. She figured as long as he was willing to help her put the bad guys away, she wouldn't argue about it.

She picked up the binoculars from the dash and scanned the warehouse one more time. She'd found a prime parking spot. Across the street and far enough away not to attract attention, she had a good view of the front door and a partial view of the side of the building with the large sliding door. Right now that door was open, but she couldn't see inside.

Movement to the left caught her attention. A dark green Chevy Tahoe pulled around the curve and followed the gravel path to the side of the warehouse. It parked next to the black Ford pickup and the low-slung red Mustang convertible. Izzy hit record on the camera mounted on her dash.

"You got the other camera?" she asked Kevin.

"Charged and ready."

In addition to being her partner, Kevin was a very good amateur photographer.

Two men climbed out of the Tahoe and Kevin lifted the camera to his eye. She heard the zoom lens whir.

"I see a bulge that looks like a gun to me," he said.

"Always go with that assumption."

"Yeah. Actually, make that two. They both have them." The shutter clicked multiple times as he snapped.

The taller one walked to the back of the SUV. "He's taking something out of the back," she said. "You see that?"

"Yes." A pause. "And that is a mighty fancy rifle." He gave a low whistle.

"Whoa," she whispered. "Score another one for Blackjack."

"We've got guns too."

She shot him a warning glare. "And we're not using them, because we're not going to get anywhere near there. At least not without backup."

"Whatever." Kevin kept the camera snapping as the men disappeared into the warehouse. He lowered the camera. "I can't see anything else from here. I'm going to have to get closer."

Izzy swung her gaze away from the warehouse to land on Kevin. "Did you not just hear me? We're not taking these guys down alone."

He reached for the door.

She grabbed the camera. "You can't take that, the shutter is so loud, you'll be discovered before you have a chance to snap the second picture."

"Fine. I'm still going to see what I can see."

She snagged his arm. "Kevin, no."

He shrugged her off. "Something hinky is going down and I want to know what it is. I've got to go now—it's still light enough the floodlights won't come on. You saw that weapon. That wasn't your average hunting rifle."

"They're probably gun runners and more. I'll call it in, but you stay put."

"I'm going. With the escalating gang activity lately, we sure don't need those guns to fall into their hands. I won't let them see me, I promise. But I'll be one of the first in as soon as backup arrives." Green eyes sparkling, he tossed her a lopsided smile. "Ryan would do it."

Ryan? His brother? "No, he wouldn't. And besides, Ryan's a detective with many years' experience," she said. "You're a rookie just two months out of the academy. Is that what this is about? You think you have to prove something to Ryan?"

"Of course not. At least I don't think so. Maybe." He paused and glanced back at the warehouse. "It's more like I have something to prove to myself."

He winked at her and her blood pressure shot up. "Like what?"

"Doesn't matter." He handed her the binoculars she'd set on the dash. "Do you see any cameras anywhere?"

She growled and slapped the lenses to her eyes. Scanning from side to side, she shook her head. "I don't see any, but that doesn't mean they're not there."

The door shut with a quiet snick. She dropped the binoculars to see Kevin sprinting toward the warehouse.

3

Kevin!" But with the doors shut and the windows up, he wouldn't hear her whispered shout. She should have lied and said the place was covered in cameras. "You're not even wearing a vest, you moron."

Izzy sat still for a brief second, muttering under her breath before grabbing her phone and calling for discreet backup. She provided her badge number first. "I don't know the situation inside the building. I know they're armed. Come in quiet. I'm dressed as a civilian in jeans, a gray sweatshirt, and black running shoes. I have on a shoulder holster and am armed. For goodness' sake, don't shoot me." Because she wasn't wearing a vest either. She hadn't known she was going to need one. She also gave Kevin's description. "Don't shoot him either, okay?"

Once she had it confirmed that officers were on the way and they'd been informed of their plainclothes status, she quickly grabbed her weapon, checked it, and went after Kevin. No matter that she was furious with him for his renegade actions, she wouldn't let him go in alone and unprotected.

He was just outside the warehouse door. She ran in a low crouch to the green Tahoe and hid behind it, glancing around the side to see Kevin with his back to the wall of the warehouse, next to the open door.

He held his weapon ready, even as he caught her eye and lifted a finger to his lips. She widened her eyes and jerked her head, motioning for him to get away from the door and join her. He shook his head and Izzy wanted to smack him. Hard.

He rounded the sliding metal door and disappeared into the interior of the warehouse.

Silence reigned.

Izzy looked back over her shoulder and prayed the others would get here soon. Until then . . .

She drew in a deep breath and jogged over to the entrance, taking the spot Kevin had just vacated. She risked a quick glance inside and noted him kneeling behind a pallet piled with boxes.

Just ahead of him were three men, each holding one of the rifles they'd seen carried into the building. They stood facing each other, their focus on checking out the weapons.

As quickly as she dared, she got a good look at the interior of the building. A plain concrete floor. Plenty of unmarked boxes piled on pallets identical to the one that sheltered Kevin. To her right, there were metal steps that led to an indoor balcony on the opposite side. It ran the length of the back wall and was packed with crates as well.

Dirt-encrusted windows kept out the light and would prevent her from seeing in to get a better picture of the interior. And how badly she and Kevin were outnumbered.

She leaned back, trying to decide what to do, when she saw two unmarked cars park across the street from the warehouse. Four detectives headed her way. A rush of relief flowed through her.

Then gunfire from inside the building jerked her back around the corner of the door in time to see Kevin fall to the floor, blood pooling on his chest. One man walked toward Kevin, his weapon held in front of him. "You a cop?"

"Police! Freeze! Drop your weapons!" Izzy yelled. She ducked when his gun spat back at her. She pulled back for cover, then waited for the gunfire to end before she once again peered around the edge of the metal door. The three men she'd seen during her brief peek through the door had scattered, firing in her direction as they ran, their bullets pinging off the walls of the warehouse.

"Kevin!" She grabbed her radio. "Officer down! Officer down!"

Running footsteps sounded behind her and she spared a glance over her shoulder. Their backup had arrived too late.

She checked back on Kevin. He lay still, the pool of blood growing in a widening circle. She looked over her shoulder to see officers decked out in tactical gear taking up positions, making sure they were out of the line of fire.

"Three suspects heading out the back!" She gave the name of the street. "I repeat, cut them off at the ba—"

Two shots came from up above.

Izzy looked up in time to see a body fall over the railing of the balcony. The thud on the concrete floor sounded like another gunshot. And then she caught a brief glimpse of a dark-haired man who was turning sideways and racing out the back door of the balcony to the stairwell. She rushed toward her partner and dropped to her knees. "Kevin!"

His eyes fluttered. He gasped. Sputtered. Blood dribbled from his mouth.

She wiped it with her hand. "No, no, don't do this."

He swallowed and whispered something. She pressed one hand to his chest and one to his stomach in a hopeless effort to staunch the flow of blood.

"Phone . . ."

"What?"

"Phone. Look at . . ." His eyes fluttered.

She looked around. There, on the floor, slid halfway under the wooden crate.

"Promise," he whispered. "Promise . . . look . . . hide it."

"Yeah. Yeah. I promise." She grabbed the phone and shoved it into the back pocket of her jeans, not caring about the blood she smeared over it. "Okay, I've got it. Okay? Now be quiet and just hang on."

"Good. Have a . . . good . . . birthday, Iz."

"Yes. I will. If you'll go with me, I'll jump all over that place. We'll jump together, okay?"

"Tell . . . Ryan . . . Mom . . . sorry . . . was . . . stupid."

"No. I'm not telling them that. You tell them."

"*Ga-ga-baahhhh . . . ga . . .*" He strained, his breathing labored, his eyes wide.

"What? Breathe, Kev, just breathe."

His eyes closed.

"Kevin!"

Detective Ryan Marshall liked football. Especially Gamecock football. He'd been debating whether to head to Williams-Bryce stadium to watch them scrimmage or go into the office and work when the call came over the radio. "Officer needs assistance. Officer needs backup." And then the details. Details that included his younger brother's name and Izzy's.

He'd grabbed his vest, badge, and gun and bolted from his home to dive into his vehicle. It should have taken him fifteen minutes to arrive to the location. He made it in nine.

Cutting everything off a mile before the specified address, he coasted in behind two unmarked cars. He'd listened to the radio all the way over and knew the situation had gone south fast. Gunshots reported. Officer down. *Officer down . . .* two words that should never have a reason to be used together.

Kevin was there. As was Izzy. Izzy, with flashing green eyes and dark hair that he'd seen all his life and just noticed in an

23

I'm-interested-in-going-out-with-her kind of way about three months ago. Izzy, who was his brother's partner and wouldn't let anything happen to him. Would she?

He threw the vehicle in park and bolted out the door.

"Kevin!"

The raw, grief-ravaged scream nearly halted him in his tracks. "No," he whispered. "Oh, please, God, not Kevin." He flashed his badge to the uniformed officers who had arrived on the scene to indicate he was backup. He had the earpiece in to allow him to hear the progress being made in the apprehension of the suspects.

But right now, his only focus was his brother. He dashed inside the warehouse, weapon ready.

Only to skid to a heart-jarring halt when he saw Izzy on the floor, covered in blood and demanding that Kevin breathe.

4

Time moved in a blur for Izzy. She knew the ambulance was there, felt hands on her shoulders moving her away from Kevin, heard the paramedics talking, saw them working on him, smelled the residue from the gunfire—and the blood. She didn't think she'd ever get the scent of the blood out of her mind.

Oh, Kevin.

She sat back and leaned against the wooden pallets that had sheltered Kevin only moments ago. A rough edge dug into her back, but she didn't care.

"He's still alive, let's go."

The words penetrated her stupor. Wait. What? He was alive? She shuddered and tried to focus. The paramedics loaded Kevin into the ambulance and squealed away.

Izzy ran a hand through her hair. She had to get to the hospital, to be with him. To . . . what?

Wait. And pray.

But first, the guy who'd fallen from the balcony. Paramedics were working on him. She slipped in for a closer look. Who was he? They'd cut his shirt from hem to collar. Tattoos covered his abdomen. The five-pointed star with the number 5 in the middle. A Bloods gang member.

A hard hand on her upper arm pulled her around to meet a pair of glittering hazel eyes that belonged to Ryan Marshall. "What was he doing here," he said, "facing these guys alone? Two months, Izzy." He held up two fingers as though she needed the visual. "He's only been out of the academy two months! You were supposed to have his back."

Izzy jerked her arm from his grasp. "Are you kidding me? I had his back, I was all over watching out for him, but it's hard to do that when the other person doesn't cooperate." She couldn't do this. Not now. Her brain and emotions were on overload. "I called for backup and followed him in." She jabbed a finger in his chest. "This isn't on me." She turned her back on him and let her eyes dart from one face to the next, but didn't see the one she was looking for.

Where had he gone?

"I have questions that you're going to answer," Ryan said.

The demand scraped her nerves and she had to bite her tongue on the words that wanted to bypass her filter. Ryan was angry, upset, scared to death his little brother was going to die. Well, so was she.

She drew in a deep breath and turned back to face him. "And I'll answer your questions. Soon." She had a full night ahead of her. Paperwork, her statement . . . praying for Kevin to live. And her own questions that needed answers. Fast. Like where had Blackjack been? The fact that he'd never shown up made her wonder.

And what had *he* been doing here? The scene ran through her mind once again. She'd entered the warehouse, seen Kevin on the floor. Raced to his side. Heard more gunshots. Saw the body fall from the balcony, heard it hit the floor. And looked up to see . . .

. . . Derek?

Maybe. She'd only caught a glimpse of his profile, but it had sure looked like him.

Izzy rubbed her forehead, the tension headache growing by the second. It couldn't have been Derek, could it? Her twin brother was also a detective in the department where she worked as well as a member of vice. And if it *had* been him on the balcony, then he'd saved her life by shooting the man who'd been about to shoot her.

And then he'd run. *Why?*

"What was he doing here?"

She jerked as Ryan's voice echoed her own mental question, and for a moment she thought he was talking about—

"Why'd you let him go in alone?" Ryan continued.

He was talking about Kevin, not Derek. "We were on a stakeout, Ryan. And I didn't *let* Kevin go in alone. I didn't *let* him do anything. He's a big boy." A big boy who'd made a very stupid, possibly lethal, decision.

All because he had something to prove. She didn't buy that he just wanted to prove something to himself. The youngest sibling of four, with one brother killed on the battlefield of Afghanistan, Kevin had always been the daredevil. He'd craved accolades and attention. In his eyes, this was his chance to be a hero. He'd gotten the information and he'd wanted to make the bust. And it had gotten him shot. Period.

She kept walking toward her car, parked where she'd left it.

With a perfect view of the warehouse.

Where her partner had just been shot.

Grief welled. She shut it down. Not yet. Not now.

A hard hand on her arm jerked her around again. And once again, she pulled out of his grasp. "You have to stop doing that or you're going to find yourself on the ground." She ignored the flash of memory that kind of touch incited. Memories Ryan didn't know about. Memories she refused to allow a hold on her. Not anymore.

He ran a hand through his hair. "Sorry. Sorry. I don't mean to be rough, but I . . ."

"What?"

He spread his hands. "That can't be the way it happened."

She froze for half a second, tempted to lash out. She drew in a steadying breath. "Well, since you were here, why don't you tell me exactly what happened then?"

He winced at the sarcasm, then shook his head. "Obviously you left him alone or you would have been shot too. Or you would have shot the guys that shot him. Or . . . or something."

"Or something?" If she kept repeating him, they'd never get anywhere. She opened her mouth to blast him, then snapped her lips shut. With effort, she reminded herself once again that he was mad, upset, looking for someone to blame and not thinking clearly. But still the words came. "So what you're saying is that if one partner gets shot and the other one doesn't, then she's not doing her job? Think about that for just half a minute, Ryan."

He flinched. "No. Of course not."

"That's what you just said. You need to stop and take a deep breath and get your thoughts together before you say anything else." She glared at him and opened her car door. "I'll see you at the hospital." She climbed in and slammed the door in his face.

Once she was on the road toward the hospital, guilt hit her. Was he right? Was there something else she should have done? *Could* have done? Had she waited too long to call for backup? Should she have followed Kevin into the building? If she'd been in there, is it possible she might have seen the gun, maybe shot first?

No. If she'd gone in, she'd have been shot too, by the suspect she'd missed seeing. The guy on the balcony who had intended to shoot her as well.

Only Derek had shot him first. If it *had* been him, her twin brother had some explaining to do. She pulled over to the side of the road, hating the delay, but not wanting to mess with her phone while she was this upset and driving. She dialed his number and it went straight to voice mail.

Izzy growled and sent him a text.

Call me.

She hesitated, then called Derek's partner, Jasmine Clark. When the woman's voice mail came on, Izzy sighed, but left a message for her to call. She then clipped the phone to her belt and pulled back into traffic while Ryan's accusations looped through her brain.

Ryan Marshall. He'd been a thorn in her side since she'd met him at the tender age of nine and he'd talked her into climbing a tree. She'd fallen out and busted her chin wide open. He'd been remorseful and begged her forgiveness. And while she'd given it, she'd hated heights ever since.

She grimaced. She shouldn't have slammed the door on him. She'd apologize. As long as he didn't say something to set her off again. No. His brother was clinging to life. Ryan deserved grace. No matter what he said, she'd hold her tongue.

Her phone rang and she pulled it from her back pocket. Only it wasn't hers, it was Kevin's. His blood still covered the screen.

With a new lump in her throat, she shoved his phone back into her pocket and grabbed hers from the clip. Izzy spared a quick glance at the screen. She didn't feel like talking, but had to check since she'd sent Derek the order to call her. Only it wasn't him. She pressed the button to connect the call. "Hello?"

"Are you all right?"

The intensity of the question struck her like a punch to the solar plexus. "Yes, ma'am." She slowed and pulled over once more. The chief of police checking up on her. As she would every officer involved in the incident.

"And Officer Marshall?"

"He's en route to the hospital and so am I."

"So he's still alive."

"Yes, ma'am."

"I have a press conference scheduled in thirty minutes on the steps of the hospital. Then I want to see you."

"Of course. I'll be in the surgery waiting room."

"I'll find you."

"Yes, ma'am."

"And Isabelle?"

"Yes?"

The line went silent for a brief moment. Then the woman cleared her throat. "I'm not the chief of police right now. I'm your mother and I'm so glad you're okay. I love you, sweetheart."

Izzy's throat tightened at the husky words. "I love you too, Mom. See you soon."

Ryan waited at the entrance for Izzy to park her car and come through the automatic door. Somehow he'd beaten her here. Officers involved in the incident were already in the waiting room. They could give their statements from there just as well as any other place. Ryan had already gotten an update on Kevin and there was nothing more he could do except wait.

Wait and talk. Find out what happened from the officer who'd let his brother get shot.

When Izzy saw him, she frowned, then took a deep breath but didn't try to avoid him. No, she wouldn't. Izzy always faced everything head on. One of the many qualities he admired about her.

"How is he?" she asked.

"They're taking him to surgery now. My parents are on the way and I'm headed in there too. I'm probably going to be giving blood. We're the same type. Walk with me?"

"Sure." She fell into step beside him and they made their way to the elevator. They were the only ones on the ride to the second floor.

"Did they catch them?" she asked. "The guys who ran from the warehouse? There were four of them. No, five." The guy on the balcony.

"They got one. If there were five, then three managed to slip away. One's dead, one's in custody."

"Is the one in custody talking?"

"He hasn't said a word, according to Charice. He just sits and stares at the wall. Like he's deaf. She said it's creepy."

Charice Mann. His partner of four years. She'd continue to keep him updated on the interrogation.

"Is he? Deaf?" she asked.

"No one knows. I don't think so, though. Charice said he's got gang markings for the Crips. If we let him sit long enough, maybe he'll start talking."

Izzy rubbed red-rimmed eyes. "What is with the sudden resurgence of gang violence? It seems to be so much worse in the last few weeks. Even random attacks on people in the street have risen."

"I know. Seems like every time we turn around there's a new dead gang member—mostly kids. Dead kids." It broke his heart.

"It needs to stop."

"The gang unit is working on it."

She paused. "Wait a minute. You said he has the markings of the Crips."

"Right."

"But the dead guy had the markings of the Bloods."

"So what were they doing together in the warehouse?"

They stepped off the elevator. "Izzy? Ryan?"

Ruthie's voice stopped them. Izzy turned and gave a little grunt when Ruthie enveloped her in a massive hug.

"I've only got about three more minutes," Ruthie said. "I was hoping to see you step off that elevator. Are you okay?" She stepped back to look her over. "I see blood. Is it yours?"

She started to examine her when Izzy caught her hands.

"It's not mine. It's Kevin's." Her voice broke on his name and Ryan felt his own throat tighten.

Ruthie's eyes reddened, but no tears fell. "I heard. He's being rushed into surgery right now. I'm going to assist. I'm headed there now, so you can rest assured there will be someone in the room who's praying." She turned her attention to him and Ryan soon found himself wrapped in a hug as well. "I'm so sorry," she whispered. "I really am."

"Yeah. Thanks, Ruthie. Just save him, okay?"

"They're waiting on you, Dr. St. John." One of the nurses stood to the side, glancing at her watch.

Ruthie stepped back. "I've got to go. But I'll have someone keep you updated as often as I can, I promise."

"Okay."

She gave Izzy one last hug and hurried down the hall. Izzy looked down at her arms and hands. Ryan's gaze followed hers to Kevin's dried blood. "I need to clean up. I can't see your mother like this."

"There's a bathroom over there." He pointed down the hall and to the left.

Izzy nodded and disappeared inside. When she stepped back out, he pushed himself off the wall. She looked presentable. She still had some blood on her shirt and on her jeans at the knees where she'd knelt next to Kevin on the warehouse floor. But the worst of it was gone.

Ryan swiped a hand over his eyes. "Before we hit the waiting room, will you please tell me what happened with Kevin?" he asked.

"Thought you'd already come to your own conclusions."

He sighed. "I'm sorry. I was panicked."

"I know." She reached into the bag she carried on her shoulder and pulled out a small handheld camcorder. "You can watch it."

His heart thudded. "You recorded it?"

"Partly. I drove my personal car to the stakeout. The last thing I needed was for these guys to catch me in a cruiser. I set up the camera as a precaution. Anyway, it doesn't show what happened inside, just outside. And I debated even showing it to you, but if it was my brother . . ." She hesitated when he tried to take it from her. "You're not going to be happy with Kevin."

"That's nothing new." He sighed. Then scowled. "I can handle it."

She placed a hand over the camcorder. "No, I mean, you're going to be livid . . . and very disappointed."

He met her frown for frown. *Livid*? That was a pretty strong word. And *disappointed*? What had Kevin done?

He hesitated. He wanted to watch the video, but he wanted an update on Kevin more. "Hold on to this. It can wait." He just needed to hear his brother was still alive. *Please, God.*

A mere two minutes after he and Izzy stepped into the waiting room, the door swung open again and Ryan turned to see his parents enter. His father's eyes met his and the absolute devastation there nearly took him to his knees. He went over and hugged the man. "He's still alive, Dad."

"Barely, from what I was told."

Yes. "But still alive." As long as he was alive, there was hope. He turned to his mother, who stood stoic, her blank stare riveted on a painting hanging on the wall across the room. Prematurely gray, her short hair curled around her temples and at the base of her neck. He took her arm and led her to a chair. "Mom? Mom. Look at me."

She blinked. Tears filled her eyes and spilled down her still-smooth cheeks like silent rivers of pain. "I can't lose him, Ryan. Not him too. My heart simply can't . . . not with Chris . . . I can't . . ."

Grief burned yet another hole in his heart. "I know, Mom."

He pinched the bridge of his nose, then grasped her hand. Two SLED detectives approached Izzy. Yeah, the state agency, South Carolina Law Enforcement Division, would be involved in this. He knew the chief, Tabitha St. John, worked closely with them. She would have been all over that. "Could we get your statement? Officers are canvassing the area and doing an all-out manhunt for the suspects, but we need your input now."

And they'd want to check her weapon. If she'd fired it, she'd have to go through all the paperwork. If she hadn't, they'd simply hand it back to her.

"Of course."

"While you're doing that," Ryan said, "I'm going to go give blood."

His mother patted his hand. "Yes. Go."

"Text me if there's any change at all. Promise."

"I promise, son," his father said.

Izzy stepped aside with the two SLED detectives and Ryan made his way to the area he'd been to several times before. Always for an officer-involved shooting. Never had he imagined it would be for his brother. Thirty minutes later, with no texts regarding Kevin, he tossed back the orange juice they handed him and took the crackers without protest. He might need them.

Ryan made his way back to the waiting room and found his mother leaning against his father, eyes closed, face ashen, tears still wet on her cheeks. He simply sat next to her, trying to ignore the thick-as-tar tension surrounding him.

Time passed with no word on his brother and Ryan's nerves stretched with each minute that ticked by.

Izzy finally finished with the detectives and returned to her seat opposite him and his mother. She leaned forward. "I'm sorry, Mrs. Marshall."

His mom opened her eyes. "Tell me what happened." She sniffed and swiped a tissue over the tears that seemed to have no end.

Ryan almost interrupted and told her not to worry about the details for now, but of course she'd want to know. She might be reeling with the news of Kevin's shooting, but she'd want answers.

"Uh, well, I can't right now," Izzy said. "I promise that as soon as I have the green light, I'll fill you in."

His mother frowned at the evasive answer, and Ryan didn't like it either but kept his mouth shut. She was shooting looks at him to back her up. She didn't want to tell his mother what had happened. And until he knew himself, he'd support her.

A woman stepped into the room. "Is the Marshall family here?"

Ryan shot to his feet. His father stood as well. "We are."

"Could you follow me, please? The doctor would like to meet with you in private."

"No," his mother whispered. "No. I'm not going." Sobs tumbled from her lips. The others in the waiting room stared and Ryan couldn't stand the pity he saw etched there. He pulled her to her feet. "Come on, Mom. I'll help you." His eyes locked on Izzy's pleading ones. He nodded and she rose to follow.

His mother let him lead her, him holding one arm, his father on the other side.

Once in the private room, Ryan lowered his mother into the nearest chair while he kept a tight grip on his grief. Izzy stood just inside the door, her hands clenched, jaw tight. Tears stood in her eyes, but he could see her fierce determination to keep them from falling.

He didn't want to be here. He knew what was coming, but for just a moment he could pretend it wasn't real. It wasn't real if nobody said it.

His father stood by the fake window with curtains that framed a painted outdoor scene. Ryan wondered if that was supposed to be comforting somehow. Then wondered why he wondered that.

His dad started to pace from one end of the twelve-by-twelve room to the other. Ryan focused on the cross on the wall. *Don't take Kevin, please, God, not Kevin too.*

The door opened and then Ruthie stepped into the room. Ryan's heart dropped. He knew that look on her face. Had seen it on his father's when he'd told him his Marine brother, Chris, had been killed in Afghanistan by an IED.

Ryan placed a hand on his mother's shoulder and felt it shake. Sobs ripped from her.

"I asked them to let me tell you." Her voice hitched. "I'm sorry," Ruthie said. Tears stood in her eyes, then tumbled over her lashes. She wiped them away. "We did all we could, but his injuries were just too extensive—"

35

5

Izzy stumbled back against the wall. Then slid down it until she sat on the floor. Kevin was dead. Her partner, her friend, a guy she'd known since birth, was dead, and there was nothing she could do about it. She couldn't turn back time and do things differently. She couldn't fix this.

Her mind raced with sporadic thoughts, each one trying to find a landing spot, but skittering out of reach at the last minute.

Except for one.

Kevin's dead. Kevin's dead.

"Izzy? Izzy?"

Ryan's voice penetrated and she lifted her head to find him holding a hand out to her. She swiped a hand across her wet cheeks and allowed him to pull her to her feet. "What?"

"You might want to check your phone. You have so many messages coming in, it's about to blow up."

She drew in a shuddering breath. How much time had blipped by while she'd been lost in her grief? His mother was still crying on his father's shoulder and Ruthie was gone. So maybe just a few minutes?

The door opened and more family entered. She recognized Ryan's sister, Cathy, and her husband, Dale. Cathy ran to Ryan and hugged him while her tears soaked his shirt.

Izzy looked down at her phone and realized she'd missed her

mother's calls as well as calls from her brothers and sisters. And twenty-four texts from her siblings and a few friends.

Her mother. She had to find her. "I have to go."

Ryan nodded. "Okay."

"Mom's here to make a statement about the shooting to the press. I need to find her before she gets in front of the cameras." She motioned to her bloody clothes. "I'm not letting them get a shot of this."

"She'll announce Kevin's death as well now," Ryan said softly.

"Yes. I'm sure." She pressed fingertips to her burning eyes and gathered her emotions into a safe place. When she was ready, she blinked and texted her mother she was on the way. Then sent a group text to the rest of her family that she was fine.

The door opened again and her mother walked in. Tabitha St. John, dressed in her chief of police formal blues—she exuded confidence, strength, sorrow, and compassion. Her assistant, deputy chief of police Felicia Denning, followed behind. The other woman was tall with blue eyes and usually wore a warm smile. Today her eyes sparked with anger and her lips were tight with suppressed emotion. Izzy understood.

She nodded to Felicia, then went to her mother and hugged her. "I was on my way to find you."

"I was just informed of Kevin's death. Ruthie called me. I wanted to come offer my condolences." She walked over to Ryan and hugged him, then did the same, one by one, for each of his family members. "I'm so sorry, Gena," her mother said. "So very sorry."

"Thank you," Ryan's mother whispered. She dabbed her cheeks with the tissue and lifted her chin. "What are you going to do about this, Tabitha? Felicia? They killed my boy." Her lips trembled, but her eyes never wavered from the two women.

"There will be a full investigation and we'll catch the people who killed him," Tabitha said.

Just flat, emotionless facts. Her mother decreed it, therefore it would be. Izzy had no doubt she would do whatever it took to bring Ryan's killer to justice.

That was fine with Izzy. She felt the same way. Felicia nodded with each word her mother said. The two women worked well together, and Izzy felt sure the people responsible for Kevin's death would soon be in custody—especially with every cop in the city also on high alert, looking for their brother's killer.

The events of the night blipped through her mind at warp speed, stopping only when she got to the man on the warehouse balcony. She played his profile over and over in her mind. He'd saved her life, then run.

Why?

She'd given her statement to the police and left Derek's name out of it since she wasn't completely sure, but still . . .

She grabbed her phone from the clip on her belt and dialed her brother's number. Four rings, then voice mail. "I'm not kidding. Call me."

She hung up.

Her phone buzzed, indicating a text. Derek.

Can't talk right now. What do you need?

A cold ball of anxiety formed in the pit of her belly.

That was you on the balcony, wasn't it?

No answer. She typed again.

I know it was you. You shot that guy.

What are you talking about?

Anger and disbelief curled inside her.

So, you're going to lie to me?

38

They'd never lied to one another. Never.

More time passed and she thought he was going to ignore her. Her phone buzzed, but her mother took her hand and pulled her toward the door. "Come with me." She excused them to the others in the room and left Felicia with the family. Once in the hall, her mother released her hand and turned. "We need to talk and I don't have much time. They're waiting on me."

"I know."

"Tell me everything that happened."

"Hasn't someone already filled you in?"

"Of course, I want it from you, though." She pulled a tube of lipstick from the pocket of her blazer and applied it expertly without a mirror.

"Okay, but quick question."

"Yes?"

"Is Derek working on something I don't know about? He missed our lunch today."

Her mother frowned. "Like what?"

"Like some undercover stuff."

"Seems like he's always undercover, doesn't it?" She rubbed her forehead as though she had a headache forming. "But no, nothing as of right this minute. He actually asked for time off." Her eyes narrowed and she dropped her hand back to her side. "Why?"

"Time off? Derek, the workaholic? Time off for what?"

"You know he and Elaine broke up. He said he needed time to clear his head and get his focus back. Not wanting him undercover in that state, I told him to take two weeks—and to let me know if that wasn't long enough."

"Seriously?"

"Yes. Why?"

Izzy opened her mouth, then snapped it shut. Was she wrong then? Maybe it wasn't Derek. "It doesn't matter."

"Yes, it does. You asked for a reason. What is it?"

She should have kept her mouth shut. "Just . . . I don't know. I have to think."

"If something's going on with Derek—"

"There's not. I mean, there might be, but it's nothing I have facts on. Nothing that I know of for sure and I mean that."

"Izzy, I know he shares everything with you—"

"Mom, please don't push. And apparently not everything. I didn't know about his leave of absence or that he and Elaine had called it quits."

Her mother raised a brow. "You didn't?"

"No."

"Then something is definitely going on with Derek."

"But I don't know what. Seriously, if I had something to tell you, I would, but I don't, so I can't. You know how Linc's always saying to have the facts before you say anything." She shrugged. "I don't have facts, just speculation."

"Speculation about what, Izzy?"

"Something at the warehouse."

"What did you see that would cause you to speculate?"

Izzy flashed back to the moment she'd seen the man on the balcony and shook her head. "Nothing I can put my finger on. It's a feeling more than anything and I don't want to base anything on a feeling, you know?"

Her mother held her eyes a moment longer, and it was all Izzy could do not to glance away. Finally, her mother nodded, looked back at the closed door to the room where grief reigned, and drew in a deep breath. "Now. About Kevin. Tell me and quickly."

"It'll be easier to show you."

"Is this something Felicia should see?"

"Probably."

"Let me get her then."

Izzy waited until the deputy chief of police joined them, then she pulled the camera from her bag and pressed the touch screen to start the footage.

Her mother and Felicia watched it. Izzy watched her mother. She didn't need to see what happened on the recording again. The thunderclouds in her eyes turned into a full-blown raging storm during the two-minute video.

She shut it off.

Her mother and Felicia exchanged a glance. "Is there any more footage anywhere?" Felicia asked.

"No."

Fingers pressed against her lips, her mother shook her head. "Is there any footage from the inside?"

"No, nothing."

"You're sure?" Felicia pressed. "Absolutely positive?"

"I'm sure. That's it."

"Okay." Her mother drew in a deep breath. "Has anyone else seen this?"

"No. I'm going to show it to Ryan, though. He knows about it, but he hasn't seen it."

Hesitating, she locked her eyes on Izzy's and finally gave a slow nod. "Fine. He can see it. If he knows about it, we both know he'll be like a dog with a bone about watching it. But don't show it to anyone else and turn it in as evidence immediately." She paused. "Did you fire your weapon?"

"No, ma'am. SLED has checked it and confirmed."

"Don't forget to call Rhianna Simpson."

"The trauma counselor? Mom, I really don't need—"

Her mother simply raised her brow.

Izzy sighed and grimaced. It was protocol and she knew it. She tucked the camera into her bag. "I'll do it first thing in the morning. Go do your press conference. I've got my laptop, so I'm going to stay here and start filling out paperwork. I'll also get the video turned in."

Her mother clasped Izzy's upper arm. "You're on leave for a few days."

"Mom—"

"No choice, Izzy. I mean it."

"Fine."

She frowned. "Be careful, darling. What happened to Kevin is tragic. I don't want that same phone call."

"Trust me, I don't want that either."

Izzy hesitated, the desire to tell her about Derek nearly overwhelming her. Only the thought of Derek's texts and Felicia's presence stopped her. She at least owed it to him to let him explain himself. Didn't she?

"Something else, Izzy?" her mother asked.

"No." Izzy cleared her throat. "Not right now. Go. It's going to be a long night."

The two women walked away and Ryan joined her in the hall. "I'm ready to see that video."

"Don't you need to be with your family right now? Don't *they* need you to be with them?"

He turned on her. "Right now, what they *need* is for me to find out who killed Kevin. Now, let's find a place to watch that video."

"Fine. But away from here. I don't want your parents or someone stepping outside and asking what we're doing."

"Izzy?"

She turned. Gabby stood twenty feet away, her fingers wrapped around the strap of her purse, white teeth chewing on her bottom lip. Her friend's uncertainty grabbed her heart. "Hold on a second, Ryan, okay?"

"Yeah."

He began to pace while Izzy went to hug her friend.

"I'm sorry," Gabby said, "I just want you to know that."

"I know."

"I won't keep you, I just wanted to see you and make sure you were all right."

"I'm not all right, but I'm not falling to pieces either. What about you?"

Gabby shrugged, then rubbed a hand across her forehead. "I'm surviving."

The woman wouldn't meet her gaze. Izzy frowned at the odd body language. "What is it, Gab?"

"I . . . need to let you know that Mick was released this morning. For good."

Izzy froze, then swallowed hard and glanced over her shoulder to make sure Ryan was out of earshot. "I see."

"He's done with the hospital and weekend visits and all that." She drew in a deep breath. "And he's faithfully taking his medication— at least he says so . . ." She lifted a shoulder. "All we can do is just pray for the best."

And keep him away from me. Izzy shuddered.

"I thought about calling you or texting you or . . . whatever. But I wanted to tell you in person."

"Thank you. Is he . . . uh . . . okay?"

"Yes. I think so. For now. But he's going to be staying with me until he gets a job, so I didn't want you popping in unannounced."

"No popping in on you. Got it." Izzy wasn't sure what to say.

Gabby rubbed her eyes. "Okay, well. I'll go. You look busy."

Izzy sighed and hugged her friend one more time. "I don't want things to be awkward with us. We'll take it one day at a time."

Relief wilted the woman's shoulders, then she hugged Izzy with a hard squeeze. "Thanks, Iz." She nodded toward the pacing Ryan. "Any word on his brother's killer?"

"Not yet."

"Did they catch everyone involved?"

"Are you asking as a friend or as campaign manager for Melissa Endicott?"

Gabby flushed. "Well, just as a friend, but if you'd rather not answer that, I understand."

"No, they didn't catch everyone."

"Any leads?"

"None that I can talk about."

Gabby nodded. "I get it. I'll talk to you later, okay?"

"Sure."

Still, Gabby lingered. "Give my condolences to the family?"

"Of course. Let's grab some lunch soon."

"You got it. See you later."

Gabby finally left and Ryan was instantly at her side. "Let's go down here."

He led the way down the hall to an empty patient room. She handed him the camera and he pressed play. His expression never changed as the video played out.

But his jaw tightened and a muscle jumped in his cheek. When the footage ended, he turned it off and handed the camera to her. He didn't say anything for at least a full minute. Izzy knew he was processing and she simply stayed quiet.

When he finally looked at her, she flinched at the hardness in his eyes. "Let's find some place we can talk."

———

Ryan didn't know what to feel. To think. To say. To do. He was afraid to move lest he simply explode. He decided *livid* was too tame a word for the description of his current emotion. "How could he do that? How could he be so stupid? I don't even know what to say to that."

The words came out in a whisper, but Izzy must have heard them. She took his hand. "I tried to stop him, Ryan, I did. I promise."

"I . . . know. I heard. I . . . I'm sorry I jumped on you earlier about not having his back. You obviously did. You did everything right. But Kevin—" He shook his head. He had no words. He finally raked a hand through his hair. "How long have our families been friends?"

"What? I don't know. Since before the Civil War probably. A long time. Why?"

"Because I want to know what Kevin thought he had to prove to himself and why he thought he would do such a lame-brained, stupid thing as to go into a warehouse full of—" He looked down and drew in a breath, then looked back up into her sad, grieving eyes. "So think back and tell me what he had to prove."

"Ry—"

"Think!" She flinched, then glared at him. He closed his eyes. "Sorry."

"I don't know, okay? I'll think about it. I've *thought* about it. But I just don't know."

He closed his eyes. "I'm doing it again. Snapping at you when none of this is your fault. I'm sorry. I'm . . . sorry."

"I know."

"Okay, fine." He paused and opened his eyes. "Were there any cameras inside the warehouse?"

"I don't know. I looked for some on the outside when Kevin was running toward it. I was afraid they'd pick him up on one as he approached, but as far as I could tell, there weren't any. Doesn't mean there weren't, but . . ." She pressed her fingers to her eyes. "I didn't even look inside. I was too busy trying to—"

"Yeah."

"What about the guys who worked the crime scene? They would know."

He nodded. "I'll call and see." Five minutes later, he hung up. "They found three surveillance cameras on the outside of the building."

"Why didn't I see them?"

"They were hidden. Tucked away in strategic places, but there was no recorded footage and they didn't find any cameras on the inside."

"That makes me wonder."

"What?"

"If the cameras on the outside were hidden, there are probably hidden cameras on the inside."

He nodded. "I can agree with that."

"Okay, forget that for the moment. What about the guy who fell from the balcony?" she said. "In all the chaos with Kevin, I haven't checked. We need to follow up on him."

"I'll call the morgue and see if he was brought in. If not, he's at one of the hospitals."

While he dialed the morgue, she walked to the drink machine and dumped in enough money for two sodas. He watched her fluid movements. Graceful . . . and pretty. He blinked at the thought. He'd known Izzy since she was a little kid. He actually remembered the day she was born and his mother made him come to this very hospital to see her. Izzy had only been a year older than Kevin, but Kevin had played around for years before deciding to settle down and join the police force.

Against Ryan's advice.

Five years Izzy's senior, Ryan had graduated high school and gone on to the police academy. He'd seen her only a handful of times in the years before she'd joined the force.

But three months ago, at a joint family picnic, he'd noticed her. And Derek had noticed him noticing. "Stay away from her," he said.

Ryan frowned. "Why?"

"Because I said so. Izzy's doing a good job on the force. She's focused, sharp. If you let her know you're interested, she'd . . . well, you'd be a distraction and she doesn't need that right now."

So Ryan had reluctantly kept his distance. He still didn't know why Derek was so adamant that he stay away from Izzy, but since Izzy hadn't shown him any encouragement, he'd kept a tight grip on his feelings. Of course, the *reason* she hadn't shown him any encouragement was because he'd held her at arm's length. At least he hoped that was why. Maybe she wasn't nearly as interested in him as he was in her.

Ryan drew in a calming breath. He needed to get his thoughts organized.

When Izzy came back, she handed him one of the sodas, then took a long swig out of the other.

"I'm on hold," he said.

She gave a low huff. "Of course you are. And you're probably calling at the worst time *ever*."

"Yeah. Because any time is the worst time *ever*," he mimicked her. Ryan knew she was as familiar with Maria Dover's work practices as he was. Maria never had time for phone calls and she made sure everyone knew it. But this was important.

Kevin . . . God, not Kevin. No, why Kevin?

"This better be important." Maria sounded irritated. Just like she always did.

Ryan didn't really care. "My brother was shot and killed tonight. That important enough for you, Maria?"

The line went silent. "Ryan. Sorry. I didn't look to see who was calling. And I heard about Kevin," she said, a softness in her voice he'd never heard before. "I'm so sorry. Truly."

Her new tone sapped his ire. "And I'm sorry I snapped. It seems to be the only way I know how to communicate right now."

"What do you need?"

"At the warehouse where the shooting took place, there was a guy. Izzy thinks he was killed. Did you get a body?"

"I got him. DOA. His autopsy is a priority, don't worry."

"Who is he?"

"I don't know since there was no ID on him. I'm sure someone's run his prints, but I haven't heard any more about him."

"Right. Thanks."

"If I hear something, I'll text."

Ryan pressed his fingers to his eyelids. "Appreciate it."

"I really am sorry, Ryan."

"Thanks." He hung up and stood silent for a moment, just processing.

"Well?"

He turned to see Izzy waiting. Ryan filled her in, then took a swig of the Coke. He tossed the can in the recycle bin. "I want to know who the warehouse belongs to."

"That should be easy enough to find out."

"Should be." He shot a text to David Unger, his go-to guy when it came to needing information fast. David had many resources. It wouldn't take long for him to find the answer. Assuming he was working.

An answering text said he was.

On it. Stay tuned.

Ryan showed her the text. "I need to get back to my family, but I really want to join Charice downtown while she's questioning the prisoner."

"You think he'd tell you anything he won't tell her?"

"I don't know. Probably not."

"Yeah." She sighed. "I'm just going to go fill out paperwork."

It hit him again.

Kevin was dead.

"He's gone, Izzy," he whispered. "I can't believe it. I told him not to be a cop. I told him he was too impulsive, that he would get himself or someone else killed. I told him that, can you believe it?"

She threw herself against his chest and wrapped her arms around his waist. Her shoulders shook and he realized she was crying. Huge, silent, body-wracking, soul-deep sobs that triggered his own tears.

Still holding her, he let his knees buckle and, his back against the wall, slid to the floor, pulling her with him. He held her while their tears mingled in salty grief.

6

At 10:30, Izzy pulled up to the warehouse and cut her lights. Before she'd left the hospital, David had texted Ryan that the warehouse had been purchased almost two years ago by a company named Second Chances, Inc. It had been a cash transaction, so there'd been no bank loan. The name on the deed showed Jonathan Gill as the buyer, but the warehouse had sat empty and the company had never gotten off the ground. Probably because Jonathan had been killed in action while in Afghanistan four months later. And Chris two months after that.

Sixteen months ago, the building had been sold to Bricks & Sticks, Inc. Ryan said he had detectives digging deeper into the corporation, but so far there was no paper trail back to the seller. At least not one easy to find, but it had to be there somewhere.

"I want to know who owns Bricks & Sticks," she'd told Ryan.

"Me too, and we're working on it, but it looks like it might be a dummy corporation for something. Charice is tracking down Gill's family to see if they have any helpful information."

About an hour after that, Ryan had called her to let her know that the prints on the dead guy in the warehouse belonged to a career criminal named Spencer Elmore. He'd texted,

He's got ties to organized crime around here, surprise, surprise. Tats for the Bloods are all

49

over him. He's been arrested on some minor
stuff, but has always gotten off.

> Must not have been in the gang long enough to
> build up his rap sheet.

Maybe not. Hopefully it won't take long to run
down his associates and nab the one who killed
Kevin.

She sure hoped so. And then Derek had texted her back. Finally.

I can't explain everything right now. I really
need you to keep quiet about anything you
think you might have seen. Please, Izzy.

So, it *had* been him.

The three-quarters moon cast shadows all over the area and she shivered, debating what she should do now. Her phone buzzed in its clip, distracting her. Chloe checking on her. Again.

U okay?

> I'm fine. Well, as fine as I can be.

Stay with me tonight?

Izzy thought about it. Chloe wouldn't expect her to talk and it might be nice not to be alone. Then again, she didn't know when she'd be finished here. She grimaced and answered,

> No. I wouldn't be good company.

Don't have to be.

> Thanks anyway.

Want me to come stay with u?

No.

Sigh . . . okay. If you change your mind, let me
know. Love u.

U too.

She replaced her phone and drew in a deep breath. Yellow crime
scene tape flapped in the light breeze, and she tugged her jacket
closer around her neck. Flashes from the shooting pinged across
her mind, and she let them come. She was desperate to remember
some detail that would be helpful. A face, a name that someone
might have shouted, anything.

But all she could remember was Kevin. Hearing the shots, seeing
him lying in a pool of blood, his life slowly draining away.

Grabbing his phone, she pulled it from her back pocket. Why
would he tell her to hide it?

Because there was something on there he didn't want anyone to
see. *Duh*. But could she handle scrolling through his selfies right now?

She checked her own phone. Nothing more from Derek. Why
hadn't he called her back? Or at least acknowledged her other texts?
Telling her he couldn't explain wasn't acceptable. If he was truly
undercover, that would make sense. But her mother said he wasn't.
So . . . was she lying for some reason? Izzy's instincts said no.

And his partner hadn't called either. She might not know anything anyway. It was really Derek she needed to talk to.

Izzy walked toward the entrance, her steps slow while her heartbeat raced at the memories. She ducked under the crime scene
tape and tried the metal sliding door. It slid on the track with no
problem. Entering the warehouse, she looked around.

Someone had left one light on inside, which illuminated much
of the space.

The building stood empty and silent now. Law enforcement had finished with it or someone would still be guarding it. Her gaze instantly went to the floor and the brown bloodstain weakened her knees. She wanted to collapse and wail out her anger and grief. Instead she rubbed her eyes, then looked around.

The crime scene unit would have covered every square inch and retrieved any evidence left behind. At least she thought they would. So . . .

She didn't even know why she was here. She'd just felt compelled to come. Izzy continued on into the interior of the building and stopped at the spot where she'd looked up and seen Derek. She replayed the moment in her head once again and still couldn't come up with a good reason for him to be there. Not if he wasn't undercover. But he'd been on the balcony, so that's where'd she start. A sound behind her brought her head up.

She spun and saw nothing, but the hair on the back of her neck lifted as she rested a hand on her weapon. Instead of calling out and revealing her location, she slid behind a pile of empty crates and slipped her weapon from the holster.

The many boxes of weapons had been taken into evidence, but the stacked wooden crates provided enough of a hiding place.

This time the noise came to her left. She turned, and a dark shadow caught her eye. Izzy pulled her phone from the clip and, one-handed, sent a text to the first person at the top of her list who could help without making a big deal about her returning to the crime scene.

Ryan Marshall.

At the warehouse. Someone is here sneaking around.

You need backup?

She breathed a sigh of relief at his immediate response.

Not yet.

I'm on the way.

Izzy tucked her phone into her pocket, afraid to snap it back onto the clip for fear of alerting the person to her presence. Then again, she had a feeling he knew she was in the building. So, go after him, or stay put?

She glanced around the edge of her hiding spot. He was gone. Great.

Izzy decided to get back to her car and call Ryan. No sense in being a sitting duck. The last she'd seen, the person had been to her left. The door was just to her right.

She headed for it, keeping an eye over her shoulder.

Izzy stepped out of the warehouse.

And an arm went around her neck, pressing against her throat. She gasped and jerked.

"Be still," he hissed. "Drop the gun."

He'd snuck out the back and circled the building. Or went out a side door. Either way, he had her. Blood pounded through her veins and Izzy thought about fighting him. Instead, she let the weapon tumble from her fingers.

"Stay out of this, you understand?" He kept his voice low, a whispered hiss. "You could get hurt, or worse."

In spite of the way he spoke, the hoarse, raspy voice sounded familiar, as did the smell of soap mingled with sweat. She knew that smell because she used the same soap. "Derek?"

He gave a low curse and shoved her from him. She stumbled away and turned to face him. "What do you think you're *doing*?" She scooped her weapon from the ground and holstered it.

"That's my question," he said. "What are you doing here?"

"My partner died here, remember? I came to see if . . ." No need to mention the cameras yet. Not until she knew what was going on with him. She threw her hands up. "It doesn't matter. I just had to come back. Now what are you doing here? That was you here earlier, wasn't it? What were you doing here with those guys?"

"I'm working on something."

"You're not undercover. I asked Mom."

He froze, then glared. "You told her you saw me here?"

"No, I didn't know for sure it was you until just now. I just asked her—" She shook her head. "Again, it doesn't matter. You shot that guy, Derek, you have to give a statement."

"Not yet. And Mom doesn't know everything that goes on in the department as much as she would like to think she does. And I *am* undercover."

She narrowed her eyes. "Mom said you're supposed to be on personal leave getting over your breakup with Elaine. That's what she told me anyway. What was that? A cover story for the under-cover job?"

He pinched the bridge of his nose. "Something like that. Please, Izzy. It's complicated and I need you to just pretend like you never saw me."

"Do you know what you're asking? I'm putting my career on the line by not saying anything."

"I know what I'm asking!" He drew in a deep breath. "And I know what I'm doing. This is my life we're talking about here, okay? Please." She could see the effort it took him to speak the words quietly.

"Your life?"

"Yes."

"Tell me."

"I . . . can't."

She simply crossed her arms and stared into eyes that were identical to hers. "Tell me or I tell Mom." She didn't care that she sounded like a petulant child. This was too important.

He groaned, then moved closer, his nose almost touching hers, his eyes flashing. "Are you a dirty cop, Izzy?"

She flinched, then placed her hands on his chest and shoved him away from her. "What? No! Why would you even ask that?"

He studied her, not answering at first, then seemed to come to a decision. "There's a list," he said.

"What list?"

"Parker Estes and Collin Howard are on it."

She gaped. "The cops who were arrested for—"

"Yeah . . . for stealing from the evidence room. And Mom's on it too."

"As a dirty cop?" She couldn't help the squeak in her voice. "Derek! You know there's no way—you can't believe—"

"I *don't* know, Izzy, that's the problem."

"And me? I'm on that list too?"

Headlights went dark before the vehicle turned into the parking area and the engine cut off. If they'd been inside, they never would have seen him.

Derek snagged her upper arm and jerked her back through the warehouse door. "You brought someone with you?"

"No—and keep your hands off of me." She yanked out of his grasp. "But I called for backup when I saw your shadowy figure trying to be all sneaky. It's probably Ryan Marshall."

He dropped his hands. "I can't be seen." He backed up slowly, toward the rear exit of the warehouse.

"What exactly are you doing here, Derek? Why come back here?"

"Don't say anything, Izzy."

"Derek! You know how this works. I could lose my job." She sounded like a broken record, but he wasn't listening.

"And I could wind up dead if the wrong person reads that report."

"Like who?"

He pointed at her, his green eyes snapping. "Keep me out of the report, Izzy, unless you want to see me dead. This is way bigger than you can even imagine. Watch your back and keep your mouth *shut*."

If he didn't quit telling her to keep her mouth shut, she was going to seriously hurt him. "Derek, I can't—"

He slapped a hand to his head and gave another groan, his frustration palpable at her stubborn insistence. "Delay it then. Wait twenty-four hours, then add it, but don't bring attention to it. If anyone says anything, the report is there."

Derek's eyes flicked toward the door as he slipped backward a few more steps.

It occurred to her why he was here. He wanted to make sure that he hadn't left any evidence behind from earlier.

She narrowed her eyes. "Twenty-four hours, Derek. If I can. If I can't, I won't."

"Iz—"

"I mean it."

"Fine. Now make sure it's Ryan and I don't have to save your life again, then I'm out of here."

Izzy pressed her palms to her eyes. Then dropped her hands. She waited until she heard the soft snick of the car door shutting and peered outside.

Ryan's silhouette stood tall in the moonlight and she let out a slow breath. "It's him."

Derek took off toward the back of the warehouse.

Now what?

She was technically withholding evidence in a shooting. Earlier, when she simply suspected that it was Derek in the warehouse, she could just make the shooter a nameless person in the report. But now that she knew for a fact that he'd shot the man, she had to add that to the file.

It was a clean shoot and he'd saved her life, but keeping quiet about it was not cool. Not if she wanted to keep her job. Twenty-four hours. That was as long as she'd give him. Maybe.

Ryan's soft footsteps approached. He entered the open door and stopped when he spotted her.

"It's okay," she said. "Don't shoot me."

"Is he still here?"

"No. He left."

"I didn't hear a car."

"I think he was on foot. Or he had a car stashed somewhere else."

Ryan lowered his weapon. "You think it was the guy that killed Kevin?"

"No."

"You seem awfully sure of that."

"I am. I saw the four possible guys who could have killed Kevin. The person who was just here wasn't one of them."

"You saw him?"

"Yes. Briefly." Time for a change of subject. "Want to look for cameras while we're here?"

"Who was it? Did you know him?"

So much for changing the subject.

She considered lying, then sighed. "I know him. He was just another cop affected by Kevin's shooting and doing some snooping of his own. I overreacted by texting you."

He studied her.

Before he could say anything else, she waved a hand to gesture to the warehouse. "Anyway, while you're here, you want to help me out?"

"What'd you have in mind?"

"There's no way that this was their home base and they didn't take precautions, have some security. I still think there are cameras inside."

He drew in a breath and she saw him glance at the floor. His eyes locked on the bloodstain the same as hers had. He turned away. "Yeah. I'll take the balcony."

He headed for the stairs and Izzy closed her eyes for a moment. He'd not pressed her on the identity of the cop and for that she was thankful. And mad. Why was Derek doing this to her? Why would he ask if she was a dirty cop? Why would she be on a list that indicated she was one? Or that their mother was? That bothered her. A lot. And not only that, but where did he even get such a list? Who'd put it together and how did he learn about it?

She shoved thoughts of her brother and the unanswered questions aside and focused on what she came here to do. She started in one corner of the warehouse and began a perimeter search. She could hear Ryan above her doing the same.

Izzy continued around the building, searching for any area that might hold a camera. Bad guys didn't play fair. "Hey, did the ME or anyone mention anything about finding a body cam on the dead guy?"

"Nope."

"Can we find out?"

He was tracking with her. "I'll text Maria and see." She and Ryan combed the warehouse, each going in opposite directions until they finally met up on the second floor. He had his hands on his hips, looking at the ceiling. "If there are any cameras hidden here, they've got to be up there."

"The light?" she asked.

"Yeah."

"All right, so how are we going to get up there to look? Or . . ." She pointed. "See that ladder that leads to the roof?"

"Yes." The metal ladder attached to the wall led to a door that allowed access to the outside.

She walked toward it and climbed.

"Be careful, would you?"

"Just catch me if I fall. I hate heights."

"Great," she heard him murmur.

"Yeah. And it's all your fault."

"What? How do you figure that?"

"Remember that tree you dared me to climb when I was nine?"

"Oh." A pause. "Hey, you wanted to climb that tree."

"I had a huge crush on you. I wanted you to think I was awesome. I climbed it because I thought it would impress you."

He fell silent. "You had a crush on me?"

"Hmm, yes. I got over it, though." Sort of.

"Oh."

Izzy smiled and kept climbing, doing her best to keep her nerves calm. Ryan was below her. If she fell, he'd do his best to catch her. If he missed, well . . . she shuddered and tightened her grip.

At the top, she turned and looked out over the warehouse. A perfect view, just like she'd thought. The view sent her stomach fluttering and nausea rose. She forced it down and focused on the task before her. Izzy ran her hand over the top of the ladder.

Nothing.

She tried the side. "Aha."

"What?"

"Found it."

She pulled it off the Velcro that held it and started down. *You can do this. One step at a time.* Her foot slipped on the second-to-last rung. "Ah!"

For a moment, she dangled, feet swinging. Then hard hands clamped down on her waist. "I've got you."

Ryan lowered her to the floor and she turned to stare up at him. His eyes narrowed and she swallowed hard. "I . . . uh . . . knew I was going to do something like that. I shouldn't have said anything about hating heights." She cleared her throat. "So . . . um. Here."

He took it and finally looked away from her to study the small object. "So if they have a camera, they've got to have a way to watch it," Ryan said.

"They can do that on their phones."

"True. Is it one of those that records footage or no?"

"I'm not sure, but I think so."

"I do too. Let's sweep this place one more time, then we can get the camera over to David and see what he can pull off of it." Only she might not want David to see what's on it. Not yet. But she didn't have a choice. They finished the rest of the building and rounded up two more cameras hidden strategically. One in a file cabinet with a hole drilled into the side for the lens and one in the storage room lock.

"Clever," she murmured. "No wonder CSU missed them. I'm surprised *we* found them."

"Yeah. I guess there's something to be said for dumb luck."

"Or divine intervention," she murmured. Then nodded. "I'll call David and let him know what's coming."

"Go for it."

She pulled her phone off the clip and simply stared at the screen.

He noticed. "What?"

"Nothing."

So why was she hesitating? This could be a good thing. If Derek was shown to be on any of the footage, he'd have to come forward and explain himself.

Right?

"Iz?"

She shot him a tight smile. "Just thinking for a second. I'll call him."

7

From the corner of his eye, Ryan discreetly watched her. With a mixture of pit-bull determination and a lightning fast brain, she was a good cop, and he expected if she wanted to make detective, she'd do so without any trouble.

She was also loyal—one of her more endearing qualities that he'd noticed at a young age. Fiercely protective of those she loved, she'd go above and beyond to take care of them. Which made him wonder who was in the warehouse before he'd arrived, who she was protecting.

He'd get it out of her eventually.

Ryan lifted his hands up to study his palms. He'd reacted instinctively to catch Izzy when she'd slipped. Holding her had sent his heart into a pitter-patter rhythm he thought he'd outgrown years ago. Then again, he must not have, if he'd thought about asking her out—which he still thought about on a regular basis. What was it about this woman that drew him so?

She hung up and rejoined him at the door. Near where his brother had pretty much bled out. All romantic thoughts dissipated like mist in the wind.

"David said he could jump on the cameras first thing in the morning," she said.

"Fine," he said. "Tomorrow first thing. I'm ready to get out of here and get back to the hospital. Mom was asking about Kevin's things."

"Of course."

Her grief-shadowed eyes pierced him. Maybe it wasn't the same grief as losing a brother, but she and Kevin—they'd been close.

He waited until she was in her vehicle before he headed to his. Once in the driver's seat he aimed for the hospital. His mother wanted to sit with Kevin before they took his body to the morgue. Ryan's father had maintained a stoic attitude, doing his best in his head-of-the-family role to comfort his wife and the others, but Ryan knew the man was on the edge of breaking down himself. He just prayed his dad could keep it together for the two of them.

Once back at the hospital, Ryan made his way to the room where his brother still lay. His mother sat next to him, holding his hand, eyes closed, while silent tears tracked her cheeks. Ryan's father sat in the only other chair, his head in his hands. Probably praying.

Ryan cleared his throat and both of them looked up at him. "We'll get them," he said. "If it's the last thing I do, I'll get them."

His mother stared at him without blinking, without moving. Ryan wondered if she was even breathing. Then she slowly placed Kevin's hand back on the bed beside him and smoothed the sheet down over his chest. She turned to Ryan and shook her head. "No. You're quitting the force."

Izzy stepped into her home and kicked off her shoes, relishing the quiet surrounding her. She never took it for granted. Even if it was just five short minutes from her parents' home, it was still enough distance to fill her with contentment.

They would have been happy to have her continue living with them, but she was twenty-seven years old and needed her space. Growing up in a large family with three brothers and two sisters, she found that having a place of her own was blissful—and essential to her mental well-being.

She'd moved into her side of the two-bedroom duplex three years ago and it had served its purpose well. And she definitely hadn't gotten tired of the silence yet. Not completely anyway.

When she needed a family fix, she simply went to church, then Sunday lunch with the rest of her siblings and extended family. And then returned home to her precious quiet.

Mozart, her miniature Eskimo Spitz, greeted her in the foyer with a happy yip, his tail wagging in anticipation of her attention. She scratched his ears and he followed her through the den, then down the hall and into her bedroom.

The quiet bothered her tonight, though.

Kevin.

Silence and grief didn't go well together—and yet she didn't want to be around people either. Climbing beneath the covers and watching a classic movie where there was no shooting, no crime, no . . . violence, sounded perfect.

A knock on her front door froze her mid-reach for her television remote. She sighed and padded back to the entrance to glance through the peephole. And smiled. Her neighbor, Mrs. Helen Spade, stood on the front porch holding a covered dish. Because she'd heard of Kevin's death, no doubt, and was offering comfort in the best way she knew how. By cooking. Izzy's grief gripped her once more as she opened the door. "Mrs. Spade, it's so late, you shouldn't have."

The woman slipped inside. "I heard you come in. Well, Mozart heard you first, but I had this casserole and I wanted to bring it to you." Mozart was technically Izzy's dog, but with her crazy schedule, her sweet duplex neighbor had agreed to help take care of him.

Derek had come over and cut a doggie door in the wall between their units so Mozart could go back and forth as he pleased. The woman continued talking while she set the food on the stove. "I know you're probably worn out, but it's all over the news about your partner. I'm so sorry, darling. Have you eaten?"

"No, not much." Not anything. Eating reminded her of Kevin devouring her food in the car. Would she ever be able to eat another roast beef sandwich? Her stomach churned at the thought.

"Then this chicken casserole is just the thing."

"Thanks. I appreciate it."

"Sure thing, honey. Now, I'm right next door if you need anything. I'm going to bed, but you know I keep my phone on the nightstand and will come running if you need me."

Izzy hugged the older woman who'd decided to adopt her from the moment she'd moved in. Her own grown children didn't call her or come by much, and Izzy knew she was lonely. "Thanks so much."

"Okay, you eat, then go straight to bed, honey. I'll see you later."

Mrs. Spade walked back over to her side and Izzy waited until she heard the dead bolt click to lock her own door. Truthfully, she didn't feel like eating but forced herself to down a few bites of the casserole. If she was going to find the people who killed Kevin, she'd need her strength. The fact that it was delicious helped.

Her phone buzzed as she swallowed the last bite. "Hello?"

"I just wanted to check on you one more time. You've had such a horrifying night," Gabby said.

"Horrifying. Yeah. That's a good word for it." She swallowed against the grief that wanted to well and crash over her.

"I'm sorry."

"Thanks."

"Anything I can do?"

"No. I wish you could, but there's nothing you or anyone can do." Gabby was about three years older than Izzy, but they'd become fast friends when Izzy started dating her brother, Mick. And then they'd stayed friends in spite of the way Mick and Izzy's relationship ended. With Mick in a psych ward and Izzy trying to deal with nightmares. She shut that train of thought off immediately. "Listen, I've got to get some rest. I'll talk to you soon."

Gabby sighed. "Fine. I can't seem to say anything right tonight. But look, I know you don't want to come over, with Mick staying here and all, but call me if you need me. I'm happy to come over there."

"I will." She paused. "And Gabby?"

"Yes?"

"Thanks for not going into how much *Mayor* Endicott would change things for the department—and stuff."

"Didn't figure you needed to hear that right now."

"Yeah."

"Hey, babe, you ready?" Izzy frowned at the male voice that came through the line.

"Who's that?" she asked.

"Oh, just a friend. I'll talk to you later."

"Okay. I want to hear about that friend."

"I'll tell you about him later. Get some sleep."

"Night."

She hung up, then rose to place the remainder of the casserole into the refrigerator and her dirty dishes into the dishwasher. With a sigh she looked around, only to see Mozart slip through his doggie door into Mrs. Spade's side. "Fine. Be that way."

A shower. She needed piping hot water beating on her back. Maybe then her muscles would unlock. She headed for the bathroom. Once under the steaming spray, she let the tears fall once again.

How am I supposed to deal with this, God?

How was she going to face tomorrow? How would she get through the next hour? The warm water attempted to chase away the cold grief that seeped into the deepest part of her heart.

When Chris had died, it had been bad enough. But Kevin . . .

While she loved all of the Marshalls like family, she'd been closer to Kevin than the other brothers.

Chris had been older, tougher, with a distant personality that kept most people at arms' length.

Except Ryan. They'd been tight.

And she'd admired Chris's dedication to fighting for what he believed in. Especially homeless vets. She'd sat in on enough conversations to know his passion for them had run deep.

But Kevin. He'd always been special to Izzy. Being so close in age, he'd been her partner in everything from sneaking out of the house at two in the morning to go swimming at the local lake, to backpacking around Europe for two months after college graduation. She'd been waffling about law school or the academy and had wanted to see a bit of the world before making the decision.

Kevin had gone with her. He hadn't known what he wanted to do either. But he knew one thing. "I want to make a difference, Izzy," he told her one night, sitting on the front porch of his parents' house—just across the street from her parents'. "I want to make the world a better place. If I do that for one person, great. If I can do that for a lot of people, even better. Like Chris and Ruthie. I just don't want to join the Army or be a doctor. I hate the sight of blood. I could be a cop, though. I just want to make a difference."

"Yes. I know what you mean."

After that conversation with Kevin, she'd chosen to go to the academy. No one in her family knew that. They just thought she'd been following in their footsteps, but that hadn't been the case. At least, not completely. And Kevin had played around for a couple of years before heading to the academy, but no matter what Ryan said, no matter that Kevin had died, it had been the right choice for him.

She thought about that particular conversation when she needed a reminder about why she did what she did, and the only thing that made Kevin's death bearable was the fact that he'd died doing what he thought would make a difference.

He'd just wanted to make a difference.

And he had, even in the short time he'd been on the force. He'd saved a young child from a burning car. She'd never forget the look on his face when he pulled that three-year-old from the vehicle. From that moment on, he was addicted.

She knew the feeling.

Unfortunately, that feeling had to be tempered, controlled. And Kevin hadn't lived long enough to learn that. Instead, it had gotten him killed.

She had to remember that part too. Not that she was likely to forget it.

When the water started to turn cold, she shut it off and stepped out. As she readied herself for bed, she thought about everything she needed to do tomorrow. Take the videos to David and finagle her way into watching them with him. Then she planned to go by and see if she could be granted permission to talk to the man who had been captured. Then what?

Go through Kevin's phone.

She pulled the device from the back pocket of the jeans she'd tossed into the corner chair and stared at it while tears wanted to fall again. She sniffed and dropped onto the bed.

Mozart jumped up beside her and nudged his head under her hand. She chuckled, even while she swiped a few stray tears. "Mrs. Spade went to sleep on you, huh? Think you'll get some attention over here now? Well, you're right." She scratched his ears and then he rolled over to give her access to his belly. Finally, she turned her attention to Kevin's phone.

And realized it was dead. She groaned and plugged it into the charger next to her bed. "So what do you think, Mozart?" His ears swiveled in her direction. "Should I have let Chloe come stay over? Or gone to her house?"

He settled his nose between his paws and stared at her with those soft brown eyes.

Probably.

Her phone buzzed regularly for the next half hour as her five siblings checked in once more. She finally sent them all a group text declaring that it was midnight, she was going to bed, and she'd see them for Sunday lunch at their parents' house.

Her phone fell silent. Forget the movie, forget Kevin's phone, she was exhausted. Izzy flopped back on the bed, rolled over, and closed her eyes.

FRIDAY

8

"Maybe I should give it up, Tabitha. Go ahead and announce my retirement."

Tabitha stood. "Eric, I'm speaking as your chief of police as well as your friend. We don't negotiate with terrorists."

"They're not terrorists."

"Actually, they rather are. But whatever name you want to put on them, we're not budging. You are *not* conceding the race. That's the act of a coward. Something you're not and never have been."

"I was hoping you'd see the action as more of a selfless sacrifice. As a way to save our city." He rubbed his tired eyes. "Bianchi's power has grown to epic proportions."

Tabitha paced her office. "I know. It seems like every time we get a shot at taking him down, he finds out and slithers away."

"Exactly."

"It should not be *that* hard to find the man."

"But it is. It's been nigh on impossible and the people in this city are terrified. It's getting worse by the day." He drew in a breath and let it out slowly. "And I can stop it."

"At what expense, Eric?" She crossed her arms and glared at him. "Why does he want you out and Melissa Endicott in so bad?"

"Becau—"

"Because he can control her," she snapped. She jabbed a finger

71

at him. "And if he controls her, he can get rid of me. And then whoever takes my place will bow to Bianchi and there will be no one in power to stand up to him."

"I know," her friend whispered. "I know." He stood and paced to the window. "I don't want to see that happen." He cleared his throat. "We can't let it happen."

"I agree. Just hang on a little longer, Eric. I'm working on bringing him down. And soon."

"I hope so." He stood and gathered his jacket. "I'm afraid for my family. I've sent them to stay with Elise's mother in Utah."

She sighed. "I understand and it's not a bad idea to be on the safe side, but I've been thinking about this."

"About what?"

"Bianchi's threats. He's done everything in his power—which, as we've discussed, is considerable—to make sure crime and gang violence are out of control. Or at least appear to be."

"Yes." He returned to the wing-backed chair opposite her desk. "And?"

"And I've come up with a plan that I think can bring an end to this mess."

Eric tilted his head and raised a brow. "All right, I'm listening. What's your plan?"

"We make it look like you're throwing the election."

"What?"

"In other words, we give Bianchi what he wants."

Izzy stood at David Unger's desk and waited for him to pull a chair around. His office, on the lower level of 1 Justice Square, was a floor below her own.

She settled herself beside him and fidgeted with the ring on her pinkie finger while he pulled up the camera footage. "Thanks for doing this on your day off."

"Sure." He shrugged. "Not like I had anything better to do."

"Except maybe sleep in?"

"Yeah, that would have been nice, but catching a killer is a priority."

He had monitors everywhere. National news played on one, local on another, the weather channel on yet another.

"Do you mind if I watch?"

Ryan's voice came from the doorway, jerking David around to look at him. Izzy found she wasn't even surprised Ryan had shown up. Subconsciously, she'd probably expected him to do so. Turning, she locked her eyes on his. "You know you can't investigate this officially, right?"

He frowned. "Of course I know that."

But it wouldn't stop him from doing what he could to stay informed and on top of the investigation.

David nodded. "Okay, grab that chair and have a seat."

Ryan seated himself and David got busy. While the man worked, his fingers moving the mouse, then clicking over the keyboard, Ryan turned to Izzy. "Charice found Jonathan Gill's family. They live about thirty minutes from here. You want to go with us after we're done here?"

"You really shouldn't be going."

"Charice will be there. I'm just going to listen."

"From the car?"

He scowled at her. "You want to go or not?"

"Of course."

Finally, a black-and-white video appeared on the monitor. David pressed play.

Izzy leaned forward. "That's the camera from the ladder. The highest point in the building."

"Yeah. I would say so. It's got a pretty sharp angle, but you can see the entire bottom floor with only a few places out of range. Like the office in the corner."

"There's a back door that leads directly into the office," Izzy said. "We won't be able to see any of that area."

And no video of the balcony.

Izzy sat back with a thud. Derek wouldn't be on this footage. She wasn't sure how she felt about that. She'd hoped she wouldn't have to be the bad guy and spill the information, but it looked like she wasn't going to have any other choice.

On the screen three men came into range. She recognized the two she and Kevin had seen arrive during their stakeout. The other man must have already been there. From the angle that he entered the video, it looked as if he had come from the small office at the back. One set his rifle on the floor and she heard the light thud.

"There's audio?" Izzy asked.

"Yeah. This is some kind of superduper spy camera. Quality stuff. They're standing pretty much right below it, so we should be able to hear everything they say."

He cranked the volume up.

"Get the pictures and get out. Understand?"

The first one, a man who looked to be in his late forties, nodded. *"It's already arranged."*

"Who are these guys?" Ryan asked.

"Don't know yet," David said. He paused the footage and took still shots of each of the men's faces. "We'll run their faces through the system and see if we get a hit. I have a feeling this isn't their first rodeo."

He let the video continue while the recognition software ran in the background.

And then there was Kevin on the screen and sneaking around the door. Ryan's breath left him in a whoosh and Izzy reached back to take his hand. He squeezed her fingers.

The men didn't see Kevin and he settled into his little spot behind the wooden crates.

The guy who appeared to be the one in charge asked about the weapons. The shortest of the three men reached into the nearest box and pulled one out. He passed it to the man, who loaded the ammo, then aimed it at the wall. He nodded. *"The buyer will be here day after tomorrow. The boss needs seventy of these."*

"They're packed in those boxes near the door."

"Good." He set the weapon aside. *"Now for other business. Are we ready?"*

"We're ready."

"You have the entry and exit points narrowed down?"

"We do."

"Good."

Another man walked up to the three. The man who had been giving orders said, *"Ready, boss,"* then started across the warehouse and walked out of camera range.

"Get these weapons ready to ship," the boss said. *"I've got a little business to take care of."* He turned to look behind him.

"What's he looking at?" Ryan asked.

"I can't tell," David said. "The angle doesn't go back that way."

The boss had turned back and was now facing Kevin's hiding place with narrowed eyes. He pulled his weapon and aimed it in Kevin's direction. The others pulled theirs as well and stepped out of his way.

"What is it?" the shorter man asked.

"There," Ryan said and pointed. "He saw Kevin move. Kevin messed up and showed himself."

"But why? Why would he take that chance?" Izzy asked. "Back it up and zoom in if you can."

"Of course I can. I can slow it down too." He did as directed and Izzy watched Kevin move his hand around the edge of the crates.

"Wait a minute," Ryan said. "That's his phone. Is he recording them?"

"Yes." Izzy leaned in.

Ryan's eyes stayed glued to the screen. "He's recording them and it looks like he moved to get a better angle of something."

"And that's why they spotted him. He risked—no, *gave* his life to get something on video." Izzy sat back with a thump. He'd recorded the suspects, had their faces on the camera. So why ask her to hide it? Was he protecting someone? Like her brother? The camera was definitely aimed in his direction. "I want to know if any of those guys are undercover."

David raised a brow. "Why?"

She shrugged. "Just curious."

"No, you're not. You have a reason for asking," Ryan said. "Do you recognize someone?"

"No." Izzy shot him a tight smile. "So just humor me, okay?"

David turned back to the screen. "I don't know if they're undercover or not. I can send the photos up to your mother's office and ask, letting her know the reason why."

"Thanks." Because if Derek was working undercover, then he might be working in conjunction with one of the other men in the video. And if that was the case, she could rest a little easier about the situation. Maybe.

She'd left Kevin's phone at home, unable to face going through it, putting it off until she could prepare herself. Now she couldn't wait to get her hands on it.

David started the video again.

The boss had seen Kevin's hand and drawn his weapon, aiming it at the crates. Now he motioned across the warehouse—probably to the man who'd left the threesome earlier—to go around the side of Kevin's hiding place. Kevin hadn't seen that part. He'd been recording the three, but had his head down, trying to stay invisible.

Izzy's heart thundered, knowing what was coming. She wanted to turn away but couldn't. Ryan's waves of tension reached her.

A shadowed figure came around the side of the crate. Kevin jerked and spun.

"What are you doing here, huh? You a cop?"

The gun popped twice and the bullets hit Kevin one right after the other. He went down, shock and surprise on his face. The camera caught Izzy at the warehouse entrance. Another spate of bullets echoed through the room and then there was Izzy, running inside to throw herself on the floor next to Kevin.

She looked away. Then took a deep breath and forced herself to focus back on the screen. Waiting.

And there it was. Another shot. A loud thud as a body hit the warehouse floor. Izzy, on screen, turning and looking up.

Ryan pointed. "What was that?"

Grief and anger roughened his words and Izzy fought to figure out what to say. She just couldn't tell him about Derek's presence. Not yet.

"What was it?" Ryan said. He looked at her. "What'd you see? You were looking right there."

"That's the dead guy in the morgue. There was someone else on the balcony. Someone who shot him and ran."

"Who?"

"I . . . don't know." She winced as the words slipped from her lips. She'd lied. Flat-out lied. Guilt rammed her and fury with Derek built within her. "I didn't get a good look at his face, he was turning to leave when I looked up." Well, that was true enough.

"We need to know who else was there and why."

"Yes," she said. "We sure do need to know why."

Ryan still stared at the screen, even though David had closed the program. Izzy had excused herself to the restroom after they were finished, and Ryan stayed seated, unable to move just yet while he tried to breathe through the pain of watching his brother get shot.

He did take note of the man who'd pulled the trigger. He needed to see the man's face. It was the only reason he'd wanted to watch the video. The only reason he'd put himself through the agony of it. But that face would stay with him forever now. Ryan would hunt it down and make sure he and the consequences of his actions had a meeting. If he lived to go to trial, fine. If not, that was fine too. But one way or another, he was going to pay.

His mother's words still rang through his mind. "You're going to quit the force." The absolute terror with which she'd said the words had kept him from responding with the instant denial that had popped into his head.

Instead, he'd drawn a deep breath, then knelt before her and taken her hand. He kissed it while tears ran down both their faces. "No, Mom, I'm going to get the person who killed him. Look into my eyes and tell me you think I can just turn in my badge and my gun and let someone else handle this. That I can just walk away. You really think I can do that?"

A low, gutteral cry had ripped from her. "No. No, you can't. I know that. But—"

"No buts, Mom."

She'd wailed a cry that still echoed in his head along with her words. He'd looked into his father's eyes and saw a chilling emptiness. "Dad?" His father simply stared, not blinking, not crying, nothing. "Dad?"

Finally, his father locked eyes with him. "You get him, son. And you make him pay. Understood?"

Ryan gave a slow nod. "Understood, Dad."

"Ryan, you okay?"

David's question sounded like a shot in the quiet room and Ryan flinched. "Yes. No. I don't know."

"Actually, that was a dumb question. Sorry."

Ryan shook his head. "It's okay."

"I have a kid brother. He's five years younger. I don't know what I'd do in your shoes."

Ryan looked up. "You'd go find the guy who killed him."

78

"Yeah. You're right about that. That's exactly what I would do." He cleared his throat. "I got a hit on three of the four faces in the warehouse."

"Who are they?"

"Guys with rap sheets, but mostly small-time stuff." He brought up the screen with all of them on it and pointed. "That guy is Peter Leahy, the one to his left is Xavier Bowles. That guy there is big time. Tony Bianchi."

"Bianchi, huh?"

"Yes. You've heard of him, I'm sure."

"I've heard of him. I should have recognized him."

David nodded. "Then I guess you know they call him The Iceman. It's rumored he's been responsible for almost twenty law enforcement deaths in the last ten years."

"And he's still out there," Ryan muttered. "No one's been able to catch him. He manages to slip away every single time. It's eerie. I've heard his name for years, but never had any dealings with him. Mainly because no one can ever find him."

"Well, he's coming out of hiding for some reason. And you're dealing with him now." He held up a hand. "I take that back. The officers who are investigating Kevin's death are dealing with him. *You*, however, are not. Right?"

"Right," the voice said from behind him.

Ryan turned to find his partner in the doorway. "Hey."

Charice stepped into the room. "I figured you might be down here."

"What's up?"

"That guy who was arrested last night at the warehouse, Carl Timmons, was just murdered."

Ryan froze. "What?"

She nodded and leaned against the doorjamb. "Yeah. I'm sorry."

Ryan slammed a fist onto the table and stood. "He was our

best lead to find the guy who killed Kevin." He looked at David. "Unless you got a name?"

David grimaced. "Unfortunately, he's the one I didn't get a hit on."

Disappointment flashed. "All right." He rubbed his eyes and looked at Charice. "Who killed Timmons?"

"Don't know. Right now, no one's talking and nothing's on surveillance video. It happened in the shower."

"Of course it did."

"One good piece of news is that we did get footage of the group of men all going into the showers at the same time. We're questioning them individually, but so far no one's spilling anything."

And most likely, if he didn't want to be the next victim, no one *would* say anything.

Ryan nodded. "It's okay. I'll find him anyway." Somehow. He told her about getting the hit on Tony Bianchi. "We need to find him. He's the one in charge of all of this."

Charice nodded. "It could be Bianchi was the one who bought the warehouse and set up his dummy corporation to run his dirty money through," she said.

"And weapons," Ryan said. They'd gotten the pictures off the camera Kevin had left in the car. Not to mention the gun that had been shown to the man in charge before Kevin had been spotted. It had been dropped in the chaos. On the plus side, it had been the catalyst for a warrant and all contents of the warehouse had been seized. If the weapons pictured there had hit the streets, Ryan shuddered to think of the damage. "So Bianchi has ties to the Crips. And the Bloods are expanding their territory, moving closer to where this warehouse is. What if Bianchi's not comfortable with that? What if the gang wars are directed by Bianchi to get the Bloods to move back?"

"It's possible. If he's funneling money to the leader, then I can see that happening easily."

"It's also possible that Timmons knew more than Bianchi was happy with him knowing while being in custody of the police."

"I'd say that's the most likely scenario," Ryan said.

"I think we can now safely assume that Bricks & Sticks is definitely a dummy corporation," Charice said. "Run by Tony Bianchi. You think it's his headquarters?"

"No way," Ryan said. "But something was important enough for him to show up last night." He paused. "So, they purchased it from Jonathan Gill—or whoever inherited the place when he died. Who would that be?"

Charice shrugged. "His family, I guess. I can ask them when I see them this afternoon."

"Good," Ryan said. "I want to know if there's a connection between them and Bianchi."

"I'll try to figure that out before I get there," Charice said. "We."

"Ryan, we talked about this and—"

"I can just tag along. I don't have to do the questioning. You can do that. We agreed. And Izzy's coming too."

Charice pursed her lips, then rolled her eyes and nodded. "Fine."

"Listen," David said, his gaze jumping back and forth between the two of them, "you didn't get any of this from me, okay? As much as I would be doing the same thing you are when it comes to finding my brother's killer, I need this job."

"Don't worry, David," Ryan said, "this is our little secret."

He wasn't technically investigating, and he wasn't interfering. He wouldn't do anything that might be construed as such. Yes, it was his brother who'd been killed. Yes, it was a conflict of interest for him to be a part of the investigation.

But he couldn't sit back and do nothing. He had to at least stay on top of what was being done to find Kevin's killers. As long as he knew what everyone else knew, he would be able to release Kevin's investigation into other very capable hands—or at least not hold on to it with such a tight fist. "I want everything to be on the up and up if this ever comes to trial. I'm simply an observer, okay?"

"Okay. Thanks."

He turned back to his computer and Charice gave Ryan a small salute. "Sorry to be the bearer of bad news about Timmons," she said.

"Yeah. Thanks."

"I'm going to go work on finding a connection between the Gills and Bianchi before we head out. Let me know if you need anything else."

"Thanks."

She left and Ryan shot a text to Lincoln St. John. As a special agent with the FBI, he had more resources than Ryan—and if Bianchi was involved, a vested interest in finding Kevin's killer. There was no reason not to ask.

> Need to know current info on Tony Bianchi.

Why?

> He was in the warehouse when Kevin was killed.

How do you know?

> I have a source.

Right. A source. I'll be in touch.

When he looked up from his phone, the local news playing on the monitor to his right caught his attention. The chief of police was standing on the hospital steps in front of a tangle of microphones.

It was recorded footage of her statement about Kevin's shooting and subsequent death. He knew because he'd seen it looping last night. The current mayor stood beside her, looking pale and worn. The lines on his face seemed to have deepened over the course of the election, but lately even more so.

That segment ended and the video switched to a live feed. Another woman stepped into view. Melissa Endicott—the woman who wanted to replace Mayor Eric Cotterill in the upcoming election. "Thank you," she said into the microphone on the podium. "I appreciate you all for coming."

Like the press would miss it. Her campaign manager, Gabrielle Sinclair, stood off to the side in the back. Ryan shook his head. He had to give Izzy props for not letting political affiliations mar her friendship with the woman.

Endicott adjusted the microphone and leaned in. "As you know, the election is fast approaching. Next week, people." She pointed to the air as though her audience could visualize the time and place. "Next week." She dropped her hand. "I want to encourage you to look at the facts. Our current mayor is a nice man, a good man." She spread her hands and shrugged. "I like him and believe he's done a good job during his time in office. But something's changed in the last couple of years. Look at the statistics, and you'll see— crime is rising, especially with the gangs. Have you noticed the rise in drive-by shootings and knifings? It's unprecedented. And our officers' salaries haven't been raised in two years. It's time to pay our officers what they deserve. In short, the police department needs a complete overhaul . . ."

The volume lowered and David set the remote next to his computer. "What do you think about her?"

Ryan shrugged. "She seems like a good enough candidate. She doesn't really fight dirty, just kind of tells it like it is." It was all she'd had to do.

He wasn't opposed to having her in office, but Mayor Eric Cotterill was a longtime friend. However, Ryan had to admit, he agreed with a lot of what Melissa said and knew others did too.

Eric should have been bringing his A-game in order to keep his position, but for some reason, he wasn't.

"Yeah. She's popular and I think she'll win," David said. "What does the chief think about her?"

Ryan frowned. "She doesn't seem to have an opinion about her one way or the other. Or if she does, she's not expressing it."

"Playing her cards close to the chest?"

"Something like that."

Eric Cotterill and Tabitha St. John had grown up together, their families often getting together to celebrate holidays and birthdays. Ryan knew this because his family was also within that circle.

But maybe some fresh blood in the office would be a good thing. His eyes went to the door Izzy had slipped out of not too long ago. And maybe he'd just keep his thoughts to himself. No sense in provoking World War III. Not while he needed Izzy's help in finding his brother's killer.

9

Izzy lost track of time as she stood at the sink staring into the mirror. There was something on Kevin's phone and she needed to know what it was.

And Derek—

The stress of keeping Derek's secret—aka *lying*—was killing her. He wasn't undercover or her mother wouldn't have been so clueless in her answer. Then again, Derek intimated that even if he *was* undercover, their mother might not be aware of the assignment.

If Derek was truly undercover, there would be an ops plan. If she knew for sure there was an ops plan, she'd feel a lot better.

She dialed Louis Harper's number. "Come on," she whispered, "pick up."

Harper had been the one to inform Kevin about the warehouse and the weapons. He'd known Bianchi was going to be there. Maybe. He might not have known about Bianchi, but he knew enough.

Her call went through to his voice mail. "Call me."

She hung up and rubbed her eyes only to jerk when her phone buzzed. "Well, that was fast." A glance at the screen showed a text from Gabby, not Harper.

> When do you want to do that lunch? Are you
> working tomorrow?

Izzy thought about it and realized that if she put her friend off, Gabby *might* take it to mean that Izzy was too uncomfortable with the situation to remain friends. She sensed Gabby's hesitation when she'd come to the hospital to deliver the news of her brother's release—and new living arrangements.

Izzy's fingers hovered over the keys. It would only be awkward if they let it be. She answered truthfully.

> No, not working until after the funeral. My first
> assignment back is the election win speech,
> can you believe it? I think I can do lunch tmrw.
> Let you know in the morning?

> Sure.

> Thanks.

A knock made her sigh. "Yeah?"

"You okay in there?" Ryan's low voice filtered through the wooden door.

"Peachy," she muttered under her breath. "I'm fine. I'm coming," she said loud enough to be heard. She stepped out of the bathroom and found Ryan waiting. "What?"

He winced and she regretted her sharp tone. He didn't deserve it. His eyes narrowed. "Tense much?"

"Aren't you?"

"Absolutely."

And she was doing to him what he had done directly following Kevin's shooting. Snapping and snarling.

She touched his hand. "I'm sorry."

"No, don't apologize. I get it."

"I know you do, but . . ." She waved a hand in dismissal of the subject. "I'll be all right. However, something occurred to me while I was watching that video."

"What?"

"That there's something on Kevin's phone."

"What are you talking about?"

She told him.

"You have his phone because he asked you to hide it?"

"Yes, while he was bleeding out on the floor."

Ryan raked a hand through his hair. "All right, we don't have time to pick it up before we go to the Gills' house, but as soon as we're done with them, we'll see what's on there."

"*We're* going to the Gills'?"

His jaw tightened. "*We* are."

Ryan decided he wasn't waiting in the car and appreciated that no one said anything when he stepped into the living room, where Charice took the lead. He'd promised to fade into the background and meant to keep that promise. Charice made the introductions to the fiftysomething couple. "Thank you for meeting with us."

"Of course," Mrs. Gill said, leading them into a recently renovated den. Hardwoods gleamed around the edges of the large oriental rug and the smell of paint hung faintly in the air. "Would you like anything to drink?"

Ryan declined.

"I'm fine," Izzy said.

Charice shook her head. "Nothing for me, thanks."

Once they were all seated, Izzy and Ryan on the love seat, Charice in the chair by the fireplace, and the Gills on the long couch against the far wall, Mrs. Gill clasped her husband's hand and studied Ryan. "Marshall?"

"Yes, ma'am."

"Any relation to the young officer who was killed?" she asked.

"My brother."

Her eyes widened. "Oh, I'm so sorry. How terrible."

Ryan cleared his throat and nodded. "Thank you."

She turned her attention to Izzy and Charice. "Now, what's this all about?"

Izzy leaned forward. "There was a crime committed at a warehouse last night."

"We saw it on the news."

"Yes, ma'am," Izzy said, her voice slightly husky. She cleared her throat. "During our investigation, we came across your son's name on the purchase of the warehouse."

"Jonathan?"

"Yes."

Mr. Gill frowned. "But how is that possible? He's been dead for almost two years."

"And the building was sold just shortly after his death. Two months after, to be exact."

Mrs. Gill's gaze bounced between the three of them. "But, I don't understand. He never owned a warehouse that I know of."

"Well, the paperwork says he did," Izzy said, her tone mild. "Or does. Do you know who Tony Bianchi is?"

"No." She didn't flinch or even blink when she answered. Her husband answered negatively as well. Charice had already informed them in the car that she'd found nothing to indicate a connection between the Gills and Bianchi. Not even something as small as using the same bank or attending the same church.

Ryan had no reason to suspect they were lying. If they were, they belonged on the big screen.

Frustration mounted. How were they supposed to connect Gill to Bianchi? Or was there a connection at all? But there had to be. How did a dead man sell a building two months after his death?

Mrs. Gill shrugged. "Who is Tony Bianchi?"

Charice rubbed her chin. "A career criminal, but forget that for a moment. Let's go at this from a different direction. I know this is painful and I apologize, but when Jonathan died, who inherited all of his assets?"

"His father and I did." She cleared her throat and a sheen of tears appeared briefly in her eyes before she blinked them away. "He wasn't married and . . ."

Her husband picked up the explanation. "Jonathan wrote a will before he left for Afghanistan and made sure his mother and I were on the safe-deposit box where he kept all of his important documents and such."

"And there was nothing in there about a deed to a warehouse?" Charice asked.

Mr. Gill shook his head. "Nothing."

Izzy frowned and looked at Charice, who shared the frown. Ryan shifted and sent a text to Izzy. He had questions he wanted answered but didn't want to be the one asking them. She glanced at her phone, then gave him a nod.

"Mrs. Gill," Izzy said, "the whole point of this visit is that we're trying to figure out how a warehouse in Jonathan's name ended up being sold two months after he died. That's all."

"I really don't know." The lines in her forehead deepened. "But for some reason, I keep coming back to the name *Marshall*," she said. "That's so familiar." She hesitated, then stood and walked over to the desk in the corner of the room. "There's a picture here, somewhere . . ." She looked back over her shoulder at Ryan. "You remind me of him. He was military, too, like Jonathan." One drawer opened, then closed. Another drawer opened. "Ah, here we go." She studied the photograph, then let her gaze rove back over Ryan's face. "Yes, there are differences, but you look very similar."

Ryan held out a hand. "Who?"

Mrs. Gill crossed the room and handed the picture to him. "I believe his name was Chris, but I may have it wrong. It's been almost two years."

Ryan looked down at the picture and the air left his lungs. For a moment, all he could do was stare at the two men in the photo. They were sitting at the kitchen table, laughing. Chris had his head thrown back in that carefree way that had been more obvious when he was a teen. Ryan didn't remember seeing Chris laugh like that since enlisting. And then he'd died . . .

Ryan cleared his throat and passed the picture to Izzy, who looked at it. She lifted her gaze to his. "How . . . ?"

"You're right. His name is Chris Marshall," Ryan told the Gills. "He's my brother who was killed in Afghanistan a year and a half ago. There were only two men in that unit who didn't die that day." He took the picture from Izzy and studied it one more time. "But Jonathan wasn't in Chris's unit. So how did they meet? What was he doing there?" Charice shot him a "shut up" look and Ryan snapped his lips together.

Mrs. Gill shrugged. "As far as I know they were just hanging out. There was another young man as well, but I can't remember his name for the life of me. Richard? Rowen?" She sighed. "I'm sorry, I can't remember. I only met him the one time, but I got the feeling Jonathan had met both of them recently."

"You don't have a picture of him?" Charice asked.

"No. I just snapped that one of those two. They looked so happy, without a care in the world." She cleared her throat. "I'm not sure where the other man went, but he wasn't in the kitchen at that time. I cherish that picture. It's how I want to remember Jonathan."

"Of course. I can't believe I never heard Chris mention Jonathan," Ryan murmured.

She shrugged. "Like I said, I don't think they knew each other very long. They had met at some charity dinner—a fundraiser for veterans—and hit it off. I think your brother was getting ready to head off overseas in the next month or so. Anyway, they came here for the long weekend in May to go hiking, and I know they spent a lot of time talking, but I really didn't pay that much attention, to be honest." Sadness clouded her eyes. "I wish I had now. I'm sorry."

"No, it's okay." Ryan studied the picture again. "He looks so happy," he murmured.

"They were laughing about a funny story Chris told."

Ryan looked up. "Probably the time he got roped into dancing with his CO's wife."

"Oh my. That sounds interesting."

A slight smile curved his lips in spite of the grief he could never shake when talking about his brother. Now brothers. "And intimidating. Chris hated dancing. He was lousy at it and his unit promised him that if he came to the dance, he wouldn't have to do anything but be there. They insisted that they were a team and if he didn't show, he was breaking up the team. Chris reluctantly agreed, and when they arrived, Mrs. Pitts decided there wouldn't be any wallflowers on her watch. She pulled him onto the dance floor and proceeded to school him in ballroom dancing. Chris was sure her feet were never the same after that night."

Ryan remembered the first time Chris had told him that story. He'd been home for Christmas and they'd sat out on his parents' front porch to catch up. His brother had been mortified, but big enough to recognize it for what it was. A funny incident that made for a great laugh.

After the fact, of course.

Mrs. Gill smiled. "I don't remember what story he told, but there was a lot of laughter that weekend. Like they did that on purpose."

"I'd like to know who the other person was," Izzy said.

Charice nodded. "So would I." She looked at the two. "Anything else you can tell us? Any small detail at all that you think may be insignificant, but stood out to you?"

The Gills exchanged a glance, then shook their heads together. "No," Mr. Gill said, "I can't think of a thing. There was nothing extraordinary about that weekend. I wasn't even here that much.

I'm an ER nurse and was working a double that weekend, I do remember that much. I was mad because I wanted to be home with my son while he was here." He shrugged. "But the flu was running rampant and I didn't have much choice but to go to work."

"Right. Not every job is nine to five." Ryan stood.

"Wait a minute," Mrs. Gill said. "I don't know if this means anything, but . . ."

"But what?" Izzy asked.

"After Jonathan was killed, we went to his apartment to gather his things and close it up. And . . . there was something odd about it."

Charice leaned forward. "What was that?"

"Someone had been there recently. Nothing was out of place except there was a coffee cup in the trash can and it still had coffee in it."

"Why would that be odd?" Izzy said.

"Because Jonathan had been gone for a month at this point. Before he died, we'd go by and check on his place every so often and we never left trash there, for sure. When I picked up the cup, it was still just a tad bit warm."

Charice frowned. "That is odd. And you have no idea who it could have been? Someone who had a key and thought they'd help Jonathan out by checking on his place? Maybe a girlfriend who was missing him and went by to feel closer to him by visiting his home?"

"No, nothing like that. But the place was locked up tight when we got there. It's not like the door was left open or anything. And like I said, nothing was out of place or disturbed. Just the coffee cup. It bothered me greatly at the time and I thought about calling the police, but"—she shrugged—"like I said, there really wasn't anything to report. But I've never forgotten that—or stopped wondering about who it could have been and why."

Charice's phone rang. She glanced at the screen and frowned. "I need to take this. Excuse me, please." She stepped into the foyer and Ryan could hear her low voice, but not the words.

Izzy nodded to Mrs. Gill. "That might be pretty significant. We'll look into it. Again, thank you for your time."

"Of course."

The couple escorted the three of them to the door and Charice followed, ending her call.

"I'm sorry for your loss," Izzy said to the woman.

"And yours," Mrs. Gill said. She hugged Ryan. "Very sorry for yours as well. Two brothers. I can't imagine the pain your poor mother is going through. The pain you're *all* going through." She shook her head, sorrow radiating from her. "You're in my prayers from this moment on."

"Yes. It's definitely a beast." Ryan swallowed against the lump that wanted to form in his throat. "Thank you for the prayers."

"If we think of anything else, we'll call," Mr. Gill said.

Charice handed him a card. "That would be great."

The door shut with a quiet snick behind them. "Well," Ryan said. "That was interesting."

They made their way to the SUV and climbed in. Ryan let Charice drive. "What do you think about that? Jonathan and Chris?" she asked.

Ryan shrugged. "Chris was very involved in that charity for veterans. The Forgotten Warriors. That must be the charity event Mrs. Gill was talking about where he and Jonathan met."

"But what about the third guy?"

Ryan sighed and rubbed his head. "I don't know, and I don't know how to find out. We might never know now."

"Maybe not," Izzy said.

"What do you mean?"

"His mother said they were all part of that charity dinner. We have the weekend that it took place. All of those kinds of functions have a professional photographer. It shouldn't be hard to track that person down. What if we got pictures from it and started looking to see who was there? See if you recognize anyone."

Ryan turned in the passenger seat to capture her gaze. "That's good thinking." It bothered him that he hadn't thought of it himself. Was his head that messed up because of all of the emotional hits he'd had lately? He sure hoped not.

She smiled. "Thanks. It might be like looking for the proverbial needle, but it's better than nothing."

"I'll text David now and see if he can help us track down some pictures. But I don't think I'd recognize anyone."

"No, maybe not. You probably need to find someone who knew both Jonathan and Chris and the people they knew," Izzy said. "Maybe someone in their units."

Ryan gave a slow nod. "I know exactly who to call for help." Lee Filmore would be next on his list.

Ryan spent the rest of the ride back to the office texting David. He'd also left a message for Lee to call him when he got a chance. Charice had just finished taking a call.

"Who was that?" he asked.

"They finally found an address for Spencer Elmore, the dead guy from the warehouse."

"And?"

"They didn't find much, not even a laptop or a tablet. He lived in a squatty little apartment in a government housing project, but he did have over three hundred grand in the bank."

"Smart," Ryan said. "No one would ever suspect it. He wasn't living above his means and could sock it away until he had enough to just disappear."

"Only he didn't live long enough to enjoy it," Izzy said.

Ryan shrugged. "It's a dangerous occupation hanging out with Bianchi. You take your chances."

"Right. They're still looking for anything that will give them a hint of where to look next for him," Charice said. "They'll be thorough and I'll let you know if I hear anything."

"Perfect." Hope sprouted. Maybe they'd figure this out before too much longer.

All he knew was that Bianchi was partly responsible for Kevin's death and Ryan would see him pay for it. One way or another.

Back at the station, Charice went inside and Ryan snagged Izzy's hand. "Let's get some food and take a look at Kevin's phone."

"It's at my house," she said.

"I'll drive."

10

Izzy climbed in his SUV and Ryan drove to the nearest fast-food restaurant that also offered healthier options. "What do you want?"

"A cheeseburger all the way and large fries."

"Wow. Wasn't expecting that one."

She shrugged. "It's two o'clock. I'm hungry." She usually stuck to the healthier stuff, but not today.

Once they had the food, she dug into the fries, passing him some as he drove. "What did David say about tracking down the photographer?" she asked.

"Said he didn't think it would take him very long."

"Is he doing okay? David, I mean?"

"I think so, why?"

She shrugged. "We're kind of asking a lot of him lately."

"It's his job."

"I know, but we're asking him to put other stuff aside to rush our needs through. I'm feeling a little guilty."

"Yeah." He fell silent and continued to work through her fries. "What about this? He's a huge Gamecocks fan. Do you think we could get him tickets to the Carolina-Clemson game?"

"Oh, he'd love that."

"I'll see if I have any strings to pull. Keep it to yourself."

"Of course."

Ryan was such a considerate guy. Always thinking of others and how to help or how best to do his job. A lot like Kevin. Thinking about Kevin brought back the lump in her throat that never seemed to completely go away. She wished she could just stop thinking, but it seemed like the only thing she *could* do. Think and see Wednesday night play out over and over in her mind. Think and try to avoid the grief that wouldn't let go.

"Iz?"

With a start she realized they were sitting in her drive. And she held a french fry in the air pointing toward her mouth. "Oh. Sorry." She ate the fry and gathered her stuff.

When they walked inside her home, Mozart greeted them, begging for attention.

From Ryan.

"Why does he like you so much?" she asked.

"He knows a good guy when he meets one," he said while scratching the dog's ears.

"Hmm."

"What?"

She smiled softly. "You are a good guy, Ryan. You're definitely one of the rare ones."

His eyes narrowed, and a thoughtful look she'd seen on occasion crossed his face. "Thanks, Izzy."

"Sure." She cleared her throat. "Let me just get the phone."

"Of course." Mozart ran in circles around Ryan's feet. "I'll just let this dude out."

"That would be great. I'll be right back."

Once he and Mozart were outside, Izzy went straight to the nightstand in her bedroom and picked up Kevin's phone. The blood on it seared her. She couldn't let Ryan see it like that.

She took it into the bathroom and retrieved some cotton balls.

Soon, she'd scrubbed as much of Kevin's blood off the device as she could.

And then she cleaned it again through a fresh bout of tears.

Finally, she sighed and pressed the home button. New emails appeared on the screen and she swiped one. Which took her to the screen to enter a passcode. He'd used the six-digits code, not the four.

Great.

Then she paused. Of course he'd use the six digits. Because his code would be someone's birthday.

She tried Kevin's.

Two-digit month, two-digit day, two-digit year.

Nope.

Ryan's.

Her phone rang and he grabbed it from the dresser where she'd set it when she'd walked into the bedroom. "Hello?"

"Izzy?"

The hushed voice captured her attention. "Louis?"

"Yeah."

"You okay?"

"Yeah, yeah."

"The warehouse. Did you set us up?"

"No!" The word exploded from him in a low hiss. "I swear."

He was telling the truth. "How did you know what was going down?"

"When I was on the inside, I was out in the yard one afternoon. The day before I was released. I overheard two guys talking about working for Bianchi. One of them mentioned he was sore about missing out on the deal going down that night. I kept listening and picked up the location of the warehouse. That's it. That's all I had."

"It's okay, Louis."

"I wouldn't turn on you, Izzy, I swear. You saved my life."

Maybe she was an idiot, but she believed him.

"Anyway," he said, "I need you to meet me."

"Why?"

"I got pictures for you."

"Pictures? Of what?"

"Not exactly sure. I took them from a file Bianchi left sitting on the bar. They were making a big deal about them, so I'm sure they're important."

She sucked in a breath. "Louis! That's too dangerous. You can't be doing stuff like that."

"He'll never know who took them. There was a bunch of us in there that day. It was crowded."

"If he's got security cameras, he'll figure it out."

Louis fell silent. "Maybe so."

"I hate to say this, Louis, but I think it's time you left the city. You may have just crossed a line." And stepped into his grave.

"I don't care. I want this guy taken down."

"I do too, but not at the expense of your life." She paused. "I've never heard you like this before. What did Bianchi do to you?"

"He killed someone I cared about."

"Oh, Louis, I'm so sorry."

"Yeah. Thanks."

"Izzy?"

She lifted her head to see Ryan standing just outside the door. He saw she was on the phone and waved his understanding, then disappeared back into her den.

"When do you want to meet?"

"Tonight. I'll text you a time. I'm not sure when I can get away." His voice lowered another notch. "Someone's coming. Gotta go."

He hung up.

Izzy changed into a pair of sweatpants and T-shirt, then picked up Kevin's phone again. What was his code?

If she tried too many times, she'd get locked out.

Still thinking, she carried the phone into the den where Ryan sprawled on her couch with Mozart resting on his lap. Izzy shook her head. "You spoil him."

"I know." His gaze honed in on the device in her hand. "Is that it?"

"Yes." She handed it to him. "He told me to hide it when I was trying to keep him from bleeding out on the warehouse floor. It was *that* important to him."

Ryan frowned and took it from her. "Why?"

"I don't know. I can't figure out the code to get into it. I feel sure it's someone's birthday, but not a clue whose it might be."

"Why didn't you tell me about the phone earlier?"

She frowned. "Can you think of when I've had a chance before now?"

"When we were at the hospital?"

"While you were grieving Kevin's death? While you were consoling your parents? While you were—"

"Izzy—"

He lifted a hand, but she cut him off. "I didn't know there could possibly be anything on it other than personal stuff until we saw the video. And that's when I mentioned it."

He sighed and shut his eyes. "Sorry. Sorry. You're right."

Izzy's surge of anger fizzled. "Honestly, I wasn't even thinking about the phone during the initial craziness. Like I said earlier, it didn't occur to me that there might be anything on the phone except Kevin's stuff. Maybe personal stuff. You know, maybe something he was embarrassed about and didn't want his family to know was on there."

"Kevin wasn't into anything he needed to be embarrassed by."

"Of course you would say that, you're his big brother. But you never know." She didn't really think so either, but people had a way of hiding things they didn't want known. Kevin was no different than her or anyone else when it came to secrets. Everyone had them. "Anyway, I was going to erase whatever 'it' was, then give you the phone. Only now, after seeing the video, I think something's on there that Kevin saw—and possibly recorded—in the warehouse."

"Yeah. I do too." Ryan tapped in a code, then shook his head.

She told him all of the ones she'd tried. "What about a girlfriend? Or someone he had a crush on in high school? Or . . . " She shrugged. "I don't know."

He tapped in his birthday, then sighed when it didn't unlock the phone. "I'll have to think about it."

"You think David could crack it?"

"I don't know."

They tried more codes until they were locked out. Waited for the minute to pass and started trying more dates. His graduation from the academy, his first day on the job, his favorite singer's birthday.

"Nothing," Ryan said. "I should be able to do this."

"I know what you mean."

"Guess we'll have to do a little more research and try again later." He started to tuck the device into his pocket.

"Do you mind if I hang on to it?" she asked.

He lifted a brow. "Why?"

Izzy shrugged. "I don't know. I kind of feel like it's my responsibility to keep it with me until we figure out the passcode."

"It could be evidence."

"True." She paused. "Okay, I'll turn it in."

His eyes searched hers. "On second thought, let's wait on that. Let me run it by my captain and see what he thinks. He'll probably want David to try it."

"Sure."

"Who was that on the phone? Sounded serious."

"That was Louis Harper."

"Your CI?"

"Yeah. He wants to meet tonight. He stole some pictures from a file Bianchi had sitting on a bar and wants to give them to me."

101

"Tonight? What time and where? You'll need backup."

"He's going to text me, but the where is at Elmwood Cemetery."

Ryan's brow rose. "Seriously? A graveyard?"

She shot him a wry look. "Not my choice, I promise. Louis is a bit weird. I just go along with it."

He yawned. "You mind if I take a nap until your guy texts?"

"Go for it. I'm too wired right now." She tossed him a blanket and he pulled it over him, leaned his head back against a cushion, and was asleep before she could blink. How in the world did he do that?

She leaned her head back and closed her eyes. When Mozart barked, she jerked awake to find she'd slept for two hours and could have slept for more if the dog hadn't awakened her.

Mozart barked at the sliding glass doors, jerking her out of her sleepy fog. "Okay, okay. You need to go. I get it."

Ryan stirred and opened his eyes. "Ignore him. I've got this."

"No, stay here. I'm already awake."

Mozart ran to the door and she opened it, then stepped out after him. At four thirty, the sky had darkened with the threat of a thunderstorm and the temperature was dropping. In Columbia, at the beginning of November, one never knew what the weather might decide to do. One day, it might be eighty degrees and the next forty. This evening promised to be a cool one.

Mozart went straight to the back of the fence and sat. And barked.

"What is it, boy?"

He turned at her voice, but quickly focused back on the gate.

Something had caught his attention. He barked again and Izzy walked toward him.

Was someone out there?

Her hand went to her empty hip. She'd left her weapon on the kitchen table.

A noise—footstep?—from beyond the gate reached her ears. A rustle, like someone trying to be quiet and not quite succeeding.

Mozart barked again.

Izzy hesitated, undecided. The fence itself had slim openings between each board. She stepped forward to peer through one and heard a low grunt. "Hey! Who's out there?"

A shadow crossed in front of her, then she heard running footsteps. She jerked back and raced for the sliding glass doors, leaving Mozart behind her, lunging and barking at the gate.

Izzy snagged her Glock from the counter while Ryan surged to his feet, weapon in his hand. All traces of his nap gone. "What is it?"

"Someone snooping around outside." She bolted to her front door, then paused to draw in a breath. Ryan took up a stance on the other side and nodded. She opened the door to see a large man climbing into a Ford Explorer he'd parked across the street from her home. "Hey!"

He didn't pause or look her way before pulling away from the curb, tires squealing on the asphalt. Izzy ran after him, hoping to get a look at the license plate. Ryan stayed at her back.

"Can you see it?"

"Yes, but I can't read it. You?"

"He covered it with something. A real good indication that he was up to no good."

"Oooh!" She bolted back into the house and called it in. No, he hadn't broken in. No, he hadn't stolen anything. No, he hadn't hurt her, she was fine.

And thinking about investing in a security system.

Her phone buzzed in her hand and a text from Louis popped up.

"Louis said to meet him at 10:00," Izzy said to Ryan.

He nodded. "That's five hours from now. I think I'm going to get back to my nap."

"You can fall back asleep? My adrenaline is still rushing so fast I'd never be able to keep my eyes shut."

He shrugged. "It's a gift."

And she doubted he was sleeping much at home. Alone. With time to think about Kevin.

He strode over to her couch and sank onto it. "I like this couch. It's more comfortable than my bed." With that, he pulled the blanket back up and shut his eyes.

"So . . . you're not worried about this guy coming back?"

"Nope, not as long as you have Mozart to sound the alarm."

"Right."

Mozart leapt up onto the couch and settled on the lower part of the blanket at Ryan's feet. Izzy rolled her eyes and took the recliner. Fine. If he could sleep, so could she. She set her phone alarm and closed her eyes. Then opened them and grabbed the book from the end table. She'd sleep later.

Four hours later, the incessant beeping from Izzy's phone woke him. He pried his eyes open and realized he'd actually slept. He hadn't thought he really would, but it had been a good excuse to stay close to Izzy. He was more shook up about whoever had been outside her house than he was willing to let on and there'd been no way he was about to leave her alone. Meeting her CI had come at a perfect time, because sleeping outside in his car had been the only option he'd been able to come up with should she have been ready for him to leave.

Ryan reached over to turn off the annoying alarm and sat up to find Izzy sprawled in her recliner, book in her lap. She stirred, opening her eyes.

"Did you sleep?" he asked.

She looked up. "I dozed."

He stood and stretched. "I'm going to go splash some water on my face."

"There's an extra toothbrush in the medicine cabinet if you want it."

"I do. Thanks."

While Ryan refreshed himself, Izzy threw together a couple of chicken salad sandwiches and grabbed a bowl of fresh fruit from the refrigerator. When Ryan returned, she blinked. Wow. He cleaned up well. When he caught her staring, he raised a brow. Heat flooded her cheeks and she cleared her throat. "Um, I thought we'd eat before we left."

"That looks amazing."

"It's nothing. Just a sandwich and some fruit."

"Exactly. It's not a burger and fries."

Izzy laughed and they settled at the table together, making small talk. She finally glanced at the clock. "I guess it's my turn. I'll be right back and we can leave."

"I'm just going to fix another sandwich to go. That okay?"

"Sure."

While he got to work, Izzy changed back into her jeans and added a sweatshirt over her T-shirt. She holstered her weapon and grabbed her purse. When she walked back into the kitchen, she found Ryan licking his fingers. "Guess that sandwich didn't make it to go?"

He shrugged. "Nope."

"You want another?"

He glanced at the refrigerator, then shook his head. "Naw. It was really good, though."

"Thanks." She smiled. It felt good to feed him, to know that he enjoyed her cooking. Such that it was. Chicken salad wasn't exactly cooking. But still . . .

"I'll drive," Ryan said. "I don't mind bringing you back."

"Great. Thanks."

Once in his SUV, they buckled up and headed toward the cemetery. "You realize how cliché this is, right? Meeting your informant in a cemetery?"

"I know. Like I said, I meet him wherever he feels safe."

The twenty-minute drive passed in silence, each of them lost in thought. When they arrived at the cemetery, the gates stood open. Ryan drove through, then followed her quiet directions, winding through the narrow asphalt paths until he reached a small parking lot. About ten yards to his right was a circle of mausoleums with a concrete patio type area that held three curved benches in the middle. Soft lights highlighted the mausoleums with a gentle glow. Ryan had to admit, it was rather nice. He climbed out and shut the door.

Izzy did the same. Darkness surrounded them. In addition to the lights near the mausoleums, the cemetery also had some low-beam lights scattered around, but in certain areas, it was black as ink. "Stay here, okay?" she said. "He might not come out if he sees you with me."

"I'll keep an eye out around here."

"Thanks."

She clicked on a flashlight and walked toward the nearest mausoleum. Ryan watched her go, no hesitation in her step, confidence in her stride. How often had she done this?

Quite often, if he had to guess. He frowned and decided she needed a keeper. *She's a big girl. She's a cop and she can take care of herself*, the small voice whispered in his head and Ryan grimaced. He knew many cops met with their CIs alone. He'd done it himself on more than one occasion.

But this was Izzy and he didn't like it.

However, since he wanted to keep all his teeth, he'd be sure not to mention that fact to her.

He shifted and squinted through the darkness, his eyes probing the area. Movement to his left caught his attention and he slid his hand to his weapon.

———

Izzy sat on the cement bench next to the mausoleum, facing the entrance of the cemetery since that was the direction Louis usually came from. While Ryan seemed to be freaked out at the thought of meeting an informant in this place, she didn't mind. To her, the cemetery wasn't creepy, it was peaceful. Soothing in its stillness. But then, she was weird.

A footstep fell to her right and she turned, expecting to see Louis hurrying to meet her. Instead, her gaze met . . . nothing.

"Louis?"

She stood and walked to the edge of the mausoleum and looked out toward where Louis usually parked. And, of course, she could see nothing in the darkness.

A quick glance at her phone showed Louis was already ten minutes late. Worry sprouted. He was never late. And he was never sneaky.

She turned just as a low pop reached her and debris from the cement stone battered the right side of her face. She cried out and went down.

"Izzy!"

Ryan's cry spun her around and she jumped to her feet to jog in a zigzag pattern in the direction of his voice. Another pop and this time the bullet landed beside her. She reached Ryan and he snagged her arm to pull her behind the nearest headstone.

"Are you okay?" he asked, his whisper low and harsh. And scared.

Her breath came quick, in pants mostly, due to the fear racing through her. "Yeah, he missed me."

"Your CI set you up."

"Either that or he's dead." She held her weapon ready, listening.

Footsteps.

A low scrape.

"What's he doing?" she whispered.

Ryan shook his head. He had his phone out and was calling for backup.

Izzy's fingers twitched around the grip of her weapon. She really wanted to capture this guy.

107

Another gunshot thudded in the center of the headstone they were hiding behind and she flinched. Ryan jerked. He peered around the edge of the stone, then pulled back. Footsteps pounded in the distance, growing fainter by the second. "He's running."

"How far away is backup?"

"Far enough."

Izzy darted to her feet. "Let's go."

Together, they chased the fleeing figure, catching a brief glimpse of him every so often as he passed a light. "Police! Stop!"

Ryan's words spurred the man on and Izzy doubled her efforts, sidestepping headstones. He finally landed on asphalt and she fell in behind Ryan.

And then he was . . . gone?

She pulled up short. "Where'd he go?"

Ryan stopped and grabbed her hand to pull her behind cover. "In case he starts shooting again. Listen."

Sirens sounded. The man who'd taken off had heard them too, no doubt. A motorcycle roared to life, the sound of the engine fading fast.

She let out a breath she hadn't realized she'd been holding. "Great."

Ryan was on his phone calling it in, telling them to be on the lookout for a motorcycle. "Suspect is armed and dangerous. Approach with caution." He hung up and turned to Izzy. "Ready to go?"

"Yeah. I'll see if I can get Louis to answer. If not, let's swing by his place."

"Got it."

Back in Ryan's SUV, Izzy dialed Louis's number four times. Each time it went to voice mail. "I'm scared for him. He's never missed a meeting."

"We'll check his house."

Fifteen minutes later, Ryan pulled to a stop on the curb of the small bungalow-type home in one of the poorest neighborhoods in Columbia. "No lights on. Does he live with anyone?"

"His sister."

Izzy walked to the door and knocked. It was late and this was important. She continued knocking until she finally heard footsteps on the other side. "Who's there?"

"Annie, it's Izzy, I need to talk to Louis."

The door swung open and a short woman wearing a T-shirt and sweats stood there with a baseball bat in her right hand. "He ain't here. He left around ten and said he had to meet someone."

"He didn't make it to the meeting and he's not answering his phone."

Annie frowned. "I don't know where he is then. He probably stopped off at Red's and had a few drinks. Could be he's passed out somewhere."

"Maybe." But Izzy seriously doubted it. "If he comes home, tell him to call me, all right? I don't care what time it is."

"Yeah, I'll tell him and you call me if you find him, all right?"

"I will."

Annie shut the door and Izzy raked a hand over her ponytail. "Now what?"

"Guess we head home and see if he contacts you in the next few hours."

"I've got a bad feeling about this, Ryan."

"I know. I have the same feeling."

Izzy climbed back into the vehicle and Ryan aimed it toward her home. When he pulled into her drive, he parked and rubbed his chin. "I don't want you here by yourself tonight. Someone was hanging around your gate and then shooting at you in the cemetery? I don't like that at all."

"Can't say I'm loving it." She yawned. "But I'm beat. I need to get some rest. Mozart will sound the alarm if anything hinky happens."

"Right." He walked her to the door and stepped inside, then shut the door behind him. Mozart bounded around his feet, tongue hanging over the side of his mouth. Ryan scratched his ears.

"And just so you know, I'm going to church in the morning with my family, then having lunch with Gabby. You can come if you want." She'd almost feel better having him there. Sort of a shield. To keep things from getting awkward. She was such a wimp.

He shook his head. "Thanks, but I'd better stick close to my family for now. I may go into the office for a bit, though, depending on if Charice comes up with anything else."

"Okay."

"Iz . . ." His eyes caught hers and her breath snagged in her chest. That look in his gaze—

"Yes?"

Then it was gone. "You've got some blood on your face."

"Probably from the cement that sprayed me."

"Yeah. Well, I'll . . . uh . . . see you later," he said. "Get some rest."

"Yeah. You too." She shut the door and leaned against it for a moment while she ordered her pounding heart to slow. Why was she developing these crazy feelings for a man she'd always considered out of her league? Why did the look in his eyes say he might be having the same feelings? Why did she want to explore where said feelings might take them when she'd sworn off men until she could trust her instincts—or at least learn to listen to them?

But Ryan was Ryan. She trusted him.

With her life.

But someone had taken shots at her tonight after someone had been sneaking around her home.

She didn't like it any more than Ryan did.

So that meant she'd be sleeping with her weapon on the nightstand and Mozart at the foot of her bed. If she slept at all.

SATURDAY

11

After a restless night with only a few hours of being horizontal, Ryan drove to his parents' home to find it crowded once again. While he appreciated the fact that people cared, he was getting tired of nodding and smiling and accepting condolences.

And the longer Ryan stayed with his family, the more his nerves shredded. And none of it was their fault. Not the visitors and not his family. It was simply the fact that he was beyond frustrated at the lack of progress on Kevin's case and he felt stifled by inactivity.

Add in the fact that his mother, while she hadn't said much of anything to him or anyone else, hadn't let him leave her side for the past two hours, well . . . he'd about had it.

"Mom, why don't you sit down and rest?" he said. "I'll get you a plate of something to eat."

She slid her hand into the crook of his elbow and said nothing. He sighed.

His phone buzzed. "Excuse me, Mom, I've got to take this."

She nodded, but didn't let go of his arm. He pressed the phone to his ear. "Grant, what's up?"

"Just wanted to let you know that Izzy had a quiet rest of the night. Nothing suspicious. She's good."

"All right, thanks for keeping an eye on her."

"Sure thing."

Ryan had called in a favor and gotten Izzy's house covered for the remainder of the night. He wouldn't have been able to leave otherwise. But now his attention swung back to his present situation.

People swarmed the house. Cops, relatives, friends, probably a reporter or two in disguise.

"Ryan?"

He turned to see a familiar face. "Lee?" He placed a hand on his mother's shoulder. "This is Lee Filmore. He served with Chris in Afghanistan."

"Oh!" His mother shuddered and for a moment, she was back, the blank stare replaced with a burst of life. She pressed her fingers to her lips, the white tissue peeking out from between her knuckles. "You knew Chris. Of course you did. I remember you."

"Yes, ma'am. I was here for Christmas about five years ago. I was going through a hard time and Chris told me I'd be welcome here for the holidays. He was one of my best friends."

Tears spilled over his mother's lower lashes, but she didn't seem to notice. Ryan's throat tightened.

"I've lost two boys now," she whispered.

"I know. I'm so sorry." Lee's eyes reddened and he looked away for a moment. When he looked back, his mouth worked. He snapped his lips shut, then rubbed a hand over his jaw. "I just came to pay my respects to your family, Mrs. Marshall. Chris—" he cleared his throat—"was a good man. One of the best."

"Yes, yes he was. And so was Kevin."

"Chris talked about Kevin a lot. He—he talked about all of you and how much he missed being home. And about how much he missed your Sunday roast."

She gasped and more tears fell.

Ryan held up a hand. "Lee, I don't think—"

"No." His mother managed a wobbly smile. "I want to hear those things. *Need* to hear them. Thank you."

"Of course." He nodded at Ryan. "I just flew in a couple of hours ago and have to leave again in a bit, but I got your message and thought we could talk here."

"Excellent. Thank you."

"What is it you do, Lee?" his mother asked.

"I'm a private pilot. I fly on demand."

"A pilot?"

"Yes, ma'am."

"Well, thank you for coming. I would love to hear more stories if you have the time."

Lee's eyes softened. "I think that can be arranged."

Ryan's sister, Cathy, slipped up beside them and put her arm around their mother. "Excuse me, Mom, Aunt Jessica and Uncle Phil are here and she's got food to put in the refrigerator. Do you think you can help her?"

"What? Now? She was just here this morning with a casserole."

"Well, now she's got more and I think she's planning on spending the night—if the overnight bag Uncle Phil was carrying is any indication."

"Oh, for the love of—" She sighed and rubbed her forehead. "Of course. Thanks for letting me know." She turned back to Lee. "Thank you again."

"Yes, ma'am."

His mother headed for the kitchen and Ryan figured that while she was tired to the point of exhaustion, she was also grateful for something to do. Lying in bed with nothing to do but think about the two sons she'd lost probably wasn't very appealing to her right now. He could relate. At least the blank stare was gone. Maybe he should be grateful for all the people surrounding them instead of being annoyed.

He turned back to his brother's friend. "How much time do you have?"

"About half an hour."

"Won't take that long."

Cathy patted his arm. "Come find me when you're done." She headed toward the kitchen.

Turning back to Lee, Ryan motioned him to the side of the room. "I just needed to ask if you would be willing to take a look at some pictures."

"Sure. What pictures?"

"I don't have them yet, but hopefully soon."

He told him about the banquet Chris and Jonathan had attended and Lee nodded. "Chris told me about going to that banquet. Told me about meeting Jonathan too. Said the two of them were planning to open up a shelter for homeless vets."

Ryan stilled. "He did? They were?"

"Yeah. He talked about it a lot while we were overseas. Said he'd already gotten the ball rolling and was ready to get out of the service and work with those vets full time."

"How did I not know this?"

Lee shrugged. "Chris was a private man. You know that better than anyone. He was leery of talking about the future, but sometimes, late at night, when it was just the six of us, he'd talk."

"I see. Do you know who the third man could have been with him and Jonathan at the Gills' home that day?"

"No." Lee shook his head. "Could have been anyone. Did Jonathan's mother indicate if the other guy was in the service?"

"No, she didn't say."

Lee glanced at his watch. "Then I couldn't begin to guess. Let me know when you've got those pictures. I'm happy to take a look when I'm in town or you can email them to me."

"Thanks."

"No problem." He saw Lee out the door, then went to find his sister. She stood at the entrance to the hall, her expression pensive. Sad. And like she'd rather be anywhere else in the world than where she was.

"What's up, Cath? Did you want to talk?"

"Not about anything specific." She started down the hall and Ryan followed her. "First Chris and now Kevin. It's not right—or fair—or—" Tears welled in her eyes, but she held them back, even as she stopped in front of Kevin's closed bedroom door.

Ryan nodded and swallowed against the lump that wanted to grow in his throat. Rubbing a hand over his face, he gathered his emotions and stuffed them into a tight ball. "I should have talked him out of being a cop, Cathy."

"You tried." She twisted the knob and stepped inside Kevin's room.

"I should have tried harder." Ryan followed her inside and looked around. "He wasn't ready. I mean, look at this room. It's like he was still a teenager." Baseball posters hung on the wall. Trophies lined his shelves and a pair of jeans still lay where he'd tossed them in the corner next to the desk that held his laptop. "What made him think he could be a cop? He wasn't even an adult yet. I should have tried harder. I should have . . ." He pressed his fingers to his burning eyes.

She huffed. "Do you really think it would have made a difference? Do you honestly think you could have changed his mind?"

For a moment Ryan didn't answer, then shook his head. "Probably not, but we'll never know now, will we?"

"Don't put this on yourself, Ry, it will just make you crazy. Kevin was a big boy and he knew his own mind."

"Yeah." Ryan walked over to the desk and pulled open the top drawer.

"What are you doing?"

"Looking for something."

"What?"

"Izzy has Kevin's phone. He asked her to hide it the night he was killed."

She gasped. "What?"

"Yeah. And I need the six-digit code Kevin used for the password on his phone." He glanced at her. "You have any idea?"

"No, but it's probably a birthday."

He paused. "Interesting. That's what we think too."

Ryan went back to searching and pulled a handful of pictures from the drawer. He flipped through them. "They're pictures of Kevin and Izzy."

"All of them?"

"Not all, but a lot. Here's one with Kevin and that girl, Miranda, he dated for a while. What was her birthday?"

"I have no idea."

"I can find it." A quick search for her driver's license and he would have it.

"It might not be a birthday," Cathy said.

"Maybe, but you know Kevin and his birthday celebrations. He loved them."

"And made a big deal out of everyone's. You're probably right."

"But whose?"

She joined in the search. "There's no journal, nothing like that. Just those pictures."

He tucked them into his jacket pocket. "I'll go over them later. Let's get back out there."

Ryan led the way out of the room and back into the den. He looked around and found his mother sitting in the wing-backed chair next to the fireplace. The vacant stare was back and she was ignoring whatever his aunt Jessica was saying to her.

His seventeen-year-old cousin, Lilianna, had taken a seat in the recliner, her attention focused on her iPhone.

"This is a zoo," Cathy whispered. "It's been two days. Why don't they all just leave?"

"I know." He hugged his sister. "They think they're helping. Just be patient and we'll get through this."

"But at what cost?"

He didn't even try to come up with an answer for that one. "I'm going to go say hey to Lilianna."

"Okay."

Ryan walked over to her. "Hey, kid."

She didn't bother to look up. "Hey."

"You ignoring everyone?"

Lilianna tilted her head at him in a practiced pose he figured she used on boys she wanted to flirt with. "Most everyone. Not you." She stuck her phone in her pocket and stood to give him a hug. "I guess the next few days are going to be just like when Chris died, huh?"

"You remember those days, I suppose?"

"Like they were yesterday."

Of course she did. It had only been eighteen months. Seemed like longer.

Her blue eyes clouded. "I'm sorry about Kevin."

"Me too."

"I overheard Mom talking and she said he did something stupid and got himself killed."

Ryan stiffened. "Where'd she hear that from?"

"I don't know. I was listening to her talk on the phone."

"I see."

"Did he?"

Ryan hung his head for a moment, then nodded. "Yeah, he did. But I hope that's not the only thing he's remembered for—and it was for a good reason. He just . . ." He shrugged.

When he looked up, she hugged him again. "Thanks for being honest with me. You're about the only one who will be."

"I'm sorry about that. Sometimes it's just hard for adults to admit something they'd rather not. Even to themselves. Don't take it personally."

"Right." She shifted and wiped away a tear. "I'm mad at him

for being stupid, but I'll remember him for all the funny stuff we used to do together," she said.

"Like the practical jokes he used to play on your dad?"

"Yeah—and the time he threw me into the pool because I swiped his phone and texted his girlfriend that he wanted to marry her."

"You did that?"

She flushed. "I was young and stupid." She grimaced. "At least I get to grow up to regret my stupidity."

"Yeah." He hugged her and said a silent prayer over her. "Hey, what was her name, you remember?"

She laughed. "I'm not likely to ever forget it. Sherry Livingston. Why?"

"You don't happen to know her birthday, do you?"

"No. Again, why?"

"It was just a thought I had. I need to look at something on Kevin's phone and we're pretty sure his password is a birthdate, but we have no idea whose it could be."

"Hmm. Me either. Sorry."

"Okay. Thanks."

"Sure."

He glanced at his phone and noted the time. "I've got to go find Izzy. You going to be okay?"

She pulled out her iPhone and waved it at him. "I'll be just fine. I have my coping mechanism to help me tune out the rest of the world."

"Yeah. I plan to do that sometime soon myself."

"We'll be leaving soon anyway. Mom said something about Aunt Gena needing some rest."

"Right."

She plugged back in and he went to find Cathy to let her know he was leaving. He found her standing in front of the fireplace, staring at the pictures on the mantel. Pictures containing two of their fallen brothers. The rage swelled. He tamped it down. "I was planning to stay the night, but now that Jessica and Phil are here, I feel better about leaving."

Cathy turned. "Where are you going?"

"To see Izzy. I need to talk to her."

"Poor Izzy. Her parents were here just before you got here. Chief St. John said they're all just heartbroken, especially Izzy. She and Kevin were like best friends. Or brother and sister."

"I know."

"Go check on her."

"All right. See you tomorrow."

Ryan said his goodbyes and slipped out the back door. As he climbed into his vehicle, he noticed Chief's car in the driveway across the street. No doubt she was working at home. Her husband, Izzy's father, was a defense attorney. He knew the husband and wife often went toe-to-toe on some of the cases that crossed his desk. And yet, they managed to make their marriage work even while they battled it out in their professional lives.

He called Izzy and got her voice mail. "I need to see Kevin's phone. I'm going to come by and we're going to try to work on his password again, okay?"

He hung up and remembered. She'd gone to church this morning, then had planned to eat with Gabby. He knew just where to find her.

12

Izzy walked out of the church with her father. It had been just the two of them this morning. She enjoyed the Saturday morning service and attended whenever she could—especially if she was going to be working on Sunday. It was a small service and more like a Bible study than a full-blown worship service, made up mostly of stay-at-home moms and other law enforcement officers. But it refreshed her spirit and she thanked God for a church that was sensitive to the fact that not everyone's schedule allowed for Sunday morning attendance.

Tomorrow was Kevin's funeral. Truthfully, she wasn't sure that she would feel like attending church with the rest of the family or even what the investigation would bring by then. She prayed they had whoever had killed Kevin in custody by then.

Swallowing against the lump the thought immediately generated, she turned her thoughts to her brother. Derek still hadn't bothered to text or call her after their initial exchange, and Izzy had already made up her mind that she simply couldn't cover for him any longer—and continue to risk her job. She'd write the update and be done with it.

Maybe.

Her father slung an arm around her shoulders and pulled her to his side as he talked to a young man who appeared to be a client.

She snuggled a bit closer and simply enjoyed being next to him, while she thought about all the times he'd been there for her. To dry her tears when one of her brothers had been mean, to wipe scraped knees and kiss her boo-boos. To hold her hand while she prepared for her court appearance after Mick had terrorized her for hours.

She shuddered at the last thought and pushed it away, focusing on the good ones.

In spite of the long hours her parents worked and the number of children in the family, she'd never felt neglected or invisible. And that was due to the fact that her parents worked hard to make sure that she and her siblings felt special, always loved.

Which is probably why she thought she could help Mick see that he had potential, that he could overcome whatever life had thrown at him and grow into the person he was created to be.

Unfortunately, that hadn't turned out well at all, and she still bore the scars from that relationship. She wouldn't make that mistake again. Mainly because she wasn't sure she had the courage to try.

Ryan's face popped into her mind and her heart skittered a bit. But Ryan was Ryan. Exactly, she silently argued. And he's trustworthy, not to mention gorgeous, and—

Movement to her left captured her attention. She focused on it while her father's voice echoed in the background. It moved again. The large oak at the edge of the church property seemed to have sprouted a piece of trunk that flapped when the wind blew.

She slipped from beneath her father's arm and walked toward the tree.

More flapping.

She realized it wasn't a part of the tree, but someone standing behind the tree, wearing a trench coat. Each time the wind gusted, the bottom part of the coat blew out, then back in.

As she drew closer, the person behind the tree moved to keep the tree between him and her.

Creepy.

Izzy lifted her chin and took another step.

The large man hiding behind the tree reached out and grabbed her arm, pulling her toward him.

"Hey!" She jerked against his grip, but he was so strong it was like a fly trying to escape a spider's web.

"Izzy!" She heard her father's cry over the pounding of her heart.

"Let me go!"

Her captor, her *huge*, ginormous captor, pulled her close to stare at her with such menace in his dark eyes that for a moment Izzy couldn't blink. He reached up with his other hand and ran it over her body. Flashes of Mick came to mind and she froze. Literally, she couldn't move.

She felt a tug on her left coat pocket. Then her frozen state melted and she brought her right fist up in a punch that landed with a solid thud on his jaw. He blinked. She punched him again and pain raced through her knuckles and up her arm.

"Izzy! Hey!" Her father's furious shout caught the attention of the other church members. "Let her go!"

Without a word, the man scowled and shoved her to the ground. She landed with a hard thud that stole her breath. He spun on his heel, crossed the street, and disappeared between the Methodist church and the park. Izzy hauled herself to her feet as her father stopped beside her.

"I'm going after him." She raced in the direction the man had gone and heard her father's footsteps pounding after her.

As she rounded the corner of the church wall, she came to a stop. Her father pulled up beside her. "Did you see which way he went?" she said.

"No. He's gone."

"Ugh!"

"What was that all about, Izzy? Are you okay?"

She looked down at her bruised hand and grimaced. "I'm fine."

She realized her father was speaking into his phone, describing what had happened and giving the police a general description of the man. He hung up and took her wounded hand in his. "Nice work."

He was trying to sound blasé, but the hand that held hers had a fine tremor and his ragged breathing said the incident had shaken him greatly.

Izzy shuddered. It had shaken her too.

"The police are on the way."

Izzy shoved her hands into her pockets and stilled. "He stole my phone."

"What?"

"My phone. It was in my left pocket." She checked the other just in case, but wasn't surprised when she found it empty. Her fear slowly fading, her pulse on its way back to normal, she frowned. "Why does he want my phone?"

"Probably a junkie looking for something to sell."

Officers arrived and Izzy showed her badge. They took her statement and promised to be on the lookout for the man. She used her father's phone to put her phone into lost mode. Unfortunately, it must have been offline, because the tracking mode didn't come up. But it would. Whoever took it would try to use it or get something off it.

When she handed his phone back to him, he put his arm around her and steered her toward his car. "Are you sure you're all right? That was pretty scary."

"I'll be fine, Dad. Yes, it was scary, but I think I was more surprised than anything."

"How's the hand?"

"Sore. I need to ice it."

"So, how about brunch with your old man?"

"I'd love to, but I already promised Gabby I'd meet her. And now I'm going to have to go shopping for a new phone."

He stopped and pulled her around to face him. "You're continuing to be friends with her?"

"Of course. What Mick did isn't her fault."

"I know." He rubbed his forehead while his eyes bored into hers. "You're right, but I . . ."

She knew what he wanted to say . . . but didn't. "Don't worry, Dad. I'm not having anything to do with Mick. I don't plan to get anywhere near him and the restraining order is still in place."

A low grunt escaped him and he rolled his eyes. "Restraining order. We all know how effective those are."

True. It hadn't stopped Mick last time and probably wouldn't again if he was determined to see her. "He was released from the hospital."

"I know."

"You keep tabs on him."

"I do."

Izzy kissed his freshly shaved cheek. "Thanks, Dad. I love you."

Strong arms wrapped her in a hug she'd loved ever since she could remember. "I love you too, kiddo." Then he let out a sigh and put her away from him. "Go meet Gabby and tell her she needs to rein in her candidate."

"Rein her in?" Izzy laughed. "No she doesn't. Her candidate is doing everything in her power to win this election and Mayor Cotterill is letting her." Izzy frowned. "What's his problem anyway?"

Another sigh. "I don't know, Iz. I went by his office yesterday afternoon and tried to talk to him. He didn't have much to say and looks worn out."

"Well, if he wants to win, he better get on the stick."

"Yeah. Maybe he's just ready to retire."

"He's only in his late fifties and he's still got two kids in college. Does he have the means to retire?"

"I . . . wouldn't think so, but let's not worry about him right now. You go . . ." He gave her a gentle shove toward her car, which was parked next to his. "And be careful, Izzy."

"I'm always careful these days. Even more so now." She frowned.

He gave her a sad smile. "Yeah."

Izzy headed to the nearest phone store and within thirty minutes had a new device and a small dent in her savings account. She'd texted Gabby to let her know she was running late. When she finally arrived at the restaurant, Gabby had just pulled into the parking lot as well.

"Hey," Izzy said, "perfect timing."

"It was no problem." Gabby hugged her. "I've been looking forward to this."

"So have I. Let's eat."

Once settled at the table with their drinks in front of them and their order placed, Izzy leaned forward. "Tell me how you're doing, Gabby."

Her friend shrugged. "I'm doing fine. Well," she gave a low, humorless laugh, "as well as I can be with Mick living with me." She waved a hand. "But the campaign is going well, as I'm sure you've noticed."

"I have."

"She's a good woman, Izzy, she really is. And all she wants to do is make the city better. Safer for everyone, including you."

Izzy played with her glass, wiping the condensation off before she answered. "She sure seems to come across that way."

Gabby paused. "You know what? Let's not talk about the election. I'm stressed enough about it that I don't need to let that bleed into our lunch."

"All right, let's talk about the guy I heard calling you 'babe.'"

A slight smile tugged at Gabby's lips. "He's a friend."

"Where did you meet him?"

"A mutual friend introduced us."

"So . . . is it going anywhere?"

Gabby shrugged. "I don't know." She rubbed her eyes. "I really don't have time to worry about a relationship right now. At least not until after the election. And even then . . . I'm just not sure." She paused. "Look, can I ask you something?"

"Of course."

Her friend hesitated, then laced her fingers together on the table. "Can we talk about Mick?"

Dread churned, but Izzy nodded. "If you want. What about him?"

Gabby hesitated, then sighed. "No, let's not talk about him either." She forced a smile and Izzy frowned.

"What is it, Gab?"

"Nothing. I just need to get through this election and hopefully things will take a turn for the less stressful."

Their food arrived and they fell silent. Izzy dumped butter on her potato and topped it off with sour cream.

A giggle from Gabby brought her eyes up. "What?"

"You do realize that you're going to have to stop eating that much butter at some point? You're practically signing your own death warrant."

Izzy laughed. "I'll take my chances. Thanks."

Gabby's gaze turned serious. "So, are you okay? I can't imagine how hard losing Kevin has been."

"Am I okay?" She sighed. "I don't know, Gab. Not really, but I will be. At some point." She shrugged. "This helps."

"What?"

"Getting out. Being around other people. Not sitting at home crying." The tears were very near the surface and she swallowed them back.

"Oh. Good. I'm glad I suggested it then." Gabby sipped her water and gave Izzy a forced smile.

Izzy put her fork down. "Okay, spill it."

"What?"

"Whatever it is you want to say about Mick."

Gabby flushed. "You know me pretty well."

"Hmm. So what is it?"

"Izzy—"

"What? Tell me."

"He wants to apologize."

"No."

Gabby's eyes turned earnest and she bit her lip, then sighed. "Please, Izzy. He's come so far and he's worked so hard with everyone at the counseling center. He's taking his medication regularly and he's just . . . I think he needs to tell you how sorry he is."

"Gabby, I just . . . can't."

Her friend lowered her face to her palms and spoke into them. "I know, I understand."

"Do you really?"

With a ragged sigh, she looked up. "Yes, actually. And it's horrible of me to ask this of you. And I wouldn't, except . . ."

"Except?"

"*Except* we've spent every last dime we have on his therapy. We're broke, Izzy. Flat, stinking broke and I'm afraid if you don't agree to let him apologize, then he'll relapse or . . . or . . . something. And there will be nothing left to help him. He'll wind up in jail—or worse. And then there's my mother. I can't pay for her assisted living after next month. She doesn't even know who I am anymore, but I can't quit my job to take care of her full time because then we'd be homeless. But I can't just *not* take care of her, she's my mother and I love her."

"Of course you have to take care of her."

Tears filled her friend's eyes. "I wasn't going to do this. I promised myself we were going to have a wonderful lunch and I was going to make you laugh." She wiped the tears away with a rough hand. "I just don't know what to do. I can't let Mick relapse. If he does, I'm done," she said on a whisper. "I'm so sorry."

Izzy didn't say anything for a moment while she chewed food she was no longer hungry for. She swallowed and looked up. "I didn't know all that."

"I know. I've tried not to think about it—or spread my misery to others by talking about it, but I've seen the improvement in him and I want to be sure I'm doing everything I can to make sure he continues to progress. Even if that means asking you for the impossible." Her words dropped to a whisper and Izzy could feel the woman's angst rolling off her.

Setting her napkin aside, she drew in a breath and let it out slowly while she considered her options. "I won't meet him in person, but he can write me a letter and I promise to read it."

Gabby's tear-filled gaze swept away from Izzy's. She finally sniffed and nodded. "Okay. That might work. I'll tell him."

"Fine." As much as she usually enjoyed Gabby's company, right now, Izzy just wanted to escape.

"So," Gabby said, "let's talk about something else . . . if you're still talking to me."

Izzy couldn't help it. She let a smile curve her lips and some of the tension left her. "I'm still talking to you." She paused. Then lifted her gaze to meet her friend's. "How about those Gamecocks, huh? They were playing pretty well until the offense dropped out of the game in the second quarter."

Gabby giggled and swiped a few stray tears. "Hey, at least they rallied in the second half and came back to win it."

"After giving me a heart attack."

"I'm sure the coach didn't pull any punches in his halftime speech."

Her friend seemed to relax while they talked, and Izzy let out a relieved sigh, even while the thought of any communication with Mick Sinclair left her feeling like she might hurl at any second. Shoving thoughts of the man aside, she focused on another fact.

She had to talk to Derek's supervisor, ask him what her brother was doing, and let him know he'd shot a man. In her defense, of course. But—

Her phone buzzed and she glanced at the screen. Ryan. She'd call him back in just a few minutes. Izzy tried to stay focused on Gabby's words, but in truth, she was in a hurry to get away. She had to do something. Anything. Even if that meant betraying Derek's wishes.

When the bill arrived, she paid, hugged Gabby goodbye, and climbed into her vehicle with a sigh of relief and checked her text messages.

Once out of the parking lot, she made a left and headed toward the station.

Locating Izzy hadn't been as easy as he'd thought it would be. She hadn't called him back, so he'd sent her a text letting her know where he was and to call him or come by when she got the message.

Scenes from the warehouse continued to blip through his mind. Planning his brother's funeral wasn't a good way to forget them. Not that he ever would. He needed to know who pulled the trigger and sent his bullets flying into Kevin's body.

Propping his feet on his desk, he leaned back in his rickety chair to stare at the ceiling and tried to prioritize his to-do list.

Charice walked in and dropped into the chair at her desk opposite his. "Hey."

He didn't take his gaze from the ceiling. "Hey."

"I've got a name for you. I know who pulled the trigger and shot Kevin."

That got his attention. He dropped his feet to the floor and spun to face her. "Who?"

"Tobias Freeman."

"You're sure?"

"Yep. He matches the guy in the video."

Ryan closed his eyes briefly. "How'd you find him?"

"Good old-fashioned legwork, and shockingly enough, it didn't take nearly as long as I expected it to. I started with the restaurants near the warehouse. Apparently he was a regular at that little café on the corner of Henry and Reeds. First waitress I talked to recognized him. She called him Toby."

"Where does he live?"

She gave him the address. "But the cops have already been there and left."

"What?"

"Four hours ago. Sorry, but I had to pass the information on to the detectives working the case first."

No wonder she'd been so evasive when he'd been calling her all morning.

"And before you get bent out of shape," she said, "Freeman wasn't there. But we've got his laptop and other things to go through and see if we can figure out where he'll go into hiding."

Ryan scowled. "I should have been there."

"No, Ryan, you shouldn't have been, because you're not supposed to be investigating it, remember?"

Just because she was right didn't mean he had to like it. "He's my brother, Charice."

"I know. That's why I didn't tell you."

Anger nipped at him. Truly, he really did understand her reasoning, but it still rubbed him the wrong way. If the roles had been reversed . . .

He sighed and dropped his chin to his chest.

. . . he would have done the same thing. She was just protecting him from himself. At least that's the way he figured *she* was looking at it. "Thanks for the update." Thanks for nothing.

He might understand, but it would take some time to get past it.

He fell silent and ran the name around in his head.

Tobias Freeman.

A name Ryan would never be able to forget now.

And it belonged to a man he'd spend his days tracking down no matter how long it took.

He ran a hand down his face and sighed. Then looked at his phone. Izzy had texted.

I'm on the way to the office. Are you still there?

Yes.

Be there in a few.

Ten minutes later, he looked up to find Izzy standing in front of his desk, staring at him with questioning eyes. Charice had disappeared during his mental absence from her, and apparently Izzy had said his name a couple of times. "Oh. Sorry."

"You okay?" she asked.

"Fine."

She dropped into the chair next to his desk. "But not?"

He sighed. "Yes."

"Okay."

"How are you?"

She crossed her arms. "Okay. But not."

"What's wrong?"

"A couple of things."

"Okay . . . number one?"

"Number one is that I was attacked at the church today and he stole my phone."

Ryan frowned as fear for her darted through him. "Are you okay?"

"Physically, yes." She flexed her hand and he noticed the bruises.

"He hurt you."

"What? This?" She held up her hand. "Oh, no. I got those when I punched him."

"You punched him."

"I did."

"Good for you. I hope it hurt him."

"Honestly, I don't think so. The guy was monster huge, Ry, like six feet five or six inches tall. Linebacker size. It probably felt like a poke to him."

Awe and respect filled him. "But you managed to land a punch?"

She shrugged. "Yeah. Two, actually."

"You deserve a cape. Izzy, that's amazing." He frowned again. "But you're sure you're not hurt."

"Ryan, please. I'm not hurt. Confused as to why he would go after my phone and not my purse, but whatever. Forget about that for a minute. This brings me to number two."

"I don't want to forget that. I mean, first someone is snooping around your house, then someone tries to shoot you when you go to meet your informant. And now this. Izzy, you could be in real danger."

She frowned. "Maybe. We'll have to think about that."

"I think you need protection."

"I think the person shooting at me just didn't want me to meet with Louis. You think he was after me for another reason?"

"I think it's a possibility."

"Like what?"

He sighed. "I don't know."

"Okay, well, think about that later. I'm still on this second item."

"Which is?"

"I need to do something and I can't bring myself to do it. So I think I just need you to say, 'Do it.'"

Ryan leaned back and gave her his full attention. He liked that she was here, that she'd come to him with a problem. He wanted to help her solve all of her problems. Or hold her when he couldn't. He didn't like the fact that someone attacked her and stole her phone but didn't bother to go for her purse. He'd have to think about that one. He cleared his throat. "What do you need to do?"

"Well . . . I can't tell you."

"Why not?"

"Because I can't betray a confidence."

Ryan leaned forward. "I can't help you if you don't tell me."

"I don't want your help."

He lifted a brow. "Okay. So you sought me out, told me you had a problem, but you don't want my help, so you're not going to tell me what said problem is."

"Exactly."

"I'll never understand women."

13

She let out a half chuckle, half sigh at his quiet words. "I know I'm being difficult and vague and I'm sorry. I'm just worried about Derek." Her eyes met his. "You haven't heard from him, have you?"

Ryan frowned. "No."

"I thought for sure I'd hear from him yesterday, but not a word. I don't like it and I don't like being worried about him."

"Did you ask your mother if she's heard from him?"

"Yes. She hasn't." Izzy twisted her ponytail around the fingers of her right hand, then let the strands drop.

"He's probably undercover," Ryan said.

"That's what everyone keeps assuming."

"But you don't think so?"

Frustration curled her fingers into tight fists. "I don't know what to think." She stood. "I shouldn't have bothered you with this."

"Sit down, Izzy, let me help."

The desire to lean into him, depend on him to fix things, crashed over her. But she couldn't. At least not yet. "I want to, but I need to talk to someone first. Let me ask him if he's okay with you helping."

"Talk to who?" He stared her down, trying to get her to tell him. She refused to look away. "Derek?" he pressed.

She made a sound that could have been confirmation—or not. Izzy pulled out Kevin's phone and set it on his desk. "I was going to take it by David just in case he could do something with it, but I keep thinking we'll come up with the password eventually."

Ryan nodded. "All right, I'll let you change the subject. For now."

"Thanks."

Her eyes never left his and he finally sighed. "I told my captain about the phone and he said to keep trying for the next day or so and see if we could crack it. If not, we'll have to take more extreme measures."

"Like what?"

"Like letting David give it a try."

She gave a slow nod. "Okay, let's see if we can get this done."

He pulled the pictures he'd found in Kevin's bedroom from his pocket. "Look at these while I work on this. I need to figure out Sherry Livingston's birthday."

She took them and settled back to flip through them. The first one hit her like a punch to the gut. Kevin's smiling face as the worker connected the bungee cord to his safety harness. He'd insisted she snap the picture. Then he'd done the same for her. Her expression hadn't been quite so gleeful. "Oh Kevin." Tears sprang to her eyes. How was she supposed to move on?

She sniffed and looked up. Ryan's gaze was glued to the computer screen. "What are you doing?"

"Getting driver's license information for all the Sherry Livingstons in a fifty-mile radius."

"How many are there?"

He clicked a few more keys. "Sixteen." He fell silent and she figured he was scanning each one. With a disgusted sigh, he sat back. "I don't remember her at all. None of them look remotely familiar."

"I don't know many who look like their driver's license picture. She could be in there and you just don't recognize her." She swiped a tear that had managed to escape and Ryan chose that moment to look up.

"Aw, Izzy, I'm sorry. I should have thought how hard it would be seeing those pictures. Put them away for another time and help me."

Swiping a tissue from the box on his desk, she blew her nose. "It's okay. It's hard, but it's okay. And help you with what?"

He picked up Kevin's phone, then turned the computer monitor so she could see it. "Start calling out all the birthdays."

It only took a few seconds before they were locked out of the phone. Ryan sighed. "I'll try the rest later, I guess, but I don't see him using her birthday."

"No. It would be someone closer to him, not someone he dated a couple of years ago." He raised a brow and she shook her head. "I already tried my birthdate and yours . . . and Chris's."

With a sigh, he slid Kevin's phone into his pocket. "Now, what's this about Derek? Let me help."

"No, that's okay. I need to think on it some more. I'll see you later." She stood and headed for the exit.

"Wait a minute."

But she didn't stop. She didn't trust herself not to confide in him, ask him for his help.

Ryan went after her.

Once outside, she paused on the brick steps.

"Hold on. Why are you in such a rush?" he said and caught her arm. "What are you going to do?"

"I'm not sure." She pulled on her arm and he released her immediately. The fact that she hadn't startled or had an instant flashback to her time as Mick's hostage stunned her for a moment. She shook her head. "But I'm not going to find my answers here."

"Izzy! Come on."

He wasn't going to give it up and she wasn't going to talk about Derek. She sighed. "Ryan, I have to think."

"Will you at least talk to me about it? Talk it out. You know, brainstorm?"

"I said I needed to think. I do that best alone."

"Brainstorming with brilliance *is* thinking."

She couldn't help it. She laughed. "You're cute, but brilliant might be pushing it."

He tilted his head. "You think I'm cute?"

"Ryan."

"I mean, I've never had any complaints." He paused. "Except from Lydia McCarthy from tenth grade."

Izzy stopped, totally pulled in by his sudden charm. She'd gone from annoyed and worried to laughing in point two seconds. "I remember her. Rich, snooty girl. What was Lydia McCarthy's problem with you?"

"She said my nose was too big, but I was willing to overlook that."

"So you asked her out anyway?"

He shrugged. "She had horses."

"What? Ryan Marshall, you only wanted to go out with her so she would invite you over to ride a horse?"

He flushed. "Yeah."

"You're sad. Cute, but sad."

Sobering, he studied her. "So are you going to tell this cute, but sad guy what you're thinking?"

"No."

At the ferocious frown on his face, she gave in to impulse and stood on her tiptoes to place a kiss on his cheek. "We'll talk later, I promise. Give your mom and dad hugs from me."

She ignored his stunned look—just glad that he no longer looked like he wanted to strangle her—then turned her back on him and headed in the direction of her car.

Izzy heard his low growl and knew he was still watching her, wanting her to turn around and come back, but she couldn't. "Izzy! What are you going to do?"

She turned, walking backward. "I'm going to think about getting a horse." She spun back around and grinned for a moment. She'd managed to effectively shut him up with that statement. Her mirth faded as her mind spun back to the problem at hand. Namely Derek. What *was* she going to do? What *should* she do? Talk to her supervisor herself? Talk to his?

No. Not just yet.

She was off-duty for the next several days and planned to take advantage of it. She'd continue to try to get ahold of Derek. If she failed, she'd have to come to a decision about whether or not to go to a supervisor.

The parking lot was fairly full and she'd parked her Chevy Tahoe at the far end, feeling fortunate she'd found a spot in the lot off Lincoln instead of having to use the parking garage across the street.

As she drew closer to her vehicle, movement in the front seat made her frown. Then she realized the driver's door was open. "Hey!" She placed her hand on her weapon.

The person sitting in the front of her vehicle jumped out and took off.

"Police! Stop!"

14

Ryan jerked at the shout. He turned to see Izzy sprinting across the parking lot, chasing a fleeing figure. Ryan's brain clicked even as he opened the car door and threw himself into the driver's seat. He backed out of the parking spot and shoved the gear into drive.

Izzy was closing in on the guy at the end of the parking lot row. If they kept going, they'd cross Washington. Ryan drove until he was parallel to the man. At the end of the lane, he swerved in front of him. The guy slammed into the side of the vehicle, rolled off the front, and kept going.

"Whoa!" The dude was *huge*. Linebacker size.

Izzy sped past Ryan as the fleeing man slipped into the parking garage at the corner of Washington and Lincoln.

Ryan pulled to a stop and bolted from the vehicle. He'd lost sight of the two.

"Ryan! Up the ramp!" Ryan followed the sound of Izzy's voice and the fleeing footsteps. "You! I said 'Stop!'"

And then it fell quiet.

At the top of the ramp, he paused. Listened.

And heard nothing.

No yelling, no footsteps. Nothing at all. The guy was hiding. Probably behind or under a car.

And Izzy was looking for him. He glanced around as he hurried to join the search. This garage was right across the street from the police department. Where were the cops? The garage would teem with them at shift change. But it wasn't time and the place was about as active as a graveyard at midnight. Now that he had a chance, he put in a call for backup, keeping his voice low while his gaze swept the area.

With his weapon held ready, Ryan peered around the edge of the cement pillar to get a look at the ramp leading up to the next floor. He couldn't see anyone, but that didn't mean the guy wasn't hiding behind the line of cars parked on either side of the ramp.

Slowly, he eased his way around the pillar, then head swiveling, began to climb. On the last floor before the next ramp would lead him to the roof, a thud came from above. A harsh cry echoed. His pulse jerked. "Izzy!"

"Ryan!"

Ryan raced the rest of the way up and turned the corner to spy Izzy on the far side of the lot, her back on the hard cement floor, with the goon she'd been chasing on top of her.

He took off running. "Police! Back off!"

Izzy jerked her head to the side when the man swung. His meaty fist grazed her ear. Pain slashed through her. She'd finally caught up with him and tackled him, wrapping both arms around his legs to bring him down. Probably not her smartest moment, but it had seemed like a good idea at the time.

Only he was big as the Hulk, strong as an ox, and had quickly flipped her onto her back. She'd slammed hard and lost her breath as her weapon hit the ground and slid out of her reach.

The good thing was that it was out of his reach too, and he didn't appear to have another one close by.

It didn't take her long to figure out this was the same man

who'd attacked her at the church and stolen her phone. His size alone was a dead giveaway. He now straddled her lower body, left hand clamped around her throat. Panic hit her hard. Flashes of her previous attack threatened to overwhelm her.

No. Don't let it take control. Think. Think.

Mick's face superimposed itself over the man's above her. Her fingers pried uselessly at his while he grinned down at her, his light blue eyes like chips of ice. "Where is it?"

"What?" Izzy managed to croak. Terror grabbed her, and she knew if he landed a blow, he'd crack her skull. Black spots danced before her eyes and she was seconds from passing out.

Izzy's lungs strained only to finally grab air. His grip had loosened so she could talk. She drew in the air and the dots faded. Keeping her eyes on his, she released her grip on the wrist of the hand around her throat and allowed both of her arms to fall to the cement floor. He blinked as though she'd confused him.

With a jerk, she bucked her hips and brought both fists up to slam them against his ears. He howled his pain and fury, and then he was off of her.

"Put your hands up!" Ryan said.

Izzy gasped in two more gulps of air, coughed, and rolled to her feet.

Her attacker lay on his side, clutching his ribs. Ryan must have kicked him in order to get him off of her.

"Put your hands up, I said!"

Ryan continued to yell orders and the guy continued to ignore him. Ryan started toward him, but in one smooth move, the hulking man made a rolling lunge, his arm outstretched toward Izzy. She spun to get out of his reach, but still weak from the attack, stumbled. He snagged her foot and yanked her on top of him. Off-balance, Izzy flinched when he got a grasp on her arm and, using her as a shield, hauled himself—and her—to his feet, his breath harsh against her ear. Her feet dangled inches from the concrete floor.

Ryan held his weapon steady. "Let her go! Now!"

Of course he didn't. Instead, he walked backward. "Put your gun down, cop."

"Can't do that. Let her go."

The guy laughed. "Right."

Ryan followed. "I mean it."

For each step Ryan took toward them, Hulk took one step back. Izzy struggled against him. Never had she felt so powerless. Except maybe when she'd held a dying Kevin in her arms. "Just shoot him," she gasped.

But Ryan wouldn't risk hitting her.

"Put your weapon down, cop, or I snap her neck."

Ryan didn't even blink. "Put her down and step. Away. From. Her."

"You want me to put her down? All right. I can do that."

Izzy felt the sun come through the side of the building. Cold dread centered itself in her belly. "Ryan!"

In another effortless move, Hulk lifted her over the cement wall and dangled her above the asphalt below. A cry slipped from her and she grasped a handful of his shirtsleeve in both fists. If she was going over, she was taking him with her. "Shoot him!"

If Ryan shot him at this point, the way Hulk was leaning over the wall, he'd simply fall over and they'd both go down.

And the guy knew it. "What are you going to do, cop? Chase me? Or save her?"

He reached over and jerked one of her hands from his wrist. She tried to grab it back. When she realized there was no way she was going to be able to hold on to him with both hands, she grabbed the wall—which was probably his plan. "Ryan!" *Don't look down, don't look down, don't look down!*

Hulk yanked his arm from her flimsy grasp and she desperately grabbed at the wall with her other hand while her feet swung above the concrete below.

Her fingers slipped. How bad would it hurt to slam into the

ground from this height? Would she feel anything or would everything just go black? *Oh God, help me, please!*

Her hand slipped farther.

Terror engulfed her.

———————

Ryan's heart jammed itself in his throat. He couldn't shoot the
guy earlier, not because the guy wasn't armed, but because if he
went over the wall, Izzy would go with him. Only now he couldn't
shoot him because the dude was running away and Izzy needed
his help. Now. He heard the noise of backup arriving and hoped
someone would see the fleeing man. Ryan threw himself toward
the wall, only to see one of Izzy's hands slip off. "Izzy!"

"Ryan!"

"Izzy! Izzy, hang on!" The cry came from the ground below and
he thought he recognized Chloe's voice.

Ryan ignored the action going on outside the parking garage,
reached the wall, and grasped her wrist. With a grunt, he leaned
over. "Give me your other hand."

She swung her arm up and clasped his forearm with desperate
fingers. He held on tight. Running footsteps and shouts reached
his ears as he hauled Izzy back onto the side of safety.

Her feet hit the floor and she fell against him, trembling, her
breath coming in panicked spurts. He helped her to the floor and
she sat with her back against the wall. "Thanks."

"Izz . . ."

"I know."

"You—"

"I *know*, Ryan."

"Talk about an adrenaline rush."

She lifted her head and glared at him.

He shrugged. "Sorry."

He kept his voice light, but she saw the fading fear in his eyes.
The incident had terrified him.

145

She knew the feeling.

He lightly touched her throat. "You're going to have bruises."

"I'll take that over death." She frowned at him. "You should have shot him."

"I wanted to. You kept getting in the way. I couldn't take a chance on hitting you."

"Right. And one more thing."

"What?"

"You can't tell my mom about this."

He let out a huff of breath. "Yeah, let's keep this one to ourselves."

"Ryan?"

"Yeah?"

"That was the guy who stole my phone at church."

He fell silent. "Then we have a problem."

She snorted. "Well, I do anyway. You think they got him?"

"I don't know. Will your legs hold you long enough to go find out?"

"I have no idea." She held up a hand and Ryan clasped her fingers to pull her to her feet. "They're still wobbly, but I think I can make it."

Once she was steady, she followed him down to the first floor, hearing the clamor of the police action going on. Paramedics and fellow officers met her on the bottom floor. "Did you get him?"

"Izzy!" She turned to see Chloe racing toward her, her K-9, Hank, loping at her side. "Izzy, that was you hanging from the building. What happened? Are you okay?" She threw her arms around her sister and squeezed.

Izzy winced, but managed to pat Chloe on the back. "I'm fine. It's okay. It's a crazy story." Man, her throat hurt.

"And one that's probably going to be on the evening news," Ryan muttered.

"What?"

He nodded toward the crowd who'd gathered. Their iPhones were still videoing. Izzy groaned. "Great. That's just great."

15

6:30 P.M.

Izzy let herself into her side of the duplex and shut the door, throwing the dead bolt home before crossing the den area to the window. Ryan had insisted she needed someone watching her home. After everything that had happened, she was in full agreement.

She'd had a full day that consisted of a quick hospital visit to ensure no broken bones, then back to the office to search for the man who'd attacked her, which included hours of sitting in front of the computer looking at mug shots and drinking bad coffee. Every muscle in her shoulders—and other parts of her body—screamed their displeasure with the misadventures of the day.

She didn't blame them. She wasn't so thrilled with the day's events herself.

At the window, Izzy pushed aside the curtain to see Ryan roll up to the curb and stop. He'd insisted on searching her car, then following her home after they'd grabbed a quick bite to eat. And she hadn't had the energy to dissuade him.

She waved and he returned the gesture before pulling away. Closing the curtain before she gave in to the temptation to beg him to stay, she closed her eyes and drew in a deep breath. Mozart shot through the doggie door and pranced at her feet. Izzy dropped to her knees to bury her face in his silky white fur. Absently, she noted he'd had a bath. Mrs. Spade had been busy.

The parking garage incident flashed through her mind and she shuddered. Touching her still sore throat, the images flickered, larger than life. Would she even be able to sleep tonight without reliving every horrifying second? She'd only been that terrified one other time in her life. Terrified and helpless. Two things she'd vowed never to feel again after her disastrous relationship with Mick. If she closed her eyes, she could still feel the edge of the knife pressed against her throat. She swallowed. *God, I know you're sovereign, you can bring good from evil, but sometimes it's hard to remember that.*

After today's incident, it was obvious that no matter what kind of promises she made to herself, she wasn't the one in control. She'd failed today.

"Epically," she muttered.

What had he been looking for anyway? He'd been thorough, emptying the glove box, the center console, even the driver's door pocket of its varied receipts and trash she'd been meaning to clean out and hadn't gotten around to yet.

Looking for cash? Drugs? What?

Where is it? He'd asked her that question. So, his search of her car had been deliberate, not random. He'd been looking for something specific.

Mozart licked her nose and went to the sliding glass doors that led out to the fenced backyard. She opened it for him, then put food and fresh water in the dog bowls and let him back inside. He went straight to his bowls and she locked the door. The pictures Ryan had shown her today flipped through her mind and she swallowed against the sudden lump. She missed Kevin.

And then something occurred to her.

She had a date to try as Kevin's password. But she'd left the device with Ryan.

Izzy pulled her personal phone from her pocket and sent a text to Ryan.

> Where are you? If you're not home yet, come by my house first and bring Kevin's phone with you.

When he didn't answer right away, she debated just calling him. But he'd said something about going by his parents' before going home and she hated to disturb him. He'd text her back when he could, and stopping by her house wouldn't be an imposition if he was already at his parents'.

He'd pass right by her duplex on his way to his condominium complex about five minutes away. He'd bought his home after she'd rented her duplex, and Izzy's father had grinned when he'd heard the news. "Us on one side of her and Ryan on the other. Couldn't ask for better protection than that."

Izzy had scowled at him. "I can take care of myself." Only to find out she wasn't so great at taking care of herself. Not when it came to judging men anyway. She shuddered. Mick Sinclair had been a huge mistake. One she was still paying for, since she couldn't seem to bring herself to trust anyone else for anything as simple as a first date.

Izzy grabbed her phone and walked into her bedroom to flop onto the bed. Mozart jumped up and settled himself at her feet.

She set her phone on the nightstand and stared at the ceiling with tired eyes. More than anything, she simply wanted to bury her head in her pillow, pull the covers over her head, and stay there until the pain went away.

But life went on. And she had killers to find.

And a phone code to crack. Could she possibly be right about the code? Impatience surged. She could just get in the car and go find Ryan. But she didn't want to intrude if he was with his family. The code could wait another few minutes.

With a sigh, she checked her phone to make sure she'd hear

it if Ryan texted or called, then turned off the lamp. In the semi-darkness she lay there thinking, drifting. Only to jerk when a sound reached her. Mozart's ears twitched, then he lifted his head to stare into the hall. She glanced at the clock. She'd fallen asleep and snoozed for two hours.

Frowning, Izzy stayed still. Sometimes the old duplex creaked as it settled in for the night.

Only this time the sound came from the direction of the front door.

That wasn't the duplex settling. Could Mrs. Spade be outside and about to knock? She waited.

Nothing.

Mozart placed his head back between his paws and huffed a sigh.

Izzy held still a moment longer, then relaxed back against the pillow. Only to sit back up when Mozart bolted to the floor with a growl. "What is it, boy?"

Had her visitor from the other day come back? The one she'd caught a glimpse of through her fence? The one that had run and no one had been able to track down?

Or was it the guy from the parking garage? The Hulk?

But probably not, since there was an officer watching. He would have alerted her to any problems. Wouldn't he? She dialed his number and he didn't pick up. Weird. Uneasiness curled within her.

She rolled off the bed, slipped on a pair of tennis shoes, and grabbed her Glock from the nightstand as well as her iPhone. She shoved the phone into her pocket and gripped the weapon, feeling its comforting weight against her palm.

Mozart had left the bedroom and walked down the hall into the living area. She stepped behind him and he gave a low bark without pulling his gaze from the front door. Izzy's adrenaline spiked another notch. She walked to the door and stood to the side, listening. She needed to look through the peephole, but wariness prevented her from wanting to stand in front of the door. Finally, after about a minute with no more sounds reaching her, she moved to look through the peephole she'd had installed after her fiasco relationship with Mick.

She could see a faint shadow off to the left. She stepped back to the side of the door.

She slipped to the window and looked out. The officer had parked two doors down in an unmarked car. The car was there, but she couldn't tell if he was still in the driver's seat or not. She tried his number again. And still nothing. Not good.

Walking through the living area to the sliding glass door, she decided she'd slip out and around to her front door to see what— or who—the shadow was. Mozart danced at her feet, anxious to go out as well. She unlocked the door and pulled. Only it didn't budge. She frowned and put more power into it.

Nothing.

"What?"

Izzy dropped to her knees and looked at the bottom of the door. Someone had jammed it. Somehow. All around the door was an odd yellow-colored substance. Insulating foam? Really? So . . . this was deliberate. Unwilling to waste any more time on a dead end, she spun and headed for the door that would lead her to the garage. Mozart followed her.

And the lights blinked off.

Ryan glanced at his phone. He hadn't heard it or felt it vibrate. Odd. But Izzy's message now glared up at him. She thought she might know the code and wanted him to bring Kevin's phone by so they could try it.

What's the code?

He waited for a good five minutes for her to answer while watching his mother. She sat on the couch with Aunt Jessica, her head resting on her sister's shoulder. All visitors had left and just family remained.

Cathy picked up a few paper plates that had been placed on the coffee table. Ryan followed her into the kitchen. "Hey."

"Hey."

"I've got to run by Izzy's for a bit. I'll see you all in the morning."

"You sure are running off to see Izzy a lot these days. Is there something going on there?"

Ryan almost smiled. Cathy had always been able to read him. "Maybe."

Her brow rose. "Really?"

He shrugged. "I like her. Admire her. She's a good cop and will make detective one day soon, I guarantee it."

"Izzy was always ambitious."

"All the St. Johns are."

She dropped the paper plates into the trash. "Well, what do you expect with parents like theirs?"

He let out a low laugh. "Yeah. The stress of being their kid has to be enormous. I'm kind of surprised none of them went over to the other side." Izzy's text beckoned and he backed toward the door. "I'll see you tomorrow." Not for the first time, he noticed the faint shadows under her eyes. "Get some sleep, Cath."

"You too."

Ryan shot another text to Izzy.

The code?

Once in his car, he fastened his seat belt and dropped his phone into the cup holder. At the entrance to the subdivision, he started to pull out when a car blew past him going at least twenty miles over the speed limit. Ryan slammed on his brakes, sending his phone flying into the floorboard.

Ryan growled, hit his blue lights, and gave chase.

16

Izzy's pulse hammered in her ears. How much time had passed since the lights went off? Five minutes? Ten? What was he doing?

When it first went dark, she'd waited, listening over the thundering of her heart. But after the power failure, there'd been nothing else.

Questions assaulted her. She moved back to the front door and noticed the shadow was gone.

Was danger really lurking outside her home? If she called it in and no one was out there . . . yeah . . . that wasn't happening. Except there was foam insulation around her door and windows preventing her from getting out that way. Someone was up to something. But what? And could she handle it herself?

Izzy looked out into the garage. She could get in her car, back out, and shine her lights on the front porch area.

Only she had no power for the garage door. She could manually pull it up, but who might be waiting on the other side? What if that's exactly what he was waiting for her to do?

But *he* who?

And how did *he* find her? Assuming there was someone actually out there.

She stopped and pressed her head against the wall. "Think, Izzy. You had a bad scare today and now something else is going down. So think."

She needed to get out and get out now. Scanning the garage once more, she decided it wasn't going to be an exit option. She'd be too exposed opening the garage door and there were no windows to enable her to climb out.

So now what?

A quick tap on her screen sent her call through to Ryan's phone—and voice mail. "Call me when you get this." She hung up. Should she call someone else? Chloe?

No.

911?

Probably.

Fear skittered up her spine and her brain spun. Using the flashlight feature on her iPhone, she moved to the nearest window to look into the backyard. The floodlights had also gone out, blanketing the area in darkness. And giving a good cover to whoever was out there.

Izzy debated whether or not to try to go out the front door. Or would it be better to throw something through the sliding glass door? And risk alerting her position to whoever was watching?

Probably not a good idea.

Then again, she had no other windows in the den area, the glass door providing plenty of light for the room.

So, she'd go out her bedroom window.

She rushed down the hall. "Ryan, pick up the phone." Of course he didn't.

She hung up and dialed Chloe's number.

Voice mail.

Great. She dialed 911 as she hurried to her bedroom.

". . . what's your emergency? Hello? Is anyone there?"

"Ah yes, sorry." She'd been so focused on trying to figure out what to do she hadn't heard the woman come on the line. "This is Izzy St. John." She gave her badge number. "I think someone's sneaking around my house and possibly looking for a way to get in. Could you send a car ASAP? I might need some backup." She didn't know that someone was trying to get in, but she had a distinct feeling someone was trying to "smoke her out," so to speak.

"Absolutely. Stay on the line with me, all right?"

Izzy went to the window and unlocked it. She gave it a tug and it didn't budge. Leaning harder into it didn't help. Her blood ran cold when it refused to move. Somehow he'd jammed her windows too? She squinted and saw more yellow-colored stuff around the edges of her windows. Insulation foam? Whatever. She needed to find a way out.

Heart hammering in her throat, she took a breath.

He'd blocked every exit except the front door. It was like he *wanted* her to come out the front door. So, that wasn't happening.

Her phone beeped, indicating she had a call coming in.

She looked at the screen.

Ryan. Without hesitation, she switched over. "Where are you?" She moved to the next window and still couldn't see anything. The streetlight closest to her was out. It had been working last night.

"Well, hello to you too. I started to chase down an idiot who needs some driving lessons, but decided coming to see you was more important. I'm about three minutes away. What's—"

Mozart barked at the front door, then raced to the sliding glass door, then back to the front door. A shadow near the bedroom window crossed her line of vision, then a face with a mask looked right in at her before it disappeared.

She let out a scream and ran into the living area.

"Izzy! What's going on?"

"Someone's trying to break into my house. Get over here, please, and bring backup."

"Are you sure?"

Gunshots sounded and bullets pelted her front door. "Pretty sure!"

"Izzy!"

Mozart went crazy, barking and growling, lunging at the door.

Fortunately, the bullets were flying above his head. At a lull in the shooting, Izzy darted and scooped the animal into her arms and spun to run into the bathroom.

Ryan was still on the phone yelling something at her.

"I'm fine. Call for backup!" Fine was pushing it, but she didn't have any bullet holes in her body, so she'd go with that.

Izzy put the dog into the bathtub. He could climb out but probably wouldn't, as he loved baths and would stay there as long as he thought he was getting one. Hopefully if the bullets started flying again, he'd be out of the way.

Heart crashing against her rib cage, she shut the bathroom door, then raced back into the bedroom to lock the door and, out of desperation, to try the windows again.

Still jammed.

Heavy footsteps sounded in her living area, and she whirled, grabbed the lamp on her nightstand, and tossed it through the nearest window.

No time to climb out.

The bedroom knob was already rattling. One hard kick and he'd be inside the room, but maybe he'd think she'd gotten out the broken window. Izzy raced back to the bathroom, shut the door, and locked it.

She stood away from the shower on the other side of the toilet and aimed her weapon at the door while her heart beat a harsh rhythm in her chest.

"All right," she whispered. "I'm ready. Where are you?"

"Izzy! Izzy . . . answer the phone!"

Ryan's voice came through the speaker loud and clear. "Be quiet, Ryan," she hissed even as she lifted the phone to her ear.

"Did he shoot you? Are you hit?"

"No. I'm locked in my bathroom." She spoke so low, she wondered if he could even hear her. "Now hush. I need to listen."

He fell silent and she lowered the phone.

According to her intruder's footsteps, he was heading toward her broken window. Would he think she went out and leave?

His steps thudded against her hardwoods again.

Heading straight toward her. He wasn't leaving voluntarily. She'd have to convince him.

Izzy lifted the weapon and aimed it at the door. A heavy thud sounded against the bathroom door and she bit back a scream. "I'm armed. If you don't want to get shot, you'd better leave now!"

"Give me that phone, Officer Isabelle St. John! Is it worth dying for?"

So it *was* the phone he was after. And that was the guy from the parking garage. She'd recognize that voice anywhere. Fear shuddered through her. "I don't know. You tell me!"

The flash of remembered terror when she was hanging over the side of the garage sent her already-rushing adrenaline into overdrive. She shoved the memory aside and focused on the man outside her bathroom door.

Another thud ripped the door from the bottom hinge. One more kick and it would fall. She fired once. Twice. Three times. He cried out. Izzy fired again, this time hitting the doorframe. The bullet sent wood fragments flying and she heard his running footsteps.

He was leaving. He was gone. She lowered the weapon to her side and drew in a ragged breath. She'd just lifted the phone to her ear once more when the building shook with an explosion that sent her to her knees.

Ryan pulled to a stop as flames shot out of her front door. He grabbed his phone and called it in as he charged toward the duplex. Mrs. Spade stumbled from her side of the building. "What happened?"

"Ma'am? Are you okay?"

She nodded, eyes wide and fearful. "But Izzy and Mozart—"

"I'll get them. Help is on the way. Get in the back of my car for now." He didn't wait to see if she obeyed. And he didn't see the officer who'd been watching Izzy's house. The car was there, but no one had exited the vehicle during all of the commotion. As he raced toward the front door, his mind replayed the gunshots he'd heard come through the line, then Izzy yelling at the intruder that she was armed. Then more gunshots.

And the explosion.

Ryan made it to the first step of the porch before he had to stop and pull back. Hot flames barred his entrance.

"Izzy!"

Ryan raced around to the side where the sliding glass door was. He tried it, but found it locked and the flames spreading toward it anyway.

"No. Come on. Izzy!"

Sirens sounded in the distance, but he had to get her out before her side of the place was completely consumed.

He ran around to the side where her bedroom was and found flames licking there as well.

Terror flooded him. He couldn't lose Izzy too. With his heartbeat pounding in his ears, he stared at the burning home and knew there was no way she'd be able to get out. "Izzy!" He went to his knees as the fire trucks pulled to a stop in front. He should have insisted she stay with her family.

Fear and grief pounded him as the flames grew higher and hotter, driving him from his knees to his feet. He backed away, desperately searching for a way in. He should have known that guy wouldn't give up so easily. "Izzy, come on, come on, get out of there."

How had the person who'd done this found her? From the car registration. But why come after her? Or send someone after her? Unless it was someone from the warehouse? Maybe she'd been seen?

Izzy had just said he was in her front seat when she'd walked out to her car. Who breaks into a car in a police station parking lot? Either someone really desperate—or someone who wasn't worried about being caught.

The guy from the parking garage definitely hadn't wanted to be caught.

So, that left desperate.

17

Izzy choked on the smoke as she tied the wet towel around her face. She had only seconds to act before she and Mozart went up in flames with the rest of her home. With the towel firmly over the lower part of her face, she grabbed the dog and pushed him out of the bathroom, stepping over the destroyed door.

The smoky haze burned her eyes. Her goal had been to make it to her broken bedroom window, but he'd set fire to her bed and the carpet around it. The flames sent her scrambling back toward the hall. An idea hit her and she hurried into the den where she dropped to the floor and shoved Mozart through the doggie door. It was almost too hot to try it, but the alternative was death.

Please, God, let this work.

She stayed low to the floor and followed Mozart through the small opening while the flames licked at her feet. She had a moment of panic when her hips became stuck, but some desperate squirming and a twisting maneuver got her through and into Mrs. Spade's side of the duplex.

Smoke followed her into the room and swirled above her, but on the floor, she was able to draw in breath. She prayed the fire wall between their two units kept the flames on her side and spared Mrs. Spade's area.

For several seconds, she lay still, not having the breath or the energy to move. In spite of the wet cloth, she knew she'd inhaled quite a bit of smoke and her head spun. She touched her pockets, first one, then the other. She had her phone. She'd dropped her weapon back in the bathroom when the explosive device had gone off, but there was no time to get it now.

Mozart ran to the door, barking, anxious to get out of the place.

She groaned and held the towel to her face with one hand while she pushed herself to her knees with the other. The smoke was getting thicker, rolling through the little door. Izzy shut it, then crawled to the front door, but paused.

What if he was still out there waiting?

Then the red lights bouncing off the walls registered. Those weren't flames, those were fire trucks outside. Grateful, she hauled herself to her feet and opened the door.

Through his tears, Ryan saw Mrs. Spade's front door open. At first he thought he'd simply snapped and was losing his mind. Then Mozart darted out and Ryan's heart thumped a bit harder in his chest. "Mozart, here, boy."

The dog ran to him and Ryan passed him to the nearest officer. "Take him to the woman sitting in my car, will you?"

He didn't wait for a response, he just took off running toward Mrs. Spade's front door and was almost there when Izzy's soot-covered face appeared. She spotted him and went to her knees. He grabbed her up in his arms while water from the hoses rained down around them. "I need a paramedic!"

"I'm okay." Her faint words reached him. He ignored them and hauled her to the nearest ambulance while coughs wracked her slender frame.

"Izzy!"

Ryan heard the chief's voice and spun to see the woman climbing

161

out of her Suburban. He ignored her too, his full attention on Izzy as the paramedic slapped an oxygen mask over her face.

The chief raced up beside him. He just now noticed the news vans and other media vehicles behind the tape that had been pulled across the road. "Detective Stiles called me. Is she okay? What happened?"

Ryan moved to allow her access to her daughter. "She's alive. A few minutes ago, she called me and said someone was outside her home and was trying to kill her. I heard gunshots come over the line. When I got here, her home was in flames."

And he'd thought her dead.

He still hadn't recovered from that emotional hit and wasn't sure if he would anytime soon.

The chief stopped a uniformed officer. "Start canvassing the area. See if anyone saw anything, if there are any security cameras aimed this way, and detain anyone who seems suspicious or evasive—or isn't a resident of this neighborhood." The officer took off and Ryan didn't bother to tell her he'd already set most of those orders in motion. The chief looked back at him. "Why would someone do this?"

Ryan shook his head. "It probably has something to do with the guys in the warehouse. It's all I can think of anyway. Izzy may have something more to add to that speculation."

The chief nodded, then stepped into the ambulance.

"Mom?"

Ryan peered inside to see Izzy had shoved the mask away. Her mother leaned over to give her a quick hug, then put the mask back over her face. "Don't talk. Just breathe."

She pushed it off again. "What are you doing here?"

"Checking on you, of course."

"I'll be fine."

The chief replaced the mask. "Take this off again and you're grounded. I'll meet you at the hospital."

Izzy rolled her eyes, but Ryan noticed she left the mask alone. "I'm right behind you," he said.

When the ambulance pulled away, the man on the hill lowered his binoculars and ignored the bleeding wound in his side. He needed to know if she was dead but didn't dare stand around with the other gawkers. The officers would be questioning them, watching for signs that the arsonist had decided to stay and enjoy his handiwork.

He grunted. Nope, no need to be stupid.

It hadn't been very hard to get inside Izzy's home. He'd done his job scouting the place and had come up with a plan that had been perfect. He hadn't planned on the cop playing bodyguard, but he'd been easy enough to get rid of. A simple tap to the head with his meaty fist had knocked the guy senseless.

And it had all been for nothing apparently.

They'd put someone in the ambulance and it looked like Isabelle St. John. How had she survived the fire? After she'd shot him, he made sure to light the gasoline-soaked rag and toss it onto the floor near her window. Then drop the same thing right at her front door. The insulation had welded the sliding door shut.

There was no way she could get out.

And yet she had.

He swore.

It was proving to be a bit harder to grab the phone than he'd thought it would be. Grab it or destroy it.

Whatever.

He tossed the binoculars into the passenger seat.

Next time he wouldn't fail.

18

Izzy paced the hospital room while she waited for Chloe to pick her up. Her chest ached from the smoke inhalation, but it wasn't anything that would keep her in the hospital. Antibiotics, an inhaler, and rest were her marching orders and she was glad enough to get them. But she couldn't go home.

Her home, her private sanctuary . . . gone . . .

Grief and fury flooded her and she wanted to cry.

No, she wouldn't think about it. She was alive. Mrs. Spade and Mozart were fine. The officer had a massive headache, but no one had been seriously hurt.

And she had insurance. In the end, after she mourned the loss of some of her favorite things and went through the rebuilding process, she would be fine. It would *all* be fine.

It would.

It really would.

Maybe she'd eventually believe it.

Chloe had insisted Izzy come stay with her, but that didn't sound like such a great idea to her. Would she be putting her sister in danger? The person who wanted Kevin's phone didn't seem all that concerned if he hurt anyone who stood in the way of his getting it.

164

A knock on the door pulled her from her thoughts and she looked up to see Ryan peeking around the edge. "Come on in."

"Are you okay?"

"I'm fine."

"You sure?"

Izzy huffed. "I said I'm fine!"

"You don't sound fine."

She crossed her arms. "What do I sound like?"

"Like a frog. An annoyed one that inhaled too much smoke."

"Oh." She touched her throat and grimaced, then dropped her arms. "Well, I'm that too. Annoyed, that is."

"I've got some good news that might cheer you up."

"Wonderful. I could use some good news."

"We got an ID on your friend, the Hulk."

She scowled. "Friend? Don't even joke about that."

He cleared his throat. "Right, sorry. His name is Lamar Young and he's not a nice person."

"I find that shocking."

"Yeah. He's affiliated with Tony Bianchi and has been suspected of several murders. Cop murders as well."

"A cop killer. Lovely." Izzy shivered. "I guess it wasn't my time yet."

Ryan moved closer. "I've checked with all the hospitals. If he shows up with a gunshot wound, we'll know it. We've also got a BOLO out on him, so all the patrol officers are keeping their eyes open. Hopefully we'll hear something soon."

"Like we've heard something on the guy that killed Kevin?"

His jaw tightened. "Everyone's looking, you know they are."

"Yes, I know."

"So . . . you do realize your entire family, except Chloe and Derek, is in the waiting room, don't you?"

She coughed, several lung-wrenching hacks, then groaned and flopped back onto the bed. "Yes," she croaked, "and they've all been back here. Every last one of them. I just kicked Brady out twenty minutes ago, claiming I needed to rest. Chloe said I could go home with her. I'm just waiting for her to get here."

"You don't want to go to your parents' house?"

"Nope."

Ryan sat beside her. "They love you."

"I love them too." She rubbed her eyes. "And it might be okay if we were all at work at the same time, but Mom said something about taking a couple of days off, then Dad jumped in and said he could take care of me. It's sweet, but no thanks. I mean, they have to work. Staying home with me is not an option."

The nurse bustled in and handed Izzy her walking papers. After a litany of instructions, she left with a hasty "Take care."

Ryan stood and Izzy put a hand on his arm. "Hold on a second."

He paused. "What is it?"

She drew in a deep breath. "I'm going to need a weapon. Mine is probably just a melted puddle of steel at this point."

"We'll get you one."

"Thanks."

"Hey, I know this isn't exactly a great time, but I got your text—I brought Kevin's phone."

He pulled it from his pocket and she nodded. "Try this date." When he punched it in, the home screen came up. "It worked," he said. He looked up to see tears streaming down her cheeks. "Where did you come up with that?"

"Our wedding day," she choked out.

Ryan gaped. "Your *what*?"

Izzy grabbed several tissues from the box next to the bed. "It's a joke."

"Tell me."

"Those pictures, the ones that you found in Kevin's room. They

166

were all the things Kevin and I were going to do on our 'honeymoon.'" She put air quotes around the word.

"Iz, I think the smoke affected more than your lungs. Could you be a tad more clear?"

"Bungee jumping, water skiing, hiking, and seeing the world," she whispered. "I would have turned fifty first."

"What?"

"And then he would have turned fifty a year later."

"Iz? You're not making any sense."

She shook her head. "I don't know why I didn't think of it sooner."

"Izzy, please! You're killing me."

She finally looked up and met his gaze. And blinked rapidly, more tears falling. He handed her some tissues and she swiped her eyes. "Sorry. The pictures reminded me of a stupid pact Kevin and I made as teenagers. I'd forgotten all about it until you showed me those pictures and said you'd found them in his room. They were things we'd done that we said we'd do again as an old married couple."

"Okay, you made a pact. Keep going. I'm still waiting for the clarity part."

She gave a low laugh that held very little humor. "He asked me to marry him when he was fifteen and I was sixteen. I told him if I was still single when I turned fifty, I'd marry him."

"Wait, I think I remember him telling me about that."

Izzy shrugged. "It was so long ago, I . . ."

"Guess he still thought about it."

"I know he did. He mentioned it the night he was killed. Wow," she breathed.

"Yeah." He tapped another sequence on the screen. "I'm going to look at videos and pictures first."

"Check the last video he took. If he was filming, it should be right there."

Ryan tapped again and drew in a breath. "And there it is."

He held the phone where Izzy could see it. The picture wobbled, then steadied. The interior of the warehouse came into view and the camera zoomed in on the three men standing in front of the glass-encased office.

"Those are the three I saw," Izzy said. "The one on the left is the one who shot Kevin."

"The one who must have gone into hiding, since we've heard nothing about anyone spotting him," Ryan said.

The camera panned upward and Izzy heard a gasp sound over the speaker. Kevin. "Derek?" he whispered.

Izzy gasped and Ryan paused the video to look at her. "Derek? Derek was there? This is what you've been struggling with, isn't it?"

"Yeah."

"And you didn't think you needed to mention it to me?"

She bit her lip and met his gaze. "I wanted to, but I promised I wouldn't. I didn't know he'd be on the video, but figured it was a possibility."

"Izzy. He's an eyewitness to Kevin's death. We needed to be talking to him!"

She didn't flinch at his accusatory tone. "Good luck with that. I can't get him to answer my calls or texts. I doubt he's going to answer yours."

Ryan narrowed his eyes. "Is he undercover?"

"He said he was, but I'm not sure."

"When did you talk to him? I thought you said he wouldn't answer your calls."

"The night Kevin died, when I texted you about someone in the warehouse. That was Derek."

"What was he doing there?"

"Looking for anything that might reveal he'd been there, I guess. I don't really know."

"No. He was looking for the cameras," Ryan said. "He was checking to make sure he stayed out of sight of them."

"Maybe."

"You should have told me."

"Maybe."

"Why do you think he might not be undercover?"

"Because my mom didn't seem to know anything about it."

"Could she just be keeping it quiet?"

Izzy shrugged. "Of course, but I don't think she is." She coughed and drew in another ragged breath.

Ryan could tell she needed to rest, so he dropped the subject. For now. He looked down at the phone. "Let's finish this," he said.

He pressed play once more. Derek stood on the balcony, looking down, taking pictures. Then he turned, seemed to listen for a brief second, and disappeared again behind one of the stacks of crates. The door at the top opened and shut, and the guy Izzy recognized as the man Derek eventually shot stepped inside. He'd missed seeing Derek by a fraction of a second.

Then the camera panned back over to the office. "Look," she said. "Someone's in there."

Ryan took the phone and squinted at the screen. "We need to zoom this." He looked up with a frown. "I don't remember anyone else being there. No one else was caught."

Izzy leaned her head back against the pillow. "No, there were only the three on the main floor and the guy on the balcony with Derek. If someone else was in there, where did he go?"

They were at the point where the voice shouted, "You a cop?"

Then Ryan shut it off. "I don't need to see him get shot again," he said gruffly. "We'll take it to David and let him see what he can pull off of it."

"And zoom in on the person in the office. He must have slipped out as soon as the gunshot sounded," Izzy said. "When I ran inside,

I never saw anything but Kevin. Then Derek." She rubbed her eyes. "Now what?"

"I want to know what Derek was doing at the warehouse and if he's undercover," Ryan said.

"Me too. I've been thinking about that."

"And?"

"I have a plan."

"Tell me about it."

"Well, I thought about trying to hack into Derek's computer to see if he had an ops plan on there somewhere, but I think it might just be easier to break into his office."

Ryan started. "Seriously?"

"Yes."

"Izzy, we need to go to Captain Bonner with this." Captain Pierce Bonner, Derek's supervisor.

"After I see if there's an ops plan. It's not like I can just walk up to him and ask him."

"Iz—"

She climbed down from the bed. "But for now, I'm going to face my family."

Izzy slipped out of the room and down the hall toward the exit, bracing herself for the reunion with her family.

It went about how she expected. After being smothered with hugs and offers of a place to live until she could figure out what she was going to do about her burned-out home, she finally spotted Chloe rushing through the automatic doors.

Brady held her a bit longer than the others. "You scared me, sis."

"I'm fine." She hoped the rasp in her voice went away fast.

"Yeah. Now. And what's this I heard about you getting tossed over the side of a parking garage?"

"Shh!" She shot a quick glance at her parents, who had moved back to give the others room to reassure themselves that she was still breathing. "That's not for everyone to know about."

"They've already heard about it. Mom forbade us to mention it to you, though."

"And yet you did."

Brady shrugged. "Just giving you a heads-up that you're going to have to face the music soon."

Izzy sighed. "I'll cross that bridge later when I have more energy. And for your information, I was not thrown over. I was . . . dangled." And it had been terrifying. She planted a kiss on his cheek. "Go back to work and stay safe." She detached herself from the rest of her family and allowed Chloe one quick hug. "I'm exhausted. Please, take me to your place. I need a shower and some clothes and some sleep."

"Roger that."

"Where's Hank?"

"In the truck."

Hank had his own temperature-controlled area in Chloe's vehicle and would be fine for as long as Chloe needed to be away from the truck.

"Where are Mozart and Mrs. Spade?"

"Her daughter came and picked her up. Mozart is at Mom and Dad's house."

"Okay, good." A place he was familiar with. She often took him with her when she was going to be spending several hours there. He loved the big yard.

With that taken care of, Izzy was ready to go. "After you."

Her mother hugged her one more time, then looked into her eyes. "Is there something you're not telling me?"

"What?"

"Besides the fact that someone tried to throw you off a parking garage?"

Izzy winced. "He didn't try to throw me over. He just—"

"I'll come back to that," her mother said. "Ryan said you called him and thought someone was trying to kill you." She lifted a brow. "Again, apparently. And then the fire happened. I'm not speaking as your mother, I'm your chief. What's going on?"

Izzy rubbed her head. The ache that had started at the base of her skull in the ambulance had now spread to her temples. "I'm honestly not sure *what's* going on." She sighed. "I had Kevin's phone. He asked me to hide it the night he died."

A low gasp left her mother's lips. "And you didn't bother to tell me that?"

"No. We just managed to get into it like fifteen minutes ago. There's a video on there from the warehouse and everyone who was there. Ryan and I are going to take it to David and let him pull what he can off of it." Izzy debated telling her about Derek's involvement, but his urgent—almost desperate—plea for her to keep quiet stilled her tongue. "Can you give us some time to figure it out?"

Her mother stared at her, her jaw tight, eyes narrowing. "Yes, but only because I don't feel like you're simply putting me off. Let me know what David says. Come by my office tomorrow and we'll talk."

"Tomorrow?" She glanced at the clock on the wall. "Seriously?"

The woman grimaced. "No, of course not. Take the day—or two or three—and see how you feel." She pressed a hand to her forehead. "I think I'm in denial. You just lost your home and this is going to take some time to straighten out. I'll contact your supervisor and let him know you're going to be off for a bit. Rest and heal, understand?"

"Yes, ma'am. Got it."

"But we *will* talk."

"About the—"

"Yes. The parking garage. It's all over the news."

Izzy grimaced. "I figured it would be. People were recording it."

172

"Fortunately, your face isn't shown. What were you *thinking*?"

Izzy scowled. "You said we'd talk about it later."

Her mother sighed. "Fine. I'm going to let you put me off for now, but don't think it's forever."

"I know, Mom, but for now, I just really want to go to bed."

Her mother's features softened and she reached for Izzy one more time for a bone-crunching hug. "You scared me tonight."

"I scared myself." She paused. "I'm sorry."

Her mother cleared her throat and nodded to Chloe. "Take care of her."

"I'll do my best."

Izzy rushed Chloe out of the hospital, desperate to get away from the questions and worry, even while she knew how blessed she was to have so many people who loved her. She did know that, and she was grateful, but she just wanted to be alone so she could *think*.

———

Ryan pulled Izzy to the side while Chloe went to get her vehicle. "You're thinking of doing this tonight, aren't you?"

She nodded.

"You're not doing it alone."

"I was hoping you'd say that."

He raked a hand through his hair and saw the chief watching them, a speculative look in her eyes. He glanced back at Izzy. "What time?"

"Late. Or early, depending on how you look at it. Like 1:30. The office is busy, but not overrun."

"All right. I'll pick you up at 1:15."

"Thanks, Ryan."

"Of course."

Chloe pulled to the door, and Ryan walked out with Izzy, staying right at her side.

"What are you doing?" Izzy asked.

"Making sure no one takes a shot at you while you're walking to the car."

She grimaced. "Thanks." She opened the passenger door and climbed in, but left the door open so she could finish her thought. "But if this guy is after Kevin's phone, then you're the one in danger now."

"Maybe, but he doesn't know I'm the one who has it, so . . ."

"True."

"Kevin's phone?" Chloe asked.

Izzy fastened her seat belt. "It's a long story."

"You can tell me after you get a shower. Be sure to roll your window down, would you? I don't want the smoky smell to linger."

Izzy gave a low huff. "I almost died and you're worried about me stinking up your truck? Thanks so much. I appreciate the love and concern."

"Well, you didn't die and I'm very glad for that. But roll down the window. Please."

In sync with the roll of her eyes, Izzy let the window down and cool air rushed in.

Ryan shut the door, watching them. He'd always been slightly envious of the easy relationship the two of them shared. It had been that way as long as he remembered.

He'd been so much older than Kevin that, while they got along and hung out occasionally, they hadn't had that deep sibling bond. Not like he and Chris had shared. Chris. How he missed him. He cleared his throat. "Be careful, will you?"

"Of course," Chloe said. She cranked the SUV and Ryan watched them pull out of the hospital parking lot. Right behind them were two unmarked cars.

Breathing a bit easier knowing Izzy was in good hands, Ryan decided to head home and see if he could grab a little sleep before taking the video to David.

Kevin's face swam before him and he pressed a hand to his

eyes. *God, I don't like this new normal. Give us all strength to get through the next few days. And years.*

Kevin's death only made Chris's memory that much more fresh, and Ryan tried to close his heart to the renewed pain. Two brothers gone. And now he had to find a way to get through another funeral.

After he helped Izzy break into her brother's office.

19

1:30 A.M.

Izzy's palms itched. Ryan drove in silence, his tension rolling off of him, so Izzy just kept quiet and concentrated on not coughing. The inhaler helped fight the urge.

Kevin's funeral was less than twelve hours away, and she almost felt like she wouldn't be able to rest without answers to Derek's involvement in what had gone down at the warehouse. He still wasn't responding to her pleas to contact her.

So maybe this would set her mind at ease. As long as there was an ops plan.

Ryan sat in the driver's seat while Izzy pulled her hair into her usual work ponytail. "I can't believe I let you talk me into this," he finally said.

"Just keep an eye out for me. If anything happens, I'll take the blame. I don't want you implicated in any way." No, she definitely didn't want to bring trouble down on his head.

"I'm not worried about that," he said. "I want to help. I'm just not sure that this is the way to do it."

"I'm not either, but nevertheless . . ."

"We're doing it."

A flash of guilt shot through her as his phone buzzed. He read the text and frowned.

"Who is it?" she asked.

"Linc."

"My brother Linc?"

"Yeah. I asked him to see what he could find out about Tony Bianchi."

"What did he say?"

"That they've opened a Preliminary Inquiry of RICO and will get back to me." The RICO Act. Racketeer Influenced and Corrupt Organization Act. "That means they've got enough evidence on him for multiple crimes." He shrugged. "I guess we'll see what shakes loose."

She nodded, then paused. "Maybe you're right. Maybe I should just talk to Derek's supervisor and be done with it."

"It's definitely the less risky option."

"Is it? Less risky for who? Derek said to keep my mouth shut unless I wanted him dead."

Ryan scrubbed a hand down his cheek and drew in a breath. "Then let's get this over with. Do you have the earpiece?"

"Yes." She shoved it in her ear and he did the same.

Ryan parked across from the Midtown Region office and Izzy climbed out of the car, eyes darting. She was pretty sure she was out of range of any cameras. At least she hoped so.

Ryan had decided to stay out of the building for as long as possible. They both knew there was no way he'd be able to go in without being recognized, since he worked out of this office. He'd watch the door and tell her if someone he thought she knew or might know was headed inside, but she was going to have to take her chances with the people already in the building.

Columbia was a large city and had been divided into several regional areas. East, West, North, South, Metro . . . and Midtown. Derek worked out of the Midtown region. If there was an ops plan tucked away in a drawer or a file cabinet somewhere, it would be in his office.

Or on his computer.

She was already considering passwords he might use for that, even though she'd originally discarded the idea. He'd probably use "Elaine" or the date they met. Or something related to her.

But first things first.

At this time of night, the place wouldn't be as busy as daytime hours, but it was still active and she'd have to be careful. She didn't visit Derek at his office often and did her best to keep a low profile when it came to her last name.

Hopefully, dressed in her uniform, she'd blend in and no one would question her presence. She pulled her cap lower over her eyes and punched the code into the pad next to the door.

Derek gave her the code each time it was changed so that she could bring him lunch on the rare occasions they got together while on duty—or so she could drop it at the desk.

"You okay?"

Ryan's voice came through the earpiece crystal clear. "I'm fine."

Izzy walked through the door and kept going. She lifted a hand in acknowledgment to the receptionist, but didn't turn her head or give the guy a chance to get a good look at her. He might wonder for a second who she was, but hopefully the ringing phone would distract him.

Passing several other officers, she kept her head down and eyes averted.

Finally, she reached Derek's cubicle. Izzy casually peered around the corner as though looking for Jasmine in case anyone was watching her and wondering what she was doing. Jasmine and Derek shared cubicle space.

With a glance back over her shoulder, she realized not a single person was paying her the slightest bit of attention. She slipped behind the partition and drew in a relieved breath.

Out of sight of the open area where most of the cops were, she went straight to Derek's file cabinet and pulled.

Locked.

Of course.

She tried his desk and the middle drawer slid out with a slight squeak. She cringed at the sound and froze. It didn't seem to spark anyone's curiosity, so she searched the contents looking for the key.

Nothing.

When it came to an ops plan, she knew every detective and every person involved in the undercover operation got a hard copy they all used in the briefing meeting. Then a copy was placed in the case file and stored with all the other ops plans. There was also a copy on the computer, but hacking into Derek's desktop would leave a trail and she'd rather avoid that if at all possible.

Which brought her full circle. There had to be a key to the file cabinet somewhere in this office. Derek was notorious for asking people to do things for him.

Like bring him lunch.

No doubt, at some point, he'd asked Jasmine to bring him a file from the locked cabinet. So, he'd either made her a key or stashed one somewhere.

Izzy pressed fingers to her tired eyes. *Think, think*. She grabbed one of the many pieces of candy from the jar on the desk, unwrapped it, and popped it in her mouth.

She resumed her search. Five minutes later, she sat back in Derek's chair and let out a defeated sigh as she ran through all kinds of possibilities of what he might do with the key. He wouldn't keep it on his key ring, as he'd want someone else to be able to have access to it. Like Jasmine or someone else he trusted.

A memory flashed. When they were teens, she'd walked in on him messing with the drawer to his desk in his bedroom. When she asked him what he was doing, he'd dropped the key to the chest he kept stuff in and yelled at her to get out of his room and quit being such a snoop.

Izzy pulled the desk drawer open once more and examined both sides and the bottom. Nothing.

Not ready to give up hope yet, she did the same with every drawer in the small cubicle.

And nothing.

"Grrrr." She wanted to slam her fist on the desk, but restrained herself. No need to draw attention to herself.

And he wouldn't be that obvious.

Izzy let her eyes drift to his partner's desk. Would he? Maybe.

She moved to Jasmine's chair and hesitated. Technically, she supposed her actions could be considered trespassing. Then again, her brother's life might be in danger and she needed to act to help him. At least that would be her argument should she get caught. Footsteps sounded outside the cubicle, right behind the chair, and she froze, even though she knew no one could see her.

Hurry up.

Izzy checked the first drawer, then the second. On the next to the last drawer, she struck gold in the form of a little key that looked like it might fit a filing cabinet. She hoped.

Quickly, aware that the more time she spent in the building, the more chances of someone recognizing her, she moved back to Derek's side of the cubicle and inserted the key in the cabinet.

Bingo. The lock popped.

"Thank you, Jesus," she breathed.

"You found it?"

She jerked at the voice in her ear. "Sheesh, Ryan. You scared me to death. You've been so quiet, I almost forgot you were there."

"Just keeping an eye on things. I didn't want my talking to you to distract you. It's pretty quiet around here tonight."

"Quiet out there, maybe. I keep feeling like all eyes are on me. It's unnerving."

"You'd make a lousy criminal."

"Good thing I never had dreams of being one," she whispered. Pulling open the drawer, she looked over her shoulder.

With no one watching, Izzy quickly scanned the tabs on the folders. Alphabetical order. At least Derek had good organizational skills.

In no time at all, she had the "Ops Plan" folder on the desk and open. Her eyes fell on the first one in the stack. She remembered this case—and she remembered Derek talking about closing it. It had been over four weeks ago and he'd been particularly happy about being a part of the raid that rescued several human trafficking victims.

But there was nothing else to indicate that he'd started a new assignment.

"Find anything?"

"No."

"Billy McGrath just walked in."

Billy and Derek were good friends and he was often at her parents' house for Sunday dinner. "Okay. I'm almost finished. I found the ops file, but there's nothing to indicate that he was working a new assignment."

"Nothing at all?"

She looked through the rest of the pages just in case he'd accidentally slipped it in the wrong place, but found nothing.

"Nothing, Ryan. So is he undercover or not?"

The file indicated not. Her mother said he wasn't. So . . . was Derek lying? Or . . . what?

Frustration clawed at her. She texted him.

> Please call me or text me or something. I need
> to talk to you.

"You probably need to get on out of there. Justine Clements is heading toward the front door."

Justine, a good friend of Chloe's and one who would recognize Izzy—and make a point to talk to her. She had to get out of there.

She replaced the file in the cabinet and shut the drawer. When she turned, she jerked. An officer was standing there watching her.

"Hey." The word tumbled from Izzy's lips and, to her relief, sounded normal, not strangled or nervous like she felt.

"Hey. What are you doing here? This is Derek's office."

"I know. I'm looking for something, but I think he's sent me on a wild-goose chase." Not an outright lie. She kept her shoulder turned to keep the woman from being able to read her name badge. She'd thought about leaving the badge off, but that would have snagged attention.

The woman laughed. "He's got you running errands for him too, huh?"

"You know him well," Izzy said, keeping her tone droll.

"Indeed. I'm Brenda." She looked expectantly at Izzy.

"Isabelle." Izzy wasn't going to lie. Not when it could come back to bite her that she'd been there.

"Nice to meet you. You don't work out of this office, do you?"

"No, I'm at the Metro region, but Derek . . ." She rolled her eyes and Brenda laughed.

"Don't fall for him. He's a heartbreaker."

"No kidding."

Brenda shrugged. "Anything I can help you with?"

"Nope." Izzy opened the bottom drawer of Derek's desk and pulled out a yellow notepad she'd seen earlier in her search. Derek's practically illegible handwriting covered the page. "I think this will do it."

"You must be a good friend."

"I am." If she could get away with not revealing the nature of her relationship with Derek, she would. She stood. "Well, I guess I'd better get out of here."

"Sure. See you around."

"You handled that well," Ryan said. "Now hop to it before you run into Justine or Billy."

Izzy kept her silence and waited until Brenda left before replacing the notepad and the key. She started to step out of the cubicle, but stopped when she heard voices that sounded like they were right next to her.

". . . get the numbers for the meeting," someone said.

"Jasmine has them," Justine said. "I'll get them from her."

Izzy froze.

"Is she here?" the first person asked.

"Not tonight, but she usually leaves them on her desk if someone wants to review them beforehand."

"Good, grab them for me, will you?"

"Sure."

If Justine walked in while Izzy was there, she was going to have some explaining to do.

The two officers continued the conversation while Izzy listened, trying to figure out the best move. They were to her right. She could possibly slip out and around to the left without being seen if she hurried.

Quickly, Izzy rounded the edge of the cubicle and breathed a short-lived sigh of relief. When she looked toward the door, Billy McGrath was leaning against the desk, talking to the guy who manned the phones.

Izzy blew out a breath. "I can't get out the door. Billy's talking to the guy behind the desk."

"Of course he is. Hold tight."

Feeling conspicuous just standing there, Izzy walked toward the hallway that held the restrooms. She kept her head down and her eyes cut toward the desk. She stopped when the guy behind the desk picked up the phone. Billy waited a few seconds, then waved and walked off.

Right toward her.

She veered right and slipped behind the next row of cubicles, her blood pumping harder. Weaving her way through the maze of cubicles, her attention fixed on her phone, she made her way back around to the front of the building.

Billy was gone.

She kept her stride steady and even, not hurrying, but giving the impression she was headed somewhere and didn't have time to stop and chat. "On the way out," she murmured.

"The front is clear," Ryan responded.

And then she was walking down the front steps and over to the vehicle where Ryan waited.

Izzy climbed into the passenger's seat and shut the door. She lowered her head to the glove compartment and Ryan knew her adrenaline was flying. He waited in silence for a full minute, then said, "You're a natural. Have you ever thought about undercover work?"

"A natural? My heart is about to pound right out of my chest."

"Of course it is."

"You're enjoying this, aren't you?"

"A bit, now that I'm not worried to death about you getting caught." He turned serious. "What did you find out?"

"Exactly what I told you. That if Derek is doing undercover work, it's not an assignment from his supervisor. At least not one that's on paper."

"He could be doing something on his own."

"He could. And if he hadn't shot that guy, I wouldn't think twice about keeping my mouth shut. But . . . the shooting . . ."

"Yeah. So what are you going to do now?"

"Write my supplemental report—and think."

"About?"

"How to tell Derek that his twenty-four hours have come and gone—and how to tell Kevin goodbye tomorrow."

SUNDAY

20

The day of the funeral dawned overcast and gloomy. A match to Izzy's mood. This was wrong on so many levels. Wrong . . . and yet fitting in an extremely odd way. Wrong that they were even *having* a funeral and fitting because Kevin had loved church, and even sang on the praise team when he was off duty. That praise team would sing for him today.

She was thankful she'd gone to church yesterday. It would've been too hard to concentrate if she'd gone to this morning's service. She dressed in her officer blues and used the lint roller to make sure there wasn't a speck of dirt on any part of the uniform.

Ironically, the uniform she now had on and one other had been at the cleaners the night of the fire. Her closet had suffered smoke and water damage, but her clothes had survived. They were now all at the same cleaners she'd picked up the two uniforms from. Until then, Chloe would ensure she didn't go without.

Izzy made sure she had tissues tucked into a pocket, then adjusted the empty holster on her hip. A quick glance at her phone showed she still hadn't missed a return call from Louis. She was worried about him.

"Ready?" Chloe stood behind her with Hank at her side.

"No. I want to stay in bed with the covers over my head."

"Yeah, make that two of us." Chloe paused. "Any nightmares?"

"Yes."

"I thought I heard you crying out in your sleep."

Izzy nodded. "I woke myself up."

"What were you dreaming about?"

"You mean which nightmare was triggered?"

"Yes."

"Mick. And the Hulk. They kept coming at me from every direction, shooting flames from their tongues and wrapping their claw-like hands around my throat." She touched the area under her chin. "What is it with guys who do that?"

"They're twisted somehow—or they lose control and regret it later. Or they don't regret it. As you know, some don't. But it sounds to me like you've been reading too much fantasy."

She thought about the latest novel she'd been in the midst of. Ronie Kendig's *Embers*. Somehow the fact that it had gone up in flames, along with the end table it had been sitting on, didn't amuse her, and no one had better point out the irony between the title and the way it had met its end. "I wish that's all it was." Izzy shut her eyes against the images, the remembered fear. She'd been held down and helpless, just like when Mick had—

"But it was just a dream." She said the words out loud and hoped they'd take root in her brain.

Chloe grimaced. "The Hulk?"

"The guy who almost killed me in the parking garage the other day." And the guy who'd stolen her phone. He must have taken it, hoping it was Kevin's. It was the only reason she could come up with.

"The one who threw you over the edge?"

"Dangled. He *dangled* me." She waved a hand in dismissal of that topic. "Anyway, he was huge. His name's Lamar Young and he's a cop killer." She couldn't believe he still wasn't in custody.

"Oh."

"He and Mick are running neck and neck for who wins as the most terrifying in my dreams at this point."

"You haven't heard from Mick, have you?"

"No. He's obeying the restraining order."

"But?"

Sadness curled inside her, even as she offered her sister a small smile. "You know me so well."

"But?"

Izzy turned to finish getting ready. "But I'm tempted to check up on him and make sure he's not terrorizing some other poor susceptible woman."

"He's not."

Izzy raised a brow. "Really? You want to tell me how you know that?"

"I keep tabs on him. When he walked out of the hospital, I was there to make sure he knew he was being watched."

"Chloe—"

"What?"

"Don't try to look all innocent. You really did that?"

Chloe offered her a small, mysterious smile. "Yeah."

Izzy shook her head. "As much as I want to deny it, there's some small part of me that wants to see him again."

"Have you completely lost it?"

"Maybe." She shrugged. "I think sometimes we let our fears build to a point where they're bigger in our minds than in reality. I think that's what I've done with Mick."

"Iz, he kidnapped you and held you against your will. With a knife at your throat."

"I know. Then ended up sobbing on my shoulder, telling me how sorry he was and how he never meant to hurt me, he just couldn't stand the thought of losing me."

"Are you regretting how it ended?"

"What? Me recommending psychiatric help instead of prison?"

"Yeah."

"No, I don't regret it." She grabbed a tube of waterproof mascara and applied it. "I really believe it was the right decision."

"But?"

"But Gabby came and said Mick wanted to talk to me. To apologize."

"No way."

Izzy turned and met her sister's wide-eyed look. "Yes, way."

"That's not an option."

"Of course it's an option. I think I'm going to have to talk to him at some point—so we can both have closure."

Chloe's lips settled into a frown. "No, you're not. There's no need for closure."

"Maybe not for you, but I might need it."

Her sister sighed. "You're so stubborn."

"It's a family trait."

"And I don't want to talk about this right now."

"Good. I don't either." Izzy picked up the weapon the department had replaced for her that Ryan had delivered early this morning. She slid it into her holster and steeled herself. "I'm ready." The truth was, she'd never be ready for Kevin's funeral. "Let's go."

Dread welled. The desire to run away and never look back gripped her. She snagged her hat, placed it just right on her head, and took one last look in the mirror. Time to go.

Chloe let Hank into the back in his area and Izzy climbed into the front passenger seat. Chloe drove to the funeral with an officer in front of her and one behind. Izzy frowned. Her mother was going overboard and playing favorites with the radical amount of protection. That didn't sit well with her, and she planned to address it as soon as possible, because if she noticed it, others would as well.

While there'd been no more attempts on her life, she'd been

surrounded by cops practically 24/7. She wasn't holding her breath that Hulk had given up. No, she had a feeling he was just biding his time.

The church came into sight and Izzy broke into a sweat. *Please, God, get me through this without a complete breakdown.* She felt selfish praying for herself when Kevin's family was completely shattered. *And be with the Marshalls. Give them your supernatural peace and comfort. Please.*

The line of police cars wrapped around the block. Officers had turned out in droves to say goodbye to one of their own and to show their support for the grieving family. Chloe parked and Izzy climbed out of the Tahoe.

Her gaze landed on her mother talking to Mayor Cotterill and she saw Melissa Endicott hovering in the background with Felicia Denning. The deputy chief looked right at home in front of the cameras, appearing concerned and nodding in agreement with whatever Melissa was saying. Gabby stood just behind them. Always present, but rarely visible. She met her friend's eyes and lifted a hand in acknowledgment. Gabby offered a slight nod, then turned her attention back to her boss.

Izzy wasn't sure whether to be impressed or disgusted at Endicott's determination to put herself in the spotlight. The election was two days away and the woman was going to milk every opportunity that came her way for positive exposure.

The animosity she felt toward Endicott didn't really make sense, as she'd only met her a handful of times, but she just didn't come across as sincere. Or maybe it was just that she was trying too hard to say all the right things.

Which is what one did when running for office. It was politics, right?

Maybe she meant every word she said and was simply out to make the city a better place and Izzy was prejudiced in her love for the current mayor.

Even though she had to admit she was afraid he wasn't going to win the election. It had been neck and neck in the beginning, but Mayor Cotterill had seemed to lose his steam halfway through the process.

And Melissa Endicott had a lot going for her with her military background and law enforcement experience. Add in the fact that she was the quintessential politician, charming and eloquent, with a dry sense of humor that drew people to her, and yeah . . . Mayor Cotterill didn't look so great in comparison.

He stood just a couple of feet from her, looking worn and tired, talking with several officers whose somber expressions and red eyes gave testament to their love for their fallen friend.

With her throat growing tight at the thought, Izzy let her gaze slide from the officers, to the two women still talking, to the rest of the commotion surrounding the church. Television crews were set up, each one vying for the best angle of the front door. After all, that's where the coffin would roll. Disgust for more than just politics churned in her stomach.

"Hey," Chloe said. "You coming?"

Her eyes fell on a man huddled under a raincoat, hands shoved into his pockets, standing on the fringes of the media. Recognition hit her. Derek.

No way was she letting this opportunity pass her by. "I'll be there in a second. You go ahead."

"You're sure?"

"Yes. I see someone I want to talk to." No need to tell Chloe if she hadn't spotted Derek herself.

Her sister shrugged and headed for the church. Derek didn't acknowledge her, which spoke volumes to Izzy. He didn't want to be seen, but he wasn't going to miss Kevin's funeral. She walked slowly, keeping her head averted like she didn't notice him.

Only when she was about to brush past him did she do a one-eighty and come face-to-face with him.

192

He startled like a doe in headlights and turned to walk away from her.

She clamped down on his right forearm. "Not so fast. You have some explaining to do."

"Not here, Izzy."

"Oh yes, right here. Very quietly and very 'do not bring attention to ourselves' right here. Understood?"

He scowled. "If I try to leave, you're going to follow me, aren't you?"

"You know me. What do you think?"

He sighed and nodded, still keeping his head down. Most people, even those who knew him, wouldn't recognize him in the raincoat and floppy rain hat. He also had a good start on a beard and mustache. But the raincoat was one she'd given him for Christmas last year. "What do you want me to say, Izzy? I can't tell you why I was at the warehouse."

"I have to write that supplemental report, Derek. I'm not jeopardizing my career any longer. I've given you your twenty-four hours and then some."

"I kn—"

"And let me just say this. I don't care who's on that list. If my name and Mom's name are on there, then it's not a list of dirty cops."

"It's oka—"

"Just because Mom and I are on some stupid list doesn't mean—"

"Isabelle Marie!"

She blinked. "What!"

"Shut up!"

Izzy snapped her lips shut and tried to calm her pounding pulse. Anger licked like fire along her spine.

He placed a hand on her shoulder and glanced around, then his gaze came back to lock eyes with her. "I don't think you're a dirty cop, Izzy."

The fire fizzled a little. "Okay. Well, thanks. Because I'm not."
She frowned. "But what made you decide that?"

"I followed you from the warehouse. You didn't call anyone or
meet with anyone—other than Ryan, but he was already on the
way before you knew I was there—or said anything about it."

The anger sparked again. "Nice. Thanks for your confidence."

"I'm serious. And to put your mind at ease about the guy I shot in
the warehouse, Bonner knows everything and is taking care of it."

"Oh. Good." The relief that swept over her was almost palpable.

"Yes." He looked away, his tension obvious.

"You really think Mom is involved in something dirty?" she asked.

"Look." He pulled his phone from his pocket, tapped the screen,
then showed it to her.

She gaped. "That's Mom meeting with Tony Bianchi!" Her low
hiss escaped on a ragged breath.

"I know."

"But . . . why?"

He shook his head. "I don't know. I haven't asked her. I didn't
want to tip her off if—"

"There has to be an explanation."

"That's not the only time she's met with him, Iz."

Izzy didn't care. There simply *had* to be another explanation.
"So, that's why you were there at the warehouse. You were following Mom?"

"Yeah, but she wasn't there this time. I didn't get a look at who
he was meeting with in his office. It's glass on the side facing the
front door, but the rest is walls. I couldn't see from my angle, and
whoever came in used the door from the outside, not the door you
and Kevin came in."

"So how do you know it wasn't Mom if you didn't see who
came in?"

"Because she was texting me, asking me where I was and to
come to her office immediately if I got that message."

"Obviously you didn't go."

"Obviously." He rubbed his tired, red eyes. "I just can't figure out what the list is. What the connection is. I'm pretty convinced at this point that it's not dirty cops—at least not all of them. It could be the two on there who were busted last week are just a coincidence, but why would this list be in the hands of . . ."

"Of who, Derek?"

"Someone involved in organized crime."

"Bianchi?"

His eyes shuttered. "No, I didn't get it from him."

She frowned. "So where'd you get it?"

"From a CI."

"Oookay."

"Sorry."

The sheer weariness in his voice and expression kept her from pressing the issue. "Fine, then."

"How's Ryan doing?" he asked.

"He's surviving. And determined to catch the guys who killed Kevin."

Derek sighed. "What were you and Kev doing at the warehouse?" he asked.

"Kevin got a tip that something was going down and he wanted to be the one to get the evidence."

"He wanted to be a show-off," Derek muttered.

"He wasn't so much showing off as he was just . . . overeager. I went along to try and keep him from getting himself killed." Tears filled her eyes and she sniffed. "I didn't do a very good job of that, did I?"

"Not your fault, Iz."

"I know."

Derek's gaze swept the area again. "I'm going to get a seat. I'm going to give you all the names and I want you to see if you can come up with a connection."

"Fine. Text it or email it to me. I'll take a look."

He cleared his throat. "Uh . . . sorry I was so heavy-handed at the warehouse. I didn't know it was you at first. And sorry I had to play the bad guy, but I just had to be sure you weren't dirty."

It hurt that he doubted. "It's all right. It's already forgotten." Or would be eventually.

He cleared his throat. "I love you, sis."

This time she hesitated. "Oh boy."

"What?"

After another nanosecond of hesitation to debate with herself about the wisdom of speaking, she said, "I broke in to your office."

He raised a brow. "You did what?"

"You said you were undercover, so I went looking for your ops plan."

His face tightened.

"So," she said, "if anyone says they saw someone in your office, it was me."

"I see."

She bit her tongue.

"And did you find it?" he asked. "The ops plan?"

"You know I didn't. I found the folder, but no plan." She hesitated. "Because there isn't one, is there?"

"No, there's not."

More silence fell between them and she sighed. "And you're not going to share why you're undercover with no ops plan and Mom doesn't know about it."

"Can't."

"Fine."

"Let's go inside. I'll send you the file."

Izzy took a deep breath and nodded. It was time to face her partner's funeral.

21

Ryan sat with his family in the small alcove off to the right of the rest of the congregation. The seating allowed a semblance of privacy for the family and a good view of those in attendance.

His mother shifted slightly in her seat and he glanced at her. The continued blank look caused a resurgence of concern. Would she even remember the funeral? With a frown, he focused back on what was going on around him.

The sorrow surrounding him threatened to choke him. How he hated funerals. He slid another glance at his mother, then over to his father. The man had been a rock through the past several days.

Usually, he never said much unless he was in full story-telling mode; however, Ryan knew his father well enough to understand that his brain hadn't shut off since he'd learned of Kevin's death.

And his poor mother. With each passing minute, she seemed to slip further away into her mind, the vacant expression appearing more on her face than emotion. Sometimes she responded to people, sometimes she didn't seem capable.

Ryan had seen it before—after combat missions when soldiers had simply suffered too much for their mind to process. So it didn't. It went to some safe place in order to retreat from reality.

Some never came back and suffered permanent mental illness. He had to make sure that didn't happen to his mother.

The service passed, a blur of words and music. Ryan appreciated the injection of hope in the message, and he fully believed he'd see his brother again one day in heaven. However, while it truly did comfort him to know that, it didn't lessen the pain of losing Kevin on earth.

Or the agony of seeing his parents suffering so greatly. And honestly, if one more person told him that Kevin was in a better place, he might just punch them. He sighed.

No, he wouldn't punch anyone. They were good people who didn't know what to say so they said the wrong thing. He just had to remind himself of that.

Within the L-shaped church, most of the congregation faced the pulpit. From Ryan's vantage point in the alcove, he could see the St. John family sitting in the first two rows. Even Derek was there, sitting a ways behind them, looking ready to bolt at the slightest provocation. Ryan noticed he'd taken a seat near one of the emergency exits.

What was up with him? But at least he would be there for security. He glanced at the door in the back to his left. It led out to the parking lot. Two officers guarded it. He swung his eyes back to the St. John family and his gaze connected with Izzy's. The pure sorrow there hit him hard. As well as the raw fury barely held in check.

He got it. He *felt* it.

Giving her a slow nod, he tried to convey his own thoughts. His agreement with the anger. Her jaw relaxed slightly and she nodded back.

The connection with her shifted something inside of him. He'd always cared about Izzy. Very much. As a teen, she'd never been that awkward, gangly person he remembered his sister being. She'd been pretty and popular, but there was a kindness in her that not everyone had. That was just a part of what drew him to her.

He also realized what he was doing. Thinking about Izzy allowed him to avoid the reality of Kevin's funeral. He didn't want to listen, to be aware, to hear everyone's final goodbyes.

Then his attention was drawn to his left as the side door opened.

A large man stepped inside, wearing a long black overcoat. A mustache and beard covered most of the man's face, but the minute his eyes connected with Ryan's, he recognized him.

Lamar Young.

The man from the parking garage.

The one who'd set fire to Izzy's home. In disguise, but it was him nonetheless. He couldn't hide that size of his.

The Hulk, as Izzy distastefully referred to him, stood still, his hands hidden in the pockets of his large coat. The door with the wooden trim and glass pane shut behind him.

Ryan stiffened and his hand went to his weapon. It was all he could do not to bolt from his chair. But if he did, would the man pull a weapon and start shooting? What was he here for?

Frozen in place, Ryan glanced to the left and caught the eye of Officer Bob Gillespie. Ryan nodded toward the intruder and mouthed, "Stop him."

Bob straightened and nudged the other officer, Marco Jamison, who stood beside him. Discreetly, they planted themselves between the newcomer and Ryan's family.

In a flash, Ryan knew the man was there to make a statement. He was watching, waiting to make his next move. The man's eyes went to Izzy, deliberate in their perusal of the people who now had their backs to him. He lifted a hand, his fingers in the shape of a gun, pointed it at Izzy, and pulled the "trigger."

Rage wanted to blind him. Instead, Ryan narrowed his eyes, dipped his hand into his pocket, and pulled out Kevin's phone. At least he could show Young that Izzy didn't have it anymore. Maybe he'd quit going after her.

Ryan waved the device at the man, who started toward him.

Bob and Marco grabbed his arms and the big man stopped, a snarl twisting his lips.

Ryan dropped the phone back into his pocket. All the while, he kept his other hand on his weapon, ready to draw it and use it if necessary. His family had turned around, watching the scene play out, gaping at the intruder.

Other officers closed in, trying to be discreet but determined to remove the man from the church.

The Hulk didn't move for a few seconds, then with one last smirk in Ryan's direction, turned and let himself be ushered out. Six officers followed him to the door and he raised his hands in surrender.

Ryan was grateful the guy didn't put up a fight, but with all of the security around the church, how had he managed to slip inside in the first place?

Ryan touched his mother's shoulder and she simply sat there, her blank stare never breaking. He leaned over. "Sorry, Mom," he whispered in her ear. "I need to take care of something."

She still didn't respond and Ryan's chest tightened. Should he go or stay? The rest of the family was looking at him like he'd grown another head.

Indecision warred within him. Marco and Bob could handle him. Ryan could interrogate him after the funeral.

But this man had something to do with Kevin's death. He looked at his father and mouthed, "Sorry."

His dad waved him on and Ryan stepped outside to find Bob and Marco picking themselves up off the ground. Young was nowhere to be seen. Ryan raced over to Bob and helped him to his feet. "Where is he?"

"Gone. He acted like he planned to cooperate, the other officers went back to their posts or the service, and then when it was just the two of us, he unleashed those massive fists on us. Once we were down, he jumped into a car he had waiting and took off."

Marco was still on the ground. He groaned and pressed a hand to his cheek. "Broken," he gasped. "Arghhhh!"

"Bob, he's the one who blew up Izzy's home. Go after him if you can and I'll call an ambulance for Marco!" Two more officers arrived. "John, you and Shelly go too."

Bob flinched as he swiped the blood from his cheek, then he and the others climbed into their cruisers and took off. Ryan could see Bob spitting words into his microphone as he raced from the church parking lot. Other officers fell in behind him. He badly wanted to join in the chase, but Marco needed him.

Ryan rushed back to the wounded man's side and knelt next to him. "Hang on, Marco." He got on his phone and requested an ambulance, then gave the dispatcher the information she needed to send more officers in the right direction after Bob and Young.

The door opened behind him and he turned to see Izzy hurrying toward him. "What's going on?" she asked.

"Marco's hurt. I've got an ambulance on the way. The press is focused on the front of the church right now, but when the ambulance gets here, they're going to know something's up. Be prepared."

"Got it." She hurried to the man's side and placed a hand on his shoulder. "Help's coming. Just be as still as possible."

He nodded and shut his eyes, letting his head rest on the ground.

Izzy looked up at Ryan. "What happened?"

"Your fri—Lamar Young, the Hulk."

She grimaced and paled. "Great. I only got a glimpse of him when he stepped inside—I thought his build resembled the dude. Wonderful. Just wonderful."

Ryan wished he could have kept the information from her, but there wasn't any sense in even trying.

"He came looking for me?" she asked.

"He came looking for something. Regardless, he knows I have the phone now."

Her eyes widened. "How does he know that?"

"I showed it to him." Taunted him with it, actually, but he'd keep that to himself.

The ambulance pulled into the parking lot, lights flashing but siren off. Within seconds, the paramedics were working on Marco—and the press was rounding the side of the church to chase down the excitement.

Ryan ignored them. Marco grunted and waved at Ryan.

"What is it?"

"Geh -ack in deh," Marco whispered. "Doan -iss deh ressss."

It was hard to understand him, but Ryan knew what the man meant. He squeezed his bicep and nodded. "Come on," he said to Izzy. "Let's get back inside before my mother decides to kill me."

Izzy shuddered. "That's not the least bit funny."

"I didn't mean it to be."

He ushered her back in. Fortunately, the only ones who noticed their exit and reentry were his family. No one seated in the pews of the church facing the pulpit could see them coming in the side door. Ryan continued to stand. Izzy stayed beside him. Lilianna turned and lifted a brow at him and he gave her a tight smile. She turned back to the musician on the stage playing the closing song.

And then it was over.

Ryan drew in a deep breath. At this point, the family would normally be escorted out to head for the graveside service, but Kevin had explicitly stated during a conversation that he didn't want one. So, now they were honoring his wishes.

Ryan's phone vibrated and he lifted it to his ear. "Yeah." He kept his voice low, even though people were stirring to leave.

"This is Bob."

"You get him?"

"No, he outran me. Totally lost me, lost all of us. We're still looking, but wanted to give you an update in case he manages to

double back. I gave a description of the car, so hopefully we'll
have something soon."

"Thanks."

Bob fell silent, then sighed. "I'm sorry, man. I didn't recognize
him and neither did Marco. If we had, he never would have gotten
through the door."

He might have, using his brute strength, but Ryan decided not
to mention that. "It's all right. The only reason I recognized him
is because he looked right at me and smirked."

"Smirked?"

"Yeah."

"Bet that made your knuckles itch."

The man had no idea. "Thanks for the update."

"Sure. How's Marco?"

"In pain, probably a broken cheekbone and jaw, but he'll live.
What about you?"

"Mine's not broken, but it's going to hurt for a while. I'll check
on him soon."

Bob hung up and Izzy slipped a hand in the crook of Ryan's
elbow. Her warmth surrounded him and he found himself glad
she was there. More glad than he probably should be.

He gave her fingers a squeeze.

"I just wanted to say goodbye and I'll see you later," she said.

His phone buzzed and he glanced at it. It was Bob texting him
with an update.

Found the car. It's stolen. Will let you know if
anything else develops.

Ryan tucked the phone back into his clip then reached out and
pulled Izzy to him. After a brief hesitation, her arms encircled
his waist.

"Can I do anything?" she said into his chest.

Yeah, you can stay right here forever.

He cleared his throat. "No." He frowned. "Maybe. Where are you going to be tonight?"

She stepped back and met his gaze. "With Chloe. Why?"

"Just want to make sure you're safe. Hulk . . . *Young* got away. That was Bob texting me. The car he was driving was abandoned not too far from here and the plate came back stolen."

Izzy sighed. "Great."

"Yeah."

"And where are you going to be? With your family?"

"Probably. For a little while."

"And after?"

He shrugged. "I'm not sure yet."

"Call me if you need anything."

"Of course." He kissed her cheek, then stepped back. "Thanks, Izzy."

"Sure." She swallowed hard and lifted a hand to the cheek he'd kissed. "Um . . . bye."

Then she was gone, weaving her way through the crowd to the back of the church. Two officers followed her and Ryan breathed a relieved sigh that she would be safe for tonight. And while his heart wanted to follow after her, he had things to do—and a killer to find.

Izzy found Chloe and the two of them walked out of the church. Chloe's eyes were red-rimmed and she sniffed every so often. Izzy knew exactly how she felt. Her own nose was clogged and her eyes scratchy from the tears. "I know Mom's expecting us for lunch, but I'm not sure I could eat a bite."

"We'll try."

"Yeah."

"Izzy?"

Her steps faltered at the voice. A voice from the past. Chloe's gasp reached her ears and they both turned at the same time.

"Mick?"

At six feet two inches, Mick looked every inch the athlete he'd once been. Pro football in college had given his nose the odd little lump in the middle, but other than that, his sparkling blue eyes and twin dimples drew women like flies to honey.

At least until he took the mask off and released his true character. Obsessive. Needy. Violent.

Chloe stepped in front of Izzy. "What are you doing here?"

Izzy grasped Chloe's arm and pulled her out of the way. "I thought I told you never to come near me again."

Mick swallowed and looked around before his gaze landed on the ground. He shoved his hands in his pockets, and Izzy settled her grip on her weapon while Chloe did the same.

When he looked up, he flinched and freed his hands. Holding them in plain view, he shook his head. "I'm sorry. I wasn't thinking."

"No. You weren't."

"I didn't come to cause trouble."

"Then why?" Izzy asked.

"I wanted to tell you how sorry I am about Kevin and that I'm . . ."

"What? Just say whatever it is you need to say and leave."

He nodded. "I wanted to say I'm sorry about . . . what happened. Between us, I mean. I was wrong."

"Yes. You were." Izzy backed toward the vehicle while Chloe kept an eye on Mick. She needed to say more. But what? "Mick, I've forgiven you. I really have. And I'm glad you're getting help."

As though her words were just what he needed to hear, his features softened and tears glittered in his eyes. "Thank you, Izzy."

And for a moment she remembered why she'd been so attracted to him, why she'd fallen for him. It had been the kindness in his eyes, the fun-loving spirit that had challenged her to live for more than the job. But now, all she felt were pity and the desire to just be away from him.

"Could we . . . maybe get coffee or something?"

Her tension returned. "No, Mick. We can't, I'm sorry. I've forgiven you, but I don't want to spend time with you."

"Izzy—" Frustration flashed and Izzy tensed, her mind spinning back to that summer afternoon at his home. He'd lured her there with a request to talk. She'd agreed because she felt bad about the way she'd ended things. Once there, he knocked her unconscious and tied her up. When she woke to a throbbing headache, double vision, and a knife to her throat, she'd frozen with horror and fear.

"I love you, Izzy," he'd cried. "I can't live without you. And if you won't stay with me, you can't live. I can't know you're out there, in love with someone else."

"Mick," she whispered. "No. Don't do this. I care about you or I wouldn't have come. Please don't throw your life away like this."

His tear-filled eyes met hers. "You care about me, but you broke up with me."

She couldn't tell him why, but she couldn't agree to get back together with him. He'd see right through the quick lie. "I know. I needed time to think."

"About what?"

"About us. About what the future would hold. What it would mean if we got married."

He stared. "You were thinking about marriage too?"

"Yes." And she had been. And she hadn't liked the picture that had unfolded each time she thought about marriage to this man. She hadn't been able to put her finger on exactly what made her uneasy about the guy. Until he'd held her hostage.

"I—I didn't know."

"I wasn't cutting you out of my life forever," she said. "I just wanted . . . time. That's all."

"I'm sorry, Izzy." He closed his eyes and groaned. "Oh no. I've messed up again, haven't I? I've completely messed up. I don't want to hurt you, I just can't deal with not having you." He leaned against her and wept.

She had compassion for him after he'd cut the duct tape binding her and handed her the knife with pleas of forgiveness. She held him until the police arrived and she'd walked out alive, physically in one piece, but emotionally shattered—and with a new inability to trust her instincts when it came to men. She'd avoided any kind of romantic entanglement for the past two years.

Izzy straightened her shoulders and stared him in the eye. "I mean it, Mick. Don't bother me again, okay?"

She climbed in the car and slammed the door. But kept her eye on the side mirror. Mick punched a fist into his palm and stared at the vehicle a moment longer, nostrils flaring, but a certain sadness, maybe even acceptance, in his eyes as well. Then, without another word, he spun on his heel and marched off.

Izzy's breath whooshed from her lungs and she shut her eyes against the dizziness that hit her.

Chloe's door shut. Her sister sat in silence for a brief moment. "Are you okay?" she finally asked.

"Yes. I am."

"You sure?"

Izzy opened her eyes and stared out the windshield. Then laughed.

"Iz?"

"I'm okay." She held up her hands. "I'm not even shaking." She'd been a wreck after testifying in court. She hadn't stopped trembling for days.

Chloe started the truck.

"That felt good," Izzy said.

"He didn't like the way that ended."

"I know, but that's okay. I think the nightmares might start to fade now." The ones with Mick anyway. She had a feeling the ones with the giant hulking killer weren't going away anytime soon. "I'm actually glad he showed up."

"You are?"

"There's something to be said for facing your fears. I've been avoiding even thinking about Mick—other than when I had a nightmare about him—avoiding facing the fact that he had a serious impact on my mental well-being."

"And now?"

"Now?" She shrugged. "I don't know. Standing up to him in court was one thing, but seeing him out, away from the whole legal setting, makes him seem . . . smaller somehow."

"He could be dangerous, Izzy."

"I know." She drew in a deep breath. "And I'll watch my back."

Chloe fell silent and Izzy pulled her phone from her pocket to open the file Derek had sent her. Anxiety pulsed through her.

Within seconds, she had the file open and started scanning the names. In alphabetical order, there were twenty-seven in all, including hers, her mother's, and several other officers she knew. And several she didn't. They had to be out of different regions. But each name had a number next to it off to the left. It made no sense to her, but Derek's name wasn't on there, and neither was Chloe's or Linc's or any other family member. But Kevin's was—he was number twenty-one.

Izzy frowned and clicked off of it.

"You okay?" Chloe asked.

"Just thinking."

"About?"

"A lot of stuff." Like why did Derek think she'd be able to figure it out if he couldn't? Because her name was on it?

One thing was certain, Derek had finally gotten it right. This wasn't a list of dirty cops, it was something else. He must have gotten it without a legitimate search warrant and couldn't use it as evidence, but finding out what it meant or was related to could send him in the right direction. She shut the file and let possibilities play out in her mind. When Chloe pulled into their parents' driveway, Izzy was no closer to an answer than she had been before she'd opened the file.

Her father stepped out onto the front porch.

"They made it home pretty fast," Izzy said.

"I'm sure they didn't feel like participating in the media madhouse going on outside the church. Mom made her statement before walking inside for the funeral."

"I missed that." It must have been when Izzy was talking to Derek.

Chloe let Hank out of his area in the back of the Tahoe, and he took off for the gate that led to the backyard. Her father waved a hand. "I'll let him back there. Mozart's been waiting for him. Your mother's setting the table."

Izzy led the way inside the front door. Chloe stepped in behind her and went straight for the kitchen. Izzy stayed still for a moment, drew in a deep breath, the comfort of home immediately washing over her. The smell of roast beef, mashed potatoes, green beans, fresh pies, and some chocolate creation hung in the air. For just a split second, Izzy let herself be transported back to before Kevin's death when all was right with her world.

Brady sat on the couch with the remote in his hand. "Is it wrong to have the game on?"

She shrugged. "Kevin would be watching it if he was here."

"Yeah." He turned it down. "I'm not in the mood."

Derek stepped out of the half bath and joined Brady on the couch. Izzy's jaw dropped. His gaze collided with hers and he gave her a subtle shake of his head. She nodded and looked past him to see her mother working in the kitchen. Ruthie set a platter of meat on the dining room table to the left of the kitchen.

The front door opened again and this time Linc stepped in and shrugged out of his coat. He tossed it over the banister post.

"There's a closet right there," she said. "It's the door on the left."

"I know." He patted her cheek and headed for the den.

Izzy rolled her eyes. Her sarcasm never did have the desired effect. He took a seat in the recliner with a satisfied sigh.

Her father was back in the kitchen with her mother. The rolls were done. "Time to eat," he called.

As one, they moved to the ten-person table her brothers and father had crafted almost fifteen years ago. But the television remained on, albeit on mute.

"They scored," Brady said, nodding toward the television.

"Kevin would be thrilled," Izzy said. She slid into her seat beside Brady, Ruthie took the one by her. With a sigh, her father held out his hands. One by one, each family member joined together until they made a circle around the table. "Father, we ask that you bless this food to our bodies. Thank you for the abundance that you've provided. And Lord, we ask for your healing touch on the Marshall family tonight. This is a tough time for them. For all of us. We need your grace, your strength, and your peace. Amen."

Amens echoed quietly.

Izzy stared at her plate, emotions swirling inside her. She knew the Marshalls did this every week as well. A family dinner. And now they would have two empty places. Kevin's funeral was over. There was nothing left to do but get through life without him.

"Iz?" Linc's soft voice reached her. She looked up to find all eyes on her. Concerned, caring, compassionate. They hurt because she hurt. Because the Marshall family hurt. "You okay?"

"No. I'm not."

"Yeah." Ruthie's right hand grasped Izzy's left. "You'll get through it."

"I know." And she did. She set her napkin on the table. "I'm not hungry, though. I think I'm going to go hang out with Mozart and Hank for a while."

She stood among protests and walked to the door that led to the big backyard she'd grown up playing in. Mozart raced to greet her and Hank lumbered along behind. He would have been more interested if she'd been Chloe.

Izzy sat on the steps to the deck and let Mozart talk her into scratching his belly.

But while she scratched, she fought the fatigue washing over her. If she didn't get some rest, she was going to crash and burn. But first she dialed Louis Harper's number. And got voice mail yet again. She had a really bad feeling about the man and was afraid the next time she saw him would be in a body bag. She stood. It was time to make a plate and head back to Chloe's house. She needed sleep to help keep up her strength if she was going to be able to fight another day.

Sitting in his parents' den once more, Ryan tried to ignore the heavy pall that had fallen over the house. When his phone rang, he grabbed it like a drowning man snags a life preserver. David. "Hey."

"Hey, I'm sorry I didn't make the funeral."

"It's all right. No need to apologize."

"The reason I didn't was because I managed to track down the photographer for that charity event. I told her a little about the case and she sent me the pictures without hesitation. I sent them to Charice just to make sure all was kosher with the investigation, but she said she would show them to you ASAP."

"David, that's great. I really appreciate it." His phone buzzed and he glanced at the screen. "That's Charice calling me now. I'll catch up to you later."

"Hope you find something," he said.

"Me too." Ryan switched over to the other call. "Hey, partner."

"Hey. I've got the pictures from the charity banquet."

"I just got off the phone with David."

"Where do you want to meet me?"

Ryan hesitated. "Let me see if I can get ahold of Lee and I'll text you."

211

"I'll be waiting." She hung up and Ryan rose to pace to the window. He peered out and noticed all the cars in the St. John driveway. Izzy's father had probably fixed a family meal.

Thankfully, his parents' house was finally quiet. He'd convinced his mother to try to sleep, and it worried him that she hadn't argued with him. Aunt Jessica was talking on her cell phone and Lilianna was lounging on the couch with her headphones in. Cathy and Dale were at the table with his father.

He dialed Lee's number and got voice mail. "Lee, I've got the pictures. Call me back and let me know when you can take a look."

Ryan hung up and rose to walk into the kitchen. His father looked up, grief shadowing his eyes even though he smiled at Ryan. "I'm heading home, Dad. I'll check on y'all later."

"All right."

He gripped his father's shoulder. "See you later, Cath. Dale."

Cathy rose to hug him. "Be careful, Ryan," she whispered.

"Always."

Once outside and in his vehicle, he sent up a silent prayer. *Please, God, let these pictures get us somewhere.*

Five minutes later his phone rang and he engaged the Bluetooth. "Hello."

"Hey, Ryan, it's Lee. I just got your message."

"You have some time to meet later this evening?"

"I'm out of town. Had to fly a client down to Florida, but I'll be back in Columbia around nine o'clock tomorrow morning. Want to meet at that little diner not too far from your parents' house? The one Chris liked."

"I'd love to. Charice will be there too. She's the one that actually has the pictures."

"See you then."

Once home, he texted Charice the plan for the morning. He'd text Izzy too. There was no way she'd be okay with being left out of this one.

MONDAY

22

Monday morning, Izzy heard Chloe leave and rolled over to glance at the clock. Five thirty in the morning and she was wide awake. Not surprising. She'd crashed into bed shortly after getting home from her parents', and while she hadn't had nightmares about Mick, the Hulk kept intruding. As a result, she'd had a less than restful night's sleep.

But at least she'd been horizontal for a while.

She yawned and kicked the covers off. She had two more days of leave, then she'd be back at work full time. Which would sorely cut into her time to work on finding Kevin's killer.

Her first day back on duty would begin with security detail at the speech the winner of the election would make. Izzy had received a reminder email before falling into bed last night detailing her assignment. Everybody who was anybody would be there and security would be massive.

In the meantime, while she knew the detectives working Kevin's case were putting everything they had into it, *she* had to do *something*. As much as she understood and knew that Kevin's death wasn't her fault, she couldn't help listening to that voice that wanted to question her actions the night he was killed. Finding his killer would go a long way toward shutting that voice up.

After a quick shower and dressing, she walked into the kitchen, grabbed a bagel and some cream cheese, and carried it to the table. She prepared her bagel and took a bite, then opened the email Derek had sent her with the list of what he'd first thought were dirty cops. Studying the names didn't help any more than it had the first ten times she'd looked at them. She picked up her phone to text Chloe and noticed a text from Ryan. She'd missed it last night.

Meeting Lee at 9:00 to look over pictures from charity event. You in?

Of course she was in.

Where?

His answer came fast, as though he'd been waiting for her to respond. He was up early too. She wondered if he was getting any sleep at all. She recognized the coffee shop.

I need a ride. Chloe brought me home, remember?

Be ready at 8:30.

Will do.

Izzy stood and walked to the window. The police cruiser that had followed them home last night still sat in its designated spot.

So, if Hulk knew she didn't have the phone anymore, was she still a target? It didn't really matter. It wouldn't stop her from doing what she needed to do to hunt down Kevin's killer, and it wouldn't keep her from doing her job. Although, if innocent people were going to be hurt because of her, she'd have to rethink some things, of course.

Like working alone. For the next two hours, she cleaned Chloe's house, raided her sister's closet for something to wear, and at 8:00, called Mrs. Spade to check on her.

"I'm fine, honey. I'm glad you are too. That was a scary thing."

"Very scary, but I'm thankful to be alive."

"I'm sure. The good news is, I should be back inside my half of the duplex sometime next week. I didn't have nearly the damage you did."

"I'm so glad you were spared that. Let me know what the deductible is and I'll take care of it."

They chatted a few more minutes and Izzy hung up to go get ready.

Her phone buzzed and she lifted a brow while she answered. "Hi, Mom."

"I'm checking on you. How are you doing?"

"I've had better weeks."

"Haven't we all?" A pause. "Have you heard from Derek this morning? I've been texting him for about an hour and haven't gotten a response."

This time Izzy hesitated. "No."

"He's not answering my texts or calls, and he managed to avoid me getting him alone to talk yesterday at lunch."

"You said he was on leave. Maybe he thinks he doesn't have to talk to you until he's back on official duty."

"I'm also his mother."

"He's also a grown man."

A huff came through the line. "I don't like it. I should have just cornered him yesterday. If you talk to him, tell him to call me, okay?"

"Of course. And Mom?"

"Yes?"

"What are you going to do if he loses?" She didn't have to specify who she was talking about.

Her mother went quiet for a moment. "What makes you think he'll lose?"

"Mom, seriously? What is there to make me think he'll win?"

"You've noticed that, have you?"

"Of course I've noticed it. I'd have to be oblivious not to."

"Good."

"What?"

"I've been asked, unofficially, of course, to stay on as chief of police even if Melissa Endicott wins the election."

"But will you?"

"For a while. I'll see what it's like to work with her."

Izzy nodded, even though her mother couldn't see her. "She's going to win, isn't she?"

"Probably. If the polls are anything to count on. She's saying some good things, making significant promises. If she wins, it might not be a bad thing—if she can—and will—follow through on them."

"But what about Eric? Mayor Cotterill? Why hasn't he done more campaigning? Why hasn't he stood up to her? It's like he wants to throw the election."

Silence echoed back at her. "That's a very good observation."

Izzy's jaw dropped. She snapped it shut. "Mom, I wasn't serious."

"I know, but if you're noticing, other people are too. Let's keep this conversation just between us for now, okay?"

"Um . . . okay." Izzy frowned. What in the world?

"Get some rest, Izzy, I'll check on you again soon."

"Okay, thanks. Talk to you later."

Just as she pulled her hair into a ponytail, her phone rang again. This time it was her dad. "Hi, Dad."

After assuring him she was fine and taking it easy, she walked into Chloe's den to watch for Ryan.

Ryan had finished off the eggs, bacon, pancakes, and hash browns his mother had fixed this morning and noted that while sadness and grief still lingered in her eyes, the vacant stare that had him so worried was gone.

However, she'd attached herself to Ryan like a barnacle, and he had to remind himself that he needed to have patience like no other time in his life.

His phone buzzed. Izzy texting him.

I'm ready.

Patience.

I have none.

I know the feeling. I'll be there in ten minutes. Exactly when I said I'd be there. LOL.

I know. I'm just antsy.

I get it. I'll leave now.

Ryan stood and carried his plate to the sink, then headed for the den to retrieve his car keys from the hook near the door.

"Ryan?" his mother called.

"Yes, Mom?"

"Where are you going?"

"To pick up Izzy and we're going to meet some people to talk about the case, okay?"

"Oh. All right then."

Ryan gave a slight sigh, then went to his mother and wrapped her in a hug. "I love you, Mom."

A wobbly smile curved her lips and she patted his cheek. "I know. I'm being a pain. Go. Do what you need to do."

"You're not a pain, Mom. Never that, okay?"

219

She gave him a teary nod and he held her for another thirty seconds before she patted him on his shoulder. "You can go now."

"You're sure?"

"Well, I would prefer to do this the rest of the day, but you have a job to do. Go do it."

He looked her in the eye. "You're going to be okay. *We* are *all* going to be okay."

Another nod. "I know. One day."

"You're strong."

"Not strong enough to lose another child, Ryan. Please remember that."

"Every second of every day. I promise."

"Okay then."

She let him go and he sent a text to Charice and Lee that he was on his way to pick up Izzy. They'd see them at the coffee shop shortly after 9:00. His next text was to Izzy, to tell her to exit the house via the garage. She'd understand why. A garage was more cover, which meant less of a chance of a sniper getting her.

Ryan pulled to a stop in Chloe's garage and Izzy climbed into his SUV. Once he was backed out, she hit the button on the remote Chloe had loaned her then slipped it in her purse. "I'm really praying this pans out."

"I am too. This investigation seems to be going nowhere fast. There's no way that Bianchi can just disappear like this. There has to be a way to track him, an associate who's willing to turn on him. *Something.*"

"You would think."

"And your CI hasn't called you back?"

"No."

It didn't take long to get to the coffee shop and park. "See anything that makes your nerves jangle?" he asked.

"No, and I've been watching."

"Me too."

"All right, then, let's do this."

"They're all the way in the back. Charice got that alcove that's like a little room."

Together, they exited the SUV and entered the coffee shop. About halfway through the diner, Izzy's eyes fell on Charice. The man with her must be Lee Filmore, Chris's friend. Ryan's hand settled on her lower back and Izzy's heart skipped a beat.

She rolled her eyes at herself. Really? The heat in her cheeks said, "Yeah, really." She focused on the chair Lee held out for her and sat. Then clasped her hands in front of her. Since when did Ryan start having such a crazy effect on her pulse? It was silly. Weird.

And kind of nice.

"Glad you all could make it," Charice said. "We got here a little early, so I let him get started." Charice had a laptop open. Lee and Ryan shook hands.

"Good to see you again," Ryan said. "Thanks for doing this."

"Not a problem. Anything I can do to help." He went back to the laptop.

23

Charice caught his eye. "How's everyone holding up?"

"Holding. Sad. Grieving."

Her hand covered his. "I'm sorry."

"I know. Thanks."

"Here," Lee said, looking up and turning the laptop to face Charice. "Reuben Yarborough."

Ryan studied the picture of the three men dressed in suits and ties, talking off to the side. They didn't even realize the photographer had captured the moment.

"Who's that?" Izzy asked.

"He was in Chris's unit," Ryan said, not taking his eyes from Lee. "Your unit."

"Yeah. He was also at the banquet that night. When you asked me about it earlier, I'd forgotten he was there, however, so were several other guys I knew. But Reuben's the only other one from the unit who knew what Chris was up to."

"So he knew about the warehouse owned by Jonathan Gill."

"Sure. I knew about it too. He and Chris were making plans to turn it into a home for homeless vets."

Ryan scraped a hand through his hair. "Apparently, everyone knew about it but his family."

Lee's gaze hardened and held Ryan's. "We *were* his family."

Ryan stilled. "Yeah. Yes, you were. And I mean, we all knew how passionate he was about helping homeless vets, but not that he'd bought the warehouse with plans to develop it." He fell silent for a moment thinking about it. How he missed his brother. Both of them. "So, what happened to Yarborough?"

With a shake of his head, Lee leaned back. "I don't know. I haven't heard from him since I got back."

"Then tell me what happened the last time you saw him."

Charice started typing on the laptop, her fingers flying, while Lee took a deep breath. "The day we were supposed to leave, Reuben had a horrible attack of food poisoning or a virus and couldn't make the trip." He pinched the bridge of his nose. "You don't know this, but Chris had a price on his head."

Ryan reared back. "What?"

"A few months back, we'd been involved in a raid that resulted in the death of the son of a very powerful, very wealthy man in Afghanistan. Amir Nuristani. Chris pulled the trigger. Apparently, there was some security footage of the raid. Nuristani got his hands on it, saw Chris was the one who killed his son, and ordered the hit."

"Which wound up being your convoy."

"Yes."

"How'd you survive?"

Lee closed his eyes and shook his head. "I don't know. Everything went black when we were hit. We had another MRAP following us. From what I understand, they were able to return fire and get to us. I woke up in a hospital. Spent a week there, then they shipped me to Germany, then home where I spent six months recovering." He crossed his arms. "I heard Nuristani took credit for the hit."

"How'd he know where you were going to be?"

Lee shrugged. "I have my theories."

"Someone sold you out."

"That's one of them."

"You think Reuben could have been behind it?"

Biting his lip, Lee looked away. "I . . . don't know. Once I learned the attack was orchestrated by Nuristani, I knew it sure wasn't a coincidence. It wasn't the first time he went after Chris. And he kept raising the price on Chris's head. All the way up to two million dollars."

Ryan blinked. Izzy gasped.

"Wow. That's a lot of incentive," Charice muttered.

"No kidding. I also learned that someone let him know where we were going to be and what time . . . and that could only have been someone close to us. And Yarborough was having a tough time financially." He rubbed his eyes. "His dad died a few months before and he had to come home for the funeral, and then as soon as he got back from that, he got word of his wife's diagnosis of breast cancer."

"That's tough."

Lee sighed. "He should have requested an early discharge due to his whole family situation but said he couldn't afford to."

"So, he needed money."

Lee gave a short laugh. "A lot of guys needed money."

"Just track with me here. What if he was the one who sold Chris out?"

Lee shook his head. "I hate to say I thought about it."

"You didn't look into it?"

"No. I . . . didn't want to believe that Yarborough, someone I loved like a brother, could do that."

"What about his wife?"

"She died just a few months after I got back. I was in rehab so couldn't make the funeral. I tried to call him, but was never able to reach him and he didn't return my calls. I haven't seen him since the day Chris died. I just dropped it. Figured it was too painful for him to stay connected with me or something."

Or something. "It's awfully convenient that Yarborough got sick when he did," Ryan said.

"I've thought about that and wondered about it myself." He shook his head. "But I was there with him while he was puking his guts out. I held his head a couple of times. No one is that good of an actor or could fake that. He was violently, terribly sick. To the point I hid his weapon."

"Ouch."

"Yeah. We were all waiting to see if he'd turn a corner and be able to ride to the airport, but it soon became apparent that his illness was going to last a while and if we waited much longer, we'd miss our flight. Finally, in between episodes of vomiting, he just waved a hand and said for the rest of us to get out of there. The medic was with him and promised to look out for him, so we left him in good hands. Then we hit the IED and that was that." He rubbed a hand over his eyes. "Some days I wish I'd stayed with him."

Charice looked up. "Reuben Yarborough arrived home three days after your convoy was hit."

"That's what I heard. His wife was dying."

"So . . . where's Reuben now?" Izzy asked.

Charice scrolled. "Uh . . . looks like he bought a place on Lake Murray."

"Whoa," Lee said. "Those houses aren't cheap."

"No, they're not." Ryan rubbed his chin. "And someone who's struggling financially doesn't have the means to buy one. I think we need to dig a little deeper into his activities since he's been home. The fact that he came home three days after Chris died and never went back . . ."

Lee shook his head. "How much did he pay for the house?"

Charice clicked a few more keys. "A little over half a mil."

Gray eyes met his. "So he couldn't afford to take an early discharge to be with his family during his father's illness and death—and he couldn't afford to be with his wife during her chemo treatments—but he could afford that for a house . . ." Lee leaned forward, eyes narrowed. "Where'd he get the money?"

"I don't know," Charice said. "I sent David an email asking him to look into Reuben's financials, but we need a warrant. He's working on that for us."

"And the sale of the warehouse?" Lee asked.

"Showing as belonging to what we suspect is a dummy corporation, but the fact that we have Tony Bianchi on video and doing deals there . . . well, let's just say I've got my theories about it all." He shrugged. "We've got the forensic accounting guys still working on tracing it back to an actual person, but if cash was involved again . . ."

"Tell me your theories," Lee said.

"Just one, really. Reuben sold Chris out, faked his illness—or did something to make himself sick—so he wouldn't be on that MRAP when it hit the IED, and he got the money for his traitorous actions. It's the only thing that makes sense."

"Guess we can ask him," Charice said. "But the warehouse . . . how would someone be able to sell it?"

"The seller would need the deed for that," Lee said. "How would he be able to get his hands on that?"

Ryan frowned. "That one has me a little puzzled. Were Reuben and Jonathan close friends?"

Lee shrugged. "Not really. I mean, they knew each other and seemed to be headed toward a strong friendship because they had a lot in common, but at the time, they were in the beginning stages of that friendship."

"That would explain why Jonathan's mother couldn't remember Reuben's name and she'd never met him before that weekend—or seen him since."

"Jonathan was a pretty private guy. It's possible that he just never introduced them—or had the opportunity to before that weekend. Does your mother know everybody you interact with or are friends with?"

226

Ryan laced his fingers together and placed them behind his head while he leaned back and studied the ceiling. "True. And no. Not even close. How did Chris and Jonathan meet?"

"Believe it or not, Reuben and Jonathan met at the gym when they were both on leave and started hanging out. Reuben introduced Chris to Jonathan because they had a lot of the same interests—like helping veterans. Which is what they were going to use the warehouse for."

Still looking at the ceiling, Ryan said, "Tell me about that."

"They were going to convert it into a shelter for them. Mostly targeting those who're homeless. Someplace they could come get three squares and a bed at night. They paid cash for the place, but were going to start seeing if we could raise the funds to do a complete overhaul of the inside. You know, put in a kitchen, bedrooms, bathrooms, all of that. They also wanted to provide jobs. Everyone who worked there would be a veteran."

"That sounds like an amazing thing. I love that idea. I can't believe he never mentioned it."

Lee shrugged. "He was excited about it. He wanted it to be successful. Talking about it made him nervous."

"Even to me?"

"Especially to you."

Ryan looked over at his brother's friend. "What? Seriously?"

"He mentioned that he wanted it to be a surprise, that he wanted to make everyone proud, but didn't know when it would all come to fruition. So . . ."

"So he kept it to himself."

"Yeah."

"It's still a cool idea."

"I think so too. Only, shortly after they bought the place, Jonathan was killed. And then a couple of months later, Chris."

"Yeah. And then the warehouse sat there for a couple more months. Until a dead guy sold it." Ryan rose to pace the floor in the small area and think. "Okay, who had the papers for the warehouse? Because Jonathan's parents said there was nothing in his safe-deposit box."

"That's weird," Lee said. "Jonathan had a copy, he told me so."

"Jonathan lived in a pretty nice area. A gated apartment complex with guards at the entrance."

Lee nodded. "He inherited some money from his grandfather. That's why they were able to pay cash for the warehouse and why he could afford the nice upper-class apartment." Lee narrowed his eyes. "What are you thinking?"

"Jonathan's mother said she noticed something weird about his apartment shortly after he died." Ryan told him about the coffee cup in the garbage. "That's bothered me ever since she told me about it."

"Okay, so what are you thinking?"

"What if Jonathan had a home safe or kept the deed to the warehouse somewhere other than his safe-deposit box? Or what if someone wanted to get his hands on it and talked Jonathan into pulling it from the box?"

"But why?"

"I don't know. I'm just speculating. I wonder if there's a way to get a list of names of those who came through the gates the day of the break-in."

"That was two years ago," Izzy said.

"Yeah, but they might keep them on record."

"Guess it wouldn't hurt to ask."

Ryan pulled his phone from the clip. "Let's make some calls."

Charice stood and shut her laptop. "Why don't you make those calls on our way to see Reuben? I'll drive. Lee, you can just ride with us if you want. We'll bring you back here."

"Good idea."

The four of them left the coffee shop and Ryan stayed glued to his phone while Izzy followed Charice and Lee to her car.

24

Izzy watched one expensive house after the other flip past her window until they finally pulled to a stop in front of a three-story brick home. "Wow."

"Yeah." Lee's voice was subdued and Izzy hurt for him. To come face-to-face with solid evidence that a man he'd trusted with his life could have been responsible for the betrayal and death of four of his other friends had to be devastating.

"Did you call him?" Charice asked.

"I tried," Lee said. "All I got was voice mail, but there's a truck in the driveway. Could be his."

Charice glanced at Ryan. "We'll hang back a bit, okay?"

"Yeah."

Izzy could tell the idea didn't sit well with him by the tension in his shoulders, the flared nostrils, the narrowed eyes . . . yeah, he was hanging on to his control by a thread.

They climbed from the vehicle and shut the doors. Lee took the lead while Izzy and Charice stayed next to the car with Ryan. They'd let Lee handle this one for now, but all of them wanted to see Reuben's reaction when confronted.

The front door opened and a man stepped onto the porch. He looked . . . haggard, Izzy thought. It was the one word that instantly came to mind. Deep grooves beside the corners of his lips, stooped posture, gray hair . . . and he wasn't that old. Maybe midforties?

His eyes landed on Lee and his face lost all color. He took a deep breath and let it out slowly. "Lee Filmore, as I live and breathe. Never thought I'd see you again."

"I guess you didn't."

"You should have called."

"I did. You didn't answer."

"Right."

"Nice place you got here. I guess the blood money was worth more than Chris's life."

For a moment Reuben paused as he looked away. His jaw worked, then he shrugged. "I guess it was."

Ryan flinched. "Well, that was easy enough. He killed Chris." He started to walk toward Lee and Reuben, but Izzy's hard grip on his forearm halted him.

"Don't," she said. "Let him talk."

"I can't deny it," Reuben said. "The proof is all around me. All it would take is for someone to go digging around my checking account. But not a day goes by that I don't regret it."

Lee's eyes narrowed. "Regretting it in style, huh?"

Reuben shook his head. "Who are your friends?"

"Just that. Friends."

"You want to come in?"

"That's all right. I think I'll stay out here where the air's not so tainted."

Reuben flinched.

Ryan took a stab in the dark. "You sold the warehouse too, didn't you?"

That seemed to take the man by surprise. "Yeah. But how did you know?"

"I didn't. Until just now."

Reuben scowled. "Who are you?"

"How'd you get your hands on the documents?" Lee asked before Ryan could answer. "You had to have the deed to sell it." Lee's mild tone made Ryan nervous.

For now, Reuben seemed content to let his own question go unanswered. "I was home on leave, waiting for my second child to be born. I needed some money. I went over to Jonathan's to ask him for a loan and he went into another room to get some cash out of his safe. I did a little snooping and saw the deed to the warehouse on his desk." He shrugged. "Didn't think anything about it at first, just noticed it. He came back in and put everything in the top desk drawer and gave me the cash. Told me it was the last time he was giving me any money. I promised him I'd pay it back."

"Like the other times you paid it back?" Lee murmured.

The man's nostrils flared. "I'd only borrowed money from him once before."

"You're the one who went in his apartment after he died," Charice said.

Reuben frowned. "Are you a cop?"

"I am."

For a moment, Ryan thought the man would clam up. He turned narrowed eyes back on Lee. "You brought cops?"

"Does it matter?"

A sigh slipped out. "I guess not. The minute I saw your number and heard your message, I concluded someone had figured things out. I know I'm done for."

"So talk."

"What do I get out of it?"

"I keep Chris's brother from killing you."

Reuben raked a hand through his gray hair and studied Ryan. "Chris's brother, huh?"

"Yeah. Like the man said, talk."

For a minute, it looked like he might refuse, then he just shook his head. "Why not? All right, I knew where Gill kept the spare key. He'd let me crash on his couch a few times when Patty and I had a fight. Anyway, I just walked in, grabbed the papers from his desk, and walked out."

"And left a coffee cup in his trash can," Charice said.

Reuben squinted. "Maybe. I don't remember that."

"Who's the dummy corporation covering for?" she asked.

The man frowned. "Dummy corporation?"

"You're not using the warehouse, you sold it. Bricks & Sticks is on the deed now, but I need a name behind that. There's no trail back to you."

Reuben's brows dipped. "Then how did you know about the warehouse sale?"

"It was an educated guess. So who'd you sell it to?"

"Why?"

"Because he killed Kevin, you traitor!" Lee said. "Chris's little brother!" Lee started for him and Charice grabbed his arm.

"Not yet," she murmured.

Lee settled down. Reluctantly.

And only Izzy's grip kept Ryan from joining Lee in going after the man. "Keep your cool, Ryan," she said.

He tamped down his own fury and turned his gaze to Reuben. "Who?" Ryan asked.

Reuben shrugged. "I'm not saying."

"You don't have to," Charice said. "We've already figured out it was Tony Bianchi."

That hit its mark. Reuben swallowed hard and shifted. "Okay, then. Yeah. I wasn't supposed to know who was buying it, but the guy was in the background while the transaction was going down. I saw him and eventually put two and two together—especially when I overheard someone say his name."

"So you got in bed with the Mafia?" Lee asked.

"I didn't know it at the time, but yeah. He had cash. I had the deed. It made for a nice deal. His money's as green as the next guy's," Reuben said without any emotion.

Ryan held on to his temper by a thread. If he went after Reuben, he'd blow the whole investigation. Izzy knew that and he knew she'd put herself between him and the man on the front porch.

"Bianchi didn't know you stole that deed, did he?" Charice asked softly. "You signed Jonathan's name, didn't you?"

Reuben shoved his hands into the pockets of the light jacket he wore.

"Keep your hands where we can see them, Reuben," Izzy said.

Moving his hands back into view, the man narrowed his eyes at Charice. "Who are you?"

"The question was about you signing his name," Lee said. "I'll make introductions later."

"I signed his name. Bianchi—or rather his henchman—didn't ask questions."

"Which is why you had to sell to him. You couldn't afford to try to sell it honestly on the market," Lee said.

"Nope, couldn't do that."

"But Bianchi would have to file the sale at the courthouse, with a witness and notary and everything in order for it to look legit."

Reuben shrugged. "I guess. I'm sure that wasn't a problem for him."

"No, probably not."

"And he probably did a whole new sale to Bricks & Sticks so that his name was removed from any of the paperwork and it would just look like a company purchased the place," Lee said.

Reuben lifted his shoulders again, and Ryan could tell the man didn't really care.

"So. I guess this is it, then, huh?" Reuben shifted, but kept his hands in plain sight.

"Yeah," Lee said. "This is it. Answer me this . . . why? Why sell us out? I mean, I almost understand. Two million is a lot of money, but I always thought you were above that. What made you turn?"

Running a hand over his face, Reuben sighed. "Because I promised Patty she'd have her dream home."

Lee frowned. "Patty wasn't a gold digger. She didn't care what kind of house you lived in as long as she was with you."

"And I felt the same way."

"So it was just for the money?"

"Yes." He cleared his throat and looked away. "Patty found out she was sick with an aggressive form of breast cancer. She was diagnosed the day after my father's funeral. That was six weeks before we were supposed to fly home. After talking to her doctor, and getting a very negative prognosis, I realized the only way I was going to be able to keep my promise to Patty was to do something . . . drastic."

"Like rat Chris out to Nuristani and collect the money."

"Yes. It only took a couple weeks to set it all up."

"Which explains your occasional disappearances."

"Right." His hard eyes turned to granite. "I'm making it sound like it was an easy decision. It wasn't. But I made a choice to sacrifice a friendship so I could give her all this."

"Sacrifice your *friendship*?" Lee's question came out in a scathing spit. "You sacrificed his *life*."

Reuben didn't even blink. "I came home to an account full of money and we closed on the house four weeks later. She lived here three months before she died."

Lee's face reverted to its expressionless, rigid stance. "You never talked about it. About Patty. I thought you were handling it okay."

"I was probably in denial. If I didn't admit it, it wasn't real."

Ryan understood that feeling.

"Was it worth it?" Lee asked.

"You do crazy things for love." Reuben's eyes met Lee's, then jumped to Ryan's. "Even betraying your best friend and becoming a criminal." He gave a humorless smirk.

Lee kept his fists at his sides, but Ryan thought they might start flying at any given moment. "You're under arrest for my attempted murder and for being an accessory to Kevin's murder and anything else Ryan can think of," Lee said.

Reuben smirked. "You can't arrest me."

"I wasn't planning on trying. Just helping my officer friends out. Ryan and Charice can arrest you."

"And so can I," Izzy said. So far she'd stayed in the background, watching and listening. She stepped forward, nostrils flaring. "It would give me great pleasure."

Reuben blew out a breath and dropped his gaze. "Part of me never really thought I'd get caught. The other part's been expecting this from day one."

Ryan shifted and unfastened the safety loop around his weapon. The guy was making this way too easy and it made him itchy.

"You see that guy back there? You already know that he's Chris's brother. What you don't know is that Kevin Marshall, his other brother, was a rookie cop who died—in part—because you sold a stolen warehouse to a guy who kills cops for a living."

"I didn't pull the trigger."

"But you know who did."

"I wasn't even there."

"Didn't have to be," Ryan said, stepping forward. "You stole a warehouse, then knowingly sold it to a murderer. You're affiliated with the men and the organization that killed Kevin. That's good enough for me."

"And me." Izzy pulled her cuffs from her belt and stepped forward.

Reuben swore, then gave a slight turn and slipped back inside the door he'd left cracked. This time he shut it and Ryan heard the dead bolt click.

"I've got the back!" Drawing her weapon, Izzy darted down the walkway and sped to the rear of the house while Ryan palmed his own Glock.

He stood to the side of the door and noted Lee doing the same, his own gun drawn. "Put the gun away, Lee, you have no authority to use it here and it's just going to cause more problems. Let us handle this. After we break the door down."

Ryan slammed a foot against the door. Lee joined him, and after several attempts, the door caved and crashed inside to the foyer floor. Charice stepped inside and Ryan backed up and took in the wide-open floor plan. Still plenty of places to hide, though.

"We need him alive, Charice, to lead us to the people who killed Kevin. Remember that."

"I got that."

Izzy's face appeared in the glass of the back door that led to a large deck overlooking the lake. She stepped inside. "He didn't come out this way."

Ryan nodded. "Let's clear this floor." He was involved now whether they liked it or not. There was no way he was going to remain in the background and chance letting a killer go free. He might get a slap on the wrist from his superior, but he'd risk it.

"I called for backup," Izzy said. "Yarborough's not coming peacefully." She walked to the base of the stairs.

"Good," Charice said. "Backup is good."

Izzy disappeared down the hall while Ryan followed to cover her back. "Stay here, Lee, or better yet, get out of sight before backup gets here."

Ryan ignored Lee's low growl of frustration. He got it. He'd been betrayed and it had gotten his best friend killed, but they couldn't jeopardize this arrest and have Yarborough get off on some technicality.

Izzy came back down the hall. "Clear."

"He's upstairs then," Ryan said. He moved toward the stairs and was happy to note Lee slipping out the back door. Ryan took the lead up the stairs and Izzy followed, weapon held ready. Charice stayed close too. They cleared most of the second floor. Then stopped in front of closed double doors.

Ryan motioned for Charice to open them, he had her covered. She did. The doors swung in and she stepped back. Ryan rounded the corner and surveyed the bedroom. He stilled when he spotted Reuben standing at the chest of drawers with his back to him. "Turn around, Reuben, and keep your hands where I can see them."

Sirens sounded in the distance. Backup was near.

"It's almost a relief, you know? To have the truth come out. I've asked God to forgive me." He paused and turned slightly to meet Ryan's gaze. "Do you think your family will be able to do so?"

"Given time, maybe, but right now, I need to see your hands."

Izzy stepped around him and to the side, giving her a better view of the man and what was in front of him. She glanced back at Ryan and widened her eyes while she mouthed, "Gun." Then motioned with her free hand, index finger under her chin and wiggling her thumb.

Great, the man had a gun to his head.

"Reuben, put the gun down," Ryan said. "No one else has to get hurt."

"No, it's over for me. I'm ready to be with Patty. I'm a dead man anyway if I'm arrested. Once you start hunting Bianchi, he'll know I told you the whole story."

"He won't care. We're already looking for him because we have him on video at the time of Kevin's shooting in the warehouse. We pulled footage from a hidden camera, so we're going to get him with or without you. But if you testify against him, you can get some time knocked off." Maybe. He didn't know that for sure but was willing to say anything that would convince the man to give up the weapon.

237

Reuben turned, keeping the gun steady, the bullet end pressed beneath his chin. "I can't. They'll go after my kids."

Heart thudding, Ryan shook his head. "Don't do this, man. Your kids need you."

"Naw, they're better off with Patty's mom. And at least they're taken care of for the rest of their lives. I've already turned the money over to my in-laws."

Ryan realized the man had been thinking about this for a long time. He wasn't quite as blasé about his actions as he wanted to appear.

"The kids might be better off with her for now, but once you get some help, life can be good again, man." Probably not, but Ryan wasn't about to voice that.

Reuben's eyes glittered with grief. "Life. What a crock. Life just didn't turn out the way I thought it would, you know? Patty wasn't supposed to die so young."

"Neither was Kevin," Izzy said. "Or Chris. Put the gun down."

It was like the man hadn't heard her. "Man, I've been living on borrowed time. This is the way it was always going to end," he continued. "I think I knew that the minute I gave the location of the convoy to Nuristani's man." He laughed without humor. "I ate some tainted meat so I'd be sick enough to have an excuse to stay back. Never been so sick in my life and wondered if I'd actually live through it." His now empty eyes met Ryan's. "My kids think I'm a hero. I can't go to prison." He lowered the weapon and Ryan breathed a small puff of relief. Then Reuben's eyes met his once more. "But I just discovered something."

"What's that?"

"I don't have the guts to kill myself."

Reuben's right hand lowered and Ryan drew in a relieved breath. The man was going to surrender. "Put the weapon down, Reuben."

"Yeah." As the man started to lower the gun to the floor, the window exploded.

Izzy cried out as red sprayed the air. She heard footsteps on the stairs and then in the hall. She spun to see backup coming into the room, weapons pointed at her. Displaying her badge, she moved to the two bodies on the floor. "Call an ambulance!"

Someone said, "Do it."

Izzy dropped beside Ryan. "Are you hit?"

He grunted and rolled away from Reuben. "No." The shot had sent Reuben flying forward to slam into Ryan, taking them both to the floor—and covering Ryan in blood and other matter. "Is he dead?"

It sure looked like it. The lower half of his face was . . . gone. A red mass of blood and tissue hung from the remains. Her stomach churned, but she ignored it and reached for his wrist. A slow thud hit her fingers. "He's still alive."

She grabbed a towel and bolted back to Reuben's side, where she dropped to her knees and pressed the towel against the missing part of his face. She didn't know what was medically possible to do for the man should he live, but wanted to give him every option to survive. Stopping or slowing the loss of blood was priority one. She knew officers were searching for the shooter and she prayed they found him. For now, Izzy concentrated on keeping Reuben alive.

Paramedics rushed into the room and Izzy moved away as they took over. She looked around for Ryan and spotted him near the bathroom. He'd grabbed another towel and was wiping his pale face and hands while talking to Justin O'Keefe, another detective he worked with occasionally. Izzy interrupted them. "Bianchi knew we were here. He had a sniper just looking for an opportunity."

"Looks like he found it."

"But that means he's got someone following us."

"Yeah."

She touched his arm. "Are you okay?"

He briefly met her gaze. "Physically, yeah."

"Right."

O'Keefe patted Ryan on the shoulder—the one that didn't have blood on it—and walked away. Ryan looked at her and grimaced. "I'd really like to puke right now."

"That makes two of us. SLED is here."

He shot her a grateful look and tossed the towel back into the bathroom. "Let's give our statement, wait on a search warrant, then get busy searching." He looked at Charice. "Can you get the ball rolling on that warrant?"

"Consider it done." She walked away, her phone already pressed to her ear.

"What are we searching for?" Izzy asked.

"Anything that might have the names of people that Reuben may have contacted who have ties to Bianchi. We find those, we find the guy who shot Kevin."

"And I know where to start."

"Where?"

"When we were clearing the downstairs, there's a room that he's using as an office. There's a laptop on the desk."

He started for the hallway.

"Out of the way, please. Make way. Let us through."

The paramedics had Reuben on the gurney and were headed for the door. Ryan and Izzy moved out of the way. Organized chaos reigned as each officer stepped into the role he or she was assigned.

Ryan nodded. "CSU will take the laptop and we'll tell them what to look for. In the meantime, let's see what else we can find." He tapped the shoulder of one of the other paramedics left. "You have some extra gloves?"

"Sure." He passed a handful over to Ryan, who pulled on a set, then handed some to Izzy. She donned the gloves and together they walked down the stairs and into the office.

"Can't touch anything until the warrant gets here," Izzy said.

"And you need to remove yourself from this area now anyway. Charice can take it from here. I can help her if she needs me to."

"I know." So he paced for the next forty minutes until an officer stepped into the room and slapped the warrant into his outstretched hand.

He handed it to Charice, who waved it in the air. "All right, folks, let's get busy."

For the next thirty minutes, they searched—and came up empty. Ryan sighed when she told him. "If he has anything, it's got to be on the laptop."

"That's my guess." Izzy pulled the gloves off and stuck them in her pocket. "What now?"

Ryan grimaced. "Lee's probably outside waiting for me."

"He's going to want to know what happened for sure."

"So, let's grab him. Then I go home and get a shower."

25

zzy walked into her mother's house that evening and plopped herself at the kitchen table. "Need some help?"

"Just peeling potatoes, hon. Is Chloe coming?"

"I think so. She had to run by the office for something, but said she'd swing by in a few minutes."

"Great." Her mother flashed her a grin and laid into the potato with the peeler once more. "Your father won't be able to make it, but it will be nice to have you and Chloe here."

On some days, Tabitha St. John made an imposing figure in her dress blues and granite expression. Other days, she simply dressed for the office in a professional, perfectly pressed pantsuit that conveyed a woman of power and confidence.

Tonight, with her still dark hair pulled into a ponytail, no makeup, and her Gamecock sweatpants, she looked at least ten years younger than her fifty-six years. Her black zip-up hoodie completed her off-the-clock outfit, and Izzy decided she liked this side of her mother better than any other. She respected her professional side, of course, but she didn't always like her in that mode.

But here, in the warmth of her home, seeing her like she once had as a child, brought Izzy comfort like nothing else could.

Only tonight, she couldn't fully relax as she figured her mom would soon bring up the parking garage incident. And Izzy wanted to talk to her about all the protection she'd been noticing. However, if she broached that subject, then her mother might start talking about the incident in the parking garage.

So Izzy kept her mouth shut for now and watched the local news playing on the small television mounted on the side of the cabinet next to the sink.

Her mother turned. "Are you all right?"

"I'm fine. Why?"

"A man had half his face blown off in front of you. That's hard to unsee."

Izzy rubbed her eyes. "You're right. It is hard. And I'll have a few nightmares about it, I'm sure. The fact that he did some really rotten stuff helps put it into perspective."

"Hmm."

"You don't believe me?"

"I believe you believe that. And if that helps you cope, then I'll go with it."

Izzy sighed. "How is he? The man who was shot?"

"Still hovering between this life and the next one. He'll never be the same, and if he lives, he'll wish he was dead." Tears pooled in her mother's eyes—not a completely rare occurrence, but odd enough that Izzy straightened.

"Mom?"

A swipe of her wrist dispelled the tears. "I'm sorry, hon, it's just sometimes I wish you'd gone into some profession that was less violent."

"Like Ruthie?"

"I'm not sure being a surgeon is any less violent some days. I was thinking more along the lines of accounting or a chef. You always did love to cook."

"Yeah."

A knock on the door pulled Izzy to her feet. "I'll get it." When she opened the door, Felicia Denning's smiling face greeted her. "Oh, hi, come on in."

Izzy's mother turned. "I wasn't expecting you."

"I texted and called your personal phone, but you didn't answer. Since it wasn't an emergency and not work-related, I left that number alone."

Her mother glanced at the phone she'd left on the table. "I've had my hands in food and haven't checked my phone. It's still on silent too."

The work number would have rung. It was never turned off and the volume was always on high.

Felicia stepped into the kitchen and set a bag of oranges on the counter. "Marcus said he was running low when I saw him at the courthouse yesterday. I was on my way home from the Marshalls' house. I saw Izzy's car outside and decided to swing by and drop these off. She shrugged out of her coat and took a chair next to the one Izzy had just reclaimed.

Her mother laughed. "Running low? That means he's down to about six in the refrigerator, then."

Izzy's father enjoyed fresh-squeezed orange juice each morning.

Felicia smiled. "Jeff got back from his trip to Miami last night." A pilot for a major airline, Felicia's husband was always bringing back goodies from places he visited.

"Marcus will appreciate it. I might have to snitch one or two myself." She turned back to the sink and rinsed her hands. "How were the Marshalls?"

Felicia sighed and shook her head. "They're coping. I think. Mrs. Marshall seemed to be much better than the day of the funeral."

Melissa Endicott appeared on the screen and Felicia nodded to the television. "Can you turn that up?"

"Sure." Izzy grabbed the remote and upped the volume.

". . . come out and vote. As you know, I'm ahead in the polls.

Let me just remind you that there's a reason for that, but I still need your vote."

"What do you think, Mom?"

Her mother sighed. "I think she'll win. She says all the right things and the people—and officers—like what she has to say. They're ready for change."

"And?"

She shrugged. "And I'll—" she shot a glance at Felicia—"*we'll* do our best to work with her."

"Exactly," Felicia said.

Izzy's phone dinged and she glanced at the text. Then sat up straight. "I've got to go."

"But you haven't eaten."

Izzy raised a brow. "It's business."

"You're off duty."

She went to her mother and kissed her cheek. "And now I'm back on."

"Then tell me what it's about."

Izzy hesitated, then shrugged. "Ryan got a lead on Tony Bianchi."

Her mother's eyes narrowed and she exchanged a glance with Felicia before lasering back in on Izzy. "Why is he telling you this?"

"Because Kevin was my partner, Mom, and I'm going to be involved in taking down his killers."

"I get that, but why is Ryan involved?"

"Don't worry, he's not. He's staying in the background, but you know he's being fed information."

"I know. I expected it, but he'd better not do anything to jeopardize an arrest when it comes to Bianchi."

"He won't. You know Ryan."

"I do. He's a good detective, but he also just buried another brother and fellow officer. He's riding an emotional roller coaster right now."

She hugged her mother one more time. "I'll watch out for him, I promise."

"Hmm."

Izzy raised a brow. "Hmm? What does that mean?"

"Felicia, what do you think that means?" her mother asked.

Felicia looked up from her phone. "Oh, no, I'm not getting in the middle of this." Izzy and her mother stared at her and she finally grimaced and set her phone on the table. "Fine, if you insist. From a purely professional point of view, Ryan shouldn't be anywhere near this case. From a personal point of view, I understand his feelings. However, that takes me back to the professional point of view. Because of those feelings, he should stay far, far away."

Izzy's mother nodded. "Thank you. I agree." She looked back at Izzy. "Do I need to talk to him?"

"No, ma'am," Izzy said, wishing she hadn't received the message at that particular moment. "I'll do it. But just to be clear, he's not doing anything he shouldn't. When it comes to Kevin's investigation, he's not handling evidence, he's not talking to witnesses or doing any kind of investigating—at least none that will adversely affect the outcome of the case or cause problems in any trial that might happen. He was involved in the search of Reuben's place today, but that doesn't have anything to do with Kevin. They're two separate cases."

"But you're not with him every second of the day. You don't know what he's doing with his time off," Felicia said.

True enough, but it irritated her that the woman would believe Ryan capable of being devious like that. She had to remind herself that the deputy chief hadn't known the Marshalls as long as she had. "Seriously, he's done nothing wrong. Everything has been strictly by the book and everyone can prove it. But I'll keep you updated."

"Where's Bianchi?" her mother asked.

"I'm not sure. I'm meeting Ryan at a Starbucks near the place."

"Any word on Lamar Young?" Felicia asked.

Izzy shook her head. "He seems to have been swallowed by the earth."

"He'll surface," her mother warned, "and when he does, he's not going to play nice. Showing up at Kevin's funeral tells us that he's either certifiable—or he just doesn't care."

"Or both," Izzy muttered.

"Exactly. So watch your back and make sure someone else is watching it for good measure."

Izzy kissed her cheek. "Apparently, that's what I have you for."

"You noticed, huh?"

Pursing her lips, she rolled her eyes toward Felicia. "Good night. Keep Mom out of trouble."

"She's not the one walking into it."

Touché.

Izzy lifted a hand in a wave. "I'll be in touch."

Ryan sat at the table and sipped his fourth cup of coffee. He'd had way too much, but at least this one was decaf. Jittery from the effects of the caffeine and the word that Bianchi should soon be in custody, Ryan waited impatiently. The building across the street housed the penthouse where Bianchi was reportedly holed up.

Izzy stepped into the restaurant and Ryan's breath caught. Out of uniform, she looked only slightly older than legal. But no one knew better than he how deceptive looks could be. He knew the sharp mind behind those green eyes. Her hair swung in her usual ponytail, and for a moment he envisioned it spread across her shoulders, the sunlight glinting off the dark strands.

He shifted when she settled in the chair beside him.

And then guilt pounded him. He looked away. What was he doing even being attracted to her? His brother had been killed and he was there to see his killer brought to justice. Romance was out of the question right now.

He just wished seeing Izzy didn't stir up emotions better left alone.

And yet, here he was.

"Ryan? Hello? Anyone home?"

He realized she'd been talking to him while he stared at the windows of the penthouse. "Oh. Sorry."

She shrugged. "Lost in thought, huh?"

"Something like that."

"Want to share?"

Boy, did he. "Just praying this goes off like it's supposed to."

She nodded and pulled her phone from her pocket and tapped the screen, then handed him the device. "While we're waiting, take a look at this list and tell me if you know any of the people on it."

Ryan scanned the list of names. "Where'd you get this?"

"Derek."

"So, this is the supposed list of dirty cops?"

"Yes."

"I recognize a lot of these names and I can tell you right now, they're not dirty."

"What about the two who are now in prison?"

Ryan shrugged. "Coincidence."

"So what else could it be?"

"I have no idea. Send it to me and let me study it a bit more." He sat up straight and pushed his coffee to the side. "They're here."

She lifted her gaze from the phone to look across the street. "I should be in there," she murmured. "I want to be a part of it."

"Let the team do its job. There are reasons we shouldn't be there." Reasons he didn't like, but . . . "I'm glad you're here with me."

She shot him a tight smile. "Yeah."

He understood. It took everything in him to sit tight and not join the unit getting ready to raid Bianchi's hiding place. But he couldn't . . . wouldn't do anything to jeopardize getting Kevin's killer. And to do that, everything had to be by the book.

The streets were being cleared. Officers in uniform and plain clothes swarmed the building, disappearing inside and around the sides. "That was Derek," she said.

"And Brady," he added, pointing.

"Go get him, guys," she whispered.

Ryan rubbed a hand across his eyes and sent up a silent prayer. If all went well, no shots would be fired and the man would realize there was no chance of escape.

He and Izzy sat in silence, the tension around them thick. So thick, he was surprised he couldn't see it. "They're going to get him," he said.

"Of course they are."

A minute passed, then Ryan said, "I want to be there. I want to look in his eyes and—"

"Stop," she said.

"What?"

"You're doing exactly what I was just doing. Like you said, let them do their jobs."

"I know."

"But?"

"Nothing."

"You're just torturing yourself."

"And you're not? You might not be saying anything, but I can read your mind from here."

She shrugged and leaned forward. "What's taking so long?"

And then the front of the top-floor penthouse exploded into a ball of fire and smoke.

26

Izzy dove to the floor and Ryan landed on top of her. Her breath whooshed from her lungs as glass and debris rained down around them. As her senses tuned her back in to her surroundings, she registered screams. Screams that came from every direction. She bit down on her own cries and tried to squirm out from under Ryan's weight.

He rolled off of her and Izzy pressed a hand to her throbbing forehead. When she looked at her fingers, blood covered them.

"You're hurt," Ryan said.

She looked up to see a gash on his cheek. "You are too." She gasped. "Brady and Derek, they're across the street."

Sirens blared and Ryan pulled his badge from his belt. "First, we need to see if anyone else is hurt in here."

Dizzy and slightly disoriented, Izzy shook her head. She desperately wanted to find out about her brothers, but . . . "I can help."

Together they flashed their badges and asked the others in the restaurant if they were hurt. No one was. Ryan and Izzy had taken the brunt of it.

Ryan pointed. "The explosion sent that metal rod through the window."

"Thank God it didn't hit anything but the glass." And embedded itself into the wall behind them like an arrow. If it had struck one of them, it would have meant instant death. She shuddered and looked at the building across the street. Fear pulsed through her. "Ryan, there's no way everyone survived. Brady . . . Derek . . ."

"I know."

Her heart tight, tears on the surface, she spun on her heel and raced out of the coffee shop, holding her badge in plain sight.

"Izzy! Stop!"

She ignored Ryan's cry.

Ambulances pulled to a screeching halt right behind the fire trucks.

Izzy darted through the mass confusion and into the lobby of the apartment building. Residents flowed from the building like ants from a hill. She tried to go against the flow, but was pushed and shoved, bouncing from one person to the next.

A hand landed on her forearm and jerked her to a halt. She cried out and whirled to find Ryan shouting at her. "You can't do this." He pulled her back toward the exit.

She jerked on her arm, but his hold was too tight. "Let me go!"

"Not a chance."

"My brothers are in there!"

"And they're my friends, but you're not going to get yourself killed running into a burning building. Think!"

The side door off the lobby flew open and three officers, faces in their elbows, bolted from the stairwell. Ryan let go of Izzy and they went to the two men and one woman. "Is anyone else coming down?"

"Yes," the first officer croaked. Sweat and blood mingled on his forehead and dripped from his chin. "The blast was pretty contained to the top floors, but it was bad."

He coughed and Izzy caught Ryan's eye. She had to put her own fears aside and get to work doing what she did best. Helping others. "Let's get them to an ambulance."

Firefighters swarmed the building, hoses trailing behind them. "Up the stairs to the nearest standpipe!" Izzy heard the orders and knew they'd carry the hoses and hook them up in the area closest to the fire, typically in the stairwell of the floor below the fire. They had their tricks that would allow them to use gravity to give them the most pressure possible for the water flow.

These thoughts and more flashed through her mind in less than a second before she dismissed them and focused her concentration on the men and women in the building and getting them out. Alive. And catching the people who'd initiated the destruction.

Once outside, she and Ryan passed the officers off to the paramedics and questioned them while they received their care.

Unfortunately, they weren't much help.

"Did you see Derek or Brady St. John?" she asked.

The woman, Special Agent Blaire Harrison, Izzy had learned, nodded. "They were there, but then the explosion happened and I don't remember seeing them after that."

"Izzy!"

She turned at the shout and found Chloe and Hank running toward her. Her sister skidded to a halt. "Are you okay? You're bleeding."

Her forehead. She'd forgotten about it. Although she noticed the throbbing in the area now that Chloe brought it to her attention. "I'm fine. Brady and Derek are inside, though. They haven't come out yet."

Chloe's face paled. She turned toward the building. Ryan had already started questioning the bystanders.

Izzy watched the water saturate the building and waited, praying, desperate to see her brothers and the others come out of the building.

Two men came out carrying a third between him. Firefighters rushed over to help and Izzy strained to see who it was.

Still not one of her brothers.

And then a firefighter stumbled from the building, a body over his shoulder. "Brady!" She ran toward them with Chloe on her heels. He was carried directly to the waiting gurney that would be rolled into the back of the ambulance. One of the paramedics slapped an oxygen mask on him. Izzy gripped Brady's shoulder. "Where's Derek?"

But her brother wasn't talking. Eyes closed, he lay unconscious, his dark lashes stark against his white cheeks. She looked up to the hovering paramedic. "Is he going to be okay?"

"That's what I'm getting ready to find out." The young man slipped the ends of his stethoscope into his ears and leaned over Brady.

Izzy backed away, fingers covering her mouth to keep her fear from erupting into sobs. Chloe's fingers curled around her upper arm, and from the viselike grip, she knew her sister was holding on to her own emotions just as tightly.

"Let's go!" the paramedic shouted and shut the doors of the ambulance.

There was nothing she could do for Brady, he was in good hands now. But what about Derek? Izzy spun away from Chloe and raced back toward the building to find Ryan talking with one of the ATF agents who'd just arrived on the scene.

She grabbed his bicep and pulled his attention to her. "Excuse me, but Derek's still in there."

"I know, Iz. So are six others. Everyone else is accounted for. It looks like the blast was pretty much contained to the two upper floors. Derek and a few others were closer to the blast. Firefighters are having trouble getting to them."

First Kevin, now . . . Izzy shook her head, heart in her throat. "No, not Derek too."

She couldn't collapse. Derek would expect her to be strong, not to give in to weak knees and trembling courage. There was nothing she could do except wait.

"Iz—"

She looked around.

She *could* do something. She could ask questions.

Izzy's gaze touched on those watching the action. Most looked pale and scared. Others filmed everything with their phones. She approached a woman who was simply staring at the burning building, tears streaking her cheeks. "Did you see anything that might help catch who did this?"

The woman turned, eyes wide. "This was on purpose?"

"Probably. Did you see anything?"

She palmed the tears from her cheeks. "No. I was a couple of blocks back when the explosion happened. I have a friend who lives in there. I haven't seen her or her daughter come out yet."

"What floor do they live on?"

"The seventh."

One floor down from the eighth-floor penthouse. Izzy placed a hand on the woman's shoulder. "I'm sorry. Don't give up hope yet."

Tears filled her shadowed eyes, but she nodded. "Thanks."

Izzy questioned several others and got pretty much the same response. They'd heard the blast and raced to see what had happened.

As she walked, she prayed. *Please let Derek be okay.* Twenty feet past the building, she stopped. Two men stood to the side near a dark SUV talking to a very large man who had his back to her. Lamar Young? His build was certainly a match. She wanted to see his face. Izzy slid her phone from her pocket and snapped several pictures of them. Until one looked straight at her.

She pretended not to notice and moved the phone as though she were videoing. Since she wasn't in uniform, he would most likely think she was simply a bystander doing the same as 90 percent of the rest of the crowd. But her mind was clicking. Who were they? They didn't blend in, didn't look like the rest of the shocked rubberneckers. Were they part of Bianchi's crew? Had they done this? And what were they doing with Lamar Young? If that was him. One of them said something to the hulking man and he turned.

She snapped another picture. He scowled and Izzy's heart gave a leap. When his eyes met hers, he pressed a hand to his side.

Where her bullet had struck him?

"Izzy?"

She didn't turn toward Ryan, who'd just approached.

"That's him. Come on!"

She took off toward Young in a dead run.

And he bolted.

Izzy tried to shove through the crowd without hurting anyone, but he was getting away. Finally, she gave up trying to be gentle. He was getting away. Again.

"Hey! Watch it!"

"What are you doing?"

Ignoring the indignant protests of those her elbows unintentionally gouged, she kept after the tall man.

Who turned a corner and disappeared.

Staying on his heels, she drew her weapon, paused wide at the corner, and worked around for a better angle without going around it. Ryan slipped up beside and slightly behind her. Izzy did a quick out-and-back peek.

Nothing in front of her but an empty alley. She buttonhooked around, weapon pointed forward in a two-handed grip, Ryan at her heels.

Young had probably scaled the low fence at the end of the alley. She hurried to it, but knew continuing the search was futile.

"He's gone."

Ryan shook the fence. "Want to go over?"

"Why? He's slipped away once again. I want to get back and see if they've pulled Derek out yet."

He nodded. "Fine. I'll call it in and we'll see if a unit can spot him in the area."

While he did that, Izzy hurried back to the building, scanning, watching. Her mother might show up, and Izzy wanted to be the one to tell her about Derek and Brady. Or, if she'd already heard, she might just head straight to the hospital to check on Brady.

By the time she and Ryan made it back to the secured area, FBI and ATF agents were in the fray. Izzy spotted Linc and went over to him. "You heard?" she asked him.

"Yes."

"You have agents in there."

"Yes."

"Derek?"

His face was pale beneath the leftover summer tan. "Still in there. Brady woke up on the ride to the hospital and is going to be fine. He's got some burns and smoke inhalation, but he's going to be fine." It seemed to help him to repeat that fact.

Izzy pulled her phone back out. "Look at these guys. Do you recognize them?"

Linc studied the pictures she'd taken of the two men by the SUV. "No, why?"

"They were back there." She pointed. "Just standing there, watching the whole thing, and they were talking to the guy that tried to burn me alive—Lamar Young."

Linc's eyes narrowed and his lips tightened.

"They looked out of place to me," she said. "And the fact that they were talking to Young raises the hair on my neck."

"Me too." He got on his phone and set it up with two other agents to detain the men for questioning—if they hadn't left yet. When he hung up, he looked at Izzy. "Nice work."

"Maybe. We'll see."

And then the lower doors opened once more and two firemen carrying a third man exited. "Derek," she whispered.

She followed Linc to the waiting ambulance. The two firefighters lowered her twin to the gurney just like Brady only a short time earlier. Or had it been hours? She had no concept of time at the moment.

Derek didn't stir.

"There's blood everywhere," she whispered. "Is he still alive?"

Linc either didn't hear her or just ignored her. A hand settled on her shoulder and she turned to see Ryan's pale face and tight jaw. "What is it?"

"Five dead. Numerous injured."

Linc looked up. "The dead?"

"Three law enforcement. Two residents on the seventh floor. A mother and her eight-year-old child. Husband is at work. He's already been called."

Izzy's heart shattered for the woman's friend, who still stood staring at the building. A child. It was always the children that hit her hardest. She swallowed and focused back on Derek.

Children and family.

The paramedics already had Derek hooked up to an IV and were working on stopping the bleeding from a wound in his side. "How bad is he?" she asked.

The paramedic looked up. "Bad." He looked at his partner. "Let's go."

Ryan rubbed a hand across his forehead and down his cheek, wincing when the action pulled the cut open again. He wiped the blood on his pants and watched the ambulance carrying Derek St. John scream away from the scene.

Izzy stood, arms wrapped around her middle. Linc was walking away, his phone pressed to his ear. Most likely, he was talking to the mayor or the chief of police—or his supervisor at the FBI. Since they had an open case on Bianchi, arson would no doubt be added to the underlying charges for a RICO indictment.

All of that flitted through his mind even as Ryan's heart broke at the sight of Izzy's sorrow. He slid an arm around her shoulders. "They're alive. Focus on that."

"Kevin was, too, when they took him away," she whispered.

Wincing, he pulled her tighter and she let him, resting her head against his chest. "We'll just pray this has a different ending than Kevin's."

"I'm sorry, Ryan, I shouldn't have brought up Kevin. I know this has to be hurting you too."

His heart squeezed at her apology. "Don't be sorry. I understand."

She looked up and he brushed stray strands of hair from her forehead. Her cut had started to scab over as well, but soot and dirt covered her face. He figured they both looked like they'd just walked out of a war zone.

He placed a light passionless kiss on her lips, surprising them both, but she took it as he meant it. An offer of comfort, nothing else. Not this time. Right now, he wasn't thinking about his attraction to her, he was just thinking he wanted to take away her pain.

He drew her in for a hug and she lay against him. He soaked in the moment before she squeezed his hand and pulled away.

"Want me to take you to the hospital?" he asked.

She didn't answer right away, then gave a slow shake of her head. "No. Mom and Dad and the rest of the family will go, but they're not going to be doing anything except waiting. I don't want to wait. I want to catch the people who did this. I don't want to miss one bit of information that comes out of that building."

As though her words were prophetic, the doors opened and two firefighters once again exited with a small sheet-covered body between them. He and Izzy stayed put, watching as each person was removed, his heart breaking, his fury and rage at the people responsible growing.

And then he realized something. "Wait a minute."

"What?"

"There was an extra body."

Izzy swiped a hand across her eyes and squinted up at him. "What do you mean?"

"There were five dead total. They brought out six bodies."

27

Several hours later, the blaze was contained. It would take some time for it to cool off, but firefighters would continue to monitor it and then the investigation would crank up to full volume. Sitting on the sidewalk in front of the Starbucks, Izzy pressed fingers to her weary and dry eyes and then pulled her phone from her pocket to dial Maria Dover.

"What?" the ME snapped.

"The bodies from the explosion earlier today. Are they there yet?"

"Who is this?"

"Izzy St. John."

"Ah. Hold on a sec." Izzy heard clicking in the background, then Maria came back on the line. "Yes, they're here. Why do you need to know?"

"I need names."

"Looks like all are identified. Max Jones, Lisa Greer and her eight-year-old daughter Kristy, Stephen Hollister, Louis Harper, and—"

"Wait, hold up. Did you say Louis Harper?"

"Yes. He was in the system and easy to identify. Prints came back in like thirty seconds."

"I know him." Izzy's legs went weak. "That's Blackjack." What had he been doing at the home of Tony Bianchi? He was the one who'd told Kevin about the meeting at the warehouse. "What was he doing there?"

"I have no idea. Now, if that's all you need, I need to get back to work."

"Sure." Izzy hadn't been asking Maria the question anyway, she'd just been speaking her thoughts out loud. "Thanks, Maria."

"Yep."

Izzy shook her head. Her CI was now dead due to being involved with Tony Bianchi.

Not good.

Her phone rang. "Hello?"

"You have a minute?"

Izzy's fatigue fled at her mother's voice. "Of course. Do you have some news?"

"Brady is awake and chomping at the bit to get out of the hospital and back to work."

"And Derek?" Silence.

Then a sigh like her mother was gathering her strength.

Fear slashed through her. "Mom?"

"He's still alive, but he's hurt pretty bad. Apparently he was one of the ones closer to the blast. Right now, it's touch and go with his left leg. They're working to save it, but—" Her voice broke and Izzy's throat tightened. "But," she said, her words stronger. "He's hanging in there. Where are you?"

"I'm still at the blast site."

"Any updates?"

"One. My CI was one of the men killed."

"*Your* CI?"

"Yes. It's a long story, but he and Kevin connected. Anyway, he'd given Kevin the information about the warehouse, he tried to meet with me to give me pictures he'd stolen from Bianchi and

I got shot at, and now he winds up dead? I don't think that's a coincidence."

"No. I don't either."

"So I'm going to stay here and see what else floats to the surface."

"Keep me posted."

Izzy bit her lip and let her gaze take in the organized chaos still going on. "I will. And let me know if I need to come to the hospital."

"Praying that won't be necessary."

"Yes. Me too."

Izzy hung up with her mother and said a prayer for her brothers before focusing back on the scene. Truthfully, she'd done everything she could here. Ryan caught her eye and she noted the fatigue on his face. She was sure hers looked the same.

He walked over. "Are you ready to go?"

"Yes."

"Bianchi got away."

"Again."

"He knew we were coming."

"Yep." She followed him to the car and noted that the two men with the SUV were gone. She wondered if Linc had managed to pick them up. She sent him a text and asked.

Got them. Questioning them. Will be in touch.

Okay. I'd appreciate being kept in the loop.

If I can.

Izzy tucked her phone away and dropped her chin to her chest and closed her eyes. *God, I hope you're here. Somewhere. Because I sure don't see you.*

TUESDAY

28

Izzy's phone buzzed, waking her out of a light doze. At first she couldn't figure out what she was doing in the recliner, then remembered Ryan had followed her home to Chloe's. Chloe had already been in bed, so she and Ryan had stayed in the den talking. That's the last she remembered.

She'd fallen asleep. Mid-sentence probably. Ryan had crashed on Chloe's couch. Probably too tired to drive home. Or too worried about Hulk showing up.

Izzy sat up with a gasp and grabbed her phone. "Derek." A quick glance at the screen dispelled her initial fear.

Ryan rolled off the couch with a thud and rubbed his eyes. "What is it? What's wrong?"

"Nothing. It's David." She lifted the phone to her ear. "Hello?"

"I need you to come in when you can. I might have something on that video from Kevin's phone."

"Okay, but I just woke up. Can't you just tell me what it is?"

Silence.

"David?"

Ryan's eyes met hers and he raised a brow. She shrugged.

"I'm thinking," David said. "And no. I think this is something you need to see for yourself."

She frowned. "Okay."

"And I need you to come in now if you can. I've been here since last night and today's my day off. I'm beat."

"I understand. I'm on duty today at noon. It'll have to be now." Polls closed at 7:00 p.m. The winner's speech wouldn't be until nine o'clock in the evening. It was going to be a long day.

"Good, I'll be waiting."

"All right, I'll get there as quickly as possible."

"Fine. See you in a bit." He hung up.

"What was that all about?" Chloe asked from the doorway. She had her hair in a towel but was dressed for the day. "Is Derek okay?"

"That wasn't about Derek. As far as I know, he made it through the night. Can you call Mom and find out?"

"Sure."

Izzy turned to Ryan. "David got something off the video from Kevin's phone. He wants us there quickly so he can show us and leave."

Chloe pulled her phone from her pocket. "There's another shower in the guest room if you want to use it."

Ryan nodded. "Thanks. I need a change of clothes too. How fast can you get ready?" he asked Izzy.

"Give me ten minutes."

True to her statement, she was ready in nine. She followed Ryan out of Chloe's house and waited while Ryan gave his vehicle a thorough inspection. "All clear," he said.

She climbed into the passenger seat. "Let's go."

Thirty minutes later, Izzy's rubber-soled shoes made very little sound on the tile floor that led to David's office. He'd sounded so odd, as though he wanted to tell her something, but . . . didn't want to.

She knocked on the door and stepped inside. Ryan followed her. "What's up?"

David turned from the monitor. "Tell me what you think about this." Izzy perched on the edge of the chair opposite the monitor while Ryan took up a spot behind her. David hit the play button on the remote and the footage began to roll.

It was the same thing they'd seen in Ryan's home, but magnified, the details clearer, sharper.

"There," David said. "See that person in the office? Watch." He let the footage play.

Izzy leaned in as though that would help. The video was taken through the glass from where Kevin crouched behind the crates. She could make out Tony Bianchi standing with his back to the glass. Every so often, he'd move slightly and she'd get a glimpse of someone seated in the far left corner.

"It gets a little grainy when he zooms in," David said, "but just keep watching."

Finally, Bianchi moved aside, leaving a clear view of the woman he'd been talking to. Izzy let out a gasp. Ryan's hand came down on her shoulder like a vise. The woman stood and snatched an envelope off the desk and looked inside. She pulled out a sheet of paper, examined it, then returned it to the envelope with a nod. She picked up her purse and headed toward the office's exit door.

Bianchi walked out of the office, conversed with the three men on the warehouse floor. David stopped the video and Izzy turned slowly to look up at Ryan, whose hand still rested on her shoulder. "What is she doing there?"

"What does it look like?" he asked through tight lips.

"So it's who I thought it was?" David asked.

Izzy nodded. "Yes. That's Melissa Endicott's campaign manager and my friend, Gabby Sinclair."

29

Izzy stood. Her pasty white face scared Ryan. "Izzy, sit back down."

She didn't seem to hear him.

"What is she doing with him? Taking money?"

"Izzy—"

"What are we going to do? What am I going to do? I have to turn her in. I have to tell someone. I have to—"

He gripped her upper arms and jerked her to a halt. Her mouth snapped shut and she swayed. If he hadn't been holding her, she would have toppled over. Her eyes met his and the anguish in their depths nearly stopped his heart. "She was there. She was there when Kevin was killed," she whispered. "She was there and she ran and she knew all along who shot him. How could she?"

Ryan shot a look at David. The color in his face was nearly identical to Izzy's. "You could have given her a heads-up, man," Ryan said.

"I—I wasn't sure what to do. I wasn't even sure if I was seeing it right and I wanted her confirmation."

"I guess you got it."

"Yeah. So, what now?" David asked.

"Derek," Izzy said. "I have to talk to Derek. He was there. He saw her. He had to have seen her."

"Iz, we need to keep this quiet for a bit. This is all just circumstantial. We don't know why she was there. And besides, Derek's not in any condition to talk right now."

"Well, it's quite possible," David said, "depending on his location in the warehouse, that he never would have seen Ms. Sinclair."

"What? How?" Izzy said.

"You didn't finish it," David said. "She actually left through the door that is attached to the office. She wasn't in the building when Kevin was shot. That happened a few seconds later."

"But she had to have heard it," Ryan said.

"And she left," Izzy repeated.

Seeing her best friend in Bianchi's office had been a massive blow for Izzy. He suspected she might even be suffering from shock. He gave her a light shake. "Don't jump to conclusions."

She shook her head, but her eyes never left the screen where her friend stayed frozen, the evidence undeniable. "I'm not. Now. No, that's not true. I'm jumping to conclusions because there's no reason other than criminal behavior for her to be meeting with Bianchi. I was—am—just shocked. But there's got to be an explanation." She turned her eyes back on Ryan. "But why would Kevin want me to hide the phone? Was he trying to protect Gabby for some weird reason?" She shook her head. "No. It had to be Derek. He was protecting Derek."

"No, I don't think he was trying to protect anyone," Ryan said.

"What do you think then?"

"I think by telling you to hide the phone, he knew you'd find a way to look at it to see what he wanted to hide and find this. Exactly what you did."

"Maybe."

"No maybe about it."

"Why didn't he just tell me?"

———

Ga-ga-baahhhh . . .

Kevin's last sound echoed in her mind. She didn't need to see it on screen to remember it. "Actually, maybe he did try," she said softly. "At the end. I just didn't know what he meant. I thought he was just trying to breathe and he was really trying to say 'Gabby.'"

"His first priority was to make sure the phone didn't fall into the wrong hands. Once he realized you had it hidden, he may have figured he would die, but he wasn't going without a fight—and without making sure you'd look at his phone."

Sobs crowded her throat. "He said to tell you he was sorry. That he was stupid and that he was sorry."

Ryan stilled. "You didn't tell me that."

"It's actually on the video," David said quietly. "I just didn't play that part for you guys."

"Let me see."

"No," Izzy said. "Maybe later. Don't relive it right now." She couldn't. It was all too much. She rubbed her eyes as waves of despair, anger, and confusion rolled through her. "I have to talk to her."

"Yes. But let's wait until after the election."

"Why?"

"It could be she's got nothing to do with him. Could be the new wannabe mayor sent him a message via her campaign manager. Could be a lot of things."

"Or it could mean the new wannabe mayor is in bed with the Mafia, and once she's in power, so to speak, things will go Bianchi's way and more cops will die."

"Could be. Let's keep looking into this. Like Sinclair's financials. As well as Endicott's."

"We don't have time to wait on the financial stuff. Gabby is in the video no matter what information comes back on the money. I say we go find Gabby and see what she has to say for herself," Izzy said.

"I have to admit, that's my first reaction too." Ryan rubbed his chin. "We'll have to be careful about how we approach this."

"Yeah, as in you can't be investigating this. Charice and I can do it." He shot her a baleful glare. "Seriously, Ryan. You don't want to jeopardize this."

"I know that. And I won't. I'm not investigating Kevin's death, I'm going after a man who's killed a lot of cops and is passing money to political figureheads. But that's not what I meant."

"So what did you mean?"

"I meant that the election is today. If Endicott had no idea that her campaign manager was cozying up to Bianchi, then we don't want to do anything to sway the election."

"But if she does know, then we sure don't want her elected!"

He sighed. "I think we need to bring Linc in on this."

"Linc?"

"Yeah. He's got a lot more resources than we do and can get information a lot faster. Let's go ahead and ask him to get Gabby's financial information—as well as Endicott's."

Izzy nodded. "That's a good idea. I'll call him."

She stepped out of the room and dialed her brother's number. He didn't pick up, so she hung up and tried again. Still no answer. "Linc, this is super important. I need you to call me ASAP."

Her phone buzzed in her hand. She lifted the device to her ear. "Hey."

"What's up, Iz?"

She told him what they'd found on the video.

"I'll see if I can get a warrant rushed through for her bank, any other financials, real property, and phone records. If she's been talking to Bianchi, that may be the opening we need to find him. Get your guy to send the video over to me."

"Can you track him through his cell if Gabby's been talking to him?"

"Possibly."

"Let me know."

"I will. Good work, Izzy."

She hung up and told the guys what Linc had said. "Now what?"

"We pay Gabby a little visit," Ryan said.

"Now?"

"Yes."

This time Ryan's phone interrupted them. "Yeah, Charice?" he said into the device. "Uh-huh." More listening. More frowning. "He's got what? Yeah, yeah, I heard you. Okay, thanks. Keep me updated with anything else." He hung up and shook his head. "Things just keep getting more and more confusing."

"What was that about?" Izzy asked.

"Charice said they watched surveillance footage to see who might have visited Timmons in prison. The only one who came to see him was one of his buddies who was at the warehouse when Kevin was killed. Peter Leahy."

"What was he doing there?"

"Interesting enough, after he finished talking to Timmons, he had a little visit with a guy by the name of Spike George."

Izzy frowned. "Who's that?"

"A member of the Bloods in prison for murder."

"But Timmons is a member of the Crips. Why would he visit his ene—" The light went on. "He got George to kill Timmons."

Ryan nodded. "Looks that way. What self-respecting Blood would turn down the opportunity to kill a Crip?" He held up a finger. "But there's more."

"What?"

"Charice got a tip on Leahy's location. She and Harry and a couple of others went to see him."

"They get him?"

"Yeah. And when she put the cuffs on him, she found fake Bloods tats on his arms."

Izzy simply stared. A gang member would never put another

gang's symbols on his or her body. "That's just . . . what? I'm so confused."

"Tell me about it." He rubbed a hand over his head. "He didn't want them to be permanent. They're henna tattoos so they'll fade in a few days."

"But why?"

"Charice didn't know, but it means something, that's for sure."

Izzy rubbed her head. Her brain hurt. "So, Leahy went to visit Timmons, who is a Crips member. Then he goes to visit George, who is a Bloods member. George kills Timmons . . . did George think Leahy was a member of the Bloods? Because of the Bloods tattoos?"

Ryan sighed. "It's very possible." He scrubbed his chin. "We may not get an answer for that, so let's go back to what we were working on before that popped up. Charice is keeping in touch with the gangs division, so she'll fill me in if she gets an update—or if Leahy decides to talk."

"Right."

"Yeah." He rubbed his hands. "Now. I think we both know who's going to win the election," Ryan said.

"Yes . . . and?"

"What time is it?"

Izzy looked at her watch. "10:15."

"Do you think Gabby would be at home? Or at the campaign headquarters?"

"I don't know. I can text her and ask if she's home." She paused. "No, wait. If we're going to do a face-to-face, I don't want to go to her house. Let's get her to meet us somewhere for coffee or something."

"I'd rather not. We don't need an audience."

"Then I'll ask her to come to Chloe's place."

Ryan sighed. "Why are you being so difficult? What does it matter?"

"Because Mick is at her house!"

"Who's Mick?"

"The man who kidnapped me and held me hostage at knifepoint for four hours!"

The stunned look on Ryan's and David's faces would have been funny if she'd been going for shock value. She hadn't been. She'd just lost control of her filters for a split second and blurted out that piece of news she and her family had worked so hard to keep quiet, out of the media spotlight, and . . . truthfully, out of her mind. And now she'd just announced it to the two men standing in front of her, who still hadn't moved or closed their jaws.

She sighed. "So, can we meet somewhere else?"

Ryan finally managed to close his mouth and find his voice. "Uh, sure. Wait a minute. What? What do you mean he kidnapped you at knifepoint? Why didn't I know that?"

"Drop it for now, will you? Let's focus on what we need to get done. I can tell you that story later."

He wanted to argue, but she was right. They needed to talk to Gabby. "Fine. Where does she live?"

"Off Summit Parkway."

"So there's probably a Starbucks nearby."

Relief flickered in her eyes. "Of course."

He searched on his phone and gave her the address. "Ask her to meet us there. Chloe's place is out of the way for her and she might not want to do that."

Izzy hit the speed-dial button. Ryan noticed the fine tremor in her fingers and planned to find out exactly what had happened to her and exactly who Mick was. Because right now, Mick was living on borrowed time as far as Ryan was concerned.

"Hey, Gabby, it's Izzy. I know you're crazy busy, but something's come up and we need to talk."

Ryan was impressed. She sounded completely relaxed and normal.

"I was wondering if you were free to meet for coffee or something in about thirty minutes. I know this is a busy time for you with the election today, so . . . uh-huh."

She closed her eyes and drew in a breath. If he'd been on the other end of the line, he never would have figured she was visibly trembling.

"I see. Your house? Gab, can't we just do Starbucks? I—you can't? You have to stay . . . yes. Well, I don't think—"

Ryan motioned for her to say yes. She widened her eyes at him and shook her head. But he was ready to do whatever it took to get Gabby to agree to meet. He nodded more forcefully. "You can stay in the car," he whispered.

Finally she sighed. "Fine. Okay. An hour?" She glanced at Ryan and he nodded. "I'll see you in about an hour."

She hung up. "Why'd you do that?"

"Because she was going to say no."

Izzy rubbed her forehead. "She's crazy busy with the election. The fact that I'm asking to meet her . . ." She bit her lip, then sighed. "I'm just afraid she's going to know something's up."

"How did she sound?"

"Frazzled."

"Good. Maybe we can catch her off guard then."

"How in the world are we going to put this together that fast?"

"Charice passed the background investigation off to another detective and is working on the warrant now, Linc can grab a tech who won't mind bringing you the wire, and I can get a team together while all that's going on."

"What if she can't get a warrant this fast?"

"We'll plead exigent circumstances with the election in progress."

"That's pretty flimsy circumstances."

"I'm willing to take my chances. Are you?"

She was. She wanted to talk to Gabby as bad as he did. She still hesitated though. "But—"

"No buts. Call Linc while I start making this happen. We'll do this if I have to call in every favor I'm owed from every person in this city."

Izzy gave a slow nod. "Okay, then. Let's do it." She grabbed her phone and dialed Linc's number.

30

Izzy, Ryan, Charice, and other officers descended upon Gabby's home in a silent and organized fashion. The majority of law enforcement stayed back. Ryan was ordered to stay in the surveillance van. Izzy reluctantly wore the wire. She still wasn't sure how she'd been convinced to do so when all she'd planned to do was stay in the car.

But she'd donned the wire on the ride over to Gabby's and was mentally trying to figure out what she would say when she saw her friend.

There had to be a reasonable explanation for Gabby's meeting with Bianchi. But she'd left the scene of a shooting—and she had fifty grand wired and pending deposit into her account tonight. The money had been traced back to an offshore account belonging to Bricks & Sticks. Tony Bianchi had paid her some big bucks for . . . what?

Izzy was determined to find out.

She looked for any sign of Mick's vehicle and didn't see one. That fact allowed her to breathe a little easier.

She walked up to the door and turned the knob. Only to find it locked. Izzy frowned. She always just walked in when Gabby was expecting her.

Izzy rang the bell, dread centering itself in her midsection.

"Officer St. John?"

She didn't recognize the voice that came through her earpiece. "Yes?"

"What's the problem?"

"She's not answering." This time Izzy rang the bell, then knocked. Loud.

The dread morphed into a full-blown sinking feeling when silence was her only answer. "She ran," she said.

That's why Mick's car wasn't there.

"Search the house," the same voice said. "Let's go."

Izzy backed slowly from the house. "Be careful. Whoever she's working with likes to play with bombs." Because there was no way Gabby was working alone. In her gut, Izzy knew her friend was a part of something bigger, something that they'd only scratched the surface of.

Izzy's comment triggered a call for a bomb dog. The dog and handler arrived seven minutes after the call, along with the rest of the bomb squad in their big armored truck.

Ryan wasn't familiar with the human and K-9 duo, but he was immediately impressed with their professionalism. Once the K-9 cleared the area around the door, Izzy lifted the welcome mat and retrieved a key. She handed it to one of the officers and he opened the door to the home.

The dog led the way inside, his nose twitching, ears swiveling. It didn't take long to clear the inside, and Charice gave the nod for the rest of the team to proceed. "Look for anything that might tell us where she's gone."

Then they were inside the house.

Ryan followed, bringing up the rear. Waiting in the van wasn't his strong suit. He'd hang back, but he wanted to see what was happening.

Each officer pulled on gloves and little blue shoe covers and went to work. Ryan followed Izzy, who went straight to Gabby's in-home office. "She took her laptop."

"Of course she did."

Izzy's gloved hands worked fast. She pulled out the top drawer and set it on the desk in front of Ryan. "Don't touch. You can watch, but don't touch."

"Right." He moved back a little.

"What are you doing in here, Ryan?" Charice asked from the doorway.

Ryan held up his hands. "Nothing. I promise. Just an observer."

Charice sighed and walked over to Izzy. "What do you have?"

"If she kept something important, it would have been on her laptop or around her desk. She's not a neat freak, but she is organized." Izzy lightly rubbed her T-shirt where the wire rested, then placed the rest of the drawers on the desk and nodded to Charice. "Let's start here." She paused. "But first, I'm taking this wire off. The tape is itching me to death."

She stepped into the hall bath and removed the wire. Red welts stared back at her where the tape had irritated her skin. No wonder she was getting distracted. What a relief to have the tape off.

Back in the office, she handed the wire to Ryan and jumped in to help with the search.

In the second drawer, Izzy found several months of bank statements that Gabby had probably been meaning to file. A thought hit her. "The bank," she said.

Ryan looked up from his spot near the door. "What?"

"She's not going to leave without taking that money with her." She gave him the name of the bank. "But which branch will she go to? The closest one? Or one a bit farther away?"

Ryan started dialing. "I've got the banks covered. You keep looking."

Izzy's phone buzzed. A text from a number she didn't recognize.

> If you don't want one of your family members
> to die, find a private place to call me and keep
> this to yourself. I have someone there watching
> you, so do as you're told.

She froze at the signature.

Gabby?

Izzy stared at the text for a few seconds while her mind blipped different options at warp speed and her heart thudded with renewed adrenaline. Tell the others or not? She looked up and met Ryan's gaze. He raised a brow.

Her phone buzzed again and she glanced back at the screen.

> I know you saw the text, Izzy. I got the little read
> notice. CALL ME on this number.

It wasn't worth the risk until she knew more. "Excuse me a minute."

Ryan frowned. "What is it?"

"I need to make a call. I'm just going to step outside."

Izzy didn't acknowledge his frown, she simply walked through the house and out the front door.

Standing on the porch, she dialed the number Gabby texted her from. Her friend answered on the first ring. "Thank you. Now listen—"

"How did you know we knew?" Izzy asked.

Gabby cleared her throat. "Several things." She sounded breathless. Nervous. "Um, but the main one being you never asked if Mick would be there. And two, I know about the video that Kevin took in the warehouse. I know that I'm probably on it. You hadn't accessed it when we had lunch that day. You were clueless, but I knew it was only a matter of time. I was . . . um . . . trying to get the phone before you found a way to watch whatever Kevin recorded."

Her former friend sounded odd. Almost as though she was reading the words she was speaking.

"So you sent Lamar Young to kill me," Izzy said, keeping her voice low.

"No, no. I mean . . . well, not kill you, just to . . . um . . . get the phone."

"But if I had to die in the process, that was okay."

"Izzy . . ." Did she hear tears in her voice? Gabby did the throat-clearing thing again. "I didn't set out on this course in life, Izzy. But my baby brother means everything to me and I can't help him if I don't have money." She paused. "Now, enough chitchat. I know you have questions, but they're going to have to remain unanswered right now."

"Where's Mick? With you?"

"Um . . . Mick's not your business anymore, remember?" Her voice trembled.

"Right." She paused. "Gabby, are you okay? I'm having a hard time believing this is all your idea."

She had to find a way to alert Ryan.

"Get the iPad from the cabinet behind my desk and bring it to me," Gabby said.

The change in subject allowed Izzy to take a deep breath. "You said you have someone here watching me. Why don't you get your friend here to bring it?"

"Izzy, the people who are in control are not nice people, in case you haven't figured that out."

"I've sort of noticed. Gab, we know Bianchi wired fifty thousand dollars to your account."

Silence, then a strangled sound came over the line. "I . . . I'm not talking about that right now. Get the iPad in the cabinet behind my desk if you want to save your father's life."

Izzy stilled. "What? My *father*?"

"Yes. They're watching him right now."

Her phone buzzed and she glanced at the text. A picture of her father sitting outside, having coffee with the mayor. No doubt supporting his friend while the voters did their duty. An easy target for someone with a rifle and a scope.

"Just do what you're told and I'll give you the information you need to save him. Get the iPad and text this number and I'll tell you where to meet me. Alone. And . . . and if anyone comes with you or follows you, he's . . . he's dead. You have five minutes."

Gabby hung up.

31

Ryan noted that the officer had finished going through the last drawer of the desk and found nothing. He stood with his hands on his hips and perused the room. Where was Izzy?

Charice had moved on to the cabinet behind the desk and was carefully removing everything in it.

Izzy stepped back into the room and stopped just inside the doorway. She scanned the room, her eyes landing on each person in it.

Ryan frowned. What was she looking for?

He almost walked over to ask her when she drew in a deep breath and headed for Charice and the cabinet. She opened the door on the right and started helping by removing the items one by one.

"Everything okay?"

She glanced at him, then at the others working behind her. "Fine."

"You don't look fine."

"Sorry. I just found out my friend is in cahoots with a killer. I'm a little stressed."

She continued to work and Ryan continued to frown. He supposed that was a reasonable explanation, but she was different than before the call. He didn't think anyone else would notice the slight difference, but he did.

His phone rang and he snagged it with one last look at Izzy. She'd crouched in front of the lower part of the cabinet and was pulling items out. He sighed. "Yeah?"

"This is David."

"Hey, what's up?"

"I . . . uh . . . was playing around with that video Kevin took and I managed to get some sound from the office. It *sounds* like Sinclair said something like, 'He expects to see it there no later than eleven o'clock Tuesday night.' Granted, I had to piece together what I could clearly hear and then fill in the blanks, but that's what I've come up with."

"Money. Whoever she's working with is expecting to see money in an account."

"That was my first thought too."

"We need to get a warrant to watch the account and see where the money comes from."

"Yep. I left a message for Charice to take care of that since you're not investigating this. Since it has something to do with Kevin's death and all."

Ryan shook his head. "No, David, I'm being good, I promise." But he would stay in the loop and make sure everything was being done that could be done.

Tobias Freeman.

A man who was still on the loose.

He drew in a deep breath. "Thanks for the heads-up, though. And good work."

Ryan hung up and turned around to see Charice still working with Izzy at her side. "Charice."

"Yeah?"

"Check your phone messages."

She frowned and pulled her phone off the clip on her belt.

Izzy sighed and leaned her head against the cabinet. Ryan walked over to her and placed a hand on her shoulder. She turned and looked up at him, tears in her eyes. "This shouldn't be happening. It's not fair," she whispered.

He wrapped her in a hug and inhaled her scent, not caring about the people in the room. They knew him. Some of them had known Kevin. They'd understand.

Only she didn't hug him back. She tugged on the front pocket of his jeans and he leaned back to look in her eyes. She tugged again and he frowned. Then she pulled away and swiped the tears that had leaked onto her cheeks. "Sorry. Excuse me, I need to get ahold of myself."

"Down the hall and to the left." The officer who spoke had a sympathetic smile.

Izzy nodded. "Thanks."

She left and Ryan watched her go. Casually, he slid both hands into his pockets and sighed, met the officer's eyes, and shook his head. She'd taken his keys. What was she doing?

"Sorry about Kevin, man."

"Thanks. Me too."

"She's taking it hard."

"We all are." As he spoke, his fingers curled around a piece of paper Izzy had tucked into his pocket after she'd palmed his keys. He got it. She was being discreet. Didn't want anyone to know what she was doing for some reason. What *was* she doing? He turned. "Charice?"

"Yeah?"

"You get that message?"

"I got it. I'll let you know if I hear anything else."

"Thanks."

With another nod to the vigilant officer, Ryan followed the route Izzy had taken and walked outside to see her climbing into the front seat of his car. What the—

"Izzy?"

Her eyes met his as she slammed the door. He pulled the paper out of his pocket and read, "Gabby called. Wants me to help her escape or she'll kill my dad. Someone here is watching. Follow me discreetly."

Ryan stood for a moment, his blood humming, adrenaline kicking in while his mind went to work on a plan. First, he needed a car. Then he'd warn Izzy's father that someone was targeting him. He spotted a detective he knew and walked over, casually. "Hey, Jack, I need your car."

"What? Why?"

"Don't ask. It's important."

Jack pulled his keys from his pocket. "You need backup?"

"Not yet, but stand by. I have a feeling things are going to get messy."

"Ryan—"

"I've got to go." Izzy's taillights came on as she slowed to turn right onto the street that led out of the subdivision.

Ryan climbed in the car and pulled away from the curb. When he looked in the rearview mirror, he noticed the officer from the room he and Izzy had been searching.

He got on his phone and called Jack.

"Yeah?" The man's voice came through his Bluetooth.

"This is Ryan. Keep an eye on the officer standing on the front porch. If he tries to call anyone, stop him. I'll explain later."

"Got it."

Ryan appreciated fellow officers who would act without question. He accelerated to stay behind Izzy and activated his phone to allow him to send a voice text. When he had the chief's number, he sent the text to her work phone. Every one of her officers had the number and it was only used in an emergency. No one dared overstep the bounds and use it for anything else. She immediately responded.

Meet me in ten minutes.

Can't. They're watching. Be casual about it, but
get Marcus somewhere safe where a sniper
can't see him.

Will do. And Izzy?

Following her. I have her back.

You need backup.

Will call for it when I know where to send them.

Be safe.

He caught sight of her just ahead, saw the taillights flicker just
before she made a left.

Ryan stayed far enough behind so that if anyone had followed
or was watching him somehow, they wouldn't suspect he was following Izzy. He hoped. For a moment, he lost sight of her as she
went around the next corner, the large church blocking his view.

Several seconds later, he turned and braked. Izzy wasn't in front
of him. Nor to the right. And not to the left. Tensing, he turned
right and drove fast, looking at every car he passed. Braking, he
executed a flawless three-point turn and went back the other way.

Still no Izzy. He returned to the place where he'd lost her. How
had she vanished so quickly?

He studied the church for a brief second, then gunned the motor
and turned into the parking lot. Where could she have gone? It was
like someone had simply snatched her and the vehicle and simply
vanished. Since that wasn't possible, he drove slowly around the
perimeter of the parking lot that led around to the other side of
the building.

And there she was. Or at least there his car was.

She'd parked in one of the back parking spaces not being used by the voters crowding the area. Ryan pulled up next to the vehicle and climbed out of his borrowed unmarked car. A quick look in through the window told him what he'd already suspected.

She wasn't in the driver's seat.

So where had she gone? Had she taken off on foot?

No. Someone had picked her up and she'd left her phone on the front seat. His gut clenched.

He'd lost her.

Izzy had followed Gabby's directions to the letter. Drive to the church and park, facing the police vehicle toward the wooded area behind the back of the building. She'd had a feeling Gabby planned to pick her up and make her leave her phone and she'd racked her brain on how to leave a trail someone could follow once they found the vehicle.

The transfer to Gabby's car had taken less than a minute and then they were off, driving away from the direction from which she'd come.

"Tell me how to save my father."

Gabby shot her a pleading look and glanced at the rearview mirror. "I can't. I don't know." She tapped her ear and Izzy understood. They were listening. Probably through the Bluetooth function of the vehicle. "Did you bring the iPad?" Gabby asked.

"Yes." Izzy pulled it from where she'd tucked it into the waistband of her pants. It had taken some maneuvering, but she'd managed to do it without Charice or anyone seeing her. While she was on the floor in front of the open cabinet, she'd pulled a sheet from the stack of printer paper and grabbed a pen from the cup on the desk. She'd written the note to Ryan, folded it, and then tried to figure out how to pass it to him without sparking interest in her interaction with him.

It hadn't been hard to bring the tears to the surface. And Ryan had reacted like she'd expected him to. With a hug of comfort. She'd deliberately pulled on his pockets in a desperate attempt to make sure he checked them. Lifting his keys had been easy, as they'd been halfway out of his pocket anyway.

"Where are we going?" she asked.

"A little out-of-the-way place that no one knows about."

"Owned by who?"

"I . . . I don't know." Another frightened glance at the mirror.

Fear curled inside her. The fact that Gabby hadn't tied her up or blindfolded her told Izzy that the threat against her father was real. Gabby knew her well enough to know she wouldn't try anything without getting what she needed to save her father. But not only was the threat against her father real if Izzy didn't cooperate, the threat to Izzy was also real. They weren't going to just let her go once they got to where they were going. No blindfold, no one other than Gabby to pick her up. What did that mean?

"Gabby, just drive me to the police station. I'll help you."

Her friend's eyes filled with tears that leaked onto her cheeks. She shook her head and gripped the steering wheel. "I can't," she whispered.

"What does he have on you?"

"He?"

"Yes."

"N-Nothing."

"Who is he?" she asked. "I think I at least deserve to know who's going to kill me," she said.

Gabby gasped. "He's not going to kill you. He said he just needed you out of the way for the plan to work."

Frowning, Izzy racked her brain and came up empty. "What plan?"

"I don't know. I'm sorry."

"Gab—"

Her jaw hardened and she sent another frantic glance to the rearview mirror. "No, I can't. Please, please, be quiet."

Izzy fell silent. Not because Gabby begged her to, but because she needed to think.

They drove for the next half hour in silence and Izzy decided that someone was definitely pulling her friend's strings. Someone had terrorized her into being their puppet—and with having her be the one to pick up the money from Bianchi and have the money trail leading back to her, it was obvious they were setting her up to take the fall should they be caught.

Now Izzy had to figure out how to escape without putting her father in danger—and figure out what they'd threatened Gabby with. Maybe that they'd hurt Mick?

While Izzy didn't know their final destination, the signs indicated Lake Wateree.

Gabby finally turned down a wooded road that led to a small house set on about two acres of property. Through the trees, Izzy spotted a lake in back, with a large basketball court–sized yard sloping gently down to it. Wind shook the few trees near the house, bending them with its force. Clouds had rolled in and it looked like a thunderstorm would soon hit. Izzy wondered if she could somehow use that to her advantage.

"Who owns this place?" she asked.

"I don't know that either. He didn't tell me."

Izzy was going to have to go with the flow for now. She had no way of knowing if the person watching her father was still there, waiting for Gabby to give the word to shoot or stand down or what.

"Those weren't your words on the phone call getting me here, were they? You were reading something."

Gabby nodded.

"What did you mean by you'll give me the information that I need to save my dad? Don't you just mean you'll call off your sniper as long as I help you do whatever it is you need me to do?"

"I don't know, Izzy! I don't know what he's doing or why he's doing it. He's obsessed with you and he's—" She snapped her lips shut and tears streamed down her cheeks. "Come on. Get out, please."

Izzy went cold, but obeyed. She opened the door and stepped out. "Mick's behind this, isn't he?"

"Yes," Gabby whispered. "And I'll protect you as much as I can, I promise."

Mick Sinclair. She hadn't realized it until now, but he was a bigger nightmare than Lamar Young would ever be. To Young, she'd been a job. But for Mick, this was personal.

Gabby's tears streamed. "I'm so sorry, Izzy, you're a cop. I was hoping you could help me."

"Tell me. Fast. We're not in the car so he can't hear us."

She shot a terrified glance at the house. "Mick and the guy I was seeing were just using me. To get as much information about the election as they could get."

"Why?"

"Get in here!"

The shout came from behind the open front door and Gabby flinched. The voice was familiar, but Izzy couldn't place it. She took Izzy's hand and led her toward the house.

Izzy slowed the pace, trying to gain as much information as she could. "What are they threatening you with to get you to cooperate?"

"My mother. They'll kill my mother."

That would do it. Gabby adored her mother. And Mick hated her because she saw right through him. Izzy had no doubt he'd follow through on his threat if he had to.

"Move it! Now!"

Gabby hurried her along. Kidnapped twice in less than two years. Izzy wondered how many people could say that. A fat raindrop landed on her cheek and she giggled as the wind whipped around her. She walked into the house and Gabby glanced at her with a puzzled look.

Izzy realized she was borderline hysterical and clamped her lips together. She had no time for that and forced herself to calm. She had to stay cool and in control of her emotions—her fear. Once indoors, she saw that the home was a typical ranch. Probably three bedrooms and two baths. Den straight ahead through the foyer, formal living room to the right, and kitchen off the den.

And a basement off the kitchen.

She noted all of this as Gabby directed her toward the den.

And when she stepped into the room, she stopped and stared. Tobias Freeman, the man who'd killed Kevin, stood next to the recliner, a gun pointed at her. He tossed the duct tape to Gabby. "Secure her and be quick about it."

"I'll do it."

Izzy froze at the familiar voice and fear crystallized in her blood. She prayed she could keep it from showing on her face. Gabby had told her Mick was there, and Izzy had tried to prepare herself for it in the few seconds it took them to get into the house. But there was no preparation for coming face-to-face with one's biggest terror. Turning, she watched Mick Sinclair walk into the room, and the cold smile on his face nearly sent her to her knees.

32

Ryan ran a hand through his hair. It was now two o'clock in the afternoon and he still didn't know where Izzy was—or how to find her. CSU was combing the vehicle, but Ryan didn't hold out hope they'd find anything. Izzy had driven here under her own power and she'd probably gotten into the other car without protest.

A fact that the security camera on the church would probably verify once the church's security team finished pulling it up.

Her phone lay on the front seat. Where was her weapon? He tried the door. Locked. She'd probably locked her gun in the glove compartment. He had no doubt her captor wouldn't allow her to bring it with her, and she'd make it as hard as possible to steal.

Brady swung into the parking lot and climbed out of his vehicle. Ryan frowned as the man limped over. "Where is she?"

"Gone. Charice is working with church security to get the footage from that camera." He pointed to the corner of the building.

"You lost her."

"Yeah." Ryan placed his hands on his hips and waited for the man to rake him over the coals for losing his sister.

Surprisingly, he didn't.

One of the CSU team members walked over holding a large rock. Ryan's heart dipped. "Blood?"

"No, not at all. It was jammed in the GPS launcher."

"What?"

"Yeah. It was weird enough I thought I'd mention it to you."

"That's my girl," Ryan muttered. "It was jammed because she wanted to bring attention to it."

Ryan hoofed it over to the front of his police vehicle and crouched in front of the grill. About a year ago, all law enforcement vehicles had been equipped with a GPS launcher that enabled officers to "tag" a vehicle that refused to pull over.

High-speed chases were dangerous for everyone involved, including innocent motorists. Once tagged, the officer simply backed off and used the computer to track the vehicle via the GPS "bullet" fired from the machine.

Ryan slapped the hood of the car. "A bullet's missing. Let's get those coordinates for that." He turned and patted the CSU member's shoulder. "Good work."

"Thanks."

Now he just had to pray Izzy still had the bullet on her somewhere and that Gabby wouldn't come across it before they could get a lock on it.

Charice stepped out of the church and hurried over to him. "I've got the footage. It's grainy, but you can see what went down." She handed him her phone and he tapped the screen to play the video.

Izzy's car pulled into the parking lot and into the spot. People moved in and out of the building. Voters. Ryan kept his focus on Izzy. She got out of the car when another car pulled in beside her. She ducked down at the front of his vehicle with just her head showing.

Making sure Gabby wasn't going to shoot her? More like she was buying time, getting the rock to jam the GPS launcher open. She stayed at the front of the vehicle for another moment. Jamming the launcher?

Gabby never got out of her car, but Izzy stood when the woman

294

rolled her window down. The two talked for another moment and Izzy gestured as she spoke. Gabby responded. Then Izzy pulled her ponytail tighter, walked over to Gabby's vehicle and got in. And then they were gone.

"Smart," Charice said when Ryan explained what she'd done.

"Yes. Let's hope it's smart enough and we can find her before Gabby and whoever she's working with decide they don't need her anymore."

Izzy's hands were taped in front of her. Mick had patted her down, her glare not affecting him in the least. She'd left her phone and her weapon in Ryan's car per Gabby's order, but at least the GPS bullet she'd slid from the launcher was still in Gabby's vehicle.

Ryan had been following her. As soon as he realized he'd lost her, the search would commence. They'd find his abandoned car at some point, she just hoped it was sooner rather than later.

Unsure who she was going to be facing once they arrived at their destination, Izzy had decided the best place for the bullet was in the car. She'd dropped it into the small storage bin on the door and prayed it wouldn't roll around. Fortunately, old napkins had been left there and all of Gabby's turning hadn't dislodged the thing from the middle of them.

Now Gabby and Freeman were basically ignoring her while Mick's stare made her decidedly uneasy. They hadn't taped her mouth, just her hands and feet. She'd managed to work the tape slightly loose around her ankles, but there was nothing she could do about her hands.

Mick stood. "I'm going to check outside."

Freeman frowned at him. "There's nothing outside. Stay put and watch her."

"You don't tell me what to do." Mick's nostrils flared and his lips tightened.

"I do until the rest of the money comes in. If you want your share, you'll do what I say. Now, keep an eye on her and shut up."

Hefting the weapon from his waistband, Mick trailed the barrel down Izzy's cheek. She refused to flinch or look away, even as revulsion curled in her belly. Mick seemed to lose interest at her lack of reaction, shot a glare toward Freeman, then walked toward the door. "My sister might bow and scrape at your every demand, but I don't. I'll be outside for a few minutes."

Gabby's eyes darted nervously between her brother and Freeman, but she didn't say anything. When Mick finally closed the door behind him, Freeman threw his glass across the room. Gabby jumped. "This is your fault, you stupid woman!"

"Toby, stop—"

His hand shot out and caught Gabby on her right cheek. She cried out and went to her knees. Izzy winced. The backhanded hit had to sting.

"Get up," he ordered. "Then sit down and shut up. I didn't think I needed to tie you up, but I will."

Gabby crawled to the chair and pulled herself into it. Freeman returned to the table and went back to whatever it was he was working on.

Carefully, afraid one of them would look up from the table and catch her, she propped her elbows on her thighs, then leaned her head against her hands and palmed her eyes.

Izzy frowned and listened. The fact that they weren't trying to hide anything from her meant they didn't plan to let her live. Or at least Freeman didn't. Mick might want her alive, but she was pretty sure she might prefer death to what he had planned. And she was relatively sure that Toby didn't plan to let Gabby live either.

"Numbers one, two, three, and four need to be taken out," he muttered into his phone. "They're closest to the stage. Once that path is cleared, it's all open."

"What are you talking about?" Gabby said, her voice shaking, hand pressed to her fiery red cheek.

"You don't need to know. Tell Mick to get back in here."

With a sigh, Gabby went to the door and disappeared. Mick reentered and Freeman motioned for him to sit and pointed to the paper in front of him. Izzy noticed Gabby kept her wounded cheek out of her brother's line of sight as she joined Izzy on the couch.

"You got these covered?" Freeman asked Mick.

"Yeah, man, they're covered. How many times you want to go over it?"

Izzy braced herself at the explosive look on Toby's face. But he held on to his rage and jabbed the paper. "These four back here and off to the side—numbers sixteen, twelve, twenty-three, and—" He paused with a glance at Izzy. "We've already taken care of number twenty, but they'll probably replace her. These right here won't be in the way. By the time they react, it'll all be over. The others will have to be neutralized, though."

Izzy froze. Number twenty? What were the numbers? They obviously referred to people. People they needed to neutralize?

Derek's list instantly came to mind. *She* was number twenty on the list that Derek had sent her. They had to be talking about *that* list?

"I got it," Mick said and pulled his laptop from a bag and booted it up. "If you're so worried about it, why don't you check in with everyone and make sure they've got the plan down."

"What plan?" Izzy asked.

"None of your business," Freeman said without bothering to look up. Mick glared at her.

Gabby whimpered and Izzy reached out to clasp her hands in hers. They were cold and trembling. The woman was terrified.

While the men were otherwise occupied, Izzy gave Gabby's fingers a squeeze, then let go and lowered her head again to her hands. She found the seam of the tape with her tongue, then tried to grab it with her teeth. She managed to lift a corner.

"What are you doing?"

She dragged her hands down her face and met Freeman's eyes. "Praying."

"Well, stop."

"Right."

He rolled his eyes and went back to his laptop. This time Mick didn't bother looking up. Izzy went back to work on the tape. Only to stop and lower her hands when Gabby reached over and started helping her loosen it. It made a slight rasp as it released and Izzy coughed. "Could I have some water?"

"I'll get it," Gabby said. She rose and went into the kitchen.

"When do you get the rest of your money?" Izzy asked.

"As soon as the election results come in declaring Melissa the winner," Mick said.

"What if Eric wins?"

"He won't. Not if he cares about what happens to his family."

Izzy sucked in a breath. "You had him throw the election by threatening his family."

"Mick? Really?" Gabby stared at her brother as though she'd never seen him before.

He rolled his eyes. "Shut up about things that don't concern you."

Gabby snapped her lips shut and dropped her gaze. She walked back into the den and sat down next to Izzy.

"Gabby," Izzy whispered, turning to her friend, "why were you meeting with Tony Bianchi?"

She frowned and handed Izzy the cold bottle of water she'd removed from the refrigerator and uncapped. "Who?"

"The man in the warehouse the night Kevin got killed."

"I was picking up some money that he owed Mick. Mick asked me to go get it for him, so I did."

"That wasn't money Bianchi owed him. It was a payoff," she whispered.

"What? For what?"

"I'm not exactly sure, but it has to do with the election."

Izzy heard Freeman speaking to Mick and tuned in. "Text the guys and make sure they're ready."

Guys? How many people were involved in whatever was going on? And why weren't they asking her about helping them escape?

Because they didn't need her help. They needed a hostage later, after whatever it was they were planning. Gabby stood and walked over to the table.

A chill swept over Izzy. "Was my father ever in any danger?" she asked.

Freeman laughed and shook his head.

"Gab?"

"I don't know." She bit her trembling lip. "Probably. If you didn't do what he wanted."

"Yes. He was in danger, but now that you're here, he's not," Freeman said. "That what you need to hear? Now shut up and let us work."

Mick turned back to Freeman, who shoved something in front of him. "Two guns come from the right and two from the left. Four from behind the stage. More Bloods will be here and here."

Freeman tapped the item in front of him and Izzy realized Mick was looking at pictures.

The night of Kevin's death came back with clarity, then her mind jumped to the security footage where Bianchi was talking. *"Get the pictures and get out. Understand?"*

Then Louis's last words to her. *"I've got some pictures for you."* He'd been killed for those pictures. "What are the pictures of?"

Freeman slammed a fist onto the table. "Oh, for the love of . . . put some tape over her mouth, will you?"

Gabby flinched and shot Izzy a frightened look. Mick spotted his sister's face and he shot to his feet. "What happened to you?"

"He hit her," Izzy said.

Toby spun in his chair and aimed his weapon at her. "Shut up or I'll shoot you!"

"Or maybe I'll shoot you," Mick shouted. He lifted his hand toward Toby and the weapon cracked.

Izzy dove to the floor and rolled when another shot rang out and Mick yelled. She turned to see a red stain spreading across Mick's chest. Vaguely, she noted Gabby's screams as she rushed to her brother. Mick sank to his knees, eyes glazing over.

Izzy's throat tightened, even as it registered that Mick could never hurt her again.

"They said I could have you," he whispered. "That was the deal. We were supposed to get the money, then I was going to take . . . you . . . away . . ." His eyes never closed as he landed facedown on the floor.

Gabby's sobs now reached her. Izzy looked up to see Toby tuck his gun into the shoulder holster he wore. With a sigh, he walked over and pulled Gabby to her feet and tucked her against him. "I'm sorry, baby. I'm sorry."

"You killed him!" she wailed.

"I'm sorry. I didn't mean to, he just . . . I thought he was going to kill me. And you."

She sniffed. "Me?"

"Yeah, babe, I couldn't let him do that. He was crazy, shooting at everything."

"One shot is shooting at everything?" Izzy asked.

When he turned to her, Izzy wished she'd kept her mouth shut. He stomped over, picked her up, and threw her on the couch. "One more word out of you and you're dead. You have other siblings that will be just as effective as a hostage. Like your sister the doctor."

He meant it.

Izzy nodded that she'd be quiet, then leaned back against the couch and closed her eyes. Within just a couple of minutes, Freeman had settled Gabby at the table and removed Mick's corpse from the floor. He didn't bother to clean up the blood.

Now the two of them sat at the table, and while Gabby's sobs broke Izzy's heart, she had to come up with a plan just in case Ryan didn't figure out the bullet was missing.

They'd mentioned neutralizing people? As in killing them? But who? The names on the list? How were they planning to do that? A bomb? Multiple shooters with automatic weapons?

Things had just gone from worse to disastrous. She'd witnessed Freeman kill a man. Technically, she might actually consider it self-defense. Mick had shot first. But she knew it didn't matter. She didn't have much longer to live unless she acted.

Their words drifted to her as she tried to visualize a way out, tried to devise an escape plan. She had the duct tape worked so that one good rip would get it going and she'd eventually be able to get free. But it would make noise and grab their attention.

"I need a potty break. It's been a while."

"No." Freeman didn't bother to look up.

"Seriously?" She shrugged. "Whatever. It's your couch."

Freeman jerked his head at Gabby, motioning for her to tend to Izzy. "But keep your mouth shut."

Gabby nodded meekly and stood. But when her gaze touched Izzy, her eyes narrowed and her nostrils flared.

Interesting. So she wasn't quite as docile as she wanted the man to believe. Good. Maybe she was ready to fight back.

"Use this and bring it back to me." He handed her a pocketknife and glared at Izzy. "If you try to take it from her or escape in any way, I'll kill her. Understood?"

"Understood."

With shaking hands, Gabby cut the tape holding Izzy's ankles together and returned the knife to Freeman. Izzy then followed Gabby down the hall to the full bath on the right.

"Give me your hands," Gabby whispered.

Izzy waited while her friend loosened the tape around her wrists. "Hold on to that," Izzy told her.

"Why?"

"Because if I don't find a way out, you're going to have to wrap it back around my wrists. Just loose."

"Izzy, I didn't know all this was going to happen. I thought I was helping Mick. He was at the house when you called and rushed us out of there. He said you were going to find a way to put him in prison. And then we got here and he was furious that he didn't get the iPad. He thought it was in the bag with the computer."

"So he came up with a plan to get me to bring it to you."

"Yes. He said something about a guy named Young who was supposed to be a professional. But he'd failed to get you."

"No kidding."

"I'm sorry, Izzy. I didn't mean to get you wrapped up in all of this."

"You didn't. My involvement started with Kevin's death."

She pressed the palms of her hands against her eyes. "I can't believe I was so stupid, so blind. I thought he liked me, but he was just using me."

"Stop. Let's go out the back right now. We'll find a window and get out."

"I . . . I can't," she whispered. "I can't leave."

"Why not? He's in there."

"I know, but . . ."

"But what?"

"He'll kill my mother if I leave."

"How?"

"He's got her bed at the assisted living place wired with a bomb. If I don't do what he says, he'll set it off."

Oh no. So that's how he was keeping Gabby under control. Freeman was so confident that Gabby wouldn't buck him or do anything to help her friend because he held her mother's life in his hands.

A bomb at an assisted living home. Izzy didn't want to even imagine the mass casualty that could be.

"Do you know the plan? Have you overheard anything?" Izzy kept her voice low, making sure Freeman couldn't hear her.

"Nothing that makes any sense to me."

"What do the Bloods have to do with this? Are the Crips involved too?" The fake tattoos. No, if both gangs were involved, there wouldn't be a need for fake tats. And there was no way they'd band together for any amount of money.

"I don't know. I promise, if I knew anything I'd tell you. This wasn't supposed to happen," she whispered. "You weren't supposed to get hurt. No one was supposed to get hurt. I was just helping Mick!" she ended with a whispered shout.

They were out of sight of Freeman, but he had to be listening for them. Izzy lifted a finger to her lips and Gabby pressed a hand to her mouth.

"So do something," Izzy said.

"Like what? What can I do that won't get my mother and all those people in that building blown to bits? You tell me and I'll do it, but I just know that I can't leave." Tears dripped down her cheeks and off her chin.

"Hurry it up back there!"

Izzy let her gaze linger on her traumatized friend, at a loss as to what to tell her.

"Come on," Gabby whispered. "He's getting mad." She wrapped the tape around Izzy's wrists leaving enough room for her to slip out when she was ready. Then Gabby hurried into the bathroom and flushed the toilet. Izzy heard the water running, then Gabby returned to her side.

Back in the den, she took her spot on the sofa once more. When she glanced at Freeman, he was watching her with narrowed eyes.

She lifted her chin and glared at him, and he scowled and turned his attention back to the object he'd been studying. A picture. An 8½" x 11" picture.

And Izzy's blood ran cold. She knew that place. The place where the newly elected mayor would give her speech.

And everything fell into place.

Terror exploded through her.

The list that Derek had found was a list of cops, all right, but they weren't dirty. They were the security for the mayor's speech.

The fake tats now made sense. She could picture it clearly. They were going to launch an attack during the speech, using a fake gang war in order to take out the cops who were the first line of protection and defense.

But why? And who was the target?

Even before the question finished forming in her mind, she knew the answer.

Her mother.

33

Ryan watched the clock. How much time did he have? Did Izzy have? Ryan's phone rang. Linc. "Yeah?"

"You find her?"

"No, but we've got a lead and are following it." He explained about the missing GPS bullet.

Linc let out a short laugh. "Clever girl." Then he sobered. "I'm really scared for her, Ryan."

"That makes two of us, but we finally got a chopper in the air, heading that way to give us some recon." He glanced at the clock. "And we're fifteen minutes away."

Linc went silent a moment. Probably controlling his emotions. Ryan understood that.

He cleared his throat. "On the good news front, we got Bianchi," Linc said.

"What? How?"

"Traced him through a number on Gabby Sinclair's brother's phone. He called Bianchi one time from his personal phone. I imagine he got raked over the coals for doing so, because he never called him again from that number. It was the only number in his contact list that we had trouble tracking, but our tech guy managed to finally get a hit and then it was legwork from there. We connected him to another dummy corporation, found the office, and nabbed him while he was doing a deal."

"Mick Sinclair is involved in this?"

"Yeah, we got a warrant for his phone info, hoping it would track us to Gabby and Gabby to Bianchi. There was no communication between Gabby and Bianchi, but definitely between her brother and Bianchi."

Relief on Bianchi's capture filled him in spite of his worry about Izzy. "I really hope it wasn't a pleasant experience for Bianchi."

"He's got two bullets. One in the shoulder, one in the stomach. He might make it, he might not."

"Okay . . . and Mick Sinclair."

"Why do you keep saying that?"

"Izzy told me about him. Now I'm really scared for her. I'd almost rather her be in Bianchi's hands than Sinclair's."

"She told you?"

The pure shock in Linc's voice raised Ryan's brow. "Yeah."

"Wow. She doesn't share that with just anyone."

"I know."

Linc cleared his voice. "All right, well, more good news. In addition to the two million in cash he had getting ready to buy another load of weapons, we picked up a lot of evidence that will be used against him should he live to see the inside of a courtroom. He's going away for a long time. If he lives."

Satisfaction bloomed. A happy ending on that score. Now, to make sure Izzy got one too.

"And Ryan?"

"Yeah?"

"One thing of note," Linc said. "We found pictures of Izzy meeting with a guy known as Louis Harper."

"He's her CI."

"And Harper is now on a slab."

"Bianchi found out Harper was feeding Izzy information and killed him," Ryan said. He told him about the incident in the cemetery.

Linc gave a low gasp.

"So, while Bianchi might be out of action, the people working for him aren't. We need to find Izzy before she winds up like Harper."

A helicopter passed overhead and Izzy couldn't help the slight leap of hope her heart gave. Had someone found the jammed GPS launcher?

"Helicopter's here," Freeman said.

He stood and Izzy's hope crashed. She couldn't let them get on that helicopter. Freeman's weapon was on the table.

"Could I have something to drink?" she asked.

Freeman slid his weapon from the table and palmed it. "Nope. Time to go."

"Where?"

"To make my first million—or the rest of it." He winked at Gabby. "She just picked up the down payment. As soon as this assignment is finished, the money is wired to my account in the Caymans and I'm set for life." He shrugged. "Or until the next million-dollar deal comes along."

"What about the money you promised Mick?" Gabby said.

"He was never going to be alive to collect it. He was useful because you told him every detail of the election. But now . . ." He turned the weapon on Gabby. "You've been very useful, but it's time for us to part ways."

"Gabby, run!" Izzy launched herself at Freeman just as his finger squeezed. The gunshot echoed around them and Gabby screamed.

Izzy and Freeman went down and she rolled, yanking her hands from the tape and leaping to her feet just as he did the same. She spun and threw a hard punch to his face, but he ducked and lunged. Izzy pivoted, trying to move out of his reach. Only she was too slow. His fingers snagged the hem of her T-shirt, yanking her off-balance. She stumbled and fell to the ground, rolling and kicking out. Her foot landed against his shin.

With an angry yell, he swung. Izzy saw it coming and rolled again. She dodged a direct hit, but his fist grazed her temple, hard enough to stun her. "Get up!"

Without waiting for Izzy to do so on her own, he grabbed her by the arm and shoved her toward the door. When she stepped outside, the wind whipped her hair into her eyes. She shoved it away as Freeman jammed his weapon into her lower back. The chopper blades pounded the air around them and, instinctively, she ducked against the wind.

The rain had held off so far, but the moisture hung heavy in the air. The pilot had the doors open as a concession to the unseasonably warm day or to help with the speed of things, she didn't know which. Probably the latter.

"Get in the helicopter."

"Tell me how to save my mom!"

"Get in or I'll shoot you and you won't have a chance to save her!"

Izzy thought fast, rolling visuals of escape options through her mind at warp speed, while the left side of her head pulsed in rhythm with her heart. She had to find a way to warn her mother. There would be a radio on the helicopter. And what about the pilot? Did he know who he was working for? She had to assume so.

"Fine." She climbed into the helicopter as best she could. Now was not the time to free them.

From the corner of her eye, Izzy thought she saw movement. Dark sedans, police cruisers, and more pulled into the drive of the house.

"Izzy!"

She heard Ryan's shout over the sound of the blades. Freeman shoved her and Izzy fell onto the open deck of the chopper. Medical supplies clearly identified it as a hospital helicopter. Freeman climbed in. "Go!"

The pilot looked back. "Get that gun off my chopper!"

Freeman jabbed the weapon toward Izzy. "You want her to die?"

The man's eyes went wide. "What?"

"I'll shoot her if you don't get us in the air!"

"It's too windy. I need to wait for the wind to die down. And what are you doing anyway? This wasn't part of the deal."

"And shooting you wasn't either, but I will if you don't get us airborne!" Freeman grabbed the set of headphones and slipped them over his ears one-handed.

"I said it's too windy!"

"And I said go!" For a brief moment, Izzy thought Freeman might pull the trigger. The pilot obviously thought so too, since he shook his head and obeyed. "And if you land anywhere other than our agreed upon destination, she dies first, then you die, understood?"

"Understood."

The helicopter lifted, swaying in the rough wind. Freeman's weight shifted to keep him from sliding off the seat. The nose of the gun dipped and Izzy kicked out, landing a solid hit to Freeman's gun hand. The weapon spun from his grasp and fell to the chopper floor.

With a yell, Freeman lunged for the gun and Izzy dove after him.

She managed to clamp down on the man's wrist just as Freeman's fingers closed over the grip. "You're done, Toby!"

Freeman jerked and it was all Izzy could do to hang on. He was a big, strong man.

"Hey, you two stop that!" The pilot's shout had no effect on either of them. Freeman refused to give up and Izzy couldn't let go of the wrist that held the gun. The helicopter dipped and Izzy rolled into Freeman. She hit the man hard and Freeman slid toward the open door, pulling Izzy with him.

34

Izzy had managed to grab on to the edge of the opening with her left hand while she kept her right clamped around Freeman's wrist. The man had stopped struggling, doing his best to stay inside the listing chopper. She had the advantage with him off-balance, but he was still stronger—and determined. For now, they were at a standstill. Freeman wouldn't give up the gun and Izzy couldn't let go of his wrist or the doorframe without falling out of the chopper.

"Freeman, let it go! It's over!"

"I'm not going to prison."

The chopper rocked and Izzy lost her grip on the door, but managed to grab the seat frame welded to the side of the helicopter.

"It's either that or die!"

Izzy gathered her strength, tightened her grip on the man's wrist, and slammed it down. Freeman cried out but didn't release the gun.

"Hold on! I've got to land!"

The pilot's cry caused Freeman to jerk. "You land, you die, understand?"

Izzy took advantage and slammed the hand with the gun one more time. The gun skittered across the deck. Another gust of wind sent them sideways—and Izzy let go to swing her other hand up to latch on to the seat.

Freeman scrambled, half in, half out of the chopper. He caught hold of the base of the seat and looked up at Izzy. Dark murder stared back at her.

Sickness and terror curled within her. If he managed to get back inside, she was dead. Izzy stood, grabbed the tether hanging from the roof, and kicked him in the head. Freeman screamed and rolled out the open door.

The chopper tilted as the pilot overcorrected and Izzy lost her grip. She tumbled to the floor and rolled toward the other side, opposite the one Freeman had fallen from. Her legs dangled through the opening and she made a desperate grab to lock her fingers around the identical metal chair once more. She caught hold, but the bobbing and weaving of the chopper had her grip slipping. "Land this thing or come back here and get me!"

Her frantic words directed at the pilot made him turn to look at her. He'd been so preoccupied keeping the bird in the air, he hadn't been aware of what was happening behind him. When he saw she was alone, his eyes went even wider in his pale face.

"Hang on, hold on! Don't let go! I'm going down!"

She didn't plan on letting go. Terror clawed at her. What was it with her and dangling from objects that if she let go, she would die?

And then there was no more time to think. The helicopter bumped the ground and Izzy's fingers gave up their hold. She dropped safely to the grass while raindrops pelted her.

Arms went around her and she realized Ryan was there, hunched against the gusting wind—generated by both the blades and the weather. "Izzy, are you okay? Does anything hurt? Do you need an ambulance?"

She tried to stand and found her legs were wobbly. "No, no ambulance. Just . . . need to . . . catch my breath."

He helped her up and held on to her as he moved them out from under the blades. "What is it with you?" he demanded.

"What?"

"You and high places that are death drops?"

And she laughed.

And laughed.

And wiped away the tears she couldn't seem to stop.

Until her eyes landed on the law enforcement agents in a huddle to her right. "Gabby! Where is she?"

"She's fine. She ran out the front door right into the arms of the FBI." Izzy wilted with relief and Ryan pressed her face into his chest. "It's over now. You're safe."

Izzy jerked back and swiped her eyes. "What am I doing? I don't have time to cry. I need to find my mother."

"Why?"

"Because she's been the target from day one, and if we don't warn her, she's going to die."

With the chief of police warned about the hit that was being planned at the winner's victory speech—and Izzy's suspicion that Bianchi was brought into the scheme due to his organized crime connections—Ryan led Izzy back into the house where the crime scene unit had descended. Izzy paced, phone pressed to her ear. He heard her sigh. "Thank you. I'm so glad. Good. We'll let Gabby know her mother and the others are out of danger." She hung up and caught him watching her. "The bomb was defused. They're safe. Where's Gabby?"

"One of the agents took her to the nursing home to see her mother."

Izzy nodded. "Good, she needed to see her."

"Are you all right?"

"Not really. I hope I'll stop shaking before much longer."

"You will."

"I know." Her eyes stayed locked on his. "How are you? Freeman's dead."

"And I didn't get to be the one to kill him."

"Yes."

He blew out a breath. "It's probably better that way. I don't need that guilt hanging over me the rest of my life."

"I agree."

"I wouldn't have minded landing a few good punches, though."

Ryan had wanted to confront him, to put his hands on the man and do serious bodily damage to him. But . . . like he told Izzy, maybe it was better this way.

The helicopter pilot had spilled his story. Tobias Freeman had used Gabby to dupe him into believing he was needed to chauffeur Melissa Endicott to a private residence where she could escape the press hounds for a couple of hours before giving her victory speech.

Protection had been put on the current mayor's family, and an intense investigation into Endicott's background was going on even as the voters still turned out at the polls.

Ryan drew in a deep breath and tried to think if they'd missed anything. Unable to pinpoint what it could be if they had, he turned his attention to Izzy once more.

She stood at the kitchen table now, gloves encasing her hands while she studied the pictures. "Something's wrong," she muttered.

He knew she was talking to herself, but he overheard her. "What's wrong?"

"What time is it?"

He glanced at his watch. "3:23."

"This isn't where the final speech is going to be made." She passed him the picture. "This is the pre-winner announcement party. Mayor Cotterill will be meeting with his supporters and giving a pep talk, my mother will be there for support, as well as Felicia. They'll all be there at the outside stage in Finlay Park. And I don't think that's safe. Toby Freeman and Mick were *not* working alone."

"Which means the threat is still there. Being outside . . . no, that's not good. It's too dangerous. When does it start?"

314

"Four o'clock," she said. "We'll never get there in time. We're at least a half hour away. And she'll be first up right at four o'clock to introduce the mayor before moving to the other location where she plans to meet with Endicott."

"No playing favorites for the chief," Ryan said, then looked at the pilot. "It's only about fifteen by helicopter."

"Let me have your phone, please," Izzy said.

Ryan passed it to her and she dialed her mother's number. No answer.

She tried her mother's work number.

Fear stamped itself on her features. "It went to voice mail. It never goes to voice mail."

"She could be talking to someone about this already."

"Who? No one else knows anything."

"She knows her life is in danger. She'll take precautions." Ryan turned to his partner, who'd been listening quietly. "Call it in to the deputy chief. Tell her we need extra security and to keep the chief off that stage."

"Got it."

Ryan nodded. "Let's go."

Izzy went to the pilot, who was still trying to explain his whole role in this. He was clueless. He had no idea he'd contracted a flight with a criminal. Izzy grabbed his arm. "It's not important. Right now, you have to get us to Finlay Park and help us stop a murder." His eyes went wide. Izzy's gaze never left his. "Please."

"It's still windy out there."

"We have to chance it or the chief of police is going to die." Maybe. Felicia would see to it that the woman received the message and was safe, but the way things had been going lately, Izzy didn't want to take any chances.

"It'll be rocky. Hope you've got a strong stomach."

"Go!"

Less than five minutes had passed and they were in the air heading toward Finlay Park. And this time Izzy was buckled in, with Ryan sitting beside her. Her mother's office was about half a mile from the park. She wouldn't leave her office until the last minute. They had time as long as there was a place to land the chopper.

Ryan was on the phone requesting clearance to land it on the roof of the building. "That's a negative," he said. "We're going for the open grassy area at the corner of Lincoln and Washington."

Izzy nodded. That was better than the roof. Using Ryan's phone, she tried Linc's, and wonder of wonders, he answered on the first ring.

"Get to Mom, Linc. It's possible she's in danger."

"What?"

"Mom! Get to Mom!" She heard the static and the call dropped. She didn't know if he heard her or not.

And then they were landing in the open area of Justice Square. She looked at her watch. Fifteen minutes had passed from takeoff to landing. It was 3:50. Just about the time her mother would be walking out of her office. Had someone reached her or not?

Izzy scrambled from the chopper and knew Ryan was right behind her.

She ran across the street and into the building, only to come to a halt as she came face-to-face with her mother and Felicia. "Mom," she cried. Izzy raced to her and threw her arms around her. "You can't go out to the park."

"What? Why?"

Izzy frowned and turned her gaze on Felicia. "You didn't tell her?"

"No."

"Why not?"

Felicia huffed. "I wanted to be sure she was totally focused on

316

this speech. I've tripled security and we've cut off all access to the stage to everyone except those cleared."

"What didn't she tell me?" her mother said with a hard look at her deputy chief.

"I'm sorry, Tabitha, I just didn't want to burden you."

"It's my job to be burdened," she snapped. Then to Izzy. "What?"

"There's a hit out on you. It's supposed to go down as soon as you walk out on the stage in the form of a gang war type thing. I don't know exactly, just that it will look like a gang war, but it's not. I'm sure you're supposed to catch a stray bullet or something."

For a moment Tabitha didn't move. Then she pulled her phone from her pocket. "Yes, this is Tabitha St. John, Chief of Police. I need you to put on all news outlets that the speech has been canceled. Yes, the one that's supposed to be happening in less than five minutes. Thank you."

"Tabitha!" Felicia's protest fell on deaf ears.

The chief's piercing gaze landed on each of them. "Let's finish this discussion in my office." She turned on her heel and headed for the elevator.

The ride to the top floor seemed to last forever. In reality, it wasn't more than a minute, minute and a half. Izzy itched to escape, but knew that wasn't an option.

Ryan hooked a finger under his collar and loosened it, but said nothing.

Felicia's phone rang. "Do you mind if I take this, Tabitha? I'll be right in, I promise."

Her mother's chilly eyes swept over the woman. Then she sighed. "Of course."

Then Ryan's phone rang and he snatched it as though it were a life preserver. "Can't talk right now, Cathy." He stilled. The elevator opened and they all stepped off with Ryan pulling up the rear. "Okay. I—I'll be there as soon as I can."

"What is it, Ryan?" her mother asked.

"Mom was just admitted to the hospital with chest pains. She's asking for me. Sorry, I have to go."

Tabitha's stony features softened. "Of course you do. Go be with her."

"I'm . . . are you sure?"

"Yes. It's nothing I can't rake you over the coals about later."

"Yes, ma'am." He looked at Izzy in silent apology. She grimaced. Oh well, she'd faced her mother's wrath before and lived to tell about it. She didn't suppose this time would be much different.

Ryan left. Once inside the office, Izzy took the seat nearest to the door. Felicia's call must not have been important, as she slipped in the door before it shut and perched herself in the next chair. Her mother rounded her desk. "First," she said to Izzy, "are you all right? Did Sinclair or Freeman hurt you?"

"No, ma'am. I didn't give them a chance to."

"Good. What about Freeman? I understand he's dead."

"He is and so is Mick, but I don't know where Lamar Young is."

"We've got a BOLO out on him. Did Freeman or Sinclair say anything about who they might be working with?" Felicia asked.

"No. Nothing. There was a ton of evidence at the house, though, so there's no telling what will turn up."

Felicia nodded and stood. "Tabitha, you can yell at me later for not wanting to worry you. It won't ever happen again, I assure you. But if it's all right with you, I'm going to see what I can find out about this evidence that might lead us to whoever Freeman and Sinclair were working with."

"We know Bianchi and the Bloods were involved," Izzy said. "That's about it for now."

"Check into Melissa Endicott's background. See what turns up."

"All right. I'll be in touch if I find out anything."

She left and Izzy's mother turned her gaze on Izzy. "Now, young lady, we have a lot of catching up to do."

35

Sitting in the hospital waiting room, Ryan clutched the iPad Izzy had lifted from Gabby's house and that David had agreed to examine. David was on his way and would be there shortly. His dad was in the back with his mother. Cathy and Dale stood off to the side talking softly.

David finally rushed through the double doors and Ryan motioned him to the table in the corner. As they were taking a seat, Charice arrived and Ryan brought her up to date.

Within minutes, David had his laptop hooked up and the iPad connected. "So, he has it password protected. Six numbers."

"Of course he does. It took us days to figure out Kevin's password—and we knew him well. How in the world are we going to crack Sinclair's?"

"I'm going to set it up to run every possible combination of numbers from zero to nine, including the possibility of repetition. It will have something for us shortly."

"How shortly?"

David shrugged. "Guess we'll find out."

"So, why didn't we do this with Kevin's phone again?"

"It would have taken me a couple of days to get to it. I was working on a project for my boss. Simple stuff like pulling video off security cameras from a murder scene I could do. Hacking phones that may or may not have evidence on them wasn't high on the list."

"Right."

"I would have done it for you if you hadn't figured it out."

The door to the ER opened and Ryan stood when his dad walked through. "Well?"

"She's got an irregular heartbeat right now. They're going to run some more tests and keep her for observation."

"But is it a heart attack?" Cathy asked.

"No, not yet."

Ryan slumped back into the chair and said a silent prayer of thanks. "Okay, I'll hang out here a bit—at least until the next update."

"Sounds good."

For the next few minutes, Ryan and Charice discussed Gabby's role in the scenario. "She's completely innocent. She was as much a hostage as Izzy," Charice said. "There won't be any charges."

"How's her mother?" Ryan asked her.

"Fine. The bomb squad got there and disarmed the bomb." She shook her head. "He was serious, Ryan. If Gabby hadn't kept him happy, he would have blown the whole place up."

"What a sick sociopath."

"Yeah."

"And we have a match," David announced. "We're in. Didn't take long because she used 9-8-7-6-5-4. Not a good password."

"Actually, I consider it very good. For us anyway." Ryan scooted around so he could see. "Izzy said Freeman was adamant that Gabby make sure Izzy got that iPad to him. What is it he had on there?"

"His text history is my guess. He kept it. Probably in case he needed to blackmail someone."

He pulled up the conversation between Tobias Freeman and— *her?*

Ryan lost the air in his lungs. "No," he said. "It can't be."

"Yeah."

"Is it really her number?"

David clicked a few more keys and brought up a match.

"It's hers."

Ryan closed his eyes. "I can't believe this. This is a huge nightmare."

The screen beeped and David lifted a brow. "And look who owns that property where Freeman held Izzy hostage."

"I've got to call Izzy. You call for backup." Ryan stood and looked at Cathy. "I've got to go. Keep me updated on Mom."

Izzy sat back after spilling her guts about everything that had happened. Her mother leaned back in her chair and let her eyes fall shut. "Wow."

"I know."

"I want to ask you a question, Mom."

"What's that?"

"Why were you meeting with Tony Bianchi?"

Her mother blanched, then her features smoothed out. "How do you know about that?"

"Derek told me. He thought you were dirty and was investigating you on his own. He did break up with Elaine, but that's not why he needed the two weeks' leave."

Her face paled. "He really thought that?"

"I think deep down, he didn't, but was afraid if the pictures were leaked or something, it would look bad. That's why he was at the warehouse the night Kevin was killed. He'd found Bianchi and was keeping an eye on things. I think he thought you were meeting him that night."

"I was supposed to. Bianchi called it off."

"So . . . why?"

Izzy's phone buzzed and she sent the call to her voice mail. She didn't want any distractions.

"When the risk is as high as it is with Bianchi, I'd rather be the one taking the risk. Mayor Cotterill is a good man. I'm not going to have his family threatened by a thug, even a powerful one."

"Does this have anything to do with the mayor's silence during all this gang violence and the election?"

Her mom shoved a strand of hair behind her ear. "We needed to give Bianchi enough rope to hang himself with. Eric wanted Bianchi caught more than he wanted to win an election, and so he stayed 'ineffective' while all this was getting set up."

"Wow." Izzy sat back with a thud. "Just, wow. Mom, he's killed cops for looking at him wrong, and you just go meet with him?"

She let out a sigh. "I had surveillance on me at all times. If I was ever to run into trouble, help was only seconds away. And I never had any trouble."

"Because he knew," Izzy murmured.

"Or at least suspected."

Izzy's phone rang again just as someone knocked on the door. Her mother rose. "Take your call while I get this. Come in."

Izzy sent the call to voice mail once more. In spite of her mother's all clear to take the call, she didn't want to be on the phone if she needed to have a conversation with someone in her office.

Felicia stepped back inside. "Melissa Endicott came back clean. There's nothing in her background that would suggest she had anything to do with putting a hit out on you. And really, what reason would she have?"

Her mother pressed her fingertips to her mouth and Izzy frowned. "Maybe she didn't," she said. "Maybe Freeman did. It was clear he was the one in charge at the house."

"But why?" her mother asked.

Izzy rubbed her head. "We have to look at it like this. Who has the most to gain if you're dead?" Just saying the words made her wince, but they had to come at this from every conceivable direction. "But we'll know soon enough. Ryan, Charice, and David have Mick's iPad. It won't take long to get into it and find out why he was so desperate to have it that he'd have me bring it to him."

Felicia frowned. "They have Mick's iPad?"

Izzy nodded. "Yes." Her phone buzzed. With a sigh, she looked at it. Someone was trying very hard to get in touch with her. Ryan.

It's Felicia. She put the hit on your mother. Call me.

Izzy froze. *Felicia?* Her mind spun. She could make an excuse and slip out of the office but didn't want to leave her mother alone with the woman who wanted to kill her. Then again, if she left, she could call her mother and fill her in and her mother could make an excuse to leave. Then they could trap the woman in the office and wait for backup.

It was the best plan she could think of.

"Izzy?" Felicia asked. "Is something more interesting on your phone than this conversation?"

She realized Felicia had said her name several times. Izzy blinked. "Oh, sorry. That was Ryan." She met her mother's gaze and tried to convey her silent panic without showing emotion. "His . . . uh . . . his mother's taken a turn for the worse. He's going to be a while. I think I'm going to go up to the hospital and sit with him if that's all right. I'll watch the election results from there."

"Of course, darling. Give him my best."

Izzy backed toward the door.

Felicia moved quickly, pulling a gun from her shoulder holster. She aimed it at Izzy and stepped in front of the door, blocking Izzy's escape.

"Felicia!" Her mother gaped. "What are you doing?"

Felicia waved the weapon at Izzy, who stilled. "What gave me away?" Izzy asked.

"You backed toward the door. Good training when there's someone you don't trust in the room. And we both know that someone isn't your mother. I'm guessing that text wasn't about Ryan's mother."

Izzy didn't move, even though she mentally kicked herself for the tell. She might have just signed her mother's—and her—death warrants. "You're behind it all, aren't you?" Her gaze slipped to her mother, who was still staring at them, shock on her white face. "She was working in conjunction with Bianchi to have you killed today."

Her mother sank into her seat. "What?"

Felicia's pleasant façade was stripped from her features. She snarled like an enraged animal. "And you ruined *everything*!" She drew in a deep breath and the anger passed as quickly as it appeared. "If Ryan and David found something on Sinclair's iPad, it looks like my job here is done and it's time for me to make a hasty exit. One thing I do know is I'm not going to prison."

She walked to the window and glanced out, while keeping her weapon expertly trained on Izzy. "They're already moving. The building is covered with cops." She drew in a deep breath.

"Cops that won't hesitate to shoot you," Izzy said. "You can end this now and we can all walk out of here alive."

"I'm not interested in being alive if it means going to prison. I'll just be killed there anyway. I need to think." She checked the window again, then crossed the office to check the other one. She never took her eyes or the gun off Izzy and her mother long enough for Izzy to consider acting.

"You know Bianchi is close to death," her mother said. "If you run, how will you live? It's not like he can transfer money."

Felicia clicked her tongue. "He already has, sweetie. It went in an hour ago. I told him it had to be pending before I'd agree to our *partnership*, so to speak."

"Why was Bianchi so willing to contribute?" Izzy asked, even though she knew the answer to the question. She just needed to buy time.

Felicia raised a brow. "Really?"

"You were going to look the other way. He was going to have the chief of police in his pocket," Izzy said. "But what about Freeman and Mick Sinclair?"

"That was money for making sure Endicott got elected. A down payment. He would get the rest once the deal was done."

"And if Endicott lost?"

"Then Eric's family would die. He was to stick it out to the end of the election, but do nothing to win. He was to look weak, swaying votes."

"Yes, that's what he agreed to do," her mother said. "Until we could expose the people behind it."

"So he was doing it on purpose," Izzy said.

"Yes."

"Why do you want me dead?" her mother asked. "You could help Bianchi in your current position almost as much as in mine."

"It's called power. I want it. True, being the deputy chief isn't so bad, but Endicott made a comment at one of her fundraisers to Mrs. Tollison, a supporter, and I overheard it. It got me to thinking."

"What did she say?" Izzy asked while her mind spun. How were they going to get out of this one?

"She said that if she won, she'd keep Tabitha as chief of police, but if something happened and she was no longer the chief, she'd ask me if I wanted the job. And I do. Simple as that."

"So, you had to make sure Endicott won and that I was out of the picture," Izzy's mother said. "What were you going to do after Endicott won and I was dead? Kill Eric too? Because there's no way he would have kept quiet about it."

"Exactly. Now, it's time for us to move. I think I've managed to come up with a plan to get out of here. Put your weapons on the desk and head out the back door."

Her mother's office had two entry doors. The one that was used most often and the other one that led down to a side exit.

Felicia gestured with the weapon. "Move."

Izzy met her mother's gaze.

"Now!" Felicia shook the gun at Izzy. "Or she'll die. After all, I only need one hostage."

"No!" Her mother rounded the desk and held up a hand. "I'll do it."

Pulling the gun from her shoulder holster, Izzy's mom then placed it on the desk, never taking her eyes from Felicia.

Izzy did the same. "Ryan knows it's you. They have Mick's iPad. All of your group text messages are on there. He also recorded your phone conversations."

"Which means I'm a desperate woman now, so don't mess with me."

Now weaponless, fear wanted to smother Izzy, but she knew she had to control it. To think. "How do you plan to get out? All of the entrances will be blocked."

"But they won't shoot if I have you as shields." Felicia motioned toward the door. "Go."

"Izzy, you first," her mother said.

"No." Felicia turned the weapon on her boss. "You first. You won't try anything with a gun on your kid's head." And Izzy realized why the woman was keeping them both alive. She knew they'd each do whatever she wanted to keep her from hurting the other.

36

The trip from the hospital to the station took a little under ten minutes. Already the chief's office had set up a mobile command unit parked diagonally to the building. They had snipers on the outside and across the street, ready to do business. He'd never seen them move so fast, but this was their chief and her daughter in danger and they weren't playing around.

Brady paced in front of the command truck. Ryan raced over to him. "Have you seen them?"

"No. And they're not answering the phones."

Ryan told him about his last conversation with Izzy. "The plan was for her to get out and get her mother out. Obviously, she couldn't do that. Somehow Felicia guessed that Izzy knew something." He rubbed his eyes. "I shouldn't have called."

"No, Izzy had to know. And so did Mom."

"Is someone covering the back entrance?"

"Yeah. We've got guys all over this building. There's no way they're coming out without us seeing them."

"She'll have them as hostages."

From the corner of his eye, Ryan saw Linc approaching. The man's tight expression didn't bode well. "What's the status?"

"Your mother and Izzy are still in the building. We've had no contact."

Linc looked around. "All the right people are here. We need eyes in the building."

"Already working on it." Special Agent Josiah Lewis—and technical analyst genius—looked up from his seat in the Mobile Command Center, then back at his keyboard. He clicked a few more keys and then gave a grunt of satisfaction. "There. I'm in the security video system."

"Not sure if that's a good thing or not," Linc muttered.

Josiah smiled. "Normally, it wouldn't be that easy. I have the passwords, so that helped speed things along."

Ryan watched the monitors as Josiah brought up the chief's office. "It's empty."

"Check the exits."

The fourth try was the charm. "There, in the stairwell. They're getting ready to exit through the back."

Ryan raced for the rear. He was going to be within shouting distance when the door opened.

Felicia stopped them just short of opening the door. "When Tabitha pushes the door open, you stay in front of me. Keep your hands on your mother's shoulders, understand?"

"I understand." Izzy had an idea of what the woman planned. She'd keep her back to the building while having Izzy and her mother in front of her as human shields. They'd inch down the building and to her car, which was parked next to the exit.

She'd moved it when she realized things might be going south and she'd need to escape. Izzy figured she'd done it when she excused herself to go check Endicott's background. A plausible ruse to set up her escape route. "Why did you come back? You could have just gotten in your car and left." Izzy noticed the weapon was now lower, centered on her back and not her head. She guessed the woman's arm was tiring from holding it so high. A fact that brought her a surge of relief.

"I knew you didn't suspect anything yet. If there was the slightest chance that I could make it work, I had to try." She paused. "I didn't know about the iPad or I would have left. That bit of information came a bit too late. Now shut up and open the door."

Izzy's mother pushed on the bar that would free them from the building. As soon as the door was open, Izzy gave her mother's shoulders a hard shove. The woman stumbled through it and fell to the ground, even while Izzy dropped to the floor. The bullet hit the tile beside her waist and she rolled.

Three pops sounded.

Izzy waited for the pain to hit. Then realized it was Felicia who'd taken the bullets.

And then Ryan was there, pulling her to her feet and away from the woman who'd betrayed them all and everything they believed in.

Ryan walked Izzy over to the ambulance where paramedics were treating her mother for a sprained wrist. She looked up when he and Izzy approached. Tears gathered in her eyes and she held out her good arm. Izzy slid from his hold and into her mother's. For a moment they simply held one another. Then Izzy sighed and pulled back. "Sorry about your wrist."

"You saved us."

Izzy grimaced. "Well, it's nothing you weren't planning to do if you'd been in my position."

She brushed a tear from her cheek. "You didn't see that."

"See what?" Ryan asked.

"I was just extremely worried about Izzy."

"I know." He could tell she wasn't really afraid the tears would make her seem weak. She was human. She and the daughter she loved had almost died today. A few tears could be expected.

She turned to Izzy. "Remind me to give your self-defense instructor a raise."

They smiled at one another. Then Izzy turned to Ryan. "Want to take me to the hospital to check on Derek and your mom?"

"Absolutely."

"Then we can go to my parents' house and watch the election?"

"Sure." He looked at Izzy's mother. "I'm glad you're all right, ma'am."

"Me too, Ryan. Thanks. How's your mother?"

He held up his phone. "Dad texted. She's doing fine. They got her heart back in rhythm and are sending her home. She'll follow up with a cardiologist in the next week or so."

"Very glad to hear it." She sighed as Izzy's father broke through the crowd.

"Izzy!"

Izzy slid from the ambulance and was enveloped in his massive hug. "Hi, Dad."

"Are you okay? Tabitha?"

"I'm fine—thanks to our girl."

He leaned in and kissed his wife, then looked back at Izzy and the ongoing organized chaos. "I saw all the commotion going on and heard some rumors floating around. I don't want to know the details right now, do I?"

"Not today," she said.

He nodded. "I'm just going to be glad everyone is okay."

The paramedic finished taping the chief's hand and she thanked him. To her husband, she said, "I'm going to be a while. Why don't you go home and fix dinner? I don't think I'm going to get around to it tonight."

He laughed, a strained sound, but at least it was a laugh. "How does pizza sound?"

"Divine."

"Get enough for Ryan and me too," Izzy said.

"And me," Chloe said. Ryan turned to see her with Hank at her side, looking pale and shaken. Izzy went to her and hugged her. "They got Lamar Young and a dozen gang members at the speech site," Chloe said. "A lot of them had the fake tattoos."

"Oh good, I'm so glad," the chief said.

So, it was over. Really over.

One by one, the rest of her siblings approached to embrace her—except Brady and Derek.

"Word spreads fast," Ryan murmured.

"Too fast sometimes."

Finally, after Izzy finished giving her statement and answering questions, they were on their way to the hospital.

After a quick visit with a recovering Derek, who was celebrating the fact that he was going to get to keep his leg, they were on the way to her parents' house.

"I'm so relieved for Derek," she said. "Working undercover and being on the SWAT team . . . that's all he's ever wanted. If he lost a leg, that would severely devastate him."

"He's got a long road ahead of him," Ryan said.

"Well, he won't travel it alone," she said as he pulled to a stop on the curb.

"You've got that right."

They stepped into the foyer and Ryan flipped on the light. "Guess it's just us for a bit. When is your house going to be ready?"

"Not for a while. The insurance adjuster left a message on my voice mail that everything was covered. I guess as soon as I get the check I can start renovations." She sighed. "Poor Mrs. Spade, I'm not sure she wants me for a neighbor anymore."

"She wants Mozart for a neighbor, therefore she'll probably keep you."

"Funny."

"I try."

What was funny was that he had a bunch of words he wanted to say to her but couldn't seem to get them past his lips. He cleared his throat. "You're beautiful, you know that?" Okay, maybe that would work.

———

A warm flush worked its way up her neck and into her cheeks. "Well . . . thanks." She walked into the kitchen and grabbed a bottle of water from the refrigerator. He followed her slowly, with soft measured steps. It made her nervous. In a good way. Two swigs later, she capped the water and his eyes caught hers.

He gave her a crooked smile. "Sorry, I guess that was kind of out of left field."

"A little. But . . . not completely."

Ryan settled his hands on her shoulders. "I like you, Izzy. A lot. We've known each other forever, but each time I'm with you, I find out some new facet of your personality that either makes me smile or want to strangle you."

A short laugh escaped her. "Uh . . . okay. Thanks? I think. Or should I be mad?"

He kissed her. A leisurely kiss that made her toes curl and her heart pound. When he pulled back, his eyes glittered. "Don't be mad."

"Okay." She grinned, then sobered. "Does this mean I don't have to buy a horse?"

It was his turn to blink. "Huh?"

"It was a joke. Lydia McCarthy? You've been dying to ask me out. So why haven't you? Because I don't have horses?"

"No!" He laughed and leaned against the wall, crossing his arms. "How do you know that I've been dying to ask you out?"

"Kevin said so."

"The brat." He said the words fondly, with just a hint of huskiness.

"So what held you back?"

"Derek."

Izzy frowned. "Now there's a brat for you. What did he say?"

He shrugged. "Just that you were focused on your work and doing a good job and I'd be a distraction."

"I'm going to hurt him."

"Why?"

She kissed him. Another sweet kiss that left them both wanting more. Then she smiled. "That's why."

"Oh."

"Yeah. Oh."

He drew in a breath and took a step back. "So. You want to watch the election?"

"What election?"

"Iz—"

"I know. I'm teasing."

"Actually, I don't want to watch the election. Watching it's not going to change the outcome—nor the fact that there will be a do-over. I want you to tell me about Sinclair."

She landed back on earth with a hard thud. "Oh. Wow. Okay."

"Unless you just don't want to."

"No, it's okay. I don't mind. There's not a whole lot to tell, actually. I met Mick when I pulled him over for speeding. He begged me to let him off with a warning, so I did, since he hadn't been drinking or anything. Turns out he was a paramedic and our paths just hadn't crossed. A couple of weeks later, they did. I was first on the scene to a drive-by shooting that left two people dead and one injured. Mick was the paramedic. After it was all said and done, he asked for my number. I gave it to him."

"Sounds . . . normal."

"I know." She shrugged. "We dated for about three months and it just wasn't happening for me. He acted really possessive right from the get-go. I told him I didn't want to see him anymore and he talked me into coming to his house to discuss it. When I got there, he pulled a knife and said how much he loved me and how he couldn't live without me."

"Izzy," Ryan whispered. He pulled her to him and she shuddered but was surprised to find that the telling didn't make her want to hurl anymore.

"So, I talked him down. He cried like a baby, gave me the knife, and let me call the cops. At the trial, I testified on his behalf and he was hospitalized. He was diagnosed with a mental illness about five years ago. When he had this particular psychotic break, he'd not been taking his meds. Which makes a huge difference for him. While he was in the hospital, he had good doctors, counseling, and got back on his medicine." She shook her head. "Now, I'm sure that was all just an act to avoid prison. He played their game and won."

"A sociopath."

"Very much so."

"But he let you go, knowing he'd be taken into custody."

"Yes. But he also knew he could manipulate me, the system, and any doctors he'd be required to see. Which he did. He got cushy hospital time instead of prison."

He gathered her closer. "Well, you don't have to worry about him anymore."

"I know."

The door opened and Izzy's father stepped inside, shutting the door behind him. "What are you two up to?"

"Just getting ready to turn on the election," Izzy said as she walked into the den with Ryan on her heels.

Her father nodded and headed for the kitchen. "I'll get the popcorn, although it's probably a waste of time watching the results. The election is invalid, if you ask me. They're just going to have to redo the whole thing due to the threats against Eric."

"Probably."

A knock on the door had Izzy doing a U-turn to answer it. She found David outside on the front porch. He shot her a smile and handed her a bag of chocolate. "Ryan invited me."

"Oh yes! Come in. We have something for you."

"For me?"

"Uh-huh. Ryan, come here."

When Ryan walked in and spotted David, he grinned. "Hey, glad you could make it."

"Sure. Glad to be asked."

Ryan reached into his back pocket and pulled out a small envelope. "These are for you."

"What?" He opened the tab and pulled out the contents. And his eyes went wide. "Seriously? The Carolina-Clemson game? On the fifty-yard line? I don't know what to say."

"We're overlooking the fact that you're going to pull for Clemson," Izzy said.

"Yeah," Ryan said, "you went above and beyond to help with Kevin's case."

David nodded and sobered. "Sorry it was necessary, but glad to do it."

They walked into the den as Chloe and Hank arrived next, followed by Brady. Even Ruthie managed to get away from the hospital, where she said she'd just checked on Derek and he was sleeping comfortably.

Izzy sank onto the leather sofa and propped her feet on the ottoman. Ryan settled in beside her and snaked an arm around her shoulders.

She leaned her head against his chest and sighed. Life without Kevin was going to be hard, but they'd make it.

Together.

———

Ryan kissed the top of her head and looked around the room at the people who'd been like his extended family. He loved them all and knew Izzy felt the same way about his family. "How long do we have to date before you'll agree to get engaged?" he asked in a low whisper.

She froze and he wondered if he'd just scared her off. Then she turned her head and put her lips close to his ear. "At least a week. I don't want you to think I'm desperate or anything."

Ryan chuckled and hugged her close.

He was the one who was desperate. Desperate to make her happy, to keep her safe, and to let her continue to grow into the person she was meant to be.

Her fingers curled around his and within minutes her breathing was slow and easy. He settled in to watch the election—and to watch her sleep.

It was a good night. She and her mother were alive.

And he and Izzy had a future to look forward to.

Thanks, God.

That was his last thought before his eyes closed and he drifted into slumber.

Epilogue

Cathy stood next to Izzy and placed a sisterly arm across her shoulders. "You've got yourself a good husband."

She smiled. "I know."

"And he got a great wife."

"Thanks, Cathy," she said softly. "That means a lot." She glanced at the building where Kevin's life had drained out of him a year ago today. "Kevin would be proud."

"He would be even more proud that you went to Xtreme Flips and did a back flip on the trampoline."

She grinned. "Yeah, he would be, wouldn't he?" She'd only done it for him. Because she hoped he'd been watching and cheering.

"I heard Reuben died."

"Yes." The man had lived through sixteen surgeries over the past year and finally succumbed to a blood infection just last week. "I hope he's at peace now."

Sadness flickered in Cathy's gaze. "Me too."

Unable to talk due to the damage to his face, Reuben had typed many letters, penning his regret and begging the Marshall family's

337

forgiveness. They'd given it. "I think he knew he wasn't going to live much longer."

"Seems that way."

Ryan stepped up to them and pulled Izzy away from Cathy. "Go find someone else to hug. I got this one covered."

Cathy laughed as Izzy happily slipped into his arms. Ryan's parents and the rest of the family also pulled into the parking lot.

Izzy's mother walked over, a smile curling her lips. "What a happy day." She turned to Ryan. "You've done a good thing here."

Ryan breathed deep. "Thanks. I almost can't believe it's really happening. All but four of the beds are filled up. We've got the cook, the cleaning crew, and a fully grant-funded doctor and nurse for at least a year. As well as therapy dogs and two rotating psychiatrists."

"People were generous," Izzy said. The fundraiser had been held six months ago.

Over the next few minutes, the crowd grew until the parking lot was full. Ryan stepped up to the podium and pulled the microphone toward him. "Thank you all for coming."

Everyone stilled and soon the chatter stopped. A news team moved closer. "As you know, my brother Chris Marshall died when his convoy hit an IED two and a half years ago. Later, my family learned that he and a friend of his, Jonathan Gill, had purchased this warehouse and planned to open up a shelter for homeless vets. This place is also where my brother Kevin was shot and killed just last year. All he ever wanted was to make this world a better place. That's all both of them wanted—and died doing."

Ryan cleared his throat and took a breath. Izzy wanted to comfort him but knew he had the strength to do this.

He looked up. "Today, I'm very proud to see their dream become a reality. Ladies and gentlemen, welcome to the Gill and Marshall Second Chances House."

Applause thundered through the parking lot as Izzy expertly

snipped the ribbon. It fluttered to the ground and the crowd cheered again.

Izzy's heart was full. That was the only way she knew how to describe it. After the failed assassination attempt on her mother, Felicia's death, the "do-over" election and Mayor Cotterill's win, and her wedding two months ago, Izzy wasn't sure life would ever settle down, but it had. A fact she was grateful for.

Lilianna and Chloe walked over. "This is amazing," Chloe said with a quick hug.

"I know."

The media pressed in. Izzy saw a young man making a beeline toward her as soon as Ryan stepped away from the microphone. "Hey, you're Isabelle St. John, aren't you?"

"I am."

"I'm a reporter for *The State*. Do you mind if I ask you a couple of questions?"

Ryan walked up and put his arm around her. "This guy bothering you?"

Izzy studied the reporter's open and guileless eyes. "No, not at all. What questions do you have?"

"Well, it's been a year since you were nearly thrown off a building, then out of a helicopter, and also kidnapped at gunpoint with your mother. How has life been treating you since then?"

Izzy bit her lip against the emotions his words brought to the surface, then she smiled and shrugged. "It's been boring. Wonderfully, deliciously boring."

"Hey! What?" Ryan spun her to face him and she laughed.

"Well, compared to being *dangled* off a parking garage, and nearly rolling out of a helicopter a thousand feet in the air, and having a gun pointed at my head, I'd say everything else has been pretty boring."

Ryan's mouth worked. Then he snapped his lips together and shrugged. "Okay, as long as you're safe with your feet on solid ground, I'm happy to go with boring."

"Me too."

The reporter nodded. "Boring it is. You got anything else?"

"Just that boring has never been more exciting and I'm looking forward to many more years of it," Ryan said.

And he kissed his wife.

Dear Reader,

Thank you so much for joining me on Ryan and Izzy's journey for justice and love. While I've set the story in Columbia, South Carolina, I have to admit to some author licensure. The city of Columbia, where I went to college at the University of South Carolina, is divided up into five regions: East, West, North, South, and Metro. In this story, since I had some dirty cops, I didn't want them to be in any of those regions, so I took the liberty of creating my own region for the purpose of this story. Midtown region doesn't exist in Columbia, so for those of you who are from the city, please know it wasn't a mistake, it was intentional. I love our officers and I fully back those in blue, so I didn't want to offend anyone by placing dirty cops in a real region! Anyway, I also took some other liberties, and those of you who are native to the city will recognize them. I hope this doesn't take away your enjoyment of the story and that you are eagerly looking forward to the next installment. Chloe and Hank are chomping at the bit to get into a book, so they're next! Again, thank you for allowing me the honor of creating these stories and for inviting me into your lives for a short time. I don't take it for granted and I'm very humbled by it. God bless you and I wish you many hours of reading.

Dedicated to all of the officers who serve daily, placing their lives on the line so that I don't have to. According to the National Law Enforcement Officers Memorial Fund, "A total of 1,512 law enforcement officers died in the line of duty during the past 10 years, an average of one death every 63 hours or 151 per year. There were 143 law enforcement officers killed in the line of duty in 2016" (the year that I wrote most of this story). *My heart breaks for those families of the fallen and my prayers go up daily for those who serve—including several of my and my husband's family members. We love you and support you. Do good and stay safe while you protect and serve.*

Blessed are the peacemakers: for they shall be called the children of God.

Matthew 5:9

READ A SNEAK PEEK FROM

CALLED TO PROTECT

THE NEXT **BLUE JUSTICE** NOVEL

Available Everywhere
SUMMER 2018

Prologue

Sixteen-year-old Penny St. John smoothed the shirt over her slim waist and turned to admire herself in the mirror. He'd like the look. Just thinking about Carson Langston made her smile. She'd never had a real boyfriend before. She'd been more interested in gymnastics and running track, but Carson had caught her eye at the mall when he'd struck up a conversation with her in line at the pizza place.

That had been three weeks ago. Tonight, he said he had a surprise for her. Anticipation swirled. She didn't fancy herself in love. She was too practical for that, but she did like him a lot. Just yesterday he'd given her the gold bracelet she now wore on her left wrist.

Penny pulled her phone from the back pocket of her shorts and tapped the Instagram app. Posing with pouty lips, she snapped a picture and posted it. Next, she grinned and posted that one. Wow. She looked good.

With a giggle, she made her way downstairs and found her cousin Linc St. John in the kitchen with her brother, Damien. "Hey, you two, don't you have anything better to do on a Friday night than sit around and talk cop stuff?"

Damien frowned at her. "What do you think you're doing?"

"Going out with a friend, why?"

"Because you need to put on something besides that pajama top. And don't you have a pair of jeans or something? Those shorts are too short."

She stuck her tongue out at him. "They are not. They come to mid-thigh. And this top is fine. It's loose and comfortable."

"It shows too much skin."

"My shoulders, Damien. My bathing suit is more revealing and you know it. Seriously. You need to get a life."

"I have one. It's my mission in life to watch out for you."

Penny rolled her eyes. "You mean harass me to death."

"Has Mom seen that shirt?"

"Yes." She walked over and kissed his forehead. "She helped me pick it out. I'll be back before midnight. See ya. Bye, Linc."

"Bye, Pen. Be careful," he said.

He was more than twice her age, but he was one of her favorite cousins.

She almost turned around and went to change, but truly, Damien knew as well as she did that the shirt was fine. He was just having a hard time coming to terms with the fact that she was growing up. And, honestly, she was grateful for his protective instincts even as she strained against them.

The shirt was fine and Carson was waiting.

"Who are you going out with?" Damien asked.

"A friend," she said again with a glance out the window. "And there he is. Talk to later. Love you."

"His name, Penny."

"Carson Langston." She stuck her tongue out and bolted out the door.

She heard him yell her name as she dashed down the walkway, but she wasn't about to give him the opportunity to give Carson the third degree. How embarrassing.

Just because Damien was twenty-four years old, he thought

that made him her keeper. She was determined to prove it didn't and that she could take care of herself.

She shot a quick glance over her shoulder as she opened the door and her eyes locked on Damien's. For a moment, she regretted the way she left and she sighed. She'd apologize to him tomorrow. For now, she was going to enjoy the night. She slid into the car, turning toward Carson. "Thanks for picking me up."

"Of course." He reached over and squeezed her hand. "Anything for you." He pressed the gas and pulled from the curb.

"So, what's my surprise?" she asked.

"I'm taking you to meet a friend of mine."

She frowned. "Okay."

He laughed. "What? You don't want to meet my friends?"

"Sure, but I just thought it was going to be the two of us."

"Don't worry, we'll have a blast. My friend is going to love you. Now relax."

Penny's worries eased at his friendly smile and twinkling blue eyes. "Fine, we'll meet your friend, but then we're going to go do something. Just you and me, okay?"

Without taking his eyes from the road, he reached over and stroked her cheek. "Okay."

Ten minutes later, Carson wound through one of the nicest neighborhoods in Columbia. "Your friend lives here?"

"Yep."

"Wow. What does he do?"

"He's in sales."

One mansion after the next passed her window. "What does he sell?"

"Whatever will make him money."

"Hmm." That sounded . . . weird. What did he mean by that?

A kernel of unease curled in her belly. Carson took her hand and squeezed it, then lifted it and pressed his lips to her fingers. She sighed and smiled at him. He was so good to her.

Then he was turning into a driveway that curved around to the front of a four-story home. "Do you want me to wait here? I'm not exactly dressed for anything fancy."

"You look awesome."

"How do you know this guy?"

"I work for him. I just need to drop something off."

"Oh."

But he got out of the car without anything. Maybe it was a flash drive or something in his pocket. Or money. But why wouldn't he just say so?

He opened her door and held out his hand. She reached for it and he laced his fingers through hers as she followed him up the stone walkway to the front steps. The door opened before they reached the top and he released her hand.

A man in his midthirties stood there with a wide smile on his face. "Come on in. So glad you're here."

With Carson's warm hand against the small of her back, Penny stepped inside the massive foyer. Marble beneath her feet and a bazillion-dollar chandelier above her head. Wow.

The door shut behind them and the man's smile faded. His eyes roamed over her and he shot a look at Carson. "Good, good. Nice."

Alarms instantly jangled. "Um . . . I don't mean to be rude, but could I use your restroom?"

The man lifted a brow, and at first she thought he was going to refuse, but then the smile returned. "Of course. Carson can show you the way."

"Thank you."

Carson gripped her hand, harder than he'd ever done before, and pulled her with him.

"What are you doing?" She jerked out of his grasp. "That hurts."

Anger flashed in his eyes for a split second, then disappeared. "Sorry."

"Did I do something wrong?" she asked. "I mean, I can wait on the bathroom if I have to." But she didn't plan on it.

Her willingness to please him did the trick and his features smoothed out. "No. Of course not. It's fine, but don't take forever." He opened the door for her. "I'll be waiting for you."

"Okay. Thanks."

Once inside the bathroom with the door shut, she pulled out her cell phone and tapped Damien's name. The phone rang twice. "Penny?"

"Damien, I think I need your help," she whispered.

"Where are you?"

"At a house in—"

The call dropped. With a frustrated groan, she glanced at the battery. It was full. She'd had it plugged in the entire time she was getting ready. She dialed her brother's number again. And got nothing. The signal on her phone was gone. Had they done something to make it so she couldn't call out? "No. Come on, come on, please."

She tapped a text to him even as she knew something was terribly wrong. Fear like she'd never felt before twisted inside her. She was so stupid. Every warning Damien had ever lectured her about human trafficking rang through her mind.

But no. Carson wouldn't do that, would he?

Flashes of his behavior tonight had her acting anyway. She pressed send on the text and got the little message that it was unable to be delivered. Tears sprang to her eyes and she drew in a breath. She would not panic. She'd keep her cool.

A knock on the door caused her to jerk. "I'll be there in a minute." She flushed the toilet and eyed the cabinet under the sink.

"Come on, Penny."

"I'm washing my hands." She turned the water on and then reached under the sink to press her hand to the inside wall of the cabinet. She did the same to the toilet bowl. Then she snagged a few hairs from her head and dropped them behind the picture on the wall. Her last act was to shut the sink off, take her cell phone, and type as much as she could before the next knock.

"Penny! Come on! Do I need to come in there?" The knob rattled.

It would have to be enough. He was going to kick the door in if she didn't hurry up. She slid the phone under the large armoire-like corner cabinet, then stood.

With a prayer on her lips, she opened the door. "What's the rush, silly? I—"

A liquid spray hit her in the face and she gasped. Exactly the wrong thing to do. Whatever he'd sprayed her with burned her lungs. Carson's face blurred. "What—"

She went to her knees before Carson caught her. "It's okay, Penny, don't fight it."

1

Officer Chloe St. John pulled her SUV to a stop on the Gervais Street Bridge behind the teeming chaos just ahead. Just as a cargo van had come off the bridge, it had crossed the double yellow line and gone headlight to headlight with an eighteen-wheeler, causing a minivan to slam into the rear left corner of the trailer. All in all, the fifteen-car pile-up had caused multiple injuries and fatalities.

She climbed out and the rain hit her in the face. Chloe shuddered. The torrential downpours that had hit Columbia over the last seventy-two hours had caused the water under the bridge to turn into a raging, turbulent force to be reckoned with. At least today only a light drizzle fell from the still swollen gray clouds.

And then the victims' terror reached her. As did an explosive splash.

"A second car just went over!"

"Help me!"

"Over here!"

Sirens screamed. Rescuers shouted orders. Chloe raced to the edge of the bridge and looked over. Divers were already in the water. One of them was probably her brother, Brady. She sent up a silent prayer for their safety.

She returned to her vehicle and released Hank, her Dutch shepherd K-9, from his special area, and he hopped down beside her, quivering with energy and ready to work. She scratched his silky ears. "Hold tight, boy. Let's get our bearings."

EMS was already on the scene, as well as multiple fire trucks and police cars. A helicopter hovered overhead. Chloe spotted a familiar face. Right where she said she'd be. "Izzy!"

Her sister turned, tension lining her features. "Chloe, glad you're here. Bring Hank."

Chloe and Hank trotted over to Izzy, who stood next to a woman holding an infant wrapped in a blue blanket. A paramedic rummaged through the bag on the ground. Chloe recognized the medic. Alice Johnson. The EMT looked at Izzy. "Can you bandage this?" A gash over the victim's left eye looked like it needed stitches.

"Yes. Go." She took the bandage.

Alice paused, then headed for her ambulance. "She needs a blanket. Hang on."

"Is your baby hurt?" Chloe asked the woman.

"No." The victim's jaw trembled and shivers wracked her. "She's fine, I think." Shock. Alice passed Izzy a blanket and she wrapped it around the woman, who hunched under it, checking to make sure her baby was still covered.

"I've got to go." Alice spun.

"Hey, I need tape," Izzy called.

The paramedic tossed her a roll. "I'll be back."

Priorities.

"What's going on besides the obvious?" Chloe asked.

"We found drugs," Izzy said. She held the white bandage to the woman's head. "This thing is way too big. I need some scissors, and of course, she didn't leave me any."

"Hold on." Chloe reached behind her service weapon into a small pocket on her holster and pulled out a Swiss army knife.

Izzy took it and used its scissors to cut the bandage to size. She handed the knife back to Chloe, then taped the bandage to the woman's head. With a soft pat to the woman's bowed shoulder, she said, "Sit tight, okay? They'll get you to the hospital as soon as they can."

Izzy stood and directed Chloe to the side of the road. "The drugs came from one of the vehicles, and we need you and Hank to figure out which one. We suspect it's the eighteen-wheeler sitting over there, but a cursory search hasn't turned up any more and we're too busy trying to help keep people alive to do a more thorough search." Izzy was a detective, but she was also trained as a first responder. "The critical ones are being transported to the hospital immediately, of course, but we're matching patients with cars, so we need Hank to do his thing. When we know which vehicle the drugs came from, we'll know who to arrest. If the person's still alive. So far we've got four DOAs and a couple of others who look close to joining them."

"Where did you find the drugs?"

"This way."

Chloe followed Izzy through the ruckus. She sidestepped two paramedics rushing past her and pushing a stretcher. Izzy stopped beside the vehicle that had slammed into the back of the eighteen-wheeler. White powder from a plastic bag lay in the middle of the lane. Which meant there was probably more where that had come from. Question was, where had it come from? The truck or the minivan or an SUV that had T-boned the van? Or had someone thrown it out when they realized cops were going to be covering the area?

"You're sure it's drugs?"

Izzy shrugged. "Figured Hank would tell us."

He took one whiff and sat. "There's your answer."

"I'm stunned." Izzy rolled her eyes. "Want to see if he can find any more?"

"We're on it." Chloe led Hank to the damaged minivan behind

the tractor trailer. "Hank, find the dope." Most commands were given in Dutch, but not this one. Hank went to work, sniffing the seats, the tires, the trunk.

And got nothing.

"This one's clean," Chloe said.

She led him around the minivan, toward the cab of the eighteen-wheeler to get the trailer doors opened. Officers Josiah Henry and Olivia Nash had the driver out of the cab and were questioning him. The man looked to be unhurt, but it was obvious he wasn't happy. "I'm going to be late making my delivery and I'm going to get fired. I need to get out of here now!"

"Where do you think you're going to go? You're trapped right now."

"I can push through if you'll just get everyone out of the way."

Chloe shook her head. What an idiot.

He spotted Hank and Chloe heading his way and his eyes went wide. He shoved Olivia into Josiah and climbed back into the seat of the cab, quick as a monkey up a tree.

Olivia went after the driver, but he had scrambled to the other side. "Stop! Police!"

The man opened the passenger door, jumped to the ground, weapon in hand, and bolted.

"Hank, *apport*!" The command to get him. Chloe pulled her weapon.

Hank shot away from her, his sleek brown-and-black body a blur as he headed back toward the minivan to give chase. Chloe sprinted behind him. The fleeing man was weaving in and out of the stopped traffic and victims, but Hank easily caught up with him. The dog lunged and latched onto the arm with the weapon, and the two of them went to the ground, with the man screaming in agony. "Get him off me! Get him off!" And yet he still clutched the gun. Victims screamed and ducked.

"Drop the weapon!" Chloe raced toward them. She was joined

by Olivia and Josiah. All three of their voices blended as one. "Let go of the weapon and I'll call him off! Drop it! Now!"

Their perp stilled and Chloe slammed her foot down on the hand that held the gun. Olivia dropped a knee into his upper back and grabbed his left arm.

He let out another howl as Chloe leaned over and yanked the weapon from his now slack fingers. "You broke my hand!"

"Hank, *los, laat los*!" The order to let go.

Hank released his bite and moved back to sit, tongue lolling as he watched the action.

Josiah shook his head. "We've got a genius on our hands. Thought he was going to outrun Hank. Who really thinks that's possible? What a dumb . . ." He continued to mutter his poor opinion of the idiot on the ground while he held him there.

Olivia removed her knee and jerked the man's wounded arm behind him.

He screamed again. "I need a doctor! That dog nearly killed me! I'm going to sue you. I'm going to sue the whole department! I'll have your badges. I'll . . ."

Chloe turned a deaf ear to the threats and the stream of curses that spilled from him while she and Josiah held him down. Olivia fastened her cuffs around his wrists.

And then a gunshot rang out.

Chloe ducked and spun. More screams rang out around her.

"Go," Chloe told them. "I'll hold on to this joker until you can put him in the back of your car." She didn't have room to transport a prisoner.

They took off. She pulled her charge to the back of the trailer and shoved him next to the large tire. Pulling her cuffs from the case on her belt, she attached one cuff to the pair around his wrists and the other cuff to a metal rail running along the bottom of the trailer. "Stay there unless you want to get shot." She glanced at Hank, who hadn't taken his gaze from the prisoner. "Or bit."

The man planted his back up against the rubber and glared at her as he yanked on the cuffs. "Where do you think I'm going to go?"

She ignored him when she caught movement in the passenger side mirror and her heart thudded. He hadn't been there only moments before when her prisoner had scrambled out of that very door. So, someone else had been inside the cab? Chloe grabbed her radio.

Pop. Another shot. Then two more. Chloe flinched, even though none of the bullets came near her. But she couldn't help wondering whom they might have hit. Saying a prayer for her fellow officers, she kept watch, her senses on hyper-alert and her gaze never resting.

Another loud crack.

The bullets were fired from the truck. Chloe glared at her prisoner. "You know who's shooting?"

"No." He scowled, his expression conveying his disgust for her and anyone who wore the same uniform she did. "This is ridiculous. I need a doctor. Take me over to that ambulance." He jerked his chin toward the vehicle sitting ten yards away on the side of the highway. The paramedics were bent over a patient and still working in spite of the gunfire, using the ambulance as a shield.

Chloe kept her weapon ready and her head down. "We've got a live shooter and you want to cross that wide-open expanse? How stupid are you?" Big-time stupid. She mentally dubbed him Stupid Man.

He winced. "At least put my hands in front of me. My arm is killing me. That beast about took it off. I need stitches. Probably gonna bleed to death."

"I'm really worried about that," she muttered as she scanned the area. She kept up the running dialogue absently, while most of her attention was focused on the action going on around her.

He called her a name she didn't consider flattering, and she flicked a glance at him. Still secure and not trying to get away, in spite of his mouthiness. Good. Maybe he was slightly less stupid than she originally thought.

Chloe peered around the edge of the truck again, letting her gaze take in the scene before pulling back. People hiding, cops planted with guns aimed at the cab. Her radio crackled with rapid-fire codes and calls. *"Two men in the cab!"* She glared at the man attached to the truck. "Who else is in there?"

His nostrils flared. "No one."

"Of course not." Liar.

As if to prove her right, the truck's engine rumbled to life. Where had the driver come from? And where did they think they were going? With the front tucked into the cargo van's headlights and a minivan slammed into its rear, the truck couldn't go anywhere.

However, Chloe released Stupid Man from the truck and hauled him to his feet by his non-wounded arm. She led him to the back edge of the trailer, away from the side mirror, wondering if the occupants of the truck's cab realized she and their accomplice were right there. If they did, they didn't care. If they didn't, she'd feel much better out of sight of that side mirror.

Once at the back of the trailer, near the two large doors, her prisoner tried to run. Chloe tackled him, and she didn't even have to give the order for Hank to jump at the man's face, snapping and snarling.

Stupid Man curled into a fetal position. "Get him away! Don't let him bite me again!"

"Hank, *stil.*" The dog backed away, his eyes still on the quivering man. "Get up and try to engage your brain," she ordered.

He complied and she refastened the cuffs to the handle of the trailer's door while she listened for more shots. And although she still heard screams and cries and harsh orders from law enforcement, she hadn't heard any more pops of gunfire.

The truck surged forward and the man attached to the back of it let out a yell before swiveling his head to look at her.

"Hey, you can't leave me handcuffed here! Let me loose!"

"Why? If he drives off, you don't want to be left behind, do you?"

The truck inched forward. Screams sounded. More shots rang out. None in danger of hitting her or Stupid Man, though, since the bullets came from the truck's cab.

The truck surged and rolled forward a good three feet. "No! Stop!" Stupid Man cried, running forward to keep from falling to the ground.

With horror, Chloe knew the cab had to be pushing the vehicle in front of it. Along with any victims in its path. She followed behind Stupid Man, ready to uncuff him if the truck was truly able to pick up any more speed.

Another lurch and the trailer separated from the minivan crunched into its rear. Chloe raced to the front of the cab on the passenger side, away from any bullets that had been flying on the other side. "Police! Stop!"

The passenger looked at her and yelled something to the driver. And then she heard, "Shoot her!"

The man in the passenger seat turned and met her gaze. She held her gun on him. "Tell him to stop right now!"

In one fluid motion, he lifted his weapon, aimed it at her . . .

. . . and pulled the trigger.

———————

Through the high-powered scope on his Colt M4 carbine, Derek St. John saw the passenger in the cab fire his weapon right at his sister's head.

And Chloe dropped like a rock. Or had she dropped before the crack? He couldn't be sure.

Terror beat at him, his finger hovering over the trigger. Just before Chloe had appeared in his line of sight behind his target, a cop, trying to get into position, had run across his line of fire, causing Derek to miss his chance to pull the trigger. He wanted to punch something. Instead, he ordered his heart to slow and his mind to focus.

He'd been given the green light. The call had gone out over the radios and no one was supposed to move. And now Chloe might be dead because an officer had blown the shot for Derek. Had the man not heard the order?

At the moment, it didn't matter.

What mattered was Chloe.

Derek wasn't exactly in the most ideal position to make the shot, but it was the only one he had.

He drew in a steadying breath. He had to focus, to be cool, be steady, and return to the zone.

Looking through the scope once more, he saw the driver raise his weapon and aim it at an innocent victim. A woman not quite hidden behind her car.

Derek pulled his trigger and a nanosecond later the bullet hit its mark. The driver's body went slack. The passenger next to him jerked and turned, aiming his weapon at the cop now hovering at the edge of the driver's door, hand on the handle, ready to yank the door open in a heroic, if dangerous, possibly stupid, move. Derek could see the cop's plan as clearly as if he'd written it out with full illustrations. He was going to open the door, pull out the dead driver, and shoot the remaining passenger.

Fortunately, the passenger moved and Derek had a clear shot. A second pull on the trigger and the threat was over. The officer dove out of sight.

Derek lowered his rifle and swiped a hand across his eyes. Two lives. He'd ended two lives. Two more faces he'd see in his dreams. But they'd made their choices, and if Derek hadn't made his, innocents would be dead instead of the two men bent on destruction.

And now . . .

"Chloe," he whispered.

Acknowledgments

As always, I wouldn't have the accuracy of the police procedural without the help of FBI Special Agent Dru Wells and FBI Special Agent Wayne Smith (Retired).

A special thanks to Mark Mynheir for answering questions and giving me invaluable feedback.

Thanks to Columbia, South Carolina's, Sheriff Leon Lotts for being patient and answering a number of my questions. Thank you for helping me figure out a way to break into Derek's office and look for an Ops Plan. Thank you, Tana Bevil and Barbara Porter, for putting me in touch with Sheriff Lotts. You're both great friends and I love you!

I have to give a shout-out to Officer Steven Moore of Gaffney, South Carolina, and cousin to my fabulous husband. Thank you, too, for your feedback, for your willingness to answer my questions, and for your service.

Thanks to Detective Chris Hammett for answering a few questions and for being willing to be a future resource. A writer can never have too many!

Thank you to Lynn Blackburn, Edie Melson, Alycia Morales,

Linda Gilden, and Emme Gannon for all the brainstorming we did on this story. Y'all are amazing—and are just as devious as I am!

Thanks to my "twin sister" (we share the same birthday) and brainstorming buddy, DiAnn Mills. You're such a special lady and I love you bunches!

Yes, I had a LOT of help on this story from law enforcement sources. That is not to say that I may or may not have taken some author licensure in a couple of places. Any inaccuracies are completely on this author's shoulders, NOT the individuals who gave me *perfectly* accurate advice.

Thank you to my family for continuing to put up with me. I love you so much. There are no words to convey it.

And, of course, thank you to Jesus, my Lord and Savior. Without you, I would be nothing.

Lynette Eason is the bestselling author of the Elite Guardians series. She is the winner of two ACFW Carol Awards, the Selah Award, the Golden Scrolls Book of the year Award (2016), the Daphne Award, the Christian Readers Best Award (2017), the Inspirational Readers' Choice Award and several others. She has a master's degree in education from Converse College and lives in South Carolina with her husband and two teens. Learn more at www.lynetteeason.com.

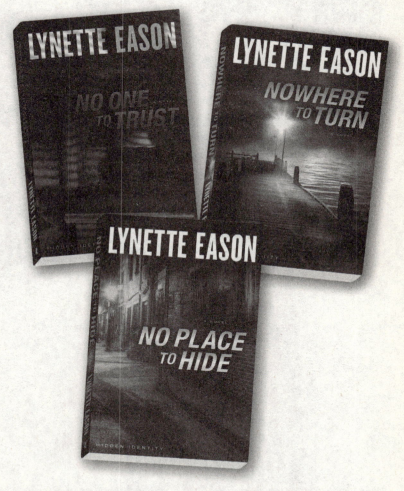

DON'T MISS ANY OF THE BOOKS IN THE
DEADLY REUNIONS SERIES

Come meet
Lynette Eason at
www.LynetteEason.com

Follow her on